I0676237

Freedom's Pride

Path to Freedom - Book Two

Pegg Thomas

Spinner of Yarns Publishing LLC

S PINNER OF YARNS PUBLISHING

Sault Ste Marie, Michigan

Copyright @2024 by Pegg Thomas
https://peggthomas.com/
Published in the United States of America
ISBN: 979-8-9866966-4-5
Cover Design by Hannah Linder
Cover Art Copyright by Spinner of Yarns Publishing

All rights reserved. No portion of this book may be transmitted in any form or by any electronic or mechanical means, including photocopying, recording, or by any information retrieval and storage system without permission of the publisher.

This is a work of fiction. Names, characters, and incidents in this book are products of the author's imagination or are used in a fictitious situation with the exception of characters listed in the Author's Notes. Any resemblances to actual events, locations, organizations, incidents, or persons – living or dead – are coincidental and beyond the intent of the author with the exception of those listed in the Author's Notes.

Praise For Pegg Thomas

Pegg Thomas possesses an extraordinary talent for resurrecting the past, skillfully weaving meticulous research into vibrant narratives. Her stories not only paint a rich tapestry of historical details but also breathe life into characters so authentic, one could easily imagine them as neighbors. In the realm of historical romance, Pegg Thomas stands out as a beacon of excellence, combining a commitment to accuracy with a gift for crafting compelling novels that transport readers through time.

~ Robin Patchen
http://robinpatchen.com

Pegg Thomas always delivers a well-researched novel balanced with realistic, lovable characters. She's one of my go-to authors for historical fiction.

~Candice Sue Patterson
Author of *Saving Mrs. Roosevelt* and *When the Waters Came*

I have been a fan of Pegg Thomas' historical fiction novels for over a decade. Her plots are well thought out and researched and her storylines are believable. The characters are realistic and easy to cheer for or despise. One of the best novelists in the genre. Highly recommend.

~ Kara R. Hunt
Award-winning Author & Host of the Cheer Up! Podcast

There are historical authors who transport readers into the past by using broad strokes to paint lush and vivid scenes. Some contrive and deliver uniquely flawed, yet lovable and sympathetic characters. Still others make readers' hearts race, their eyes weep, their fists clench, and their sides ache with laughter. But rarely do you find a singular author who encapsulates all of these finely honed skills. Pegg Thomas is that author.

~ Jericha Kingston
Author of *Prevailing Hearts* series

MORE BOOKS BY PEGG THOMAS

Salem Village
The Ragpicker ~ prequel novella (May 2025)
The Carpenter (September 2025)
The Midwife (January 2026)
The Brewer (May 2026)

Path to Freedom
Freedom's Price
Freedom's Pride
Freedom's Promise

A More Perfect Union
Emerald Fields
Cobalt Skies
Silver Prairies

Forts of Refuge
Sarah's Choice
Maggie's Strength
Abigail's Peace
Henri's Regret ~ A Prequel Novella

Individual Novellas
Worth Fighting For (Releasing January 2025)
Anna's Tower
Her Redcoat
In Sheep's Clothing
Embattled Hearts

Join Pegg's Newsletter
writing updates – sneak peeks – fiber arts updates – personal content
https://www.subscribepage.com/PeggThomas

This book is dedicated to my husband, Michael.

We lived an adventure during the months I was writing this book.
He retired, and our son got married and purchased the farm from
us. We were homeless! We lived out of our 16-foot camper for a few
weeks, then in my family's hunting cabin for five weeks, and then in
an efficiency apartment for another five weeks before we bought a
house. Our "new" house was built in 1895, so he's been very busy with
renovations ever since. Without his steadfast support, this book might
not have made it to print on time.

I love you, Sweetie!

Acknowledgements

Thank you to the readers who enjoy early American novels! I've been blessed to hear from many of you, especially those who subscribe to my newsletter, and I appreciate you all.

And a special thank you to Paul Roberts for all his assistance in gathering the best resource materials. It's wonderful to know a library expert! You've made things much easier for me.

Author's Forenote

The Quaker use of thee is not the same grammatically as the Old English use. The Quakers did not use thou, only thee and thy, a variation that they considered more plain.

Chapter 1

Greenesville, North Carolina—January 1801

MARK ALLEN TEED'S HOPES crashed with a thud to the frosty ground at his boots. He pointed at the flea-bitten gray horse and stared at Arthur, the Whitefords' coachman.

"*This* is what he is giving me?"

"Indeed. The master picked out this horse himself."

"From which slaughter yard?"

"Come now, Mark Allen. The master owes you a horse as agreed upon. What did you imagine he would purchase? The Godolphin Arabian?" The older man snorted.

Mark Allen rubbed the back of his neck. "How am I supposed to start my journey on a broken down—"

"Enough of that. I have been over him myself. He is a bit long in the tooth but sound on all four, and he has good wind." Arthur thrust the lead rope into Mark Allen's hand. "And he is a far sight better than the horse you had yesterday."

Mark Allen ground his teeth. After five years at Daniel Whiteford's estate, caring for horses of the finest quality, it had never occurred to him that the horse he'd be given at the completion of his indenture would be a worn-out sack of bones with a dull hide stretched across it. He squeezed the rope until the coarse fibers bit into his palm.

"The saddle?"

Arthur lifted his chin toward the stable. "Hanging on the hitching rail. 'Tis old, but the leather is in good shape. Same with the bridle. I found an old blanket in the tack room. You can take that too." Arthur strode to the stable and disappeared inside.

Mark Allen followed but jerked to a halt when he reached the end of the lead rope.

The horse didn't move.

He gave the rope a sharp tug that got the horse moving. "Come on, you jughead. This morning is not going to get any better for standing here."

What had he expected? A royal send-off? He flung a glance over his shoulder at the manor house. It was the day he turned twenty-one years old and, as per the agreement of indenture, he was a free man. Master Whiteford had provided a new suit of clothes, ten dollars in cash, and a horse.

Mark Allen frowned at the pale creature. Something like a horse.

He tied the animal to the hitching rail and lifted the saddle. The leather was worn butter-soft. It smelled of saddle soap and oil. Arthur. The coachman must have been up half the night bringing the relic back to life.

A knot thickened in Mark Allen's throat. He'd miss Arthur. The bandy-legged little man had taught him everything he knew about horses.

Mark Allen saddled the animal and left it tied while he climbed into the stable loft one last time to retrieve his bundle of belongings. It wasn't much of a bundle. He'd brought nothing with him when he'd arrived, and other than two changes of clothing and a blanket rolled in an oiled square of canvas. All he owned he could carry in his pockets. He looked around the slant-ceilinged room. It could've been worse. He'd chosen indenture over being apprenticed to the drunken barrel maker as his father had wanted.

That was the past. The first day of his future awaited. The start of his journey to find Gwen Morgan. Her pale face surrounded by a riot of black curls danced in his memory and tightened.

Nothing else mattered.

"He has not left yet, has he?" Cook's voice carried from the stable below.

"He will be down directly." Arthur's reply was accompanied by the familiar *scritch* of a match against his boot heel. Pipe smoke greeted Mark Allen as he climbed down.

"There he is." The rotund Cook, her mobcap askew over gray curls, clasped a sack to her chest. "'Tis a sorrowful day. Whatever shall we do without you? Nobody left but us old servants." She sniffed and stretched up to pat his cheek.

Mark Allen would miss her as well. He couldn't remember his mother, who'd died of a fever when he was very young. Cook was the closest thing he'd known.

"Do not embarrass the lad," Arthur said around the stem of his pipe.

Cook wrinkled her nose at the coachman. "I prepared a little food for your trip." She handed Mark Allen the cloth bag, which weighed considerably more than his bundle of belongings.

He cleared his throat. "I'm much obliged."

"Pshaw. 'Tis no more than you deserve." She extended her arms, and he leaned into her ample embrace. "But I would not be waving it around where the master might catch a glimpse of it, were I you." She pulled back, a twinkle in her eye.

"I have another sack for you to tie on behind that saddle." Arthur handed over a burlap bundle. "He will look a mite better with a bit of oats in his belly."

Mark Allen swallowed a lump as he took the heavy sack of feed.

"'Twouldn't hurt to tie your own bundle on top of that one as well." The old man winked.

The lump in his throat refused to stay down. As much as he couldn't wait to leave, standing before him were the closest thing he had to family.

Until he found Gwen.

He strode out the door and tied his bundles—his canvas-wrapped clothing on top—behind the saddle. He untied the lead rope and slipped the bridle over the horse's head. Foot thrust into the stirrup, he swung astride.

Cook wiped her cheek. "When you find that girl, give her our love."

The smoke from Arthur's pipe made a white wreath around his head in the crisp January air. "Take care of yourself, lad."

"I will." He turned the gray horse, and with a few kicks, urged the animal into a bone-jarring trot.

"Godspeed!" Cook called behind him.

He lifted his hand in farewell and muttered, "Only if this jughead does not trip over his bottom lip before we clear the drive."

Edinburgh, Scotland—January 1801

They were finally going home. Elation and dread fueled Faye Morgan's rushed packing. Paul McClure had given her and Madam scant notice after he'd booked their passage on the ship that would take them home. There was no time for him to even hire a girl to help with the packing.

Ship.

The very word sent a stab of fear that went from the back of her throat to the backs of her knees.

She'd crossed the ocean twice in her seventeen years, most recently two years back, when she and Madam and Paul had sailed for Edinburgh so that Paul could complete his education in the field of medicine. A voyage she'd never wanted to make but had been in no position to refuse.

But the trip when she'd been twelve years old is what caused her fear, the voyage that was supposed to give them a brand-new start. Faye's father, her sister Gwen, and she had left Wales with high hopes for a better life across the ocean. Instead, Father had died onboard, leaving Faye and Gwen orphans. They'd been sold into indenture by the ship's captain to a different captain, who'd kept them in a stinking ship's hold until he'd hauled them out, half-starving, and shoved them into a chute filled with other wretched humans bound to be sold to the highest bidder. It was there Faye had lost her sister. Gwen had been sold first and ripped away from Faye forever.

Stepping aboard another ship would bring more frequently the nightmares that still stalked her. On the voyage to Scotland, she'd rarely had a full night's sleep.

But it would be worth it to get home.

Pittsburgh would have grown in their absence, of course. Construction had been constant before they'd left. She was almost afraid to imagine how much larger it was, yet that size could be an important advantage for her. Growth meant more citizens. And while she'd left as a child, Faye Morgan was returning a young woman.

Of marriageable age.

Madam—the way Faye referred to Martha McClure—would surely see the need to present Faye to fashionable society when they returned. After all, becoming a Quaker didn't mean she couldn't marry well. They'd met a number of wealthy Quakers in Scotland, and everyone knew Pennsylvania was full of Quakers. They may dress plain and speak using *thee* and *thy*, but they were not against living well.

Faye intended to continue to live well.

Almost as traumatic as being sold like a horse. Faye remembered being hungry and cold, squatting on a dirt floor, clutching Gwen and hiding from Father when he'd been drinking.

She tossed a rolled petticoat into the trunk she was packing. Perhaps that was why she despised the beasts as much as she did. Even the smell of a horse repulsed her. In Pittsburgh, she'd look for a husband wealthy enough to provide her with a proper carriage and a liveried driver, not some wagon or cart where she'd have to look at the beast pulling it.

"Faye?" Madam's voice reached her before the tap of heels on the aged wood flooring of the rented house.

"I am still packing," she called out the open door of her bedchamber.

"Oh, good." The older woman appeared in the doorway, one hand on her chest, the other fluttering as she spoke. "I know not how Paul expected us to get everything done by this evening. Two years of living here to pack up in a single day. Thank goodness for Olivia."

Madam's maid had come to Scotland with them, but the rest of the household servants had come with the house.

"But I had a thought, my dear"—Madam plunged on with barely time for a deep breath—"about thy more elaborate dresses. There really is no need to pack them. That will save us both time and space, I should think."

Not pack her best dresses?

"But the balls in Pittsburgh." Faye pointed to her armoire where her most prized dresses still hung. "Surely I shall require such dresses to attend them."

"I know thee loves these pretty things." Madam moved to the armoire and ran her fingers over the satin and lace garments in an array of colors that they had collected for Faye before Paul convinced Madam to join the Quakers. "But we shall have no use of them now. Should Paul consent to thee attending the balls, thee will wear gowns befitting the Society of Friends."

Faye fumbled for words but came up with nothing. Leave her dresses behind? She'd accumulated these dresses for the expressed purpose of finding a husband. Dresses she'd hung her hopes on each time she'd hung a new one beside the others. Dresses denoting her status as the ward of Dr. Paul McClure. And dresses she needed to reach her ultimate goal.

She planned to become the wife of a man who would take care of her for the rest of her life in the manner to which she'd become accustomed. At least, the manner she'd lived before the turn to Quakerism.

Any hope of arriving in New Bern before midnight fled Mark Allen by mid-morning. He rubbed his gloved hands together for warmth. Sleeping outside was out of the question. He glanced over his shoulder for the third time in less than half an hour at the heavy clouds that hung in swirls of pewter and charcoal. With any luck, they carried snow and not rain. He pulled his coat collar higher on the back of his neck. The cold was bad enough. Getting soaked in these temperatures would be miserable.

Another hour down the road, slushy raindrops splattered across his back. He tugged his hat lower on his brow. Jughead—the name had stuck—quickened the pace as the drops plastered against his tail. Mark Allen thumped the animal's bony ribs with his boot heels, and he lumbered into a canter. At least the horse appeared as eager to get out of the weather as he was.

They rounded a stand of trees, and the scattered group of shabby buildings making up Durgantown came into view. *Any port in a storm.* Mark Allen rode behind the tavern, ducked beneath a wide doorway, and urged the horse straight into the stable. A Negro boy in a tattered, too-small coat hurried to his side.

"Do you know if the tavern has a room available for the night?"

"Yessah."

Mark Allen dismounted as the comforting odors of horse, hay, and dust closed around him. The horse blew out its nostrils and shook its head, spraying Mark Allen's coat with horse sneeze.

"Jugheaded horse." Mark Allen wiped the front of his coat with his gloved hands.

The boy reached for the reins.

"Nay, I will take care of him." The animal might not amount to much, but Jughead was his. He led the gray to an empty stall and eased the saddle off. Pungent steam rose from the wet hide. He poured a double handful of oats into the manger, borrowed a brush and dry sack from the boy, and worked over the gelding's wet coat while it plunged his nose in the oats.

"You may not be much to look at, and you have got a trot fit to separate me from my back teeth, but Arthur was right about one thing. You are more horse than I had yesterday." He slapped the well-rubbed rump and grabbed his bundles. "Toss him a large armful of hay, will you, boy?"

"Yessah. He could surely use it."

While the lad staggered by with an armload of hay so high he couldn't see over it, Mark Allen was satisfied his horse was in good hands. At the doorway, sleet blew almost parallel to the ground. He tugged his hat tighter and sprinted for the tavern, boots splashing icy slop in all directions.

Reaching the back door, he pushed through into a blast of warmth.

Gabe Dunkley turned from the blazing hearth and wiped his hands on the streaked gray apron around his bulging middle. "Mark Allen Teed." Firelight gleamed from his smooth head, and his smile sported as many gaps as teeth. "What errand is so important that Daniel Whiteford sent you out in weather like this?"

"I'm on no man's errand save my own." Mark Allen swept the hat from his head and straightened to his full height, his hair brushing the low kitchen beams. "I'm a free man today. My indenture has been met."

A low whistle shot through the gaps in Gabe's smile. "Your own man at last. Come in and sit." The proprietor of the tavern scooped up two tankards and filled them before leading the way to the front room and dropping his bulk onto a bench. He set the tankards on the table and motioned for Mark Allen to sit across from him. "Now, tell me of your plans."

A pair of narrow windows let in precious little light with the dark clouds overhead. One oil lamp smoked on the counter, and a meager fire in the wide hearth gave them enough light to see by. They were the only people in the room.

"I'm off to find Gwen Morgan."

"Ah." Gabe leaned into the table. "Have you any idea where to start?"

"Aye. Arthur showed me the house in New Bern where he left her three years ago."

"Three years? Has it been that long?" Gabe planted his elbows on the table. "The lass could be anywhere by now."

Mark Allen ground his teeth and stared at his wavy reflection in the dingy window. His Gwen was out there somewhere, and he was going to find her. Three years he'd waited. Three years he'd remembered his promise. *You know I will help find your sister as soon as I'm free.*

"I made her a promise. I intend to keep it."

Gabe smacked the table with his meaty palm. "I like a man who is true to his word. That I do. But three years is a long time, lad. You know..." Gabe lowered his voice as if someone were in the room to overhear. "She could be married with a couple of youngsters tuggin' on her apron strings by now."

Gripping the tankard, Mark Allen shook his head. "I cannot believe that." *I will not believe that.*

A log tumbled in the hearth, sending a shower of sparks up the chimney.

"What am I blatherin' on about?" Gabe pushed himself to his feet. "You are wet through, and here I am, talkin' your ears off. I will bring you a bowl of stew for supper. And you will be wantin' a warm, dry bed for the night. I will toss an extra blanket in the first room. Likely you be the only guest. Nobody will be out on the road in weather like this."

The tavern owner disappeared into the kitchen, still talking, and Mark Allen leaned against the rough wall beside the window.

What if Gwen hadn't waited for him? He squeezed the bridge of his nose. What if he couldn't find her?

The answer was simple.

He had to.

His whole future depended on it. He'd worked out all the details years before. He'd find Gwen and her sister and see them reunited, purchase Gwen's indenture from whoever had bought it from Daniel Whiteford, and then he and Gwen would marry and start a family. They'd put down roots. They'd belong somewhere.

Not belong to some*one*.

Belong some*where*.

He'd never belonged anywhere before, not with his father, and not with Daniel Whiteford. To both of those men, he'd been property, someone to order around, someone to do the work.

But on this day, all that ended. And as soon as he found Gwen...

His future would truly begin.

Chapter 2

NEW BERN SPRAWLED BEFORE Mark Allen, washed clean from the rain and melted snow of the day before. So much had changed since he'd last been there with Arthur more than a year prior. New homes rose on both sides of the wide street that had once been a country road. An unfinished steeple stabbed the sky behind a screen of bare tree branches. The town had burst its banks and flowed outward, swallowing fields where farmers once grazed their sheep and cattle.

Jughead ambled along, Mark Allen content with the pace as he took everything in.

How could a city change so much in that span of time? He rubbed the back of his neck. Nothing looked the same. A sign above a shop door displayed letters instead of a picture to show the shop's purpose. Letters meant nothing to him. He could scratch out enough to make his name, but that was the limit of his schooling.

A freight wagon clattered toward him. Guiding Jughead out of the path of the six-horse hitch, he moved the gray horse to the edge of the street. The wagon passed and cleared the view to a familiar building behind it. He clicked, and Jughead broke into his washboard trot, but that didn't dishearten Mark Allen. Ahead was the corner he'd been searching for. He reined the horse to the right and resisted the urge to gallop down the crowded street.

He wove between buckboards and buggies, ignoring the scowls and colorful language tossed his way. He was close. Arthur had pointed out that house with its four chimneys, and that bakery with the large front window. He remembered it like it was yesterday. And there was the picket fence where they'd slowed to watch a fetching young lady hang rugs to air.

Mark Allen searched for the corner apothecary shop he remembered. Finding it, he turned left onto another street and stood in the stirrups. The chill breeze blew the scent of the river in his face. This was the right street. His heart hammered, keeping time with Jughead's choppy pace.

The brick houses sat close to the street, many raised on high foundations near the bay. Huge trees that no doubt shaded the houses in summer stood like skeletal sentinels. Little traffic busied the quiet street.

Mark Allen tugged Jughead to a walk, then stopped in front of a three-story structure. Imposing front steps led to a pair of intricately carved doors where twin black wreaths hung, one on each.

The sign of death.

The scream that woke Faye had come from her own lips. She gasped and clung to the ship's bunk as it pitched and rolled in the frigid cabin. But it wasn't the storm that had frightened her.

"My dear, are thee all right?" Madam's voice came through the pitch darkness, it being too risky to light a candle or oil lamp in such conditions.

"I am." But she wasn't. It was the same old nightmare that had tormented her for years. Gwen reaching back for her, screaming her name. The foul smell of the auction building. The horrible man who had picked her up and heaved her onto the platform in front of all those watching—those waiting to purchase another human being. The memory of it made Faye want to scream again.

"Was it the nightmare?" Sympathy carried in Madam's voice.

"Aye." Faye shuddered. "After all these years, I had hoped for it to have lessened."

"'Tis the ship, I expect, as happened on our previous crossing."

"I hope this will be the last time I ever set foot on one." And it would be if she had any control over things. She'd find a man to marry who lacked a yearning to travel. Spending the rest of her life in Pittsburgh sounded like perfection to her.

"I am rather in agreement with thee," Madam said. "I wonder that Paul insisted we travel in the midst of winter. It seems we could have waited for fair weather." A weary sigh whispered in the darkness. "Poor man is regretting his decision now, I vow."

The ship rose and dipped again, and Faye held fast to the bunk, grateful neither she nor Madam had succumbed to motion sickness. Paul had not been so fortunate, and Olivia had gone to his cabin to attend to him.

Faye untwisted her blanket and pulled it around her as best she could while holding onto the bunk. The ship's pitching and groaning didn't frighten her. Well, not much. What she feared far worse was ever being in a position again where she was hungry and cold and hopeless. Where she was powerless to help herself, little more than prey to the human vultures who would snatch her.

If not for Madam's agent, Mr. Oster, she might have been a servant these past few years with no hope of release until she turned twenty-one. While visiting New Bern, he'd been pulled into the auction building by an acquaintance as Faye had been thrown onto the platform, falling to her knees with a cry. It had moved him, and he'd made the decision to purchase her without Madam's approval. A bold move, but one for which Madam had handsomely rewarded him.

Had Gwen fared as well? Had the man who'd purchased her indenture treated her as one of his family? Or was her sister a servant somewhere, scrubbing floors and cleaning chamber pots and... who knew what else? Faye shivered, not entirely from the cold cabin or the raging storm.

Would she ever see her sister again?

She had a slim chance of finding her in the large and growing country of the United States of America. But once Faye was married, perhaps she could talk her husband into making inquiries. Pittsburgh was a long way from North Carolina—if Gwen were still there—but Faye wouldn't give up hope. Not completely.

The ship groaned and rolled and threatened to dump Faye from her bunk.

"Oh, my," Madam said. "Sleep will elude us anymore tonight. 'Tis challenging enough to simply stay off the floor."

"Aye." Faye didn't favor sleeping again and courting the return of the nightmare. She needed to focus on her goal—to find a husband in Pittsburgh who would take care of her for the rest of her life. A man who would bring her security and peace of mind.

It was the only thing that would make the nightmare stop.

Mark Allen's heart, already beating like an owl caught in a leg trap, threatened to knock through his chest.

Not Gwen. The black wreaths couldn't be for Gwen.

He slid from the saddle, tied Jughead to the hitching post, and then raced halfway up the steps and stopped. His worn coat and muddy boots wouldn't do. He grimaced and retraced his steps. Tugging Jughead behind him, he strode around to the back of the house. He tied the horse outside the plain door and straightened his coat as best he could before hammering on the thick wood.

Hand raised to knock again, Mark Allen drew it back when the door creaked open a few inches, and the wizened face of an old woman peered at him from beneath a colorful head scarf.

"What you want?"

"I'm looking for Gwen Morgan."

She squinted at him, lips puckered into a tight frown. "What you want with that chil'?"

"Is she well?" He shifted his weight from one foot to the other. "I saw the wreath and I—"

"Them wreaths not for the girl." She started to close the door.

"Wait!" Mark Allen tore his hat off his head and beat it against his leg. "I need to see her, speak with her. Tell her—"

"She doan live here no more." She started to close the door again, but he slipped his hand into the opening.

"Please. I need to find her."

Maybe it was the note of desperation in his voice. The dark face pulled away from the narrow opening, and the door swung wide. Standing before him was a wisp of a Negro woman wearing a drab homespun dress under a stiff white apron. She planted her fists on each hip.

"Come on in. You look half froze." Her gaze flicked from his hat to his boots. "I 'spect you could do with a bite to eat."

He stepped into the tidy kitchen.

"Evie, you cain't be lettin' nobody in here. Not now. It ain't right." A taller Negro woman stood fence-post rigid against the back wall.

"What ain't right about it? Missus Cummings been two days dead. Feedin' this here boy ain't gonna bother her none." The old woman named Evie marched to the hearth.

Mistress Cummings was dead? Mistress Whiteford's sister?

Evie ladled something that smelled just short of heaven into a bowl and plunked it on the table. "Come. Eat and tells me how you know Gwen."

Mark Allen sat on the bench. Steam rose from the thick potato soup, and his stomach growled. He hadn't stopped to eat all day. When Evie pushed a plate of biscuits toward him, he broke one and dipped it into the soup and bit into it. Delicious. He chewed and surveyed the room before swallowing.

"She was here, was she not?"

"She was."

"Gwen and I were both servants for Daniel Whiteford." He tore off another chunk of biscuit and dunked it. "She never came back. And Master Whiteford never told us why."

"He never said?"

"Not a word. But I know." He leaned into the table. "You know why she came here. He could not risk bringing Gwen back to Greenesville because she knew about his daughter's baby. Master Whiteford did not want people knowing about that."

"That sure 'nuff is truth."

"I know not what he did with the baby, but I'm sure it is somewhere nobody will ever connect it with Master Whiteford."

Evie's eyebrows rose until they almost met her head scarf. She exchanged a glance with the woman still standing like a silent guard against the back wall. "Why you searchin' for Gwen after all this time?"

"I'm twenty-one now and free of my indenture. I promised Gwen that, when I was free, I would help find her sister."

"I see. You got feelin's for Gwen?"

Mark Allen choked on a spoonful of soup. The two women passed one of those looks that only women could interpret, the kind that makes a man's face flush and the hair on the back of his neck dance.

Evie grasped his arm with strength that belied her appearance. "You find her, boy. It won't be easy, but I tells you what I know."

"Anything that will point me in the right direction."

"She left with a Quaker couple name of Baldwin. Thomas and Betsy Baldwin. She traveled with them to the new free territory up north."

The potato soup turned to lead in his middle. "Why?"

The taller woman took a step further into the room. "Your massa, he want her and—"

"It be jus' like you say." Evie cut the other woman off. "He want her and that secret far away from his daughter."

Mark Allen rubbed the back of his neck as the women stared at each other across the room. There was more. They weren't telling him everything.

"I need more than that to go on. The Northwest Territory is vast. Please. Whatever you can tell me that will help me find her."

"I heard tell they took a ship that spring. Ships keep records. They may tell you somethin'."

"Do you know the name of the ship?"

Two heads wagged in response. Mark Allen pushed the soup bowl aside and rested his chin on his hands. Evening's final rays slanted across the kitchen floor.

Now what?

"You stay in the stable out back tonight. Doan nobody sleep there no more. You may have to chase out the spiders. Fetch him blankets, Sapphira." The little woman flapped her hands at the taller one and shooed her on her errand.

"Doan give up, boy. That girl is with them Quakers, and Quakers won't be hard to find." Evie patted his shoulder. "You come on back to this kitchen in the mornin', and old Evie will make you a fine breakfast. But then you best be on your way. The Whiteford family be here tomorrow, I 'spect. Best you be gone before then."

Mark Allen nodded. The last person he wanted to encounter was Daniel Whiteford.

The man who'd sent Gwen away.

Chapter 3

T YING JUGHEAD TO THE hitching post outside the shipping office, Mark Allen hoped nobody would steal the bundles behind his saddle. The sack of food Evie had pressed into his hands that morning made Cook's look stingy. Of course, Evie had no master or mistress to stop her generosity until Mr. Whiteford showed up to claim her as Mistress Cummings' next of kin.

Activity on the docks bustled around him, most of it carried out by dubious-looking fellows wearing little better than rags. Mark Allen's four bundles might be a tempting target. He thumped the gray horse's neck. "You stay here. I will return shortly."

He ducked under the low doorway to the shipping office manned by a twig of a man in a checkered vest who stood behind the counter.

"Can I help you?" the man asked without looking up from his work.

"I need to inquire about some passengers who sailed from here three years ago this coming spring."

The clerk glanced up, thin eyebrows arched above his round spectacles. "Is that all?"

"They were Quakers."

"Half of the passengers heading north are Quakers." He sneered at the name. "I have neither the time nor the inclination to search our manifests for any of them." He bent beneath the counter and brought out a brown book. Blowing dust off it, he slapped it on the counter. "This is the manifest from spring 1799. Look through it yourself."

Heat rose from under Mark Allen's collar and seeped into his cheeks. He clenched his fists at his sides. A book. Filled with scratchings he would never understand. The heat built into a roaring in his ears before he spun and barged back out onto the street.

An urchin in a tattered coat lunged at the bundles behind Jughead's saddle.

Before Mark Allen could raise a shout, Jughead pinned his ears and lashed out with a cow kick to the boy's stomach.

The boy landed on his back, clutching his middle.

Mark Allen reached him in three long strides and hauled him to his feet. "What do you think you are doing?" He held the boy's coat collar high enough that his heels didn't touch the ground.

"Leggo o' me!" The spitting tomcat swung a fist that connected with Mark Allen's ribs.

His simmering anger reaching its boiling point, he lifted the boy by his ragged collar and shook him like a dirty rug. The collar ripped free, and the boy tumbled into the street.

A book slid from his coat pocket onto Mark Allen's shoe.

Mark Allen snatched it up. "I suppose you stole this from someone else's saddle."

"Gimme that." The boy scrambled to his feet.

"Not likely. I shall turn it over to the sheriff. He can try to find the owner."

"'Tis mine." Moisture glimmered in the boy's eyes.

Mark Allen turned the book over in his hand. "Yours, huh?"

"Me name's in the front. Go ahead and look." Tears or not, the boy squared his shoulders and thrust out his chin.

Mark Allen opened the front cover. There were scratchings there. His anger smoldered. He slammed the book shut and pushed it against the boy's chest. "Keep the book and stay away from my horse."

"Not to worry, mister." The boy rubbed his stomach. "He packs a wallop."

The boy couldn't be more than twelve years old. Reed thin, pants too short, and his already tattered coat now hung lopsided across his shoulders. A gust of wind, ripe with the tang of cold seawater, fluttered a mop of straw-colored hair in need of shears.

"Where are your folks, boy?"

"Gone."

Mark Allen grunted. By the length of the boy's hair and the shortness of his pants, they'd been gone for at least a year. "Dead?"

"Aye." The boy's chin sunk to his chest, and he crossed his arms tightly, holding each elbow with the opposite hand.

"Where do you live?" Not that it was any of Mark Allen's business.

The boy shrugged.

"How do you provide for yourself?" Definitely not his business.

"'Tis probably best you don't ask."

A thief then, but it was hard to hold that against the boy, an orphan trying to survive on his own. "When was the last time you ate?" A loud gurgling answered him, but the boy didn't look up. Mark Allen blew out a long breath and contemplated the scuttling clouds. He untied Jughead and led him away from the docks. "Come on." He didn't look back, but Jughead's swiveling ears told him the boy followed.

He tied the horse to a hitching post near a building that blocked the worst of the wind and unpacked the bundle Cook had given him while the boy stayed well beyond the horse's reach. Mark Allen sat on a bench along the front of a shop. A tanner's shop, it didn't smell the best, but it would have to do.

The boy sat on the other end of the bench, his wide eyes intent on the bundle of provisions.

"What is your name?"

"You already read it." He patted the pocket he'd slipped the book into.

Mark Allen ground his teeth. "Do not sass me, boy."

The boy hunched his shoulders. "Bran Hogan."

"How old are you?"

"Fifteen."

Mark Allen snorted and pulled a round loaf of bread from the bundle. The boy sat up, his eyes following the loaf Mark Allen bounced on his palm. "Tell the truth, and I will give you half."

"Be fourteen come spring." When Mark Allen started to slide the bread back into the sack, the boy thrust out his hand. "'Tis the truth.

Always been small for me age."

Since he wasn't an expert on children's ages, Mark Allen tore the loaf in half. The boy—Bran—snatched it from his hand and crammed a huge chunk into his mouth.

"Slow down, boy. Nobody's going to take it away from you."

They ate in silence, broken only by the rattle of a wagon passing and the screech of a seagull. Mark Allen stuffed most of his half loaf back in the sack. He slumped against the bench and stared toward the docks. How was he going to find Gwen? All that scratching on the manifest meant nothing to—

The boy had a book.

"How did you learn to read?"

Bran wiped his mouth with the back of his coat sleeve. "Me ma taught me. She were a school marm before she met Pa."

"You read good?"

"Aye. Enough to read the Good Book." He patted his pocket again.

"What about names on a ship's manifest?"

"I reckon."

Mark Allen shot to his feet. "Come with me then. You can earn your supper tonight."

With Jughead secured in front of the shipping office again, Mark Allen shoved Bran through the door ahead of him. The boy's heels skidded across the rough floor planks.

Mark Allen didn't wait for the clerk to notice him. "I would like to see that manifest again."

The little man pushed his spectacles higher onto his nose and grimaced, but he hefted the large book onto the counter without a word.

"Here, boy."

"Bran." His arms were crossed, and mulish gray eyes met Mark Allen's.

"Bran. Right." He pushed the book closer to the boy. "Look for the names Gwen Morgan and Thomas and Betsy Baldwin. They left in the spring, three years ago."

Bran looked at the book and then shot Mark Allen another glare, but he opened the pages and started rifling through.

Mark Allen all but bounced on his toes. How long would it take? How difficult was it to pick out a name? He had no idea. He paced to the tiny slit of a window. Jughead dozed at the hitching post. He'd already proved he could protect himself, so Mark Allen returned to hover over Bran's shoulder.

After an eternity of flipping pages, Bran stopped and cocked his head. "Here." He jabbed a finger at a spot of scratching in the book. "All three names and plenty of others, bound for Alexandria, Virginia."

Mark Allen slumped against the counter.

The pinched-faced clerk scowled at him, but he didn't care.

Alexandria. How would he ever find her in a city like that? No. The slave woman had said Gwen was headed for the Northwest Territory. Alexandria must have been a stopping point. Or a starting point. He pulled off his hat and jammed his fingers through his hair.

"Are we goin' to Virginia?"

Mark Allen blinked. *We?*

"She is still seaworthy, and that is what matters most." Paul had joined Madam and Faye for dinner. He was pale and had dropped weight, but his smile was genuine.

The storm had raged for days, and more than once Faye had wondered if they'd meet their end in the water. Madam had prayed—silently, as was the way of the Quakers—while Faye had worried. She'd agree to join with Quakers along with Madam and Paul, but she wasn't convinced it made much difference. They were still believing in the same God.

Who hadn't saved her mother or brothers or father or kept her sister with her. Faye had no illusions of being under any divine protection.

"What did the captain say?" Madam asked.

"Minor damage for the most part. We can thank God we did not lose a mainmast or the foremast, and the crew was able to repair the mizzen. Now, let us thank God for the food as well." Paul bowed his head.

Faye did the same and waited until he cleared his throat, signaling the end of the prayer.

"The crew is patching canvas. Several sails were ripped even lashed in place as they were. The flying jib and inner jib took the most damage and may not be repairable. Not having them could slow our journey."

"Better to arrive in one piece than not at all." Madam shook out a napkin and laid it across her lap. "'Twas a frightful storm, all that pitching about."

Paul pressed a hand to his middle. "Please, Mother, let us not speak of that at the table."

"How thoughtless of me." She reached across the table and squeezed her son's other hand. "Forgive me."

"Nothing to forgive. You ladies have proved yourselves to be the superior sailors in the family." He lifted his coffee cup in tribute.

Such happy family banter. Faye relaxed against the back of her chair. Maybe now was a good time to broach the subject she most wanted to discuss with Paul.

"Now that I am seventeen and we are returning home, have you given thought to officially introducing me to society?"

"Thee are still struggling with the Quaker speech, I see." Paul scooped a spoonful of the stew and looked at her over it. "It has been months, Faye."

Months in which she'd resisted that particular change, but if it meant she'd be launched into society to find a husband...

"Pardon me, of course. 'Tis only that the subject is so dear to me." She smiled at him in the way that generally melted a reprimand, although all Paul's reprimands were gentle enough.

"Of course it is." He chewed the thick stew they'd been served.

The meat was tough, and the cook had a heavy hand with the salt, but for shipboard food, Faye shouldn't complain. And she wouldn't protest a squeak if Paul responded how she hoped.

"She is of marriageable age, my son." Madam supported Faye's plea. "Time for thy ward to be thinking of such matters. In fact, I was betrothed to thy father even a year younger."

Faye scooted to the front of her chair. "So you—thee—understand my eagerness to meet the right people in society."

"Indeed, we both do." Paul put down his spoon. "But I wonder if we will move in the same circle of friends that we did before we left. We left as Presbyterians, and we are returning Quakers."

Faye's stomach dropped. Why hadn't she thought of that? Why had she assumed that returning to Pittsburgh meant returning to what she'd always known? The things she'd grown to love and expect. She'd understood about leaving her fancy dresses behind, even if she hadn't liked it. Quakers didn't dress fancy.

But did that mean her old friends would abandon her?

"I cannot think that all our old friends will shun us." Wrinkles gathered on Madam's brow. "We have known many of them our entire lives."

"People may react to us differently now." Paul waved a finger at Faye. "But I suspect thee would receive invitations to balls if thee spoke not a word and wore nothing but sackcloth. A pretty lass such as thee will never go unnoticed."

"Oh, Paul." Madam dabbed her mouth with a napkin. "The things thee says at times." She turned to Faye. "He means well, but thee will not be wearing sackcloth. Plain clothing does not mean ugly clothing, it means modest and unassuming. Surely there will be young men aplenty in Pittsburgh who see the value in a modest and humble young woman."

Faye fervently hoped so.

As Paul's ward, she enjoyed many advantages, but she wouldn't be his ward forever. At age twenty-one, she would be her own woman. And while Paul would never toss her to the street, she was not real family to him, and she couldn't expect him to shoulder the burden of her care forever.

A scene from the nightmare flashed before her, the faces of the men who would have bought her. Greedy faces, hungry with a look she hadn't understood then and didn't fully understand yet. But she was wise enough to know that without the intervention of Mr. Oster, her life would have been much different. Madam and Paul had shown her what a family could be.

She desperately wanted a family of her own and the security a husband would bring.

Bran's eyes never left Mark Allen's face. The boy's torn coat hung lopsided on his thin frame. Those too-short pants and worn shoes would never protect him from winter's cold in Alexandria. Mark Allen knew enough geography to know it was in the northern part of Virginia.

But Bran could read.

"Come on." Mark Allen headed out the door and pulled the gray horse's reins free. He swung into the saddle and held his hand out to the boy.

Bran took a step backward.

"Come on. Jughead will not hurt you if you behave yourself." At least he hoped that was true.

Bran grasped his hand, and Mark Allen pulled him up behind the saddle. "Hang on."

"Are we goin' to Virginia?"

"To the auction yard."

Bran wriggled behind him, causing Jughead to dance sideways.

"Hold still."

"You ain't sellin' me at no auction."

"Never intended to. I need you to do some more reading."

Bran stopped struggling, and the horse resumed its calm plodding.

Sell him at auction indeed. What type of man did the boy think he was?

They rode in silence until the looming structure of the auction barn came into view. Shadows from its irregular shape poured darkness across the street. A shiver crept up Mark Allen's neck as he pulled Jughead to a halt.

Bran slid off the horse before Mark Allen could grab him. The boy stood just beyond reach while Mark Allen dismounted and tied Jughead.

"Come on."

"What type o' readin' you need done in there?" Bran poked his thumb at the hulking structure.

"Gwen Morgan and her sister were sold into indenture there in May of 1796. Gwen was purchased by Daniel Whiteford. I need to know who purchased her sister, Faye Morgan."

Bran cast a glance at the dark building and hunched his shoulders around his ears.

"If I read it for you, will you take me to Virginia?"

"Why do you want to go to Virginia?"

"I hear a man can find work in the north."

Mark Allen stifled a snort. A man maybe, but not a runt of a street urchin. "You read for me, and we will talk about it after."

Bran followed him up the steps and into the dank room beyond. The clerk behind the counter rose from a stool as they approached. A pair of chins lapped over his wrinkled stock. His waistcoat was smudged with ink stains, as were his pudgy fingers.

"Can I help you?"

"I would like to see your sales records from May of 1796."

"What for?" The clerk tried to look down his nose, even though Mark Allen stood at least a hand's width taller.

"I'm searching for a young woman sold into indenture."

"All sales here are legal and final."

"I'm not questioning that. I merely wish to know who purchased her."

The clerk's mouth twisted into a disapproving frown, but he turned to the shelves behind him and pulled out a square black book. "Here." He laid it on the counter.

Mark Allen pulled Bran forward, ignoring the raised eyebrows and the disdainful sniff of the clerk.

Bran put his nose down like a bluetick hound on a raccoon's trail. His fingers traced over the scratchings, and his lips moved even though he didn't utter a sound. While he studied each page, Mark Allen wore a path on the floorboards between the counter to the door.

"William Oster from Alexandria, Virginia," Bran said, "an agent for Martha McClure."

Mark Allen spun from the door. "What?" Two long strides had him looking over Bran's shoulder.

Bran pointed at the scratchings. "It says—"

"I heard you." He ignored the boy's huff of irritation. "Alexandria."

"Reckon this means we be goin' to Virginia for sure."

Chapter 4

MARK ALLEN PULLED THE last of the bread and cheese from Cook's sack, divided it, and handed Bran half. They sat on the same bench outside of the tanner's shop. It didn't smell any better than before, but it was still out of the wind.

Bran crossed his legs Indian-style on his end of the bench, his bare legs sockless to his shoes. Mark Allen tore off a chunk of cheese and chewed it.

Alexandria.

The clerk at the shipping office had told them it was three hundred and fifty miles north by land. With Jughead in poor shape and toting another rider, even as slight as the boy was, they'd need all of two weeks to make the trip, probably more. Traveling north into the heart of winter. He let his head rest against the building behind him.

He should leave the boy in New Bern, but who would look out for him? He cast a quick sideways glance at Bran, but he was too busy eating to notice. He'd need warmer clothing, something that fit. He'd eat his weight in provisions. But he could read, and Mark Allen couldn't.

He ground his teeth through another piece of cheese, an idea forming.

"Could you teach me to read?"

Bran swallowed a mouthful of the stale bread. "I reckon so. Ain't hard."

Mark Allen grunted and finished his own share of bread. He had ten dollars and a broken-down horse to his name. He was crazy to think about taking on the boy. But to be able to read...

"Finish up, boy."

"Bran."

"Bran, finish up."

"Where we goin'?" He crammed the last fistful of cheese into his mouth as he got to his feet.

"To the mercantile." Mark Allen dusted the crumbs from his hands and gathered Jughead's reins. He swung into the saddle and reached for Bran's hand. The boy settled behind him on top of the bundles like he'd been riding there for a month.

They dismounted in front of the mercantile just as the sun was setting, but the proprietor greeted them with a smile all the same.

"What can I do for you, gentlemen?"

Mark Allen poked a thumb toward Bran, who had his nose inches away from the line of candy jars. "He needs a whole new outfit, including boots and a coat."

Bran's head snapped around, his mouth dropping open.

"And we require provisions for a two-week journey."

While the proprietor scurried around collecting things off the shelves, Mark Allen picked up a small pot, two forks, two cups, a coil of rope, a ground tarp, and a wool blanket. He searched the store and added a slate and a packet of chalk. By the time he'd made his choices, Bran was wearing his new clothes, sensible pieces that would keep him warm.

A smile creased the boy's face, exposing the gap between his front teeth.

Mark Allen paid for everything, doing his best to keep his face blank. By himself, the trip wouldn't have cost him half as much. The boy's clothes were priced higher than he'd expected. Still and all, it would be worth it if he learned to read. Of course, he had no idea how long that would take, but he also had no idea how long it would take to find

Gwen. Or if finding her sister would lead him to Gwen. He sighed and pocketed the few coins remaining of his ten dollars.

He'd make it work somehow. He had to. He'd promised Gwen.

Mark Allen gathered their provisions into two sacks, tied them together, and slung them over the front of his saddle. He left his clothing and oat bundles behind the saddle for Bran to sit on. Jughead could use the padding to protect his bony hips. He patted the gelding's neck and swung aboard.

Gray eyes squinting, Bran folded his arms across his chest. "What be your name?"

Mark Allen blinked. "What?"

"You ain't told me your name, mister."

"Mark Allen Teed. Most folks call me Mark Allen."

Bran tilted his chin. "Am I most folks?"

"I suppose so."

"Then I want to thank you, Mark Allen, for the new clothes."

"You are welcome, boy."

"Bran."

"Right."

Mark Allen leaned down and hauled the boy up behind him, then pointed Jughead north.

The boy—Bran—was bound to keep things interesting.

Faye anchored her hat with one hand and shielded her eyes from the sun's glare with the other. The cold gust of wind whipping across the river held no trace of saltwater brine. She sucked in the clean air while their ship bobbed toward the buildings of Pittsburgh. Faye stretched onto her toes. February's stark landscape didn't lessen her excitement. In spite of the storm, they'd made excellent time.

They were home.

"Thee cannot see the house from here." Paul's voice held more than a hint of teasing.

"Of course not. I'm trying to see if Clancy is waiting with the carriage."

"He had no way to know we would arrive this evening. When we dock, I shall send a runner to the house. We should not have to wait long."

Paul's retreating footsteps thumped over the deck planking. Faye kept her attention locked on the docks and the town that sprawled into the hills beyond. Unfamiliar brick structures rose from the landscape two and three stories tall.

They had missed so much. Two years wasted in Scotland, stuck in Edinburgh while Paul finished medical school. While she'd withered away in that dreary land, Pittsburgh had blossomed.

Was there still a place for her here? Would their friends welcome the Quaker McClures back? Uncertainty warred with her eagerness to step off the ship.

The ship nudged against the dock, and Faye whirled from the rail. Across the deck, a light blue hat covered Madam's silver hair, its wide brim flapping in the breeze. Faye hurried to the lady's side.

"Madam, we're here."

Martha McClure squeezed Faye's hand. "'Tis good to be home."

"So much has changed. If not for the fort, I would not recognize it."

"I was speaking with the captain this morning after breakfast, and he has had reports that the population of Pittsburgh has increased dramatically. He claims there are as many as fifteen hundred people living here now."

"Fifteen hundred?"

"So he assured me."

Faye clenched her free hand behind her back. The town had almost doubled in size since they'd been gone. What if they'd lost their standing in society while Paul chased after his medical degree and religion? She bared her teeth in what she hoped would pass for a smile. "'Twill be good to see old friends and become acquainted with the newcomers."

Paul joined them, the dusting of silver at his temples gleaming in the sun's last rays. "'Tis good to be home. I cannot wait to sit down with Dr. Bedford and discuss—"

"Yes, dear, we know." Madam patted her son's arm.

He grinned in return. "I shall save my lengthy ideas on the topic of medical advancements until I see him, lest I spoil the delicate sensibilities of my two favorite ladies." The loading ramp thumped onto the dock, sending a shudder through the deck beneath their feet.

Paul crooked his elbows toward them, eyebrows arched toward the peak of black hair at the center of his forehead. "Shall we disembark this vessel?"

Faye snugged her hand into the crease of his coat sleeve. When her shoes struck the ramp with a hollow clunk, a nerve twisted and twitched along her spine.

The image of her sister's face flashed in front of her. The memory of another ramp tightened her throat, one lowered at New Bern almost five years past. The sour smell of stagnant salt water, the fear in her sister's attempts to soothe her, and the crush of humanity around them as they were shoved into the high-sided chute... She tightened her grip on Paul's sleeve.

"Are thee all right?" He bent and whispered under the brim of her hat.

"Perfectly fine." She cocked her head and smiled at him. "And happy to be back where we belong."

Please, let them still belong.

Dusk gave way to full darkness. Jughead plodded along the road, his hooves crunching through an icy layer forming on the mud. Mark Allen didn't fancy sleeping under a tree. His toes tingled and his nose and ears were numb from the wind. They needed shelter, but he couldn't afford an inn. They'd passed a number of farms closer to the city, but those were thinning now.

Jughead stopped abruptly.

Bran's head knocked between Mark Allen's shoulder blades.

The boy snorted and asked around a yawn, "Why we stoppin'?"

"Ask Jughead. 'Twas his idea, not mine."

The horse swung his head to the right. Mark Allen squinted through the gloom. The silhouette of a roof loomed at the end of an overgrown trail. He reined the horse in that direction and let the gelding pick his own path through the darkness to an abandoned shack. The porch had fallen off the front at one side, but it was a sight better than sleeping under a tree. He helped Bran slide down before he dismounted.

"That horse really stop all on his own?"

"He did." Mark Allen scratched the gray's forehead.

"Smart one, ain't he."

As with Jughead's kick when Bran tried to steal the bundle from behind his saddle, there was more to Mark Allen's horse than met the eye.

"He will do. Here." Mark Allen handed over the sacks. "Put these inside and see if you can find some dry wood for a fire."

Bran did as he was told, which Mark Allen took for a good sign. With the boy busy, he unsaddled Jughead and gave him a double handful of oats. He brushed the horse down with a twist of dried grass.

"You have been on the road before, and that is a fact." Mark Allen slapped the gray's neck. "'Twill come in handy on this trip. And the way you protected my gear... well done." He rigged a picket line and left the gelding where he could reach plenty of winter-cured forage.

Bran had a tendril of fire licking some moss and twigs in the fireplace when Mark Allen entered the shack.

"How did you start the fire?"

Bran held up a small piece of flint before slipping it into his pocket.

Mark Allen grunted. The horse and the boy were proving to be more useful than he'd first assumed.

Maybe things would go easier than he'd thought.

Smothering a yawn, Faye picked up a delicate china plate with pink roses and gold edges. She chose a puffy scone from the sideboard and added a spoonful of strawberry preserves. With a steaming cup of tea balanced on its matching saucer, she joined Madam at the table.

"Good morning, my dear." The older woman smiled over the rim of her cup.

"Good morning." Faye hid another yawn behind her fingers. "'Twas heavenly to sleep in my own bed last night. But I wish the floorboards were not rolling under my feet this morning."

"That shall pass in a day or two. Remember, we felt the same way when we reached Scotland."

If only she could forget about Scotland altogether. "Where is Paul?"

"He was off to Dr. Bedford's at first light. He likely found the poor man still in his nightshirt. If I were the good doctor, I would have sent him back home and told him to return at a civilized hour. But then, I suppose doctors must be used to being pulled from their beds at the most inconvenient times."

"Indeed." At least Paul was filling someone else's ears with his boring medical talk. Faye leaned forward. "What are your plans for our first morning at home? Are we calling on any of our friends? Or shall we visit the shops? I did not recognize half of those we passed on the way home last night."

Madam set her cup on its saucer and folded her hands in her lap. "No, my dear. I plan to go through my wardrobe with Olivia to see which of my gowns can be altered and made more plain."

Faye pressed against the back of her chair and stared at her untouched food. She'd held on to hope that, once they were home, all the Quaker foolishness would come to an end. All the fuss about using *thee* and *thy* and dressing little better than the servants.

"I know how much pretty things mean to a young lady. Believe it or not, I was young once myself." Madam's pale blue eyes twinkled. "But now that I have experienced a true fellowship with Christ, I would not trade it for lace or pearls or golden threads."

"Of course." But Faye would. In the wink of an eye.

Madam rose and laid her embroidered napkin on the table. "If thee wishes to join us, Olivia and I will be in my chambers all morning." She left the room.

The last thing Faye wanted to do was spend the morning stripping lovely gowns of their beauty with Madam and her maid. Plenty of well-to-do Quakers still dressed according to their station in life. Not all of them were shunning elegance for drab colors and wide white shoulder scarves. At least, not in Scotland.

Resisting the urge to hurl her plate against the sideboard, Faye laced her fingers in her lap. A lady did not behave that way. And she may not have been born to that station in life, but she had every intention of living as a lady for the rest of it.

"Miss Faye?" The McClures' housekeeper, Mrs. Hooper, stopped just inside the door to the dining room. She clasped a silver tray in her hands against her scrawny middle, her stooped shoulders rolled forward as if to hide the tray's contents.

"Aye?"

"While you were gone, miss, these letters arrived for you."

"Letters? For me?" Who would have sent a letter while she was abroad? All of her friends knew her whereabouts. Faye forced her fingers to uncurl and relax in her lap as she waited for the bent woman to shuffle across the carpet. Madam should have retired the old housekeeper before they left for Scotland. The woman had gone to bed before they'd arrived the night before and hadn't even risen to greet them properly.

Faye lifted the envelopes. The handwriting was unfamiliar. The first revealed her name in the bold strokes of a man's script. The second had the wobbly lines of a child's hand. She stood and brushed past the housekeeper.

"Miss Faye, you have touched not a morsel of your breakfast."

"I'm not hungry." Faye waved a hand at the table. "You can clear it away."

In the privacy of her room, Faye settled onto the chair in front of her desk by the window. She picked up the letter addressed in the man's handwriting first. She had not been old enough to entertain gentleman callers before they left for Scotland, but perhaps an acquaintance had anticipated her return. She plucked her letter opener from the desk. After a quick slice with the smooth pewter instrument, a single sheet slid into her hand.

It wasn't a fine linen-blend stationary. Who would write her on such a common sheet of paper? She glanced at the signature and gasped. One hand pressed against her throat, Faye read the brief note.

My dearest Faye,

You cannot imagine my joy in having discovered your whereabouts, only to be disappointed when I learned that you are currently out of the country. I am free of my indenture and traveling to the Northwest Territory with a wagon train of Quakers. I will send word when we settle and let you know where I am. I have so much to tell you. I long to be reunited with you.
Your loving sister,

Gwen

Her sister. Faye read the note a second time. The handwriting was unmistakably male. Someone had written it for Gwen. Probably one of those Quakers.

She let the letter drop into her lap and gazed out the window while memories beat against the window of her mind. Gwen's anguished face, her arms reaching for Faye, the scream torn from her own throat as Gwen was pulled off the auction block and out of her sight forever.

Deeper memories came, Gwen holding her on the ship as their father's shrouded body slipped into the waves. Gwen's arms wrapped around her at the cemetery as their two little brothers were laid to rest. And before that, Gwen facing Faye and their brothers, saying she would take care of them, while behind her on the bed laid the sheet-draped form of their mother.

A bright red bird landed on the branch outside Faye's window, its beauty a contrast to the ugly memories. She lifted the letter again and ran her fingers across the writing. Gooseflesh cobbled the skin on her arms.

Her sister was alive, free of her indenture, and looking for her.

She sliced open the second envelope. The same scrawled writing from the envelope filled only the top of the page.

My dearest Faye,

I am writing to thee from the territory of Ohio in a place called Mount Pleasant near the Pennsylvania border. We have settled here. There is so much I wish to tell thee. I am learning to read and write. When I hear back from thee, which I pray will be soon, I will write a much better letter.
They loving sister,

Gwen

The paper crinkled in Faye's trembling hand. The words *thee* and *thy*, in their spidery script, stared back at her.

Gwen was a *Quaker*?

Chapter 5

F AYE SNATCHED THE FIRST letter and scanned the bold handwriting for *you* and *your* and the date, April 3, 1800. The date on the letter written in Gwen's hand was October 10, 1800. More than four months had passed since her sister had written it.

Faye laid both letters on the desk. Never had she expected to see or hear from Gwen again. Her sister was part of her past.

Faye looked around her bedroom. With its delicate Hepplewhite cherry bed and matching curved-front armoire, it bore no resemblance to the cramped cottage in Wales where she'd been born. She ran her fingertips over the striped muslin of her day gown, so different from the rough woolens of her childhood, a time of constant hardships, hunger, and grief.

The letters before her were an opening to a past she'd worked very hard to rise above.

Tears weighted her eyelashes, and she dashed them away. She would not cry over what was or what might have been. Tears were for babies and the helpless.

Faye was neither.

While she loved her sister and always would, her plans went in a different direction. She snatched the letters off her desk and crammed them, with their envelopes, to the back of the narrow desk drawer.

After a quick look in the mirror to tidy her hair, she pulled her heavy shawl from its peg by the door and descended the stairs. She'd pay a visit to Cecelia Croft. If anyone could lift her spirits—and fill her in on the social activities of Pittsburgh—it was her dear friend Cece.

The past needed to stay in the past.

Faye needed to secure her future.

"I'm hungry. Are we stoppin' to eat soon?"

Mark Allen crossed the reins over Jughead's neck and rubbed his gloved hands together in a futile attempt to warm them. The tepid sunlight threw a feeble shadow on the road underneath them. He supposed they should stop for a meal, although if alone, he would have pushed on.

Jughead snorted and shook his head.

"We will stop by the next water we find."

Bran stretched to peek over his shoulder. "I hope so. My insides are pinched up somethin' fierce."

Only a week on the road and they were running out of food. Mark Allen hadn't purchased enough. Cook's provisions and Evie's were both gone. Where did the boy put it? Mark Allen's stomach rumbled. If he owned a musket, he'd hunt for something fresh to eat.

"There." Bran pointed to their right. "Looks like a line o' willows along a creek to me."

Mark Allen turned Jughead off the trail. As soon as they reached a narrow creek, he pulled the gray to a stop, and Bran slid down the horse's tail.

"You will get kicked doing that one of these days."

"Nah. Jughead and me got us an understandin' now." The boy ruffled his fingers in the horse's mane. "What we got to eat?"

Mark Allen stripped the horse of his saddle and gear. "Poke through the sack and see what is left. Probably salt pork and hard biscuits."

Bran wrinkled his nose and dug into the sack while Mark Allen led

Jughead to the creek to drink. He knelt beside the horse and cracked the skim of ice off the edge before taking a long drink of the cold water. February wasn't the smartest time to travel north. He stomped his boots and then bounced on his toes until the blood tingled through them. When Jughead had his fill of water, Mark Allen let the horse roll and then picketed him to graze.

The rank odor of scorching fat reached him as he approached the small fire Bran had blazing, two pieces of salt pork smoking and snapping in the frying pan. Mark Allen grunted as he squatted beside the fire, moved the pan off the hottest part of the flame, and then held his hands out to the warmth.

"This be about all of it," Bran said.

"Then I shall have to find work in the next town or village. 'Twill slow our journey, but we must eat."

Bran poked at the salt pork. "'Tis my fault, ain't it." Not a question, but a statement of fact, and the stoicism in the boy's eyes plucked at something inside Mark Allen.

He'd never had a little brother, but in the days they'd traveled together, he'd begun to look at Bran that way. "'Tis no one's fault. We need to eat. 'Tis as simple as that."

"After you find work and refill that sack, you could ride on and be leavin' me behind." Again, the stoic look, the resolution that something bad was about to happen, but Bran would meet it with a kind of honor and dignity at odds with the street urchin he had been just days ago. Or at least, the street urchin Mark Allen had thought him to be.

A street urchin who could read, write, and teach? Mark Allen glanced at Jughead where the horse grazed. He needed to remember that first impressions were rarely to be trusted.

"Then who would I continue my learning with?" Mark Allen pulled the slate and chalk from the sack. "And while we have time..."

The gap-toothed grin erased Bran's stoicism in an instant. They plunged into another reading and writing lesson that ended as they usually did, with Mark Allen frustrated at his lack of progress and Bran *tsk-tsking* it as well.

Why were letters and words so difficult to learn?

"The salt pork is done. We should eat and move on." Mark Allen put the slate and chalk away.

It didn't take long for them to wolf their food and saddle Jughead.

They were on the road heading north when a bone-chilling rain started. Mark Allen tilted his hat to the side so the rain didn't drain back into Bran's lap. But within minutes, the only dry area on either of them was the seat of their pants.

Miserable hardly began to describe it.

If the trip had been for anyone other than Gwen, Mark Allen would have stopped long ago. But the memory of her dark curls and gentle eyes filled with sadness over the loss of her sister had him urging Jughead to a quicker pace.

As darkness gathered, lights shone ahead, the dim shapes of roof lines in the distance. With luck, someone would hire him and give them at least a barn to sleep in on such a night.

A man was walking from a barn to a house on the outskirts of the town, shoulders stooped, a lantern swinging from his hand.

Mark Allen reined Jughead in his direction. When he was close enough to be heard over the rain, he called a greeting.

The old man stopped and squinted at them.

"We are seeking a place to spend the night in exchange for our labor this evening," Mark Allen said, "or perhaps a chance to work for a few days and earn some coins for our journey."

"Where are you boys from?"

"Greenesville, North Carolina, sir, traveling to Alexandria, but I must confess, I'm not sure where we are at the moment."

"You have made it into Virginia. This is Jerusalem." He pointed to Jughead. "Your horse looks about done in."

That was a fact. Poor Jughead's nose was almost to the ground. He needed rest and the last of the oats Arthur had sent along. Carrying double was wearing down the old horse.

"He is."

"Name's Will Hackett." He nodded toward the barn. "There be an empty stall and hay in the mow. Tend to your beast and then join us at the house for supper."

Mark Allen touched the soaked brim of his hat. "I'm Mark Allen Teed, and this is Bran Hogan. We appreciate the offer, sir."

"You mustn't dawdle. The wife will have her supper hour observed in a timely manner." His tone was gruff, but kind.

"Yes, sir." Mark Allen pointed to Jughead to the barn, and the old horse trotted in like he owned the place.

"I sure hope his wife is a better cook than us," Bran said.

"Anyone would be a better cook than us." Which was true. Eating something other than scorched salt pork or gnawing on hard biscuits would be a treat.

They worked together to strip Jughead and put him in an empty stall between an old cart horse with white hairs on its face and a doe-eyed dairy cow. Bran scampered up the ladder for hay while Mark Allen shook the last of the oats into the manger. They were on their way to the house in minutes.

Mark Allen knocked on the door. It needed a fresh coat of white-wash, as did the rest of the house, but it was solid under his knuckles.

It opened. "Come in, and welcome." The old man waved them in.

Mark Allen removed his hat and stamped his feet before stepping inside, making sure Bran did so as well.

"This is my wife, Mrs. Hackett."

"Ma'am." Mark Allen tipped his head, then elbowed Bran to do the same. Not that Mark Allen could blame the boy for gawking. The inside of the house was beautiful and smelled of roasted chicken and fresh bread.

"We are pleased to have you join us." Then Mrs. Hackett gestured to the table. "Do have a seat."

Mark Allen and Bran sat opposite each other on the longer sides of the table in well-made chairs, not the typical benches one would expect. The couple took their places on the ends. The table was well crafted, too, and worn smooth until the woodgrain shone, as was the cabinet nearby and several other pieces of furniture. While the outside of the house needed attention, the inside was immaculate.

Mr. Hackett cleared his throat, bowed his head, and uttered a heart-felt prayer of thanks. Then he helped himself to a piece of chicken and passed the platter to Bran. "You need some meat on your bones, boy. Better take two pieces." Again, the combination of gruff and kindness.

Bran didn't need a second invitation, helping himself as directed.

Once all the food had been passed and each plate filled, Mr. Hackett turned to Mark Allen. "What draws you to Alexandria?"

"I'm searching for someone, the sister of a friend who was sold into indenture and taken north."

"Sounds like a tall order," the old man said.

"'Tis, but I made a promise."

A smile creased the man's face. "A man should keep his promises." He gestured between Mark Allen and Bran with his fork. "And now you are looking for work?"

"I am, sir. And if Bran can find work, so much the better."

"Hmm." The man chewed a bite of the savory chicken. "For help around here, you are welcome to the barn for shelter and two meals a day with us, morning and evening. The tack room in the barn is snug, and there are blankets in there." He took another bite and chewed. "Your best opportunity for work would be with Joshua Bellinger. He runs the local sawmill. Always short of workers because he will not pay a decent wage, but if you work off your room and board here, you will be able to put by whatever he pays you."

"Thank you, sir." Mark Allen looked at Bran, who nodded, and then back to Mr. Hackett. "We would be happy to work off our keep here and just as hard for Mr. Bellinger."

"A man who keeps his word is worth more than a wagon load of gold, if you ask me." The old man winked. "Now eat up, I have plans to keep you busy, so you will have need of it."

Mrs. Hackett smiled. "'Twill be a pleasure to cook for a couple of youngsters with an appetite again. I will make something special for tomorrow. Maybe an apple pie."

Bran's mouth fell open.

Mark Allen managed to keep his shut, but just barely. How had they stumbled upon such an obliging couple?

"Donald McMasters and John Donnelly are both off the market too." CeCe paused for a quick breath and a sip of coffee. "John married a perfectly awful woman from Philadelphia when he could have had his pick of any young woman in Pittsburgh." She huffed, setting her delicate cup and saucer on the table. "I tell you the truth, if you had not returned with Paul, we would lack enough eligible men to fill the dances this spring."

The situation was more dire than Faye had feared. She wrung the linen napkin on her lap. "What of Ethan Gower and Charles Talbert?"

"Gone, both of them. Heaven only knows where." CeCe flicked her wrist to the west. "They were among the men who could not stop talking about the Northwest Territory as if 'twere paved with gold and filled with orchards. And, of course, the Quaker men all took off to those free lands. They should know their Bible well enough to realize that slavery is not a sin." CeCe's puckered lips twisted.

So did Faye's stomach. When she'd arrived in Pittsburgh, she'd been introduced as Paul's ward. Nobody in the town, not even her dearest friend, knew of her brush with fate on the auction block. Even the thought of slavery set her nerves afire.

On that one matter, she silently agreed with the Quakers.

"At least Andre had the good sense to stay put." A smug little smile played at the corners of CeCe's mouth. Her friend had never made it a secret that she intended to secure Andre Chandler as her husband. Faye couldn't help but wonder why it hadn't happened in her two years' absence.

Their conversation turned to the lesser topics of the day until Faye rose to excuse herself. Madam was expecting her to return for tea. The friends hugged and promised a longer visit soon.

Outside, Faye pulled her woolen shawl tight and headed home against the stiff February wind. She cast a glance at the heavy clouds and quickened her pace. Even so, snowflakes were surging against her by the time she turned onto Smithfield Street. Dressler opened the door as she climbed the front steps.

"Has tea been served?" She handed the butler her shawl.

"No, Miss Faye. Mister Paul returned only moments ago. Tea will be served in about twenty minutes."

"Very well." Faye climbed the stairs, pulling the pins from her hat as she went.

Paul stepped out of his room and into the hallway in front of her. "Hurry along, Faye. I have news to share. I shall tell thee and Mother at the same time." He sidestepped around her and clomped down the stairs.

News to share. Probably more boring doctor stuff.

She sighed and put her hat in its box. The only good news she could think of would be a dance and a room full of eligible young men to choose from. The right kind of young men, of course.

The kind who would guarantee her future.

Chapter 6

"**Y**OU EVER THINK MAYBE someone be watchin' over us from above?" Bran asked as he forked dirty straw from the dairy cow's stall. "Like it says in the Good Book?"

"What?" Mark Allen looked up from the old farm horse's hoof he was trimming. Arthur would have had a fit if he'd seen the condition of the poor animal's feet, so Mark Allen had begun his morning's work on them.

"You know," Bran continued, "that maybe God be lookin' out for us."

Mark Allen straightened and let the hoof down. "Why would God do that?"

Bran stabbed the pitchfork into the dirt and leaned against it. "Ma used to pray with me every night. She said God listens and answers when we pray."

Mark Allen wanted to snort, but the earnestness in the boy's face stopped him.

"The preacher used to pray up a storm every Sunday." Bran warmed up to this subject. "In the summer, sweat would be rollin' off him by the end."

"What did he do in the winter?"

"Oh, he still prayed long and loud." Bran flashed his gap-toothed grin. "But I expect the good Lord knowed he needed a break from the heat."

Mark Allen moved to the horse's other side and lifted a hoof.

"You 'spect them Quakers will be prayin' folks?"

"I suppose we will know when we find them."

"I hope so." Bran dug the pitchfork into more dirty straw. "There be a comfort in knowin' someone be prayin' for you."

They finished their work in the barn in silence, but Bran's words stuck with Mark Allen. He didn't mind the idea of someone praying for them, but he had no idea how to go about it himself. If there was a God in heaven watching over them, why didn't He just tell them where Gwen and Faye were? Why make it all so hard?

He listened extra carefully to Mr. Hackett's prayer over breakfast, but there didn't seem to be anything special about it, just a lot of thanks for food the old couple had worked for and raised themselves.

Mr. Hackett had told them where to find the sawmill, and they set out on foot after the meal, giving Jughead a good rest in the small paddock beside the barn.

"Reckon they will hire me too?" Bran asked.

Mark Allen shrugged. Even if Bran was almost fourteen—and Mark Allen still doubted it—he was a scrawny lad. A sawmill would need strong workers, men able to lift logs and stack boards. He flexed his fingers inside the thick gloves Mrs. Hackett had pressed into his hands before they left. He'd need them to handle wood.

There was no mistaking the smell of fresh-cut lumber as they rounded a thicket of leafless trees covered in vines. The sawmill rose from the bank of a fast-moving stream, its huge wheel scooping and pouring the sparkling water. Long sheds fed off the main building, open on the side they were approaching. The *whir* and *buzz* of the spinning blade made the hair on the back of Mark Allen's neck dance.

Everyone knew sawmill work was dangerous. He hoped they'd turn Bran away. That spinning silver monster was as tall as the boy.

A man approached them as they drew near. "Hello."

"Hello. Mr. Hackett said you might be hiring."

"Always." He thrust out a gloved hand. "Joshua Bellinger, owner."

Mark Allen shook the hand and gave his name.

"Name's Bran Hogan." The boy offered his hand as well. "I be lookin' for work too."

Mr. Bellinger looked at it, then shook it. "While 'tis a pleasure to meet you, I'm afraid I have no jobs suitable for a boy your age."

Bran puffed up like a partridge. "I'm a good worker, and I ain't afraid."

"And that is the problem." Mr. Bellinger's smile was firm. "Someone who is not afraid of that"—he pointed toward the saw blade—"will be hurt by it. But I heard the boy who helps at the butcher shop broke his arm. You might try there if you can handle the sight of blood."

"Sure I can."

Mr. Bellinger told Bran how to find the butcher shop, then grasped Mark Allen by the shoulder and all but hauled him into the sawmill, giving instructions at a rapid pace.

It wasn't going to be easy, but once again—with hard work—Mark Allen's needs were being met. When he found the time, he'd have to think on that as well as Bran's questions about praying.

"Here she is at last," Madam said, "Now thee can share the news."

Paul winked at Faye. "Another moment or two, Mother. Let the girl be seated, and we shall thank the Lord for the refreshments first."

Faye summoned a half-hearted smile and took her seat at the table. She bowed her head and tried to suppress a grimace as they sat in silence. She wished they would go back to the routine prayers they had uttered aloud at mealtimes before they'd gone to Scotland. Before turning Quaker.

"Now, Paul, I cannot wait another moment," Madam said as soon as Paul cleared his throat, signaling the end of their silent prayers.

"Dr. Bedford had a copy of the final issue of the *Pennsylvania Gazette*."

"What do you mean, the final issue?"

"Shush, Faye. Let him tell his story." Madam nodded at Paul to continue.

"The final issue, my dear ward, because the newspaper has gone out of business."

"Why?"

"Faye."

Paul raised his palm toward his mother and said to Faye, "I'm sure I do not know." He placed both hands on the table. "The important thing is, there was an advertisement in that issue, a place in Ohio advertising for a physician to come and reside at a new Quaker settlement."

Madam clasped her hands under her chin. "God provides."

God provides? What was she talking about? Faye leaned into the table. "What does that have to do with us?"

"I'm applying for the position."

"What?" She sat back in her chair with a thump.

"There are two physicians in Pittsburgh besides Dr. Bedford. The town cannot support a fourth."

Madam nodded, her face serene.

Faye's heart twisted like a sheet in a windstorm. Surely not. They had just arrived home. Home. Where they belonged. Where *she* belonged.

"What is the name of the settlement, son?"

"Mount Pleasant."

That wasn't possible. Faye's breath came in short pants. She pressed both her hands to her stomach. Surely it couldn't be—

"Are thee ailing?" Paul's voice echoed as if from a tunnel.

Faye took a sip of water. "Nay, 'tis just the excitement." As exciting as watching her future slip away could be.

"Exciting indeed," Madam said. "When will thee send off a letter?"

"I already have. Dr. Bedford was kind enough to provide me with the stationery. I posted it on the way home."

Faye's world spiraled around her.

They couldn't go to Mount Pleasant—where Gwen was—to a Quaker settlement. Faye had no plans to marry a Quaker and settle down to a life of *thee* and *thy* in some backwater territory where danger and hunger were only a step away.

And no proper gentleman would ever consider her for a wife if he knew her sister had been an indentured servant.

She ignored the twinge of guilt that threatened to close her throat. She loved her sister, but she hadn't seen her in years. People changed. Faye had changed.

And she didn't want to go back to how she'd been before.

Mrs. Hackett held out a sack to Bran. It was bulging with enough food to last them for several days. She'd been more than generous, and Mark Allen felt a little guilty, considering how much he and Bran had eaten over the past two weeks.

"We can buy provisions now, ma'am," he said. "We needn't deplete your larder."

"Nonsense, we have plenty, especially with Bran bringing home so much meat."

The largest part of Bran's pay had been in fresh meat from the butcher. Mrs. Hackett had cooked enough that even Bran's britches were snug around the waist, and they still had extra meat to smoke for later.

"Take it, boys," Mr. Hackett said. "My missus would worry otherwise."

Bran snatched the sack and held it to his chest. "We surely do appreciate it, ma'am. We ain't so good at cookin' on our own."

"'Tisn't charity either. You have worked it off." Mr. Hackett pointed toward the barn. "The place looks like it did when I was ten years younger."

"More like twenty." Mrs. Hackett gave her husband a fond smile.

The old man raised an eyebrow at his wife but turned his attention back to Mark Allen and Bran. "Godspeed to the both of you. Good luck in finding the young ladies. We shall keep you in our prayers."

"You remembered to pack that extra blanket?" Mrs. Hackett asked.

"We surely did, ma'am." Bran beamed at her. "'Twill come in mighty handy up north."

"Thank you, sir, ma'am, for everything." Mark Allen swung astride Jughead, who had also filled out with plenty of rest and hay.

"Bye, ma'am, sir." Bran grabbed Mark Allen's hand, keeping the sack to his chest, and scrambled to his seat behind the saddle.

With a touch to the brim of his hat, Mark Allen turned Jughead and started toward the road.

"They be nice folks," Bran said. "You remember when we talked about prayin'?"

"I remember." Sawmill work plus farm chores had left him little time to ponder it much.

"I like knowin' they be prayin' for us. 'Tis a comfort."

Mark Allen turned Jughead onto the road heading north. Birds were singing, the winter sun was bright, the road was firm, and its footing good. No reason they wouldn't make good time toward Alexandria. But winter could be fickle, and the farther north they went, the colder it would get. It was comforting, knowing that Mr. and Mrs. Hackett were keeping them in their prayers. He wasn't going to argue that.

He wasn't convinced it would do them any good, though.

According to Mr. Hackett, they had a hundred and seventy miles yet to go—more or less—before they reached Alexandria. With good roads, good weather, and if Jughead stayed sound, they could be there in eight days. Every step brought him closer to finding Gwen and Faye.

But a lot could happen in eight days.

"'Tis the first ball since we returned." Faye forced herself not to wring her hands in her lap. "We simply must attend."

Madam sat her teacup on its saucer. "We have spoken of this. The Society of Friends frowns on such frivolous activity as dancing."

"But we have always attended the balls." Faye failed to keep the whine from her voice.

"Before. That is the difference." Madam sighed and leaned forward in her chair. "Can thee not feel the difference now that we have experienced the Inner Light of Christ and have accepted the Quaker way?"

"I do feel differently." *Stifled, to be exact.*

"I thought so. The changes are something we all need to adjust to."

"But not all Quakers stop going to balls or wearing pretty clothes."

"Ah, to be young and denied such diversions. Some Quakers are indeed less stringent about these things. I will speak with Paul when he returns. He will make the final decision."

Faye stopped the protest that wanted to burst from her. Paul was the one who had gotten them into the whole Quaker mess in the first place. He seemed to take delight in being the strictest of Quakers.

"Once we are moved west to the Quaker settlement, these issues will no longer trouble us." Madam picked up her cup and sipped.

Faye retrieved her own cup and hid her gritted teeth behind its rim. She had no intention of moving west, not now, not ever. She'd lived on the edge of civilization back in Wales. She'd been poor. She'd been hungry. She'd watched her loved ones die one by one.

All but Gwen.

But Gwen was out west now, at the edge of civilization, and she would probably meet the same fate as the rest of their family.

Faye wasn't going to be around to watch it happen.

She simply must find a way to attend the ball. It was her best chance of meeting a gentleman, which was her only chance of living a safe and secure life right there in Pittsburgh.

Chapter 7

MARK ALLEN SNEEZED SO hard that Jughead spooked, and the old horse danced sideways for a few steps on the icy trail.

"Sorry, old boy." Mark Allen patted the animal's neck before wiping his nose on his coat sleeve, not that it stopped the dripping. He sneezed again. They should be almost halfway to Alexandria. He didn't have time to be sick.

"I'm thinkin' we need to find us a shelter and make a fire," Bran said. "You ain't sounding so good."

He didn't feel so good either. Between the nonstop drip at the end of his nose, the rasp in his chest, and the way his cheeks burned, Mark Allen knew Bran was right. But they hadn't seen a house since early that morning, and he was beginning to think they should have stayed on the main road. A farmer had recommended the shortcut they were on to bypass Richmond, but it was little more than a wilderness path. They'd been on it for hours, however, so it didn't make much sense to turn around and lose all the ground they'd covered.

Another bone-rattling sneeze shook him.

Bran pointed. "Maybe we can shelter in the rocks up ahead."

Mark Allen blinked, then blinked again because the rocks refused to come into focus.

Bran was right, they were large and tumbled together like some giant had been tossing them in a game of dice. All he and Bran needed was somewhere for a fire to reflect off their surfaces and radiate heat. A shiver shook him. Heat would be a wonderful thing. He urged Jughead to go faster, and then winced at the bone-jarring trot.

He hurt all over.

It hadn't been bad that morning, just a sniffle. Nothing to worry over. But the sun hadn't gotten much past its peak before he'd started to feel worse. It was nearly suppertime now, and all Mark Allen wanted to do was crawl under his blankets and sleep.

"There, ain't that a cave o' some sort?" Bran pointed to their left.

It wasn't a cave exactly, but there was a large rock that had fallen over and rested against another rock, making a lean-to of sorts. It was the best shelter they were likely to find in this patch of wilderness.

Jughead stopped, and Bran slid off the horse's back end. "I will see to Jughead, and then scout some wood for a fire. You just unroll the blankets and crawl under that rock."

"I can take care of my horse." But when Mark Allen's feet hit the ground, his knees almost buckled, and Bran had to steady him.

"I can see that." A smirk colored the boy's voice.

If he hadn't been feeling so poorly, he'd have given the upstart a piece of his mind. But the thing was, he couldn't seem to focus his mind or his eyes on much. He took the blankets and tarp Bran pressed into his arms, and then the boy turned him around the gave him a push toward the rocks. Like he was some kind of doddering old...

A violent sneeze nearly blew him off his feet. He gripped the blankets to his chest and stumbled to the rocks, falling to his knees. He crawled under the overhang, spread the tarp on the ground, then fell on top of it, his hot cheek pressed against the cold canvas as he pulled a blanket over him.

What would he have done without Bran?

CeCe hadn't exaggerated. Faye surveyed those dancing in the hall,

most of them married couples. The list of eligible men present con-
sisted of no more than five. Paul, she didn't count, and since CeCe had
at least marginal rights to Andre, that left three. Faye recognized one
of the gentlemen from before, but the other two were strangers to her.

She clenched her hands together inside her fur muff. One of those
gentlemen might have noticed her if she hadn't been draped head
to toe in a moss-green muslin gown stripped of any adornment. It
hung from a high waist to the floor without a ruffle or a scrap of lace
anywhere. She remained mindful not to stand near a window lest she
blend into the curtains. The white scarf gracing her shoulders was
of finest cashmere and not plain cotton. She'd won that battle with
Madam, at least.

"Here comes Andre." CeCe nudged her shoulder. "Surely he will
introduce you to the gentlemen with him, since Paul seems distracted."

Faye resisted the unladylike urge to snort. Paul had practically
dropped her at the door when he spied another doctor present. Those
two stood nose to nose across the room, discussing who knew what
type of gruesome treatment or another. If not for Andre...

"And here are a couple of Pittsburgh's finest young ladies." Andre
extended a hand toward them. "Faye Morgan and Cecelia Croft, let
me introduce you to William Addison and Hugh Spears."

William Addison bowed, the top of his head gleaming through long
strands of hair combed back and tied at his nape. His velvet waistcoat
stretched across an ample middle that stopped just short of being
pudgy.

Hugh Spears inclined his head in the briefest of bows. His ginger
hair curled around his face, refusing confinement. His dark coat lacked
any hint of embellishment as did his double-breasted fawn waistcoat,
but his fine linen stock was edged in lace, matching lace on his shirt
cuffs. He hiked one eyebrow above hazel eyes that gleamed with
humor or mockery.

Unsure of which, Faye turned her face away from him.

"Pleasure to meet you, ladies." The warm baritone of Hugh's greeting washed over Faye.

She peeked at him.

His mouth pulled to one side and tilted up at the corner.

"The pleasure is ours, gentlemen." CeCe stepped beside Andre and
slipped her fingers into the crook of his arm. As the musicians struck

the opening notes to a lively reel, Andre and CeCe departed for the dance floor.

Hugh moved aside, allowing them to pass in the crowded corner and effectively stepping between William and Faye. "Miss Morgan, are you free for this dance?"

"I am." She slipped her left hand from her muff and laid her fingers against the brushed wool of his coat sleeve. They slipped into the familiar steps of the dance without another word.

When the dance ended, Hugh stood by her side and clapped his appreciation to the musicians before turning toward her.

"I have been in town for six months. How have I missed the pleasure of meeting you before now?"

Faye summoned her well-practiced smile. "We have been abroad." That sounded important, perhaps enough to impress him.

He ushered her toward a pair of vacant chairs near the French doors. "Abroad? Were you in London? Paris?"

"Neither." Faye battled to keep her smile in place, wishing he hadn't asked. "We were in Edinburgh."

He stopped abruptly several steps short of the chairs. "Edinburgh?"

"Indeed. My guardian attended a physician's university there."

"Ah." He led her to a chair and held it while she sat, then took the other seat for himself. "I heard they have one of the finest for that noble profession."

Faye curled her toes in embarrassment at the way he mouthed the word *profession*.

"Paul has always felt drawn to help those in need in any way he can." She glanced at Paul, still deep in conversation.

"Then Paul McClure is your guardian?" At her nod, he continued. "Fine fellow. I met him briefly the other day. A Quaker, I believe. I'm surprised to see him in attendance."

Faye straightened in her chair. "That change is rather newly made. We attended the Presbyterian Church here before we left for Scotland. Would you mind? A cup of the cider would be most welcome right now." If only to steer the conversation elsewhere.

Hugh left and returned with two cups and handed her one.

She took a small sip. It tasted of apples, cinnamon, and too much sugar.

"Miss Morgan," he said, "what was it that drew you to the Quaker faith?"

Faye choked on the oversweet beverage. She turned her head and coughed. Tears streamed down her face as she struggled to suck in a breath between coughing spasms. Then someone slapped her back.

"Lean forward," Paul said close to her ear as he bent her over his arm. "There now. Breath in through your nose."

Faye did as he said and the spasms calmed. She took the handkerchief he pressed into her hand and mopped her face.

"I shall take thee home now."

"Nay." Faye reached for his sleeve, but he'd turned away to ask a servant to fetch their carriage. Faye refused to look up from her lap. From the corner of her eyes, she saw the skirts and trousers of the crowd moving away. Not even CeCe came to her side. Heat rose from her chest and burned across her cheeks. She'd made a spectacle of herself, and in front of Mr. Spears, no less.

She squirmed in her seat. At least she didn't have to worry about facing anyone in this crowd at church the next morning. One slight blessing for attending the Quaker Meeting House.

But what if she'd ruined her only chance of staying in Pittsburgh? What if Paul wouldn't allow her to attend another ball?

He had to. He just had to.

Water trickling over rocks somewhere nearby set off a raging thirst in Mark Allen. He blinked eyes filled with grit. A fire roared in front of him, its light glinting off the rock above him. Stars peppered the sky beyond.

Where was he?

"Mark Allen, you woke up yet?"

He knew the voice, but he couldn't put a name to it, and then a face drawn tightly in worry lines pressed close to his.

"Are you?"

"Aye." The single word came out little more than a croak and sent a stab of pain from his chest to the back of his tongue. "Water."

Bran—he remembered the boy's name—scrambled to the fire and dipped water from their pot into a cup.

Mark Allen would have preferred cold water, but he slurped down the fire-warmed drink and pressed the cup back to the boy. "More." He drained two more cupfuls before collapsing back into the blankets.

"You feelin' any better?"

Was he? He vaguely remembered Bran fussing over him, wiping his face with something wet, talking to him. Always talking, yet Mark Allen couldn't remember a word of it.

"How long... have we been here?"

"Three days and half a night."

Mark Allen groaned as a chill wind scooted under the rock and ruffled his blankets. They'd need to get back on the road come daylight. They must be growing short on provisions. He tried to add the days up in his head from when they'd left the Hackett's place.

Eight? Had it been eight days? And they were still no more than halfway to Alexandria.

Frustration gnawed in his middle, or maybe it was hunger. Whatever it was, it wasn't powerful enough to keep his eyelids open. But he couldn't fall asleep either.

Where was Gwen? How was she? Did whoever held her indenture treat her well? He shivered and pulled the blankets tighter. Was she warm enough? Did she have enough to eat?

Did she think of him as often as he thought of her?

"I vow, I was never so humiliated in my life." Faye buried her face in her hands.

"As you can imagine"—CeCe hugged Faye to her side on the settee they shared in CeCe's parlor—"I was horribly distraught when I saw what had happened. But your guardian reached you first and had everything in hand. 'Tis an advantage to have a doctor in your household."

Advantage? Maybe if he weren't a Quaker doctor who wanted to take her away from everything she held dear. Everything other than Gwen, of course.

Faye straightened, lifted her chin, and met CeCe's sympathetic eyes. "How was the rest of the ball for you and Andre?"

CeCe released her and plopped against the settee's back, hands clasped in front of her. "It could not have been better. Dear Andre danced with me a total of eight times. Eight! And I do not mind telling you that several of the old ladies were tittering behind their hankies when he escorted me out for the last dance." Her friend heaved a dramatic sigh and cut a glance at Faye. "He has asked me to join him for a drive on Saturday, or a sleigh ride if it snows. Does that not sound perfect?"

"Indeed, perfect is the word." Faye did her best to be excited. After all, CeCe had been trying to entice Andre for years. But it was difficult to squash the flash of jealousy.

It wasn't that Faye was drawn to Andre. She wasn't. He'd never seemed very genuine to her. More than once she'd feared he was stringing CeCe along only to dump her friend if someone from a more well-to-do family came along. Faye had never been a temptation for him, being a lowly ward, and she'd been glad of it.

But marriage to Andre would be better than life on the frontier.

"Do you suppose he will escort you to the McCarthys' ball the following Friday evening?" Faye asked.

CeCe slapped a hand over her heart. "'Tis my greatest wish."

"'Twould send the old women's tongues wagging for sure."

"And then Andre would have to propose to me, do you not agree?"

"Of course I do." Faye hugged her. "I will be so happy for you."

"And then, of course, we must find a husband for you. And 'twill be easier once I'm married, because I shall be able to introduce you to all of Andre's friends. He has a surprising number who never frequent the balls."

Faye drew in a breath, paused, and then let it out in a rush. "The thing is, I may not have that much time."

CeCe sat up straight. "What do you mean?"

"Paul intends to move us to the frontier, some place in Ohio that needs a doctor."

"Oh, my. But we need doctors here in Pittsburgh."

"He says there are already too many here, and he sent a letter applying for the position already."

CeCe gasped. "Then we have no time to lose. Be sure that I will inquire about Andre's eligible friends at the first opportunity. Indeed, if he cannot entice them to attend the ball, I will find a way to arrange introductions."

Faye hugged her friend as if she were a lifeline.

Chapter 8

T HEY WERE FOUR DAYS behind schedule, and the weather was turning colder. Mark Allen hiked the collar of his coat higher on his neck against the cold wind and coughed. He needed another day or two of rest, but their provisions were almost gone. He hadn't purchased much to add to everything Mrs. Hackett had packed, which would have been plenty if not for his illness.

He should be thankful to be alive. More than one man had succumbed to fever and sickness on the trail. Those found at all were generally found too late to help.

But he had Bran, who had taken care of him and Jughead. When he'd plucked the boy off the street in New Bern, he'd never imagined they'd grow as close as they had. Some days, it seemed he'd always been a part of Mark Allen's life. Like he'd been lurking in the shadows and just waiting to appear at the right moment.

Or maybe the fever had addled Mark Allen's brain.

Jughead snorted and tossed his head.

"What it is, fella?" Mark Allen patted the gray neck.

"Looks like a farm," Bran said.

Not much of a farm, just some squat log buildings and fields barren for winter, but Mark Allen pointed Jughead in that direction. "Maybe we can sleep in the barn."

"Maybe the missus will have some fresh bread we could barter for chores." The wistfulness in Bran's tone matched the emptiness in Mark Allen's middle.

As they drew near, a man appeared holding a rifle across to his body the way a man did if he wanted it clear and easy to swing and shoot.

"Hello." Mark Allen called.

"This is private property," the man said.

"We are looking for a place to bed down for the night," Mark Allen said. "We are good at barn chores. I am a stableman by trade."

The man jabbed the butt of his rifle toward the house, where someone moved, a dark-skinned man in ragged clothing. "Got my own workers. You two can move on."

Mark Allen wasn't too disappointed. He wasn't sure he'd have wanted to stay near the man who hadn't lowered the rifle. "Can you point us to the closest town?"

The man pointed with the barrel of the rifle at the road in the direction they'd been traveling. "That way."

Mark Allen tipped his hat and urged Jughead on.

"I seen a badger once," Bran said once they were back on the trail. "'Twas a mite friendlier than him."

"The way he clutched that rifle, like it was always in his hands, I would not have rested easy in his barn."

"Me neither. And that darky by the house, he looked half starved." Bran's stomach rumbled as if in sympathy, although he had to be hungry too.

They had enough food for that evening and the morning, but that would empty the sack. If there was a town up ahead, Mark Allen had coins left in this pocket, but he'd rather work off a meal whenever they could. They might need cash money once they reached the big city of Alexandria.

Mark Allen coughed again, still a deep wracking cough, but at least his throat wasn't on fire anymore. They plodded along, darkness draping down around them, until they saw another farm in the distance. The buildings were larger and surrounded by a fence.

After the last cold reception, it was tempting to just move on, but it was almost full dark, and Jughead was tiring. Mark Allen pointed the horse toward the house and called out, "Hello."

Three little dark girls squealed and raced from behind the fence to disappear around the house.

An elderly slave man hobbled toward them, making a shooing motion with both hands. "Go off with you. Ain't nobody givin' handouts here. Go on."

Did they look like vagabonds? Mark Allen glanced at his coat and britches, both covered in dust and trail dirt. Maybe they did.

"We were looking for a barn to sleep in tonight and—"

"Ain't no room here. You got to move on." The old man shook his head. "Massah doan want the likes of you hangin' round here."

"Who are you to—"

Mark Allen elbowed Bran to shut him up. There was no need to argue with the slave. It was his owner who didn't want people around.

His owner.

Mark Allen tipped his hat to the old man. "We will move on. You have a good night." Then he lifted the reins, waking Jughead, and clicking to get the old horse moving again.

"That man could have been more friendly." Bran huffed and squirmed.

"He was just following orders."

"Well, he could have followed them more friendly."

"Be thankful that you do not understand."

"What do you mean?"

Mark Allen sighed. "I was indentured, owned by another person as that man is. I had to do whatever Mr. Whiteford told me and ask no questions. But I was able to work my way free." A sadness settled over him. "That man back there, he can never do that."

Bran remained quiet after that.

They found a sheltering grove of trees and made camp as the last of the sun's rays disappeared overhead. Maybe it was good that Gwen was in the Northwest Territory with the Quakers. It was free territory with no slaves.

It would be a good place to start a new life for him and Gwen.

"Oh, my dear. She has grown into such a lovely young woman."

"Thee remembers Mrs. Downey, Faye?" Madam asked. "From Alexandra?"

"Indeed." Faye curtseyed to the plump matron seated beside Madam. "What a pleasure to see you again."

"Oh." Augusta Downey fanned her face and looked between Faye and Madam. "She has not changed her speech to reflect the Quakers?"

"Generally she does, but we all slip from time to time. 'Tis challenging to change a lifelong habit"

"I suppose so." Mrs. Downey sounded anything but sure.

Faye fought the urge to cringe. Mrs. Downey was one of only a handful of people who knew Faye's true background. What was she doing in Pittsburgh? And who might she talk to before she left?

"Augusta came at once after receiving my letter regarding our plans to move." Madam patted her friend's hand. "The most difficult part of moving is leaving our dear friends behind."

"'Twill be very difficult indeed, Madam." Faye sent a sympathetic look toward Mrs. Downey. "Perhaps we should rethink the whole idea."

"You must, Martha. Do rethink this. To have you so far away..." Mrs. Downey pressed a handkerchief to her mouth. "And you barely returned from abroad."

Faye could've kissed her.

"Now, do not start that." Madam fumbled for her own handkerchief. "Paul is quite adamant that he is going, and I cannot abide being separated from him for the few years I have left on this earth. He is all I have except for Faye."

The pounding of boot heels down the hall alerted them to Paul's arrival, just when Faye might have an ally in Mrs. Downey. She ground her teeth at his unfortunate timing.

"Great news." He shook a folded paper from his outstretched arm. "They have accepted me. Mount Pleasant's leaders have agreed to provide me with a home in return for my agreement to move there and stay at least five years." He shook the paper again. "'Tis all in here."

"Gracious." Madam pressed her hand to her breast. "We were just discussing that very thing."

"God's timing, Mother. God's timing."

"When will we leave?"

"As soon as the river allows. I should think by the first of April. We shall take a packet boat as far as"—he consulted the letter in his hand—"Robert's Landing. From there we will travel by wagon to Mount Pleasant."

With each word, Faye's heart dropped another notch in her chest. After her disastrous collapse at the ball, Paul had so far refused to let her attend another. She had no hope of a suitor approaching her before they left unless CeCe could arrange something. If only she could convince Paul to let her stay in Pittsburgh. But how?

And then there was Gwen. She'd love to be reunited with her sister, but not permanently. Not in the back of beyond on the frontier. Not when it meant leaving everything that was security behind her.

She must find a way to remain.

"Think 'tis gonna snow?"

"Aye." Mark Allen cast a glance at the clouds building low on the western horizon. "Hopefully, not too soon. Maybe we will make it to the town up ahead."

"Here. 'Tis the last of it." Bran handed over a hard biscuit.

Mark Allen's stomach lurched at the sight, but he took it and dropped it into his cup of heated spring water to soften. What he wouldn't give for a loaf of Cook's bread, or a bowl of Evie's soup, or a slice of Mrs. Hackett's pie. And coffee.

"Got that slate handy?" he asked.

Bran rolled his eyes and dug into the pack with one hand. The other kept a tight hold on his cup and biscuit. He pulled out the slate and a stick of chalk. "Here. Practice them letters I showed you whilst I gnaw on this."

"'Tis not letters I want to make," Mark Allen muttered and blew out a plume of frosty breath. "I want to make words."

"You cain't make one 'til you learn the other. Letters is like the logs you need to build a house. No logs, no house. No letters, no words."

Mark Allen scratched the letters across the slate, his concentration on that task diverting his mind from the tasteless biscuit. When finished, he handed the slate to Bran.

The boy eyed it with a frown. "Not bad, but you got the stick on the wrong sides of the b and d. On the b it goes *before*, and on the d it *don't*. That's how you remember it." He shoved it back at Mark Allen.

Growling under his breath, Mark Allen smudged out his first attempt with his thumb and made the changes.

Bran smiled. "Now you is ready to start on them words."

Mark Allen scanned the sky. "Tonight. We need to put some miles behind us before the weather changes." He wasn't accustomed to the weather this far north, but he'd heard enough about snow clouds to suspect that was what approached.

At an alarming speed.

They packed their gear, saddled the horse, and started down the road. The sun was only halfway to the tops of the trees when the wind whipped its needle teeth into the side of Mark Allen's face.

Those clouds gathering on the horizon meant business. They were traveling in a densely forested area and hadn't passed a cabin since they'd broken camp. Carrying double, Mark Allen had mostly let Jughead walk to conserve his strength, but all three of them would sleep better that night if they found a friendly homestead with a barn soon. If they reached the town, he'd have to pay out for a room and stable, but with the weather turning, they had little choice. He clicked and urged Jughead into a trot. Bran's chin connected with a sharp thump between his shoulder blades.

"Hang on, boy."

"Bran."

"Right."

"Don't worry none about me. Ain't nothin' gonna make me come off o' Jughead."

Snowflakes, wafers the size of a man's coat buttons, slanted toward them.

"I hope you can live up to your boast." Mark Allen kicked the gray into a canter until the ominous clouds unleashed a swirl of blinding white and they had to slow to a walk. They topped a low rise, and an opening in the forest appeared ahead. The sketchy outline of a rooftop rose against the backdrop of snow. Jughead's ears pitched forward. The old horse responded without further urging, heading directly for the building.

Mark Allen pulled him to a halt in front of the log structure.

"I sure hope these folks is friendly," Bran said.

The door eased open. A woman with hair as white as the snow stood in the narrow opening, a blanket wrapped around her shoulders.

"Ma'am." Mark Allen pulled his hat from his head. "We are caught out in this storm. Do you have a barn where we could take shelter?"

"Aye. 'Tis round back."

"We are grateful, ma'am, and—"

The woman closed the door before he could finish his sentence.

He didn't blame her. It was too cold to be exchanging pleasantries. He reined an eager Jughead around to the barn nestled snugly against a hill. Bran hopped down and wrestled the door open while Mark Allen dismounted and led the horse inside. Darkness and the ammonia stench of filthy straw greeted them.

"Stinks in here." Bran pulled the collar of his coat over his nose.

"Would you rather stay out in that?" Mark Allen jabbed a thumb toward the open door.

"Nay."

"Then close the door."

Mark Allen's eyes adjusted to the dim barn. A sad-faced cow stood in the corner, her head hanging almost to the manure piled deep in her box stall. A half dozen shaggy sheep eyed him from the opposite corner, their wool coated with dirty straw and filth. He led Jughead into one of two empty tie stalls, thankful it was clean.

"Look." Bran pointed into the cow's stall.

A dead calf, at least a full day dead by the look of it, lay on the manure. The cow's udder was swollen to a painful red. Poor old gal.

"I better let the lady in the cabin know." Mark Allen finished stripping the gear from Jughead. "Give him a good rub. I will return directly."

He tugged his coat collar a notch higher, stepped into the storm, and trudged through snow already above his ankles. He stomped off what clung to his boots on the narrow porch and rapped on the door. The old woman appeared, still wrapped in her blanket.

"The calf's dead."

The woman's face, already a chalky white, blanched even paler.

"If you hand me a bucket, I can milk out the cow."

She pressed her hand to her mouth to cover a wracking cough. Her body, the blanket not disguising its frailness, shook with each hacking spasm.

"Can I step inside for a moment, Ma'am? So we can shut this door."

She nodded and stepped back, still coughing.

He followed and surveyed the tidy one-room cabin. A man sat in a chair across the room, his leg resting on a pillow atop a wooden crate. Even in the flickering light of the fireplace, the swollen foot made Mark Allen wince.

"Sir." He touched the brim of his hat.

The old man nodded, grizzled beard bobbing against his chest.

"Sorry to see you are laid up, sir. As I told your woman here, the calf is dead in the barn. I would be happy to milk out the cow for you."

"Much obliged. My missus kept up with things pretty good until she went and took sick. Now, we are quite the pair."

The old woman, her coughing under control, handed him a wooden bucket with a frayed rope handle.

"'Tis mighty cold out there." Mark Allen took the bucket. "Do you have any objection to us making a small fire on the dirt floor of your barn? We will tend it proper."

The old woman looked at her husband.

He grunted and tilted his head, sizing up Mark Allen from behind hooded eyelids. "I suppose you are not likely to burn it down when 'tis the only shelter for three miles around."

"Nay, sir, we will not."

"Wood is stacked beside the barn. Help yourself."

Mark Allen touched his hat brim again and slipped out the door with the bucket. Snowflakes attacked him. He stumbled over a couple of logs near the door. Not nearly enough to keep the old couple warm through the day, much less the night. He battled the now howling wind back to the barn.

"Took you long enough."

"That old couple is in a pinch. He is laid up, and she is sickly." He thrust the bucket at Bran. "Milk that cow while I haul in some firewood."

Bran backed away from the bucket. "I ain't never milked no cow."

"What?"

"You heard me." The boy crossed his arms, hands on his elbows.

Mark Allen rubbed the back of his neck. "Get the wood then. The old man says 'tis on the side of the barn."

Bran scrambled outside like the devil himself was nipping at his backside.

A milking stanchion stood near one of the cobweb-encrusted windows. Mark Allen found a rope hanging on the wall and secured it around the cow's head. The pitiful creature bawled and balked the length of the barn. He got the cow's head in the stanchion, but that didn't quiet her. Pulling both gloves off, he tucked his hands inside his coat and under his arms. Chunks of ice would have been warmer. He danced from foot to foot, glad Bran was outside fetching another armload of wood at the moment.

The door banged open, and Bran blew in with a swirl of snow.

"Shut that fool door."

Bran kicked the door shut and shot the latch over with his elbow. "Ain't you got that cow milked yet?"

"Still warming my hands."

"What for?"

"Would you like me to grab hold of your underside with these cold hands?"

Bran took a step away from Mark Allen, his eyes huge in the dim light. "Not likely."

"Neither would she. I do not aim to be kicked for my trouble."

Bran dumped the wood near the center of the barn.

"While I milk her out, carry at least that much wood to the porch and stack it by the door. Enough to get them through until tomorrow morning."

Bran nodded and turned toward the door.

"On second thought, knock and offer to stack it by the fireplace. That way the old woman needn't come out in the cold."

Bran nodded again, his hand on the latch.

"And keep your distance from her. I do not want you taking sick with whatever ails her."

"I ain't stupid." The boy huffed. "I stayed healthy when you was sick, did I not?" Then Bran disappeared in another gust of frozen white.

The cow ignored the handful of oats Mark Allen found and tossed in the manger of the stanchion. She rolled her eyes toward the rafters and strained against the neck braces.

"'Tisn't going to be fun for either one of us. But it must be done." A good milk cow might make the difference in those two old people surviving the winter or not. He rubbed his hands one more time under his coat before he started to massage the poor beast's tight udder. Quick as a striking snake, the cow unleashed a hind hoof.

A few choice words and a couple of bruises later, he had the cow stripped of milk. Bran approached the barn as Mark Allen stepped outside to pour the milk into a growing drift of snow.

The boy gaped at him through the blowing snow. "Why throw that out?"

"'Tis no good. Tomorrow's milk we can drink. Get inside."

Mark Allen shoved the door shut behind them. "Start a fire. Keep it small and rake any loose straw away from the flames." He ignored Bran's pointed glare. The boy hated to be told the obvious, but Mark Allen wasn't about to let the barn burn down around their heads. He led the cow to the clean tie stall beside Jughead. Climbing into the loft, he found hay for the animals. They'd have to melt snow for them to drink. The way the sheep attacked their portion of hay, he doubted they'd been fed in a couple of days. Not since the calf died anyway.

The last thing he wanted was yet another delay. Knowing both Gwen and Faye were—or at least had been—in Alexandria burned like a brand. But how could he abandon the old couple in their need?

A gust of wind shook the barn. Drafts made the flames dance on Bran's fire. At least they had a place out of the wind for the night. He sighed and squinted out the window, not that he could see anything through the storm's white murkiness.

First the kid, then running out of provisions, then his sickness, and now an old couple with a barn full of neglected chores. At the rate he was going, he'd be lucky to make Alexandria before the spring thaw.

Chapter 9

"Delay." CeCe wagged her finger at Faye. "Delay any way you can. Paul will come to his senses in time."

Faye wished it were that easy, but everything seemed against her. "He means it. He plans to uproot us and plant us in the wilderness for five years." As if two years in Scotland had not been enough exile for any one person. "Five years, CeCe! I shall be an old maid by the time we return."

CeCe tapped her finger to her lips. "But you shall be of majority age before then, shall you not?"

Faye nodded. She'd be two and twenty by the time Paul fulfilled his agreement with the Quaker settlement.

"Then do you not see? You shall be free to return before they do. By then, I should be in a position to invite you to stay with Andre and me."

"Has he proposed then?" Even amid her despair, Faye was genuinely happy for her friend.

CeCe glanced away, an unreadable emotion flitting across her face. "Not yet, but I do expect it soon." There was a smugness in her voice that said she was more than expecting, she was certain.

Faye squealed and hugged her friend. "'Tis wonderful. I will love to see thee—you—happily settled, at least."

"'Twill happen for you as well. We shall see to it, one way or another."

Faye sobered. "'Twouldn't be easy for me, a young woman alone, to travel back to Pittsburgh."

"Indeed, but I should think Paul would accompany you. And would Mrs. McClure not want to come and visit with her friends as well? To check on the house?"

CeCe made sense. They must return to Pittsburgh at some point. After all, five years was a long time to leave the house to the servants who would be left to manage its upkeep. And after her twenty-first birthday, Faye would have every right to decide to stay on her own. Paul would no longer be legally responsible for her, but neither would he refuse to allow her to live in the house. He was a good man and would see her cared for even after his legal responsibilities were met.

"You have lightened my spirit, both with your assurance of a betrothal and your wisdom about the house." Faye stood. "I must return. Madam requested me to lunch with her today. I believe she wishes to go over plans for moving."

"Persevere, my friend." CeCe came to Faye's side. "'Tis only a setback, nothing that cannot be overcome with patience."

Patience. Not something at which Faye excelled. Or even mediocred, if that were a word.

She took her shawl from the Crofts' butler, wrapped it tightly against the winter's chill, and stepped outside. It was nearly March, and the landscape was as bleak as her outlook had been before talking with CeCe.

She could be patient, as it appeared she must be, and there was something good that would come of the years until she reached her majority.

She'd be reunited with Gwen.

With a renewed lightness in her step, she returned home to face whatever Madam wished to discuss with her. And perhaps follow CeCe's other advice—to find a way to delay their departure.

Quiet woke Mark Allen. He sat up and looked around the barn, which was considerably cleaner than when they'd arrived, thanks to three days of work they'd done. No wind shook the siding or rattled the rafters. He pushed his blanket aside and went to the window. Pink and blue interlaced on the horizon, promising good weather. Finally. It was time to move on.

"Get up." With the toe of his boot, Mark Allen tapped the blanket-wrapped bundle partially buried in a pile of straw.

The bundle contracted, twisted, and wormed its way deeper into the pile.

"Come on. We are leaving here today." Mark Allen blew the embers of their fire to life and added a twist of straw until it flamed. He fed it kindling until it popped and snapped.

Bran emerged from the bundle, his coat askew, hair spiked with straw, looking oddly like a blond porcupine.

"You want to cook breakfast or milk the cow?"

Bran sent a sour look toward the cow, back in her own stall since Mark Allen had dragged out the dead calf, and fully recovered from the trauma they'd discovered her in. The cow blinked at him, its doe-brown eyes framed by incredibly long lashes.

"Breakfast."

Mark Allen chuckled and grabbed the milk bucket. "Suit yourself." At least they had fresh milk to wash down the oats from the stash in the barn that they'd cooked for every meal.

After breakfast, Mark Allen carried the milk bucket to the house. The old woman opened the door before he knocked. She wasn't draped in a blanket that morning, and her cheeks held a flush of pink. The aroma of freshly baked bread almost buckled his knees.

"Come in." She waved a hand at the table, and he set the bucket down.

The old man was on his feet, a gnarled staff in one hand supporting him. "I cannot thank you enough, young man. God sent you to us in our hour of need."

Mark Allen blinked. God? He looked from the old man to the old woman and back again. "We were just passing through on our way to

Alexandria and got caught in the storm. It would have gone bad for us if we had not found shelter here in your barn."

The old woman smiled and patted his arm. "God works in mysterious ways."

Mark Allen was pretty sure that was true. He'd never been able to make heads or tails of any of God's business, although he seemed to be pondering on it more recently. He shrugged and hoped that would do for a response.

"I expect you and your brother will be moving on today," the old man said.

"We are not brothers."

"No?"

"We met in New Bern last month and, well, he did not have anyone to look after him." Mark Allen shrugged again. He needed to find a better way to express himself. But how did one explain Bran?

"I see." The old woman's eyes crinkled at the corners. "God has been using you quite a bit lately, 'twould seem."

"I know nothing about that, ma'am."

"Trust her, son. My Margaret, she has a way of knowing these things." The old man winked.

Mark Allen mustered a smile, but he took a backward step toward the door. "Well—"

"Come by the cabin when you are ready to leave," the old woman said. "I shall wrap two loaves of bread for your journey."

Part of Mark Allen wanted to decline, sure the old couple didn't have enough to share. But the part that inhaled the tantalizing fragrance nodded instead. He touched his hat and hurried to the barn.

Bran brushed Jughead in his stall. Their gear was packed and the fire gone, dirt shoveled over where it had been. The sheep and cow all munched their hay.

"Looks like you have everything ready."

"Just waitin' on you."

Cheeky kid. Mark Allen pulled his saddle off the stall wall as Bran backed Jughead out. The horse had benefited from a few days of rest and plenty of food. His gray coat shone from Bran's attention. He even tossed his head when Mark Allen slipped the bit between his teeth. Maybe the days of the storm hadn't been wasted after all.

They led Jughead around to the cabin porch, where the old lady handed them a sack too large to be just bread. Bran took it and thanked her proper like while the old man looked over at Jughead.

"No gun, young man?"

"No sir."

"Wait a moment." He clomped into the cabin with his staff and returned shortly, a musket under his arm on his good side, a leather bag and powder horn in his hand. "Take these."

"I could not—"

"You can. I have no need for them anymore. My Margaret and I will be moving in with our son in a few weeks. We should have gone last fall, right, my dear?" At the woman's nod, he continued, "If you two had not come by when you did, we might have frozen to death." He nodded to the pile of firewood stacked high on their porch. "God sent you to us in our need. We shall be forever grateful."

Mark Allen took the gifts, unsure what to say.

"Always you shall be in our prayers." The old woman pressed against her husband's lame side and smiled at them. "Bless you both."

"Thank you, sir, ma'am." Mark Allen handed Bran the musket, pulled the powder horn and shot bag straps over his head, and mounted before giving Bran a hand up. He looked at the old couple and touched his hat.

"Go with God, son," the old man said.

They rode in silence until the cabin was out of sight.

"They really think God took us there?" Bran asked.

"I guess so."

"I think He did."

Part of Mark Allen wanted to agree, but they'd been turned away from as many houses as those that had taken them in. If God was directing their path, why the rejections? It didn't make sense.

Of course, if the others had taken them in, would they have reached the old couple time? Or would he and Bran have perished in the storm—and the old couple as well? More to ponder.

"Now we got a gun. We can hunt for fresh meat." The glee in Bran's voice coaxed a smile from Mark Allen.

"Until we rig a scabbard for the saddle," he said, "try not to shoot me in the back."

Bran snorted.

The old musket was a relic from the war. Who knew if it even worked? But if it did, it would liven up their diet, and Mark Allen was in favor of that.

"I do not see what all the hurry is about." Faye placed her fork beside her plate and met Paul's low-browed stare from across the table. She squared her shoulders and raised her chin.

"The river will be prime for travel soon. With such a light snowfall this year, it may be too shallow to ferry our belongings in another month." He whisked his napkin off his lap and dropped it onto his empty plate. "We have been over this."

"Thee cannot expect Madam and me to arrange to move this entire household on such short notice. 'Tis preposterous."

"The letter came almost two weeks ago. In all that time, I have yet to see thee raise a finger to help Mother with anything."

"That is enough." Madam rubbed her forehead. "Faye, I know thee are unhappy about the move. I believe I understand why."

"Then allow me to stay behind. I can manage this house by myself while thee are away." Faye gripped the edge of her seat.

"While we are away?" Paul's eyebrows shot upward. "'Tisn't a trip. We are moving. The house will be sold after we leave and settled into our accounts."

"Paul." Madam shook her head.

Sell the house? Faye pressed her hand to her throat. Nobody had spoken of selling the house. Surely Paul would come to his senses and move them back here after his five years of service.

"She needs to face the truth, Mother. All of it." Paul raked his fingers through his hair, exposing the peak that marked the center of his forehead.

"There's more?" She whispered the question. It was either that or scream. And a lady never screamed.

Madam aimed a faint frown at Paul. "We are selling the house along with most of our belongings. The elderly servants will each receive a stipend to see them through their remaining years. Olivia and Bridget have agreed to move to Ohio with us."

"One maid and the cook? That is all? How will we find trained help in the wilderness?"

"While I shall miss Dressler's assistance, I am very capable of looking after myself." Paul stood and straightened his jacket. "And I dare say, we shan't be dressing for dinner much on the frontier."

"The truth is, my dear, we shall be making do with only Olivia and Bridget once we are settled. Things are different out west. We shall adapt and learn to be more self-sufficient."

Faye's mouth dried to dust.

Paul left the room before she could work up enough moisture to protest.

"I know 'tis not what thee would wish." The compassion in Madam's eyes didn't hide her determination, which sent a shaft of fear through Faye's middle.

"How can this be what thee wish? To leave all thy friends, home, comfort, thy life for—what?"

Madam bowed her head a moment before meeting Faye's eyes. "For the opportunity to see my son established in the profession he loves."

"What about me?"

"The frontier is full of men. God will provide thee with the one whom He chooses."

"You—thee—would see me married to some hardscrabble farmer or smelly fur trader?"

"If that is the man God has chosen for thee, then indeed, I would. 'Tis time to change thy thinking on such matters. Think not on a man's wealth, but on his godly attributes and commitment to Christ."

"'Tis not a sin to be rich."

"No. But 'tis a sin to be proud. Be not too proud to embrace our new life, my dear. 'Tis the path thy guardian has chosen, and I believe 'tis the proper one." Madam made her excuses and left the dining room.

Faye remained seated for a long time. The servants cleared the table and straightened the room. Who would be doing that from now on? Not her.

Not Faye Morgan.

She may have been humbly born, but she had risen above it. Madam herself had seen the potential in Faye when she had insisted that Paul declare her as his ward.

Although she'd spent years pushing the memory away, she closed her eyes and let the scene play out in her mind. The dapper little man in the flat-topped hat who had purchased her. Bought her like a horse at the market. The ship that carried her to Alexandria still haunted her dreams. The rough planking under her cheek, the abrasive blanket that smelled of vomit and fish, the nasty gruel fed twice a day that she couldn't keep down, and the fear that ate through her soul.

Stepping off the ship into the blinding sunlight, the first thing she'd brought into focus had been the plumed hat of Madam. A handkerchief held over her nose, the elderly lady stopped when their eyes met. Even though she'd wanted to cringe and look away, Faye had refused to crumble before anyone. Never again. She'd drawn herself to her full height and matched the lady stare for stare. The handkerchief had slipped, and Madam had stepped forward, Paul following behind. Within minutes, the dapper little man handed her over, and Faye was riding in a coach such as she'd never seen.

That day had decided her path. She was sure of it. And her path didn't involve marrying some backwoods lout who reeked of sweat and horse and had permanently dirt-encrusted fingernails.

She was absolutely sure of that.

Chapter 10

ALEXANDRIA SPRAWLED BEFORE THEM, the acid tang of coal smoke clinging to the air. Mark Allen squinted against the mid-morning sun and stroked Jughead's shoulder. "How are we going to find anyone in that mess of people?"

Bran snorted and slid off the gray's rump, a brace of rabbits draped over his shoulder. "You ain't been around cities much, have you?"

"And I suppose you have?" Mark Allen dismounted.

The boy sent him a glare that would have stopped a runaway team. "I was doin' right fine by myself 'til you come along."

Mark Allen's view of *right fine* looked considerably different than Bran's.

"Give me a day, and I will find the girl for you if she be here." The cocky lad swung the rabbits off his shoulder and onto the ground at Mark Allen's feet. He pawed through their belongings and pulled out the ratty old coat he'd kept and used as a pillow. He took off the coat Mark Allen had purchased for him, stowed it in the bag, put on the old one, and then set off on foot for the city.

"Wait a minute." Mark Allen grabbed the rabbits and tugged Jughead along behind him. "Where are you going?"

"To find you that girl."

"Why are you wearing that old rag?"

Bran whirled and crossed his arms over his chest. "Trust me. I know how to learn things. You wait here." He jabbed a finger at the ground. "Have those rabbits cooked when I get back come dark."

"Now wait a minute—"

"You done me a good turn, so I owe you. I will find that girl to set us square."

"I'm going with you."

"The people I got to talk to won't talk with you around."

"What?"

Bran tilted his head. "Trust me."

"How are you going to find them?"

"'Tis probably best you don't ask." The boy's eyes were serious.

Mark Allen looked at the city before them. If he had to, he'd go door to door asking after Mrs. McClure and Faye. That would take more than a week, maybe more than two.

Bran didn't shifted an inch.

Trust him? Did Mark Allen have a choice?

"Be back at sunset then."

Bran marched off without another word.

She'd had to leave her prettiest dresses behind in Scotland, and now Faye had to witness the desecration of those remaining. Madam had sent Olivia to remove every scrap of lace and ribbon from the dresses she could before they left.

Permanently.

The house to be sold, Faye's only chance to return, gone. Ripped away from her.

It was so unfair.

She snagged another dress from the armoire, a favorite moss green gown that she'd worn in Scotland, and thrust it at Olivia.

"Miss Faye," Olivia's voice was soft. "I am sorry this distresses thee so." The woman had embraced the Quaker way along with Madam and

Paul. Even Bridget, the Irish cook Paul had met and hired upon their return to Pittsburgh, was a Quaker.

"How can it not?" Faye swept her arm over the dress-strewn bed. "Such beauty destroyed. And for what?"

"To prevent us from being prideful." Even in her softness, the censure came through.

Madam had all but accused Faye of being prideful too. But she wasn't. Nobody understood more deeply than Faye the lowly state to which she'd been born. There was no pride in that. If there had been, she wouldn't have worked so hard to overcome it. Why couldn't others see that? At least, those who knew her story.

"'Tisn't prideful to wish to improve, is it? Is not the point of life to mature and grow and improve?

"It depends upon what thee considers improvement, I suppose."

Faye squirmed on the inside. During one Quaker meeting, a gentleman had expounded on the benefits of improving one's relationship with the Almighty to be able to see others as He saw them, to enable one to do more earthly good with a more heavenly perspective.

But how could wearing a bit of lace or ribbon interfere with that?

"Perhaps a brisk walk will *improve* my morning." Faye waved at the remaining dresses in the armoire. "Do what you must."

She headed downstairs, where she wrapped a shawl around her shoulders, tied on her white bonnet, stepped into a pair of thick leather boots, and donned her felted wool cloak. Her first full breath of the frosty air almost changed her mind, but she needed to move, to walk off her frustration.

Faye snugged her cloak tighter and walked on. What would have happened to her if Madam and Paul hadn't taken her in? Someone else would have purchased her. She might be working as a house servant or even as a field hand.

But they had taken her in, and she owed it to them to live up to their expectations. She'd done her best to fit into their family. To be accepted by their friends as an equal. To improve herself. To become one of them.

And now they wanted to rip all of that away.

Who was Faye Morgan underneath the trappings she'd come to rely on?

That was the question that sent her out to pound her frustrations into the paving stones.

She wandered into the Quaker part of Pittsburgh, though that hadn't been her intention. Numerous people were out and about on such a cold day. The women wore mostly gray dresses under gray cloaks, although some were dark blue and one a dark green. All wore a wide white shawl around their shoulders as if it were some sort of uniform. But no, it'd been explained to her by Madam that the shawl was a symbol of modesty and was always bare of any type of lace or trimming, of course. The men wore equally plain clothing in gray and black and blue, their shoes having plain buckles of pewter, not engraved or detailed silver. Several held walking sticks without a silver knob.

People nodded to each other in passing, and several nodded to Faye as well. Their smiles seemed genuine, although she knew none of these people. A woman caught a young boy by the back of his coat and drew him close, bending low for whatever she had to say to him. Further down the street, three old men sat on a bench outside a shop, smoke from their pipes filming the cold air. A girl swept the porch of a house while two younger girls chased a puppy in a fenced yard, their gray skirts swirling and laughter carrying on the breeze. It seemed a happy enough place.

Would the town in Ohio—Mount Pleasant—be much the same way?

Of course not. It was on the frontier. It would be surrounded by savage Indians, wolves, bears, and who knew what other form of wild beasts. The houses would be made of logs, not lumber. They'd be lucky to have a cedar shake roof instead of leaking split bark. And there would be no paving stones, just dust in the summer, ice in the winter, and mud in between.

Faye turned, head down as she walked into the stinging breeze, and headed home. She had to try one last appeal to CeCe for help. She couldn't give up on her dream of marriage and children and security.

Olivia had spoken of improving herself, but the only improvement Faye wanted—or even understood—would be found in a fine husband.

The sun disappeared behind the trees, yet there was still no sign of Bran. Mark Allen rotated his head and shrugged his shoulders. Had he been a fool?

Jughead blew a snort and bobbed his head.

"Reading my mind?"

A shadow moved in the distance. The horse snorted again, and Mark Allen chuckled. "You have better eyesight than I do in the dark, I will give you that."

Bran strode up to him, a wide grin exposing the gap between his front teeth.

"Well?"

"She ain't here."

A weight bore down on Mark Allen's shoulders. He shut his eyes.

"But I know where she went."

He glared at Bran. "Where?"

"Pittsburgh."

Farther north. A lot farther north. "How do you know that?"

"Boys at the big houses talk. Seems Mrs. McClure was a regular visitor here until a couple of years ago. But the boy heard it himself, from an upstairs maid, that their mistress is there visitin' the McClures right now. In Pittsburgh."

"Is that so?"

"Yup. Visitin' the McClures and Miss Morgan."

Mark Allen's heartbeat quickened. "Faye."

"No—Miss Morgan."

"That is Faye."

"You said she was a servant?"

"Of course."

"You ever heard a servant called *miss* anything?"

Mark Allen rubbed the back of his neck. "Maybe they do things different up north."

Bran made one of those faces people reserve for crazy aunts and village idiots.

Mark Allen pointed to the city. "How did the boy you talked to know all that?"

"You serve a big house?"

"Of course, but—"

Bran tipped his hat back. "Did the family have any secrets from the servants?"

No. Dinner in the kitchen was full of talk about what the Whitefords had done that day. Talk about their comings and goings, their friends. The boy made sense. The weight lifted a bit, and Mark Allen's stomach growled.

"You burnin' those rabbits or cookin' 'em?"

Mark Allen stomped over to the fire and turned the stick suspending the rabbits. Black streaks marred the side that had been over the fire. "Done. Fetch some water from the creek back yonder and we will eat."

They'd run out of the bread and cheese the kind old lady had packed for them. Without the musket, they'd have gone hungry tonight. There was something to be said for traveling on a full stomach, even if neither one of them could pass for a cook.

Tomorrow morning, they'd go into town and learn the fastest route to Pittsburgh.

I'm coming, Faye Morgan. And when I find you, I shall figure out a way to get you to Gwen. To get us both to Gwen.

"You sure any female be worth this?" Bran leaned against a tree and scraped mud from his boots with a broken branch.

"Gwen is." Mark Allen dug the packed mud out of Jughead's hooves.

"But we are chasin' after her sister. You ain't never even seen her. She might be ugly as a toad and smell worse than a pole cat."

Mark Allen couldn't help but chuckle. "Gwen said they looked much alike. But even if she were 'ugly as a toad,' I still aim to keep my promise to Gwen."

Bran snorted. "How much longer, you reckon?"

Mark Allen stretched his back. They'd left Alexandria a week before. By his figuring, they should have arrived in Pittsburgh yesterday. He wasn't about to admit that to the boy, however. At least they'd finally reached what he calculated to be the Monongahela River.

"Soon." He pulled the musket from their makeshift scabbard. Mark Allen's father had taught him to shoot and hunt, mostly so the man could stay home and drink. Mark Allen had instructed Bran. "See if you can flush something to eat."

Bran grinned and grabbed the musket. "Maybe a turkey. I heard an old gobbler callin' to his sweetheart back yonder."

Mark Allen pointed to the northwest. "Jughead and me will keep going along the riverbank. You should not have any trouble following us." Not when they sank ankle-deep in frosty muck with each step.

"Right." And with that, the boy melted into the forest. For a city-raised urchin, he'd taken to hunting like he'd been born with that musket in his hand.

They'd bought provisions in Alexandria but they were running low, and so were the powder and shot. Pittsburgh better be close.

He tightened Jughead's cinch and swung into the saddle. They'd been walking beside the horse for the past hour. With the grain long gone, Jughead had lost weight. Carrying double for such a long journey had taken its toll on the old horse. "Not much farther." Mark Allen rubbed the gray's neck. "I hope."

They ambled along the river's edge, Mark Allen letting the horse pick the pace. The rocking motion lulled him into a state of drowsy relaxation. They hadn't traveled more than half an hour when the distant boom of the musket sounded to their left.

The clatter to their right, however, wiped the grin off his face. He thumped Jughead's sides and reined the horse behind the cover of trees.

Voices drifted over the water, followed by another clatter of wood against wood.

Mark Allen dismounted and tied the horse well back from the river. He crept forward, keeping the trees between himself and a bend in the river. He crouched behind a thick stump and waited.

A box-shaped vessel floated around the bend. It looked like a cabin on a raft. Men with poles in their hands walked along its sides, four men on each side of the cabin. They walked to the front near another man, who stood looking forward. When the lone man yelled, the eight men plunged their poles into the murky water and leaned their shoulders into the poles. Then they walked back to the other end.

Nobody held a gun.

Mark Allen eased out from the cover of the trees. He cupped his hands around his mouth. "Hello!"

"Ahoy!" the lone man shouted back.

"Where are you headed?"

"Pittsburgh."

Mark Allen looked back the way he'd come and pointed. "'Tis that way?"

"If it ain't moved since we was last there, aye!" The man on the strange vessel laughed, the others joining him.

Mark Allen's ears burned at the coarse remarks that followed. He moved back into the woods and untied Jughead. He'd overshot the town. They'd come to the river too far west. He ground his teeth. Bran would never let him hear the end of it.

But at least he knew where Pittsburgh—and Faye—were.

Chapter 11

T HE MASSIVE HOUSE ON a quiet street in Pittsburgh looked nothing like the Whitefords' manor in Greensville, but there was no mistaking the air of affluence behind its iron-fenced front. Each arched window was tucked under a fan of brickwork as fancy as anything back in North Carolina. Four chimneys rose against the mid-morning sky, a trickle of smoke smudging the early spring air. A lane to the back of the house was bordered on both sides by a thick hedge, ensuring the privacy of the manor houses on both sides.

Mark Allen removed his hat and wiped a sheen of nervous sweat from his forehead. This had to be the right house. It matched the description they'd been given at a tavern on the city's edge.

"Looks like the right sort o' place to me." Bran turned and headed for the back entrance, hauling Jughead in his wake.

The front door swung open before Mark Allen could follow. A woman in a gray gown with a white shawl over her shoulders slipped onto the porch and wrapped a gray cloak around herself. She closed the door behind her and looked both ways before scurrying toward the street.

Mark Allen squinted. The woman must be young to move so nimbly. She turned her head and he caught a glimpse of black waves collected at the back of her neck, peeking out from under her bonnet. She reached the street, turned, and hurried toward him.

The breeze flipped the front of her bonnet up and an emotional fist knocked the breath from Mark Allen. "Faye." He barely breathed the word. It could be no other. The resemblance to Gwen was unmistakable. He stepped into her path.

"Faye Morgan?"

She jerked to a stop, her eyebrows arched and her mouth a circle of surprise. The dark curls that framed her pale face reminded him so much of Gwen, but her eyes were nothing like her sister's dreamy blue. Dark brown and stormy, they glared at him as she overcame her shock.

"What are you doing sneaking out the front door?" Mark Allen grabbed her elbow and pulled her behind the hedge of bushes that boxed in the lane.

"Who are you?" Faye wrested her arm from his grip and stepped back toward the street, out of his reach. "What do you think you are doing?"

"What do I think I'm doing? What do you think you are doing, coming out the front door like that?" He jabbed a finger at the manor house. "What if Mrs. McClure or one of the senior servants caught you? Do not be a fool, girl."

"Leave at once, or I shall scream."

"You won't neither." Bran snorted. "You was takin' too much care not to be seen comin' out o' that house. You be hidin' from someone."

Mark Allen looked at Bran, then back at Faye. "He is right. What if someone caught you using the front door?"

Faye drew herself up to her full height, which lacked Mark Allen's by at least two hand spans. Her gaze flicked between him and the house. "What are you talking about?"

"A servant like you would be in a heap of—" The crack of her palm across his left cheek rocked him back on his heels. Bran's boyish whoop and chortling fueled the heat rushing to Mark Allen's ears. He stared at the spitfire in front of him.

"Never call me that," she said.

"Call you what?"

"A servant. I am the *ward* of Dr. Paul McClure. Although why you and that—"—she waved a hand at the still smirking Bran—"That ill-bred boy should need to know is beyond me."

What was she talking about? "Faye Morgan, I'm a friend of Gwen. I promised her I would find you and reunite the two of you. That is what I aim to do, no matter who you pretend to be."

"Pretend?" Fire leaped from the dark eyes in front of him.

The mention of her sister brought none of the softening he'd expected.

"I know who bought you." He drew back as she raised her hand again. The desire to turn her over his knee and administer his palm over the rounder side of her person had him clenching his fists.

She looked both ways along the street before stepping closer to Mark Allen. "Go back to Mount Pleasant and tell my sister that I have a life here. A good life. One I plan to keep. I shall write her soon."

Mark Allen rubbed the back of his neck. "Mount Pleasant?"

"Or whatever that frontier outpost in Ohio is called."

"Ohio?"

She crossed her arms over her middle, snugging the white shawl around the curves of her body. "Are you simple-minded?"

Between the curvaceous bundle of indignation in front of him and the now raucous chortling of Bran behind, Mark Allen's words melted into a dry-mouthed cough. He rubbed his hand down his face and drew in a deep breath.

"I know not what you are playing at," he said, "but I made a promise to your sister."

Faye's breath hissed between her teeth. "Then tell her you found me and that I'm fine."

"I promised to reunite the two of you."

"Impossible."

"I think not. It may take me some time, but I shall find a way to purchase the rest of your indenture."

The pale face before him reddened to an alarming hue. "I am not a servant." The words weren't loud, in fact, not more than a whisper, but the clarity and detail of every syllable was etched into the air around them. She meant it.

How could that be?

The front door of the house opened and banged shut. Faye jumped.

"Go back to Gwen." Her firm chin wobbled for a moment. Then she squared her shoulders and met Mark Allen stare for stare. "I will answer her letters. I promise." She whirled and rounded the hedge toward the house.

Letters? What letters? Gwen couldn't read or write.

Bran nudged Mark Allen's elbow. "So that be the girl we traveled all this way to find?"

"Indeed."

"She ain't exactly what you was hopin' for."

Not even close.

"Where are you returning from?" Paul glanced toward the street, and Faye hoped with all her being that the oaf and his urchin had the presence of mind to keep themselves concealed.

"I went for a walk." She let her cloak sag off her shoulders. "'Tis warmer than I'd realized."

"A nice day to be out in the sunshine, but how goes thy packing?"

Faye pasted on a smile. "Fine."

"Good. I hope thee will help Mother this afternoon. There is much to be done and precious little time left to do it." He patted her shoulder before striding down the walk.

When he turned toward town, Faye held her breath. Surely those two had moved off by now. She closed her eyes and strained to hear any sound other than the birds chirping in the stately oaks that fronted the house. Nothing. With a sigh, she entered the front door.

Imagine that lout reprimanding her for using the front door. And because of his untimely interference, she'd lost the opportunity to slip off to see CeCe. Her friend had been ill and unable to entertain her on her last visit. Who knew when Faye would have time to slip away again? Her mission to enlist CeCe's aid to remain in Pittsburgh had failed. All due to an ill-smelling rustic who dared—dared—to accost her on the street. Who did he think he was?

A friend of Gwen's.

Faye hurried up the stairs to her room. She whipped off her shawl and tossed it onto the bed. Rifling through her desk, she pulled out her sister's letters. She didn't need to read them again. Each word was engraved in her memory.

She should have responded sooner. Maybe if she had, Gwen wouldn't have sent someone after her. Faye pressed the heel of her hand to her forehead. No. She couldn't have answered soon enough to stop that. The letters had been waiting for quite some time before they returned from Scotland.

What would it be like to see Gwen again? To fall into her arms and cry on her shoulder like she had when they were children? Faye blinked back the sting in her eyes. She didn't cry anymore. Tears never solved anything.

And leaning on someone else only led to that person being ripped away.

Faye must secure her own future.

She wasn't about to give up everything she'd planned for. She pushed the letters back into the drawer, planning to visit CeCe as soon as possible. She wasn't going to change her plans.

Not even for Gwen.

"What are we goin' to do now?" Bran crossed his arms, Jughead's reins looped over his shoulder.

"Let me think." Truth was, Mark Allen didn't have a clue. He's assumed Faye would be surprised by his appearance. After all, she knew nothing about him or his promise to her sister. But he'd thought she'd be happy to be rescued from her indenture. He didn't know what else he'd expected, but it wasn't a spitfire who'd have tossed him out on his ear if she could have.

He hadn't expected to be treated like an intruder.

A plainly dressed gentleman walked past them on the street. He stopped and backed up a step. Centered in the opening between the hedges, he cleared his throat. "Can I be of some assistance?"

"You live here?" Bran jerked his thumb toward the house Faye had disappeared to.

"I do."

"We could use a bit of food. Provisions been slim." The boy's gap-toothed smile took on a wistful appeal.

"We will work for it, of course." Mark Allen stepped forward, shooting a hard stare toward Bran.

"What kind of work do you do?"

"I'm a stableman by trade."

The gentleman rubbed his chin. "And the boy, is he your brother?"

"Nay, sir. But he is with me." It was probably best to remain vague on that score.

"I see." The gentleman walked toward them. "A stableman, you say."

"Yes, sir. I worked for Mr. Whiteford in Greensville before coming north."

"Go round back and introduce yourself to Clancy. He is the stableman here. Tell him I said to work you good today and feed you better."

Bran's grin almost split his face.

"Thank you, sir." Mark Allen half-lifted one hand. "Who shall I tell him sent us?"

The gentleman chuckled and patted Bran on the shoulder. "Paul McClure." And then he was gone.

Mark Allen let his hand fall back to his side. "So that was Paul McClure." The son of Mrs. McClure—and a doctor—according to those he'd spoken to in the tavern.

"So he said. Time to find that Clancy fellow. Bet they got a cook here who don't burn everything."

Mark Allen followed Bran and Jughead down the hedge-lined lane until a two-story brick stable stood before them. Whitewashed shutters framed each window and whitewashed doors stood open to let in the spring breeze. The scents of horse, leather, and hay carried on the same breeze. It smelled like home. Or as much of a home as Mark Allen had ever had.

A bandy-legged man in a battered cap appeared in the doorway. Mark Allen rubbed his eyes and looked again. It wasn't Arthur, but it might have been his brother. The creases that fanned his eyes deepened when he spied them standing there.

Mark Allen stepped forward. "Are you Clancy?" He waited for the little man's curt nod. "Mr. Paul McClure said to find you. He asked for you to put us to work in return for our supper."

"He said to feed us good," Bran added.

"Did he, indeed?"

"Yes, sir. He be a good hand with horses." Bran tipped his head toward Mark Allen. "Almost as good as me."

Mark Allen knocked Bran's cap off his head. "Enough of your sass."

Clancy chuckled and dug a pipe from his pocket. He tamped some leaves into its bowl and scratched a match across the sole of his boot, then drew in several puffs.

"Suppose you know one end of a pitchfork from the other, young man?"

"That I do, sir." Bran knocked the dirt from his hat and crammed it back on his head.

Clancy nodded. "Start with the front stall and work to the back. Everything you need be inside the door. Dump the manure in the pile out back."

"Yes, sir." Bran scampered into the barn.

Clancy ambled into the yard and stood before Mark Allen, eyeing him up and down. "Now, then. You say you are a stableman?"

"I am."

"Where did you work last?"

"I was indentured to Daniel Whiteford in Greenesville, North Carolina. I completed my obligation this past January." He looked Clancy in the eye. "I'm a free man."

Clancy nodded.

"I know my way around horses. I can ride and drive a coach and four. I know how to care for leather and can mend it when needed. I can trim hooves and file teeth, but I have never set a shoe. I'm fairly good at doctoring, although Master Whiteford's horses rarely fell ill."

Clancy ambled over to Jughead, who dozed in the sunshine. He ran his fingers around the old horse's bridle and looked into his mouth. His leathery fingers examined the saddle before he bent over and lifted each of Jughead's feet in turn. He walked around the horse again, the flat of his hands pressing against gray hide.

"He is a mite thin," Mark Allen said, "but he has carried us a long way."

"Hm." Clancy rested with his elbow against Jughead's hip. He removed his pipe and tapped out the spent tobacco before grinding it into the dirt with his heel. "He carried the both of you from North Carolina?"

"He did. He is more horse than he looks like."

Clancy's eyebrows shot up, almost meeting the bill of his cap. "He looks like plenty of horse to me. He be twenty if he be a day, and sound enough to carry double more than halfway up the country."

Mark Allen glanced at Jughead again, seeing him with a slightly different perspective.

"Turn him out in that paddock." Clancy pointed to an empty square enclosure next to the barn. "Then we will talk. I have my suspicions about why Mr. McClure sent you to me."

Then at least one of them did.

Chapter 12

MARK ALLEN LEANED OVER the wash tub and sluiced tepid water across his face, letting it run across the back of his neck and drip into the tub. A gentle breeze blew under the overhang at the back of the stable, warm for so early in the year. He grabbed a clean piece of sacking off the bench and dried what dampness the breeze left, wincing as he straightened. The McClures owned two teams of horses, one heavy and one light, and two riding mounts. Mark Allen's lower back and the backs of his legs reminded him of all twenty-four hooves he'd cleaned and trimmed. And that was after he'd soaped and oiled both sets of harnesses under Clancy's scrutiny.

Bran pushed in beside Mark Allen and plunged his head into the wash tub. He resurfaced and shook like a mongrel dog.

"Watch it." Mark Allen wiped another layer of water off his face and scowled at the boy. "Is it possible that you have any manners whatsoever?"

"Never seen a need for 'em."

"Find one." Mark Allen slapped the wet sacking over Bran's head.

Clancy ambled around the corner of the stable and eyed the pair up and down. "Come along. Best we not keep Bridget waiting."

"Who be this Bridget?" Bran asked.

"Only the best cook you will find in all of Pittsburgh. Maybe all of Pennsylvania."

Bran tried to dodge past, but Mark Allen caught him by the back of his shirt. "The least you could do is look respectable." He grabbed the sacking and dried Bran's hair the best he could, slicking it down in some semblance of order with a curry comb when he was done. When Mark Allen was satisfied, he and a mulish-looking Bran followed Clancy to the house.

Halfway across the yard, the aromas reached him. Mark Allen wiped the back of his hand across his mouth. The savory scents pulled him like a robin on a worm. He wanted to whoop and race Bran to the kitchen.

Clancy chuckled. "I guess you boys have worked up an appetite by now." He climbed the three steps and went through the open kitchen door.

Mark Allen dragged another deep breath in through his nose and followed Bran into the kitchen. A willowy woman in a long white apron stood in front of a huge blackened hearth. Her red hair escaped her mobcap, creating a fringe of curls the same color as her freckles. She nodded to the newcomers.

Clancy pointed to a bench, one of four that framed the square table in the middle of the room.

Seated around the table were a tall woman in her middle years, a wizened old woman with more wrinkles than face, and a squarely built man with the straight-backed posture and blank expression that Mark Allen assumed all butlers wore.

Clancy dropped to the bench beside the other man. "This here be Mark Allen and young Bran. Mr. McClure said to feed them well. Did I get that correct, Bran?"

"Yes, sir." Bran sat straighter on his bench. "And from the smell in here, I reckon we cain't go wrong."

The squarely built man coughed into his hand and stood. "I am Dressler." He gestured toward the tall woman. "This is Olivia, Mrs. McClure's maid." He gestured to the old woman. "And this is Mrs. Hooper, the housekeeper. Bridget is our cook." Dressler sat, and Bridget brought another platter to the already loaded table before taking her seat.

Mark Allen tried to remember the names, but tantalizing steam from the dish in the middle of the table was his undoing. How could one think of names when heaven was placed on a platter in front of him? Bran reached for the bowl of bread rolls, but Mark Allen caught his wrist and pulled it under the table, hoping nobody else noticed.

Dressler met his gaze and nodded. No such luck. Dressler cleared his throat and bowed his head. After a prayer lengthy enough to put a congregation to sleep, Dressler picked up the first dish, helped himself, and passed it around. Mark Allen retained his manacle-hold on Bran until the dish was passed to him.

"Where are you from, Mark Allen?" Dressler asked.

Mark Allen's first bite of creamy chicken with carrots and onions stopped before it reached his mouth. He lowered the spoon. "Greenesville, North Carolina." He raised the spoon again.

"What did you do there?"

Ate dinner undisturbed most evenings. He put the spoon down. "I was indentured as a stableman. But I met my obligation this January past."

"He be well trained." Clancy pointed at Mark Allen. "Whoever taught him knew his way around horses."

Mark Allen nodded to the old stableman and picked up his spoon.

"What are your plans now that you are a free man?" Clancy asked.

Mark Allen sighed and lowered the spoon again. "My plans are undefined at the moment." Severely undefined by the curly-haired young woman who clearly didn't need—or want—his interference in her life.

Bran grunted around a mouthful of the savory-smelling chicken.

Mark Allen resisted the urge to kick the boy under the table. At least with his mouth full, he wasn't talking.

Clancy put his spoon down and pinned Mark Allen with a quizzical look. "Ever think about heading west?"

"West? Sure." That's where Gwen was, after all.

"Mr. McClure is packing up the family and heading to Ohio. He is going to need a good horseman along. Me, I'm too old for an adventure like that. The missus is gone, God rest her soul, but my sons live nearby and, well, I have no taste for leaving the grandchildren behind." His speech done, Clancy resumed eating.

"Eat up now, afore 'tis cold as winter's kiss." Bridget smiled from across the table at Mark Allen.

He picked up his spoon and shoveled in a mouthful before anyone could ask another question. He pushed the notion of going west out of his mind for the moment. Right then, the only thing that mattered was the meal before him. He'd forgotten how good food could taste.

But the idea of a paying job that would take him west toward Gwen eventually superseded even the feast before him. And if the McClures were going west, then so was Faye. That was perfect.

Perhaps he could see that she reached Gwen after all.

Faye was late coming downstairs to the parlor before supper. She'd spent the day packing her belongings with Noreen, the part-time maid who came three days a week. It wasn't a total waste of time and energy. She'd need her belongings packed to move over to CeCe's anyway, as soon as she convinced CeCe to approach her parents about taking Faye in. Surely they would.

When she joined Madam in the parlor, Paul beamed at her from across the room.

"There she is. All finished packing?" he asked.

"Very close."

"Excellent. I spoke with the captain of our keelboat today. He says we shall be ready to sail on Friday."

"Friday?" Faye sank onto a chair. Three days. She had only three days to avert this disaster. "'Tis only the end of March. You—thee—said we would leave in April."

"Indeed, ours shall be one of the first boats on the river for the season."

"Come." Madam stood. "Let us finish this discussion over supper, shall we? We have kept Bridget waiting long enough."

Faye rose and followed. If only she'd made her escape that morning. If only that odious man hadn't stopped her. Instead, she'd been forced to spend the day packing, unable to postpone it another day. She clenched handfuls of her skirt at her sides and took her seat.

They bowed their heads for the silent prayer. Faye couldn't pray and seethe at the same time. And right then, she'd rather seethe. Why couldn't they just voice the prayer as they'd always done in the past? Yet another Quaker thing she despised.

Paul cleared his throat to signal the prayer's end. "I may have found our new stableman today."

"New stableman?" Faye looked from Paul to Madam and back again. "Has something happened to Clancy?"

Paul helped himself from the platter of fish and passed it to his mother. "He's getting on in years and does not wish to move west."

Who did? Faye took the platter and stared at the poached fish in dill sauce. The stableman had more rights than she did. It wasn't fair. She stabbed a piece of fish and flopped it onto her plate.

"We shall need help with the horses and someone to do the general gardening when we are settled. Clancy tells me the young man—and I quote—'will do.'"

Madam chuckled. "High praise, indeed, from Clancy."

"'Tis not like we will have all of this." Paul pointed his fork around the room "The house will be much smaller and the garden hardly anything at all."

"We shall need a patch for the kitchen vegetables, of course. And perhaps a small spot for my roses."

"Never fear, Mother. We shall take cuttings from thy roses."

Faye nudged the fish around her plate. Memories she wanted to forget pushed their way through. A small house with a dirt floor. Her mother, middle rounded with her fourth child—or perhaps her fifth—hunched over a hoe and whacking at the dry dirt of the garden while a very young Gwen scrubbed clothes in a battered washtub in the yard.

"Faye?"

Faye blinked at Paul staring at her over the top of his water glass. What had she missed?

"What has thee so distracted, my dear?" Worry lines fanned from the corners of Madam's blue eyes.

Faye shook her head and sat taller on her chair. "Just woolgathering."

"Speaking of woolgathering." Paul reached for another roll. "I understand that Quaker farmers around Mount Pleasant raise sheep as their primary livestock. I wonder if we should invest in a spinning wheel to take with us." He took a bite of the roll and pointed the rest at Faye while he chewed and swallowed. "Thee could learn to spin."

Right after I learn to fly. She shoved her plate and its untouched fish away.

"I'm sure there will be an ample supply of dry goods available in Mount Pleasant and no need to create our own." Mrs. McClure frowned at Paul then turned to Faye. "The fish is quite delicious, my dear. Do try a bite and see."

"I'm not hungry."

"Bridget will be upset if thee does not at least try it. 'Tis a new recipe, one she hoped thee especially would like."

Faye sighed and retrieved her plate. She took a tiny bite of the fish. The tangy dill mingled with a hint of lemon, but it might as well have been ashes on her tongue. She took another bite, and Madam smiled before turning to Paul to continue their discussion about the move. Faye took another bite. She must eat to keep up appearances and her strength.

She'd never get permission to stay with CeCe if Paul or Madam questioned her health.

Paul McClure walked away, leaving Mark Allen stunned. He'd been offered a job that matched his desire to take Faye west and perhaps—if his luck held—find Gwen. Or maybe it was like the old couple had said. Maybe God was at work in his life. Or maybe it was answer to the prayers Mr. And Mrs. Hackett has promised to say for them.

Bran elbowed him. "You goin' with him?"

"Aye."

"Why?"

Why? Because according to her sister, that's where Gwen was. His Gwen. "He offered me a job."

Bran snorted. "There be plenty of jobs right here in Pittsburgh."

"Not near Gwen."

"That other gal? The one you ain't seen in four or five years?"

"Three years." Three years, three months, and a handful of days. Mark Allen sighed and faced Bran. "Are you coming with me?"

Bran crossed his arms and looked away. "Ain't been asked."

"I'm asking."

Bran fixed him with a squint-eyed stare. "Why?"

Mark Allen blinked. Why indeed? He shifted his feet and resisted the urge to rub his neck. Bad habit, that. He met the boy's eyes for a moment and something—was it fear?—lingered in their depths.

"You are right handy to have around sometimes." After all, Mark Allen was reading, albeit slowly still.

The tension melted from Bran's shoulders. He lowered his hands to his waist, bony elbows poked out at his sides. "They takin' that cook with 'em?"

"I believe so."

"Jughead too?"

"I would not leave him behind."

Bran gave one firm nod. "That bein' the way of it, I guess I might."

Mark Allen bit back a grin. The boy was no kin to him, but it felt right to keep him close. Better than leaving him here in a strange city to fend for himself, maybe revert to stealing. Not that the frontier was an easy place to live, yet Mr. McClure—Paul, he wished Mark Allen to call him—seemed convinced that Mount Pleasant was a growing town. There'd be a home built by the Quakers waiting for them—for the new doctor.

Quakers. Mark Allen snatched his hand away from the back of his neck. He wasn't sure what to make of them. They seemed like decent folks, but all the *thee* and *thy*...

He for sure didn't know what to make of that.

But he could put up with it to find Gwen.

Chapter 13

"P AUL IS MAKING US leave on Friday," Faye blurted as soon as the Croft's butler had closed to door to the parlor.

"I hate that you must go." CeCe flopped onto the settee. "It will be frightfully dull for me with you so far away."

Faye sat next to her friend and placed her hand over CeCe's. "You know I have no wish to do this."

"Indeed. And who could blame you?"

"You are my last hope."

CeCe shifted to face her. "Whatever do you mean?"

"Ask your parents to let me stay here." Faye squeezed her friend's hand. "With you."

A myriad of emotions whisked across CeCe's expressive face too quickly for Faye to sort through.

Her friend jumped to her feet and paced to the bow window which overlooked the street. She stopped with her back to Faye, arms gripped across her middle.

Silence hung like a damp blanket over the room.

Faye's heartbeat eclipsed the sound of passersby on the street. A trickle of perspiration slid an itchy path from behind her ear to the collar of her gray dress.

"CeCe?"

"I cannot."

"Why?" Faye's single word carried the weight of her disappointment, not in its volume but in the desperation that saturated it.

CeCe whirled around, tears washing her cheeks, leaving their splotchy red footprints across her pale skin.

Faye rushed to her, and CeCe fell into her arms. Faye hugged her friend, alarmed at the quaking of her body. It couldn't be entirely due to her leaving.

"What has happened?"

CeCe stepped back, raised her chin despite its tremor, and looked Faye in the eye. "I'm with child."

Faye rocked back on her heels. With child? Panic pushed against her throat, blocking any attempt to respond.

"I was not going to tell you, what with you leaving and all. I was going to write you a letter. But you have to know, I want you to understand that I'm not denying your request because I do not want you here. I'm denying it because... I will not be here."

Faye panted as if she'd run for miles. This couldn't be happening. Her last chance was melting away. CeCe had been her only hope. "Where will you go?"

"Andre and I are to be married, very quietly, Monday morning." CeCe stifled a sob. "And then we are leaving for Boston that afternoon."

"Boston?"

She nodded, wiping her eyes with a lace-edged handkerchief. "Andre's brother lives there. He owns a shipping business. It has been arranged that Andre will work for him."

"Does his brother know about—"

"Not yet. Only my parents, Andre and his parents, and now you."

"I shall not tell a soul."

CeCe swiped more tears off her cheeks. "We may never see each other again."

Faye's heart, beating so loudly only moments ago, nearly stopped. She clutched to her until the shadows lengthened outside the window.

Another parting. Another person she loved wrested from Faye's arms. She wanted to scream. She wanted to howl. She did neither. She'd done both before, and it had changed nothing.

Without another word, she slipped out of the parlor, retrieved her shawl from the table by the door, and left the Crofts' home without a backward glance. For the last time. She sensed CeCe still standing in the parlor window, but Faye couldn't look back.

She reached the McClures' home on wooden legs, not remembering a single person she passed or hearing the birds that flitted among the trees lining the street. She dragged each step up the staircase and made it into her bedroom before she collapsed onto the bed.

There was nothing left for her.

"We honestly goin' to float down that river on one them box boats?" Bran leaned his pitchfork against the wall and crossed his arms.

"Paul said so." It felt odd—wrong—to call his employer by his first name, but that was how Quakers preferred things, Mark Allen was learning.

"Well, then, I ain't goin'." Bran's face took on the mulish expression Mark Allen was getting to know all too well.

"Whyever not?"

"I cain't swim."

Mark Allen finished straightening the freshly oiled riding tack on pegs along the stable's wall. "I figure to ride on the boat, not swim along behind."

"I ain't gettin' on no boat. Boats sink."

Mark Allen didn't want to leave the boy behind. Partly because he still had a lot to learn about reading and writing, even though he was stringing words together on the slate. But mostly, Bran was like a younger brother to him.

"If the worst happens and the boat sinks, you stay with old Jughead, and he will get you to shore."

Bran tilted his head, proof he was listening, but the skeptical squint hadn't left.

"Horses are strong swimmers, and there will be seven horses on the boat with us. All you would have to do is grab onto a mane, or even a tail, and let a horse pull you to the riverbank. Easy as that."

The boy shifted and then ran a hand over his jaw. "Easy as that, you say?"

"I do."

"Can you swim?"

Like a fish, but it didn't seem the time to brag on that. "I can stay afloat, but I will be with the horses too, so if the boat goes down, I will do the same thing, let one of them pull me to shore."

Bran grabbed the pitchfork and headed to the next stall. "Guess I be goin' with you then," he said over his shoulder.

"Going where?" Clancy asked as he entered the stable.

"West." Mark Allen pointed in that direction.

The old stableman grunted. "Good thing. Place here be gettin' too crowded. A young boy like that, he will do well on the frontier, needs room to move and grow." There was a wispy note to his voice.

"Do you wish you were going too?"

"Oh, the young buck inside me does." Clancy shook his head. "But the old man knows his place. The frontier be for the likes of you and the boy. There be land for the takin' if you work hard and make a place for yourself." He clasped Mark Allen's shoulder in a strong grip that belied his age. "Find a way to work for yourself and not another man. Not that the McClures were ever anything but good to me, but if I were younger, I would do things differently. That I would." He gave a last squeeze and turned away, disappearing outside.

Find a way to work for himself? Doing what? He was trained as a stableman, but horses cost, both to purchase and to feed. He could take care of someone else's animals, but affording his own—other than Jughead—was out of the question, at least for the foreseeable future.

But maybe not forever.

Maybe he and Gwen would be able to claim a tract of land. People said that the government would give away land in some places—free of charge—to those who would work it and prove out a claim. He'd have to ask about that when they arrived. Until then, he was guaranteed wages working for Mr.—Paul.

And with regular wages, a man could get himself married.

Friday morning dawned amid gray skies and a thick mist that clung to Faye's skin like an oozing wound. She took her seat in the carriage and refused to look back at the house she'd called home for five years. Even while living in exile in Scotland, Pittsburgh had been waiting for her. Pittsburgh had been *home*.

Once again, she was homeless.

The carriage rumbled down the street lined with trees and tall houses tucked into their hedged borders. The fresh scent of early lilacs lingered in the damp air. Birdsong offered a sweet refrain to the steady clomp of the horses' hooves. But none of it lifted Faye's spirit. And she doubted anything ever would again.

"'Tis a shame we do not have finer weather to begin our journey." Madam sat across from Faye, her gray dress and plain bonnet almost fading into the newly reupholstered carriage. Plain brown coverings replaced its former burgundy and black splendor.

"Paul assured me," she continued, "we will have more than adequate space aboard the keelboat to be out of the weather."

Faye glanced out the window. She was being rude but was unable to bring herself to respond.

"Perhaps we shall finally have time to finish *An Arabian Tale* along the way." Madam patted the satchel beside her.

Faye leaned back against the drab cushions. She had nothing left to say and no desire to make an effort at small talk. She was behaving badly, but the spirit had been sucked out of her. Dried from the inside out, she was a fragile husk of the young woman of three days ago when she'd learned CeCe couldn't come to her rescue.

She almost wished herself in CeCe's predicament. With her parents' discreet intervention, CeCe could weather her situation and return to Pittsburgh in a few years as a respectable married woman with none the wiser.

Faye would be moldering in a crude hut on the frontier.

The carriage arrived at the docks and stopped with a jerk. Clancy was losing his touch in his old age. Leaving him behind was probably for the best. Faye lifted Madam's satchel off the floor where it had slid.

Paul pulled open the door, still holding the reins of Storm, his favorite horse.

"The boats are ready and everything we sent last night has been loaded aboard." He took his mother's hand to help her out of the carriage. "As soon as we have thee ladies aboard the keelboat, and the carriage and horses aboard the flatboat, we shall set sail." The enthusiasm in his voice was nauseating.

Faye took his hand next and stepped from the carriage just in time to see the urchin who had been with that impertinent man in the hedges taking the reins from Paul.

"Stop him," she cried.

"Stop who?" Paul looked around.

"That boy. He is taking your horse."

"Ah, yes. Thee have yet to meet the new stableman I hired." Paul gestured toward the man climbing down from the driver's seat. "Faye, this is Mark Allen Teed, our new stableman. Bran—the boy with Storm—is with him."

The lout from the alley.

Her breath left in a gust of indignation. "You hired"—she pointed at Mark Allen as one would point at a flea—"him?"

"Faye." Paul's dark brows drew together. "What has come over thee?"

"We met earlier." Mark Allen touched the brim of his hat.

"We did not." She raised her chin before pivoting to put her back to him and face Paul. "I saw him and that boy near the house one day. We did not meet."

Paul cocked his head. "Thee have now."

"Come, dear." Madam took Faye by the elbow and started for the boarding plank. "Whatever has come over thee?"

"I do not like him."

"Clancy gave him the highest recommendation."

"Clancy is getting old, you said so yourself. Perhaps his judgment is off."

Madam stopped, took hold of Faye's shoulders, and gave them a little shake. "Thee needs to stop behaving thus. It ill becomes thee."

"But what do we know of those two? The boy, he looks so…"

"So what, dear?"

"So unsavory."

"He looks like a perfectly normal boy to me."

"And what does Paul mean, saying the boy is with the stableman?" And would they blab to Madam or Paul about Gwen? She didn't want to imagine their reactions to her having ignored her sister's letters.

Or even their reactions to learning she had a sister at all. "Are they related?"

"I'm sure I do not know, but what matters that to us? Paul hired Mark Allen to handle the horses and tend our gardens. Besides"—Madam sent a fond smile over Faye's shoulder—"'twill be nice to have a young man about the place."

Faye stepped around the older woman and stomped up the ramp and into the boat. A barefooted sailor wearing the short, baggy pants of his trade opened the door to the narrow cabin in the middle of the vessel. Faye brushed past him and stalked into the single room.

Madam murmured something to the sailor before joining her. They stood in the middle of a wooden box with four narrow windows, six narrow bunks, and three rickety chairs that didn't match. Their trunks, shoved tight against the back wall, told Faye she hadn't been mistaken when she'd entered this room. Even though she dearly wished she had.

"This is it? We are to travel in... this?"

"I admit that I expected something a bit grander myself." Madam sat her satchel on the lumpy mattress of the closest bunk. A puff of dust rose around it.

Faye coughed and waved the dust away from her face. "We are to be stuck in here for weeks?"

"Not at all," Paul said from the doorway. He ducked and entered the cabin. "If the Lord favors us, we shall dock at Roberts Landing within the week. From Roberts Landing to Mount Pleasant should be only a day's journey in the carriage if the road is dry."

If the Lord favors us.

When had the Lord ever favored Faye?

She wrapped her arms around her middle. At least that stableman and his boy would be on the barge with the horses.

The keelboat lurched under her feet, and she sat on one of the rickety chairs with a thump.

She had a week to devise a way to keep those two quiet about her sister once they landed.

Chapter 14

T HE FLATBOAT WADDLED ALONG in the current, trailing far behind the lighter, sleeker keelboat. Mark Allen stretched until his joints popped. He gave Jughead a final pat, tucked the grooming tools into their box, and stowed it in the carriage before walking the length of the barge to the crude cabin at the bow.

Sixty feet long and twenty feet wide, what the flatboat lacked in beauty it made up for in sturdiness. Constructed of thick oak boards, it hosted two long sweeps attached to the flat top of the cabin and a steering oar at the back. The stout oar in front of the sailors was called a gouger. Mark Allen didn't understand how it worked, but the sailors claimed it would keep them off the sandbars and away from rocks and snags.

The musky odors of the river blended with the scents of early pollinating trees along the riverbank and swirled in the humidity of the late afternoon. Sunlight gleamed off the river's surface, its blinding rays accounting for a sailor's perpetual squint.

Mark Allen tugged his hat lower, but it didn't help much.

The two sailors manning the sweeps nodded to him before he

ducked into the low doorway of the cabin. Bran lay sprawled across one of the dozen narrow bunks that lined the walls of the dingy room. Lacking true windows, narrow slits allowed a meager amount of sunlight in. The room looked more like a fort than a cabin. When he'd asked why, the short sailor with the barrel chest had grunted a single word. "Injuns."

A trickle of smoke wafted in through one of the slits in the forward wall of the cabin. Mark Allen breathed in the scent.

"It ain't Bridget's cookin' but if it tastes half as good as it smells, 'twill do." Bran swung his legs over the edge and sat on the bunk. "Do you know how they cook on a boat?"

Mark Allen shook his head.

"They got a metal box half-full of sand that they build the fire in. Ain't that somethin'?"

"I admit I have never thought much about cooking aboard a ship. Never thought I'd be on one, for that matter."

"Me neither, and the thought of all that water still makes my insides hurt, but I think I could get used to it if the food be good. Maybe I will hire on with a crew once we get to this Ohio place."

Mark Allen didn't like that idea. It wasn't as if he had any say-so in the matter. Bran was free to do as he pleased. But he'd gotten used to the boy being around—liked having him around. He'd had an older brother and sister, but both had died before he was born, and his mother had died while he was too young to remember her. His father was his only family, if the old man hadn't drunk himself to death yet. "Pull out that slate and the new chalk I bought. Paul says we will be a week on the river. Might as well put the time to good use."

"You already write pert near as good as me."

"Then fetch your book to read."

"Why you so fired up 'bout learnin' to read and write anyway? You never did say."

Mark Allen dropped onto a chair and leaned forward, elbows on his knees. He rubbed his hands down his face and then met Bran eyes. "I have been working for other people all my life. First my father, then Master Whiteford, and neither paid me for my labors."

"Paul be payin' you. And he don't care can you read or not."

"I shall save every penny I earn."

Bran scratched his head. "What use is it to work for pay if you ain't gonna spend it?"

"When I have enough money, I plan to start my own business."

Bran's eyes widened. "Honest?"

"Aye."

"What kind o' business."

Mark Allen cleared his throat. "I have not figured that out yet."

"Whatever it is"—Bran thumped his chest—"I will work for you. For pay."

A warmth settled in Mark Allen. To hire someone to work for him was a thought that made him want to sit taller. "A businessman must be able to read and write. Fetch your book."

It felt good to say those words aloud. *A businessman.*

With Gwen by his side.

Three days on the river and Faye couldn't sit in that stifling cabin another minute. If she had to listen to Madam, Olivia, and Bridget prattle on about the new house another afternoon, she'd go mad. It was all speculation anyway, and unlike the other women, Faye expected the worst. She pushed open the door.

"Where are thee going?" Madam asked.

Faye shut her eyes. Her options were perfectly obvious. She either walked around the deck or she jumped overboard. At the moment, one didn't seem much better than the other. Both were preferable to staying inside. "I need fresh air."

"Find Paul and stay by him, my dear."

She nodded without turning and stepped into the blinding light. At least compared to the dim interior of the cabin it was blinding. When her eyes adjusted, she spied Paul near the rear of the vessel, feet braced with each step as if the river ripples were rolling ocean waves. At least he wasn't heaving over the railing on this trip. She joined him.

"Ah, thee has emerged into the daylight."

"Indeed. I have begun to appreciate the poor life of a mole."

Paul chuckled. "'Tis only for a few more days. The sailors tell me we are making excellent time."

Faye tried to form a smile but failed. Leaving the confines of the boat for a lonely life on the frontier hardly lifted her spirits. She watched the larger boat behind them for a long moment. While too far behind to make out faces, by his clothing, the person standing at the flat front was the new stableman. She watched him until they sailed around a bend in the river and lost sight of the flatboat.

"What troubles thee to glare so?"

"I'm not glaring. Just watching, the same as you."

Paul pulled off his hat and ran his fingers through his hair before replacing it. "I have not said anything to thee before because Mother insisted thee would adapt and change. However, we shall be arriving at Mount Pleasant in a few days. 'Tis a Quaker community, Faye. 'Tis time thee dropped the use of *you*, and adapted to the Quaker term, *thee*."

"I do not see what all the fuss is about. They mean the same thing."

"True. But the Quakers have decided, universally, to adopt the plain term for their use. 'Tis a way to identify ourselves as set apart."

Faye rolled her eyes. "Set apart for what?"

Paul took her by the shoulders and turned her to face him. His arched brows drew down into a level line. His brown eyes radiated concern. "Set apart for the Lord. Did thee not attest to that when thee joined with the Quakers beside Mother and me?"

"Of course." Faye couldn't quite meet his earnest eyes. "But to change my manner of speaking... I have tried. It seems so unnatural."

Paul held her shoulders for a long minute more, then sighed and released her. "'Twould please me if thee would conform on this issue. Is that requesting too much?"

Faye hung her head. Without Paul and Madam, where would she be? Had she become such an ungrateful wretch? Heat poured into her cheeks as she laid her hand on Paul's coat sleeve. "Not at all. I will do my best."

His beaming white smile tightened the band of guilt around her heart.

She turned back toward the front of the keelboat as one of the sailors uttered a strange cry and tumbled off the roof of the cabin, his hands clutching a wooden shaft protruding from his chest.

Faye gasped. In the next instant, the air filled with shrieks.

Paul grabbed her around the ribs and pulled her tightly to his side as he ran, keeping his body between her and the river's edge. She had one glimpse of a fleet of canoes approaching before he shoved her through the open door of the cabin. She cried out as her ankle twisted beneath her, and she spilled onto the rough floorboards.

They were trapped on a boat surrounded by Indians.

The shriek that ripped through the tranquil river basin brought the hairs on Mark Allen's neck to attention as he rested in the shade of the cabin of the flatboat. Bare feet slapping the wooden decks and sailors shouting added to the confusion.

Bran appeared at his elbow, mouth a grim line.

At the squeal of a horse and hooves hammering wood, Mark Allen whipped around to the back of the vessel. "Go calm the horses." He shoved Bran in that direction as gunshots rang out from ahead.

A sailor grabbed Mark Allen's sleeve. "Git topside." He jerked a thumb toward the roof of the cabin. "Help Skeeter man the sweeps."

"Indians?"

"It ain't yer granny." The sailor spun away.

Mark Allen heaved himself onto the flat roof. One sweep already had two sailors handling it. He joined the lone sailor on the other and pulled with all his might. With the third stroke of the giant oars, they cleared a small bend in the river. Before them floated the keelboat with canoes aimed at it like floating arrows. Puffs of smoke preceded more gunshots.

"Faye." Mark Allen stepped toward the bow of the flatboat.

His sweep partner caught the fabric of his shirt and held him. "Stay here. The quicker we reach 'em, the better."

Mark Allen put everything he had into hastening the cumbersome barge through the water, sending a glance toward the horses.

Bran was holding a grain bucket, hand-feeding the horses to distract them. Good lad.

The unnerving shrieks of the Indians ceased.

Mark Allen pulled on the oar but craned his neck to see the canoes retreating toward the shore. "They are leaving."

"Ain't no guarantee they won't return. Injuns is like that." The sailor spit over the side of the boat. "Tricky devils."

An Indian reached into the water and pulled another one into the canoe. That one didn't move.

Mark Allen's throat tightened. Were people on the keelboat hurt? How could he face Gwen if her sister came to harm on their journey?

They hauled the flatboat up beside the smaller vessel.

"How fare all on board?" The captain of the flatboat shouted across the half-dozen yards of water to his counterpart on the other vessel.

"One of the crew is dead, two others with injuries, and a passenger in the cabin is hurt."

"Who?" Mark Allen asked the sailor he shared the sweep with, the one called Skeeter.

The man shrugged. Of course he couldn't know.

The captains decided the flatboat could spare one sailor to replace one of the injured men on the keelboat.

"I could go."

The sailor cocked an eyebrow at Mark Allen.

Mark Allen stiffened, hands clenched. "What I do not know I can learn fast enough."

"Maybe so." The sailor tipped his head toward the rear of the flatboat. "But those critters is your responsibility, not ours. You tend your horses, and we will work the boats."

"You were glad enough for my help moving this barge."

"Aye. Any strong back will work in a pinch. But we know nothing of horses." He shoved a stiff finger into Mark Allen's chest. "That is your job, mate."

Of course, Paul had hired him to care for the horses, not Faye. But he had to know if she was the one injured, and if so, how serious the injury was.

Paul stepped out of the keelboat's cabin. Mark Allen cupped his hands around his mouth to shout over and ask after Faye, but he let his arms drop to his sides instead. What would his new employer think about his stableman asking after his ward? Faye wasn't a servant. Clancy had confirmed her claim. However it had happened, she was part of the family.

Mark Allen was the servant.

The gulf between them was much wider than the water separating them now.

Faye shifted on the lumpy mattress and sucked a sharp breath between her teeth. The pillow under her ankle did nothing to alleviate the joint's pulsing throb. "Are you—thee—quite sure 'tis not broken?"

Paul nodded. "But a bad bruise can be more painful than a clean break."

Madam knelt beside the bunk. She took the damp cloth from Faye's ankle and rinsed it in a bucket of water before smoothing it back in place. The cool river water brought a moment of relief.

"My poor dear. That thee had to witness such a horrible event." Madam's hand trembled.

Faye shuddered. The cry. The sailor's fall. That indescribable shrieking. Paul shielding her. He'd protected her.

"There, there." Paul patted her shoulder. "The captain has moved our vessel farther from the bank. The current is a little stiffer here, but nothing this keelboat cannot handle. He has assured me the Indians will not return."

"How can he know that?"

The corners of Paul's eyes tightened, and the muscles in his jaw ticked. She wasn't the only one shaken by what they'd seen.

"Experience, I presume," he said.

Faye wasn't impressed with the captain's experience. It hadn't stopped him from floating them right into a pack of those savages. "I want to go home."

"We are going home." Paul's lips firmed. "More than ever, I'm convinced the Lord has called me to be a doctor in Mount Pleasant. Imagine facing the dangers of the frontier without access to medical help. If today is any indication—"

"'Tis an indication we should turn around and go back to Pittsburgh." Faye rose on her elbows. "We could have been killed out there." Her voice rose and wavered with each word.

"Oh, my." Madam's face paled. "We knew there may be risks."

Faye's vision blurred with unshed tears. "I care not about risks. I only want to go home." She pounded the mattress with her fist. "'Tis safe at home."

"Here, drink this." Paul pushed the cool rim of a cup against her lips. "'Twill help the pain and settle thy nerves."

Faye gulped the bitter draught, then twisted away and coughed. The acrid taste clinging to her tongue made her want to gag.

Madam fussed with the pillow and then urged her back against the mattress. She freshened the cloth and reapplied it to Faye's ankle.

In a short while, the dim room turned fuzzy, and Faye's eyelids refused to remain open. Voices came at her as if from a distant shore.

"'Tis the shock of it all," Madam said.

Paul sighed. "Nay. She never wished to come."

"She will adapt. She is young. Once we are settled and she makes a friend or two, she shall feel at home there."

"I hope thee are correct, Mother. But I fear she has her heart turned inward."

"Give her time. The poor thing has been through much in her short life. All alone. Sold like an animal at auction." The older woman clicked her tongue.

"Thee has spoiled her for all those reasons."

"Perhaps a bit, I have."

Paul's snort hinted at humor. "Perhaps much."

"Now we have uprooted her from what she had grown to love and hold dear. Is it any wonder she resents it?"

"I suppose not. But I feel called to this position. What could I do? Leave her behind to fend for herself?"

Yes. That is precisely what you—thee—should have done. Faye could think the words but her tongue was too thick to make the sounds. Her lips refused to move.

"Of course not. One does not ignore the leading of our Lord."

Why not? With that silent protest, her mind succumbed to the same blissful rest that her body had already accepted.

Chapter 15

"**S**HE IS COMING ROUND." Madam's fingers pressed against Faye's cheek. "Bring me a cup of water, Olivia. Paul said she would awaken thirsty."

The glug of water filling a cup rousted Faye more than the voices. A nasty film coated her tongue and tasted like a wedge of goat cheese gone rancid. Licking her lips gained her no moisture. She tried to rise on one elbow, but dead weights had replaced her muscles.

"Let me help thee." Madam's face swam in and out of focus as she steadied Faye.

"Water." Was that croak her voice?

The cup's rim barely connected with her lips before Faye gulped down its contents. "More." That sounded more like her.

"'Tis enough for now. Let it settle, and then I shall give thee more."

Above her sweet smile, worry wrinkles fanned from Madam's eyes. Faye had known from the start that Madam loved her like a daughter. The woman's worry and tender care didn't surprise her. But Paul's protectiveness, the way he'd thrust himself between her and danger—that had surprised her. She'd always thought of herself as an obligation to Paul. She'd assumed that with his money and influence, she was nothing more than a charity case he'd undertaken to please his mother.

"Ready for another sip?"

Faye took the cup, her hand shaking as she sipped. She let the moisture seep between her lips and bathe her mouth before swallowing. Then she gulped the rest and handed back the empty cup. "Where is Paul?"

"He went out shortly before thee awoke. Are thee in much pain? Shall I send Bridget to fetch him?" Those worry lines deepened.

"The pain is much reduced. There is no need to summon him." Although she wanted to speak to Paul, she wasn't sure she wanted to do so in front of Madam, Olivia, and Bridget. And she wasn't exactly sure what she'd say. Despite her sour and ungrateful attitude, he might have saved her life.

How did one thank a person for that?

"He shall return before long. 'Tis almost supper time."

"I believe I would like to sit up for a while." Faye leaned forward and Madam fluffed and settled the pillows against the wall that framed the bunk. Once Faye was as comfortable as she could be under the circumstances, she reached for the older woman's hand. "I owe thee an apology."

"What for, dear?"

Faye looked down at the lap. "For the way I acted this afternoon."

"'Twas only the shock, I'm sure."

"A lady never shows her temper. You—thee—taught me that, remember? 'Twas one of our first lessons."

"Indeed. Thee were a diamond in the rough when we brought thee home." Madam cupped Faye's cheek with her palm. "But so eager to learn. Such a joy to teach."

Faye raised her head. "I will be forever grateful to you—thee."

"It pleases me no end to hear the Quaker *thee* in thy speech."

"I am trying." Faye pressed the heel of her hand to her forehead. "I heard what Paul said before I fell asleep, that I never wanted to come on this journey. It was the truth—I do not want to live on the frontier. But 'twas no excuse to behave so badly. I feel..." Finding no words adequate to end her sentence, she shrugged.

Madam took Faye's hand and patted it between her own. "Thee has faced so many frightening things in thy young life. I cannot imagine.

Truly, I cannot. But this time, my dear, thee are not alone."

Faye hadn't been alone on board the ship that sailed from Wales, either. But her father had died on that journey. His body sewn into a rough sack, the captain had muttered a few words before tipping the board on which the body lay. It slipped beneath the ocean surface with a small splash, the first wave erasing any sign of his burial spot. Gwen had clung to her and promised her—promised her—that they would always have each other. Less than three weeks later, the auctioneer's gavel struck and her sister was gone.

She shivered in the muggy closeness of the closed cabin.

How long before Madam and Paul disappeared from her life as well?

The keelboat had been out of sight since they hoisted the anchors that morning. The fog, which usually dissipated by midmorning, encased the flatboat like a shroud. Its clammy fingers muffled the sounds of the sweeps and carried the musky scent of the marshes along the riverbank.

Mark Allen rested his forearms on Jughead's back, squinting into the murky world ahead of them.

"The girl be fine, just sprained an ankle. You heard the sailors talkin' same as me." Bran stopped currying Storm, Paul's black gelding. "Why you still moonin' over her?"

Mark Allen shot his best glare at Bran. "I'm not mooning over anyone. Least of all Faye Morgan."

Bran cocked an eyebrow under the too-long bangs that tumbled across his forehead.

How could the boy think he'd have any interest in Faye when her sister waited in Mount Pleasant? But then, Bran had never met his Gwen. Mark Allen cleared his throat and slapped Jughead's side. "Look how this fellow has filled out with a little rest and good fodder."

"He ain't the bag o' bones we rode into Pittsburgh, that be a fact."

"I shall be driving the carriage from Roberts Landing to Mount Pleasant. Paul will ride Storm. 'Twill be up to you to ride Jughead and lead Ginger. Think you can manage?"

Bran delivered that baleful look he reserved for Mark Allen's questions. He poked his thumb at the matched team of sorrels, Ben and Buster, the heavy horses that pulled the wagon. "Who be goin' to drive them and the wagon?"

Mark Allen had wondered about that too. "I suppose Paul will hire another driver at Roberts Landing, or perhaps he can handle a team himself."

Bran's chest pushed against the front of his shirt. "I could drive 'em."

"Have you handled a team?"

"Not yet."

"Paul is a man mighty particular about his horses. Why do you think Clancy put me through the paces like he did? Not sure he will give his team over to a novice."

"I ain't a novice. Ain't I been carin' for them for days already? You can teach me to drive." The boy thrust his chin out. "'Tis only fair, seein' I learned you how to read."

Bran had proved early on to be a good hand with Jughead—after their initial meeting. He was respectful of the animal but fearless.

And the lad was right. Mark Allen owed Bran a debt for the learning.

"Pull the harness reins from the carriage. We have a couple of days to teach you how to handle the lines."

Bran grinned, scampering under the rails that created the makeshift horse stalls at the rear of the flatboat.

Mark Allen looked down the murky river again. He couldn't see much past the boat's bow. Teaching Bran to drive would keep them both busy enough not to worry about another attack.

Bran climbed onto the wagon after Mark Allen attached the reins to the low railing that formed the sides of the flatboat. The boy tugged on his leather gloves while Mark Allen climbed up beside him, and then a shout echoed through the mist. They looked at each other as another shout followed the first. Then the metallic clang of someone beating on a kettle rang across the water.

"That ain't Injuns." Bran's voice held an undercurrent of fear.

"Stay with the horses." Mark Allen leaped off the wagon and ran to the forward cabin. He swung himself onto its top. "Do you need help on the sweeps?"

"Yup." Skeeter stepped aside and made room for him. "We gotta slow this crate down."

"What is happening?"

"'Tis a distress signal comin' from the keelboat."

What else could go wrong?

Bridget had been setting a cup of tea on the low table for Faye when the boat lurched beneath them.

Faye grabbed the bunk and held on as the boat spun to one side, then seemed to right itself, before swinging back the other way and lurching to a stop. The cup crashed to the floor, tea spraying across the boards.

"Whatever was that?" Madam clutched her needlework, her stool having slid partway across the floor.

Shouting from the sailors reached them, but Faye couldn't understand the words. She glanced out the window but could see nothing other than fog. There was no storm to toss the boat around.

The keelboat groaned, as if its wooden hull were a living thing, and then it shuddered and moved again.

"I have a bad feeling about this," said Olivia, who had been stalwart during their trips across the Atlantic, even during the worst of storms.

Faye was about to agree when the clanging sounded from outside.

"Oh, my," Madam said.

After a sharp rap on the door, Paul rushed inside, a grim set to his mouth.

"What is it, dear?" Madam asked.

"The boat has hit a snag and is taking on water." He held his hands out, palms toward them. "Be not alarmed. The captain assures me the sailors can keep it afloat, but he also bids us to move onto the flatboat for the remainder of our journey.

The flatboat? With that stableman and the boy? She couldn't.

"If we are in no danger of sinking, then why—"

"Because the captain has decided 'tis the safest option for thee ladies." By the look on Paul's face, Faye knew better than to argue.

But she wanted to. She'd rather the keelboat sink and take her chances in the river than share the flatboat with that stableman. The man who knew Gwen. Who knew that Faye had a sister.

A sister she'd never told the McClures about.

"Pack thy things, and I shall return to assist thee in the transfer." He pointed at Faye. "I shall carry thee when all is ready. Stay off that foot as much as possible."

After he left, Olivia and Bridget stuffed items into their trunks. Madam packed her needlework. And Faye did her best not to show the emotions raging through her.

The enormity of her omission was about to come crashing down on her. When Madam learned about Gwen—and she must before they arrived in Mount Pleasant—she would be hurt, maybe disappointed, or even angry. Faye couldn't blame her for any of those reactions. And Paul? How would he react?

He wouldn't turn her out, of course, he wasn't that kind of man.

But she'd deserve it for not being honest with them, and she had only herself to blame.

When the eerie silhouette of the keelboat materialized out of the fog, Mark Allen and the sailors on the sweeps slowed the flatboat enough to ease alongside the other vessel, which sat still on the water, its anchors dropped. Shouts broke out as the sailors tossed ropes from one boat to the other, lashing them together. The sailors leaped off the cabin to the deck below and hustled to make the two vessels secure.

Mark Allen hopped down to the main deck.

Bran appeared at his elbow. "What happened?"

"I told you to stay with the horses."

Bran flicked a hand in the direction of the animals. "They be fine."

Skeeter walked by and grabbed both of them by their sleeves. "Come on, we gotta clean out the cabin."

"What for?" Bran asked.

"The keelboat hit a snag. A bad one."

"Will it sink?" Bran's voice held a note of terror.

The ropes attaching the two boats creaked. Mark Allen doubted the wisdom of lashing them together. What if the keelboat sank and took the flatboat down with it?

"The crew will keep it bailed out enough to make it to a port for repairs. But the captain says we are to transfer the passengers here.

We got to make room for 'em in the cabin."

"Where will we sleep?" Bran asked as he followed the man into the low cabin.

"Under yer wagon or in yer fancy carriage, be my guess."

Bran might fit in the carriage, but it would never hold Mark Allen's length. Not that it mattered. The women needed the cabin. He gathered his scant belongings and pushed them into Bran's arms. "Stow all this in the carriage for now."

More sailors entered to grab their gear. They would likely be forced to sleep on the open deck, so Mark Allen shouldn't complain.

He went outside where a plank had been rigged between the higher side of the keelboat and the flatboat's low deck. Pitched at a fairly steep incline, it was obvious the passengers would have to slide down it.

Female passengers.

Chapter 16

"I'M FULLY CAPABLE OF walking, Paul. If you—thee—will simply lend me thy arm for assistance." Faye closed her eyes and held up her hand. She didn't know which was more frustrating, struggling to adhere to the Quaker *thee* and *thy* or trying to convince Paul she didn't need to be carried to the flatboat. Neither seemed to be working in her favor.

"Come now. Thy ankle is half again the size it should be. Putting weight on it will only prolong thy recovery."

"Having thee carry me past those sailors, my feet and ankles dangling over thy arm, is most indecent."

"Agreed. I will cover thy skirts and limbs fully with a blanket." He leaned close to where she still lay on her bunk. "Trust me, Faye."

The brotherly concern in Paul's eyes along with the half-humorous upward tug at one side of his mouth finally convinced her. That and bumping her ankle against the frame of the bunk as she sat up. She bit the inside of her top lip to keep from crying out.

"As you—thee, oh, let us get on with it."

Paul dragged the blanket she sat upon around her legs and enveloped her like a cocoon. A sticky cocoon in the heat and humidity. She hoped to be free of its smothering clutches as soon as they reached the flatboat. He was giving the blanket a final tuck when the keelboat lurched to the starboard side.

Faye gasped. "I thought you said there was no danger of sinking."

"'Tis only the two boats bucking against each other."

"'Tis only," Faye murmured under her breath.

Paul leaned over her again. "Clasp thy hands behind my neck. And worry not, I am perfectly capable of carrying thee."

Faye did as he said and breathed a sigh of relief when he stood straight and solid. She was no great size, but Paul wasn't used to such physical exertion. Unlike the broad-shouldered stableman, Paul worked with his mind, not his body. Not that she didn't think he could carry her, exactly, but it was reassuring to feel the stability of his balance.

He carried her to the port side of the keelboat, and they stopped in front of a single long plank that fell from the rail of the keelboat onto the deck of the flatboat below.

Faye tightened her hold on Paul's neck. "Surely thee do not mean for us to walk down that." She pointed just as the new stableman stepped to the plank on the flatboat side.

"Of course not. 'Tis far too steep to walk down. We shall have to slide."

"Slide?" Her voice rose above the grinding of the ship hulls as they rubbed together, shifting the plank to a slightly lesser incline.

"Oh, my." Madam joined them at the railing, Olivia and Bridget close behind. She peered over the rail. "Is there no other way?"

Paul jostled Faye a bit. Had his arms begun to tire?

"I'm afraid we have no choice, Mother."

"Paul?" The stableman called from below.

"Yes?"

"If you would but wait a moment, I could toss you a rope. We have several long enough in the wagon."

"The women cannot swing down a rope."

"No, sir. Of course not. But 'twould give them something to hang onto to slow their descent as they slide down the plank."

"Excellent. Thank you, Mark Allen."

The stableman ran to the wagon at the rear of the flatboat while Paul jostled Faye again.

"Put me down, Paul. I fear I am too much burden for thee to hold this long."

"Nonsense. Mark Allen is already on his way back. 'Twill be but a moment now."

Mark Allen called to a pair of sailors who stood by watching. He had them stand back away from the railing and anchor the rope. Then he nodded to a trio of sailors who stood behind Paul on the keelboat. Mark Allen flipped the end of the rope toward them, one man caught it, and they anchored it at the top.

"Set the lass on the plank. She can grasp the rope in both hands and ease her way down."

"I think I should come with her," Paul said.

"'Twould be more strain on those of us securing the rope. Better to come singly."

"But she is injured. Her ankle."

"I shall lift her off the plank at the bottom."

"He most certainly will not!" Faye clung to Paul. "You go first, and then you—thee—can lift me off."

"If I went first, who would set thee on the plank?"

"I shall settle myself on it."

"Nonsense. Hold on now." Paul hefted her over the railing, and her backside thumped onto the plank. Her blanket-wrapped feet pointed toward the bow of the two ships. Behind her, there was... nothing. She clutched at Paul's shoulders.

"Take the rope."

"I cannot."

"Have no fear, Faye. 'Tis not far and Mark Allen will gather thee safely at the bottom."

And he said to have no fear. As if sliding into the arms of that ill-bred lout was nothing to be alarmed over. She cast a glance down. At least the man was more used to lifting and toting than Paul was. It was a small sort of comfort.

"Take the rope."

She did. The coarse hemp chaffed against her sweating palms. Paul held her around her waist.

"Now, when thee are ready, ease thyself down, keeping a tight hold on the rope."

Faye squeezed her eyes shut and took a deep breath. She let herself slide a bit, then squeezed hard on the rope and stopped. She had let herself slide another few inches and stopped again. It wasn't as bad as she'd feared. She looked down.

Mark Allen nodded his encouragement and lifted his hands as if to catch her. Faye snapped her gaze away and looked straight forward. She let herself slide another few inches when the ships bucked against each other again. The plank shifted steeper. Her blanket caught on something, and she started to twist. To her horror, the twisting caused the blanket to unwrap.

"Oh!" Faye dropped her right hand from the rope and grabbed the blanket.

"Hold the rope, Faye!" Paul shouted from above. "Hold the rope!"

The warning came too late. The twisting turned into a tumble when her lone hand on the rope wasn't enough. Squealing like a pig caught under a fence, Faye half-slid, half-rolled the rest of the way down the plank.

Mark Allen caught her. A whoosh of breath left him when her hip collided with his stomach. Her flailing left elbow collided with his forehead, sending a shaft of prickling agony through to her fingertips. They tumbled to the deck. Mark Allen landed flat on his back. Faye landed seated upon his stomach, her skirt hiked almost to her knees, the blanket unwrapped at her feet, and her injured foot thumped against the wad of cloth. Pain screamed from her heel to her hip.

Paul slid down the plank and landed on the deck beside her. "Are thee hurt?"

"Of course I'm hurt." Tears flooded Faye's vision. She didn't think she could move her leg, much less her foot.

A gasping wheeze beneath her shook her backside.

Paul scooped her up and removed her from Mark Allen. He set her on a trunk that stood against the flatboat's cabin.

Faye fussed with her skirts to cover her ankles.

"Wait here." Paul returned to the stableman.

As if she was going anywhere on her throbbing foot with those leering sailors ogling her.

Mark Allen had rolled over and was pushing to his knees, his breath like a bagpipe deflating.

Paul hunched over him. "Let me help."

"'Tis nothing," Mark Allen managed between shuttering breaths. "She merely pressed the wind from me." He staggered to his feet, one hand on his forehead.

Faye's face caught fire at the look Mark Allen gave her. His gaze swept to her skirts and back to her face. She crossed her arms and looked away. What an insufferable man. He may have stopped her fall, but he had seen far too much of her person in the process.

And he smelled like a horse.

Mark Allen helped the sailors rig a rope seat that could be hoisted by the sweeps. It took most of an hour, but they lowered the three remaining ladies onto the flatboat without incident. Without so much as another ankle exposed—much less a knee.

Although it had been a startlingly beautiful glimpse of that knee before Faye had tumbled on top of him. And he'd be less than a man if he hadn't noticed the roundness of her backside when it pressed into his middle. If she'd been a bag of bones, he might still be wheezing, but she was more than adequately rounded in all the right womanly places.

"Pay attention," the sailor on the keelboat hollered as he sent another trunk down the ramp. Mark Allen caught it and slid it onto the flatboat's deck. So many trunks there wasn't space for them all in the cramped cabin, so they stacked them against the cabin's back wall until that was full.

"That be the last of them," the sailor yelled and left the keelboat's railing.

Mark Allen wrestled the last two trunks down the deck and under the wagon, leaving just enough space for him to sleep between them. He crawled out from beneath the wagon and stretched his back.

Paul joined him carrying a bundle of bedding. "Is there room for one more?"

"Right here, sir." Mark Allen pointed to the space between the trunks. He'd have to squeeze under the low-riding carriage.

"Excellent." The makeshift sleeping arrangement didn't diminish the doctor's easygoing smile. "Even towing the keelboat, we should not be more than two days from landing. This will do fine."

"How is Faye?"

Paul's eyebrows rose.

"Miss Morgan." Heat crept up Mark Allen's neck. He had to remember she wasn't his equal. It was difficult when he'd thought of her as such for so long.

"A trifle embarrassed, but no worse for her tumble. I expect by the time we land, she shall be walking on that ankle." He grasped Mark Allen's shoulder. "And thee were correct to refer to her as Faye. We Quakers do not hold with titles of any kind." He chuckled. "But I must confess, we are new enough Quakers that I sometimes forget."

"I am glad Faye's injury was not made worse by her fall." He should have caught her without being bowled over, but with her tumbling around, he'd been uncertain exactly where to grab hold. The warmth crept higher along his cheeks.

Paul looked out over the river and then back at Mark Allen. "She is unhappy. 'Twas not her wish to travel west. Perhaps thee, someone near her age, could encourage her on the advantages of this move. If thee have the chance, of course."

Paul wanted him to spend time with Faye? He hadn't expected that. In fact, he'd expected to be told to keep his distance.

"I am eager to reach Mount Pleasant and see what opportunities await there," Mark Allen said. "Perhaps I can speak with her about that before we land."

"I would appreciate it." Then Paul spread a straw-filled mattress he must have brought over from the keelboat under the wagon. He fumbled with the blanket and sighed. "Would thee fetch me a pillow from the cabin? I neglected to bring one, and I know Mother has an extra."

"Aye." Wait until Bran learned he'd been encouraged to speak with Faye. As if the lad weren't cheeky enough already, he'd find a way to tease Mark Allen about it for sure.

Faye still rested on the trunk outside of the cabin as Mark Allen approached. She glared when she noticed him.

"Paul assured me you took no further injury. I'm relieved to hear it."

"Indeed." She cleared her throat and lifted her chin a notch. Any higher and she'd look like one of the Blue Herons that dotted the riverbanks in the evenings. "We need to talk."

"We do?" It'd surprised him when Paul had suggested it, but Faye suggesting it nearly knocked his breath out again.

"Of course we do."

She looked around so he did too. The sailors were busy at their posts, Paul and Bran were talking near the horses, and the rest of the ladies must have been inside the cabin.

She cleared her throat again before whispering, "About my sister."

"Gwen?"

"She is my only sister." She huffed. "The point is, the McClures are not aware of her."

"They know nothing about your sister?"

"Keep your voice down." She hissed the words between her teeth, eyes darting toward the nearest sailor who was too far away to overhear. "I never told them about Gwen."

Mark Allen snatched his hand from the back of his neck. How could Faye not have spoken of her sister? Gwen had talked of little else than Faye. It made no sense.

"I never expected to see or hear from her again. The McClures assumed me to be alone in the world, and informing them otherwise would have served no purpose."

Mark Allen clenched his fists at his sides. "They may have looked for her. May have been willing to free her as well."

"'Twasn't like that." Faye turned her face from him.

"All Gwen ever talked about was you. Her little sister. She risked being caught away from the Whitefords' house—and severe punishment—to find you. And I promised to help her any way I could."

"You should have stayed in Mount Pleasant."

"I have never been there."

"What?" She looked directly at him for the first time, her brown eyes wary.

"I knew not where she was. She was sold from the Whitefords' three years ago."

"And you have not seen her since?"

"Nay."

"And yet you still came after me? Not knowing where she was?"

"I knew she was in the Northwest Territory with a band of Quakers." He half-raised his hands and then let them sink back to his sides. "I thought once I found you and worked to buy your freedom, we would find her together."

Faye's mouth dropped open. She stared at him for so long, he wondered if he'd sprouted a set of horns.

"You thought I would travel into the wilderness, to an unknown destination, unchaperoned, with a strange man?"

The heat returned to Mark Allen's face. "I did not think it through all the way."

"I should say not."

"But now you are properly chaperoned, and we are going to Mount Pleasant. So it worked out. But how did you know she is in Mount Pleasant?"

"She wrote to me."

"You mean she found someone to write for her? Gwen cannot read or write."

"She can now."

Mark Allen took a step back as if punched in the gut. "What?"

"The first letter that came was written by someone else. But the second letter was a different hand, and she told me she wrote it herself."

"When?"

"When what?"

"When did she write a letter with her own hand?"

"Last fall, why?"

Gwen could write. His Gwen.

Yet she hadn't written to him.

He concentrated on what Faye had said. "She wrote you two letters, and you still did not tell the McClures about her?"

"Shhh." Faye glanced away again. "'Tis complicated."

He snorted. "'Twill be more complicated when they meet her."

"Please. Do not mention her. Let me tell them in my own way and in my own time."

None of it made sense to him. But the unexpected sheen of tears in those brown eyes stilled the indignation churning in him for Gwen's sake. It wasn't his business to tell them anyway.

And he still needed to fetch the pillow for Paul.

As he walked away, all he could think about was that Gwen hadn't written to him.

Not once.

Chapter 17

"SO WHY DOES HE want you to spend time with her?" Bran asked.

Mark Allen knew he shouldn't have told the boy, but it being a fair evening, they'd decided to sleep out on the deck. Lying under the stars he hadn't been able to sleep, and before he knew it, he'd spilled the whole story.

"He thought if she spoke with someone closer to her age, she might change her feelings about moving to Ohio."

Bran snorted, then a bony elbow connected with Mark Allen's ribs through the coarse blanket. "Maybe you and her will spark up more than just a conversation." The grin was loud and clear in his voice.

"'Tisn't like that." But his face heated in the darkness at the memory of her curves pressed against him. She looked so much like Gwen, the same dark curls, the same height, even the same shape to her face. But where Gwen was soft and gentle, Faye was—

"Ain't no reason for it not to be like that. After all, these Quakers believe everyone is just as good as everyone else."

Was Faye a Quaker? She seemed to use *you* and *your* more than *thee* and *thy*. But it didn't matter, because she was nothing more—could be nothing more—than Gwen's sister.

"I am keeping a promise to return her to her sister."

"A sister you ain't seen in years. She could be married with a whole passel of younguns by now."

Bran could not know the pain he'd unleashed inside Mark Allen.

Mark Allen rolled onto his side, back to the boy.

Gwen had written to her sister last fall. If she'd written him too, he'd have gotten the letter long before he left the Whitefords' in January. But she hadn't.

What if Bran was right? What if she had married someone else? What if she'd forgotten all about him? What if... what if all his hopes and dreams were about to be shattered? What would he do?

What sort of a future would there be without Gwen?

Faye hobbled out of the cramped flatboat cabin, leaning on Bridget's strong arm for support. The damp morning air carried wildflower scents mixed with the pungent odors of the river—a huge improvement over the cabin's stale air. Water gurgling past the boat was a calming contrast to the endless speculations of Madam and Olivia on what their house in Mount Pleasant would look like. As if they'd be lucky enough to have something grander than a two-room shack with a servants' lean-to on the back.

Bridget helped her settle onto the same trunk she'd been seated on the day before after the disastrous transfer from the keelboat. The cook placed a pillow behind Faye's back.

"Thank you."

"Any time, miss." Her cheerful smile coaxed one from Faye in return before the cook returned to the cabin.

Faye's smile faded when Mark Allen approached.

"Faye." He touched the brim of his hat.

Rudeness wouldn't produce his cooperation, so she faced him and scooted to the edge of the trunk. "Will you join me?" It didn't seem right using thee with him. He wasn't Quaker, after all.

By his expression, she might have asked him to pet a viper.

"Come. Sit. I am no danger to you." She tempered her words with a soft chuckle. It must have worked because he sat on the other side of the trunk, keeping daylight between them. Was he afraid of her, or repulsed by her? Had she been so awful? She stifled a grimace, knowing the answer.

"Please excuse my behavior yesterday, and the day we met." She couldn't suppress the next grimace. "And the day we boarded the boats. I have not been at my best."

"Not at your best?" The question was bland, but she heard the humor underneath the words.

"You know what I mean. All three times we have met I have been under difficult circumstances."

"Because you do not wish to move west to be near your sister?" This time, his voice carried censure as plainly as if he'd snapped his fingers in front of her face.

"'Tis not about Gwen." She twisted on the trunk to face him. "I love my sister. She means the world to me. I would have answered her letters in time and—"

"You did not answer her letters?"

"I worked hard to build a new life in Pittsburgh and I—"

"While Gwen scrubbed floors, washed clothes, worked day and night while pining for you." He turned away from her.

Faye touched his arm, and he jumped.

"I did not mean to startle you, but I cannot talk to the back of your head." Exasperation had crept into her tone, despite her best efforts to remain calm. After all, did she owe him an explanation? No. But the waves of disapproval wafting off him made her want to... What? Validate herself to him? A man who smelled of sweat and horse, a man who knew her sister. A man with hazel eyes that seemed to see right through her.

He swung around. "I do not understand how you can look so much like Gwen and be so completely different at the same time."

"I'm afraid 'twas always the case. As the oldest, and Gwen was forced to be the responsible one at an early age."

"Because your mother died."

So he knew some of their family history at least. "That was a big part of it."

He raised an eyebrow.

"After she died, our father started drinking. 'Twas Gwen who kept the family going. She became our mother, cooking and cleaning and caring for me and our brothers. After they died, Father sank deeper into the bottle."

Something sparked in the amber depths of his eyes. "That must have been hard on both of you."

"'Twas, but I had Gwen to lean on."

He sat back against the outside wall of the cabin, staring across the water. "And Gwen had no one." His voice was laced with sorrow.

"She was the strong one."

"Her greatest wish was to gain her freedom and find you." He faced her again. "'Tis all she spoke of, finding her sister."

Shame washed over Faye. "And she did."

"Yet you did not answer her letters."

Faye squirmed on the hard trunk. "Why do you care?"

"I care about Gwen."

Oh. That could explain a lot. "Do you love her?"

"Everyone loves Gwen." But the russet in his cheeks said something more.

"Why did you not answer her?" Mark Allen asked, turning the conversation away from his feelings for Gwen.

Faye stiffened beside him. "I do not see 'tis any business of yours."

"You have asked me to keep her a secret from my employer."

"I asked only that you not volunteer the information."

"Which is the same as keeping a—"

"Fine." She crossed her arms and looked angry enough to chew nails. She was a feisty one. That was the word for Faye—feisty. So unlike Gwen. "I did not answer because I did not wish to be removed from Pittsburgh."

"Why?"

She tipped up her nose. "I do not suppose you would understand."

He understood all right, understood that she thought herself far above the likes of him. He stood and looked down at her. "I understand that you do not deserve Gwen's love and devotion." He'd taken just two steps when her words stopped him.

"What do you know about anything?"

He whirled around. "I know loyalty, or more to the point, I know the lack of it."

Her face blanched as white as a frog's belly. For a moment, he feared she might swoon. But in the space of a few heartbeats, the fiery spirit was back in her dark eyes, and she sat forward on the trunk.

"You know nothing. If my plans had come to pass, I would have had the money to purchase Gwen's indenture and set her free."

That took the wind out of Mark Allen's sails.

The notion of purchasing Gwen's indenture had occurred to Faye—not been her main reason—but the anger and disapproval drained from Mark Allen's face. He returned to the trunk and resumed his seat beside her.

"My apologies. I should not have assumed selfish motives for your actions. 'Twas wrong of me."

Selfish motives. Exactly what she'd held until forced onto the keelboat by Paul's insistence and CeCe's abandonment. Maybe they sprang from her deep-seated need for a secure future, but they had been selfish. She was ashamed that an almost stranger had seen through her so easily. But not ashamed enough to own up to it... yet.

"'Tis true that I wished to secure my future in Pittsburgh. A woman would be foolish to discount the need for a husband's protection and provision. And to purchase my sister's indenture." Because she would have asked it of her would-be Pittsburgh husband at some point.

"Can we start over?" He turned his hazel eyes on her again. "'Twould seem neither of us got off on our best foot. Perchance we might even become friends."

Friends with the stableman? But the Quakers didn't feel any man—or woman either—should consider themselves above any other. She *had* agreed to become a Quaker, and at least for the near future, Mark Allen was the only person near her age she would know in the new town. He couldn't be a bad sort, or Gwen wouldn't have been his friend.

She offered her hand, and he shook it, then they sat in silence for a while, listening to the river and the birds in the trees that lined its banks.

"I'm sorry you had to leave the place where you wished to stay." He said at length. "But I'm glad you will be reunited with Gwen. I know how much it means to her."

An emotional fist pushed into Faye's middle. "I miss her. She was more than my sister. She was also my best friend."

"Then why did you ignore her letters?"

Must he return to that again? Just when they'd reached a truce.

"I did not ignore them. I read them over and over." So many times, she'd committed them to memory.

"But you did not answer."

Faye squirmed on the seat.

"You cannot understand. As a man, you can always earn your own way, as you are by working for Paul. You are never dependent on someone else for your future." Her excuse rang hollow, so she tried again. "I would have answered her letters, in time, once I was settled and in a position to do so." That sounded a little better.

He relaxed against the outside wall of the flatboat's cabin. "You are right. I do not understand. But you are also right that 'tis different for a man. I can see that."

It wasn't much common ground, but it was something, and Faye felt a little better. Maybe having a friend in Ohio—even if he was a stableman—would make life more bearable. Maybe he'd even be able to smooth over her reunion with Gwen.

Because if he blamed her for not answering the letters, surely Gwen would too.

"What do you hope to find—other than your sister—in Mount Pleasant?" Mark Allen asked, ignoring the faces Bran was making at him from across the flatboat. He was just trying to help Paul, and probably Gwen too, by befriending Faye.

"I have no hope of finding anything at all."

"There must be unmarried men in Mount Pleasant, someone who would interest you if you are set on finding a husband."

She swiveled to face him, mouth open, then jerked back and crossed her arms. "I have no intention of marrying some frontiersman who must scratch out a living from the dirt."

Oh. When she'd said she wanted a husband, she'd meant she wanted a *rich* husband. Anger rose again as he thought of Gwen scratching out an existence toiling for whomever held her indenture.

"What is wrong with hard work and living off the land?" He didn't try to keep the anger from his voice.

"What is wrong with a nice house and pretty clothes and a husband who does not smell like horse and—" She snapped her mouth shut and looked away from him.

Smelled like what? Mark Allen looked down at his clothing, littered with horse hairs and dusted with the very earth to which she objected so strenuously.

Gwen had never looked down on him for working with horses or getting dirty. If his condition was good enough for her, why did her sister look down her nose at him? And why was it making him angry?

He caught sight of Bran again, the boy sitting cross-legged on the deck near Jughead's feet, watching him and Faye as if he were at a fancy theater. Farther down the boat, Paul leaned against the railing, also keeping an eye on Mark Allen and Faye.

Well, he'd not signed on to be the boat's entertainment.

He rose and dusted off his shirt, loosening the horse hairs and sending them swirling in the breeze. Some landed on her dress, but he wouldn't apologize.

"I will leave you to enjoy the rest of the journey in peace." He knew his tone was surly even before her eyebrows rose, but he stomped away, feet making a satisfying thump on the wooden deck. He avoided both Bran and Paul as he grabbed a pair of brushes and started in on Skip's bright bay coat.

"So she is too proud to marry a man who works for a living. What is that to me?" The gelding flicked an ear in his direction. "Gwen had no problem with me being a stableman. She accepted me as I was."

But she hadn't written to him.

She'd written to Faye.

Chapter 18

F AYE HAD KEPT TO the cabin for the past two days to avoid both the drizzle and Mark Allen. But she was back on her perch on the trunk and swatting away gnats awakened by the warmer weather.

"Ah, Faye," Paul said as he joined her. "I'm glad to find thee here."

"Where else would I be?" Faye swept an arm out toward the boat. "The accommodations are hardly spacious."

Paul cocked an eyebrow at her. "'Twas a matter of speech."

"My apologies." She knew herself to be out of sorts but the whole situation was intolerable. Still, Paul didn't deserve her ill temper. "What can I do for thee?"

"How is thy ankle this morning?"

"I shall be ready to dance at the first ball in Mount Pleasant."

Paul crossed his arms, lowered his chin, and stared at her.

She'd be dancing at a ball soon if he weren't moving her to the edge of civilization. Beyond the edge. But that didn't excuse her surliness. She sat straighter and smoothed out her skirts.

"'Tis more stiff than painful this morning."

"Excellent. We should reach the dock at Roberts Landing sometime this forenoon. I should like to unload and move out for Mount Pleasant straight away, if thee are able."

"I'm sure I shall be as comfortable in the carriage as I am on this barge."

"The roads will not be as smooth as we are accustomed to, I'm afraid. Thee likely will be bumped around some."

"I'm not made of spun glass. I shall be fine." She gripped the edge of the trunk in an effort to keep a smile in place.

"Splendid. Glad to hear it." Paul rubbed his hands together before making his way to their wagon and carriage near the horses at the far end of the barge.

She envied him the excitement that danced in his eyes. The spring in his step. He truly wanted to live in the forsaken backwater country they were headed to. Called to, he'd said. He felt called by God. How did God call someone? And why did He care where they lived or what they did? Maybe He only cared about certain people.

For sure, He'd never cared for her. If He had, her mother, brothers, and father would still be alive. Faye wouldn't have been left an orphan.

Except for Gwen.

How was she going to explain Gwen to Madam and Paul?

And when?

She'd been looking for an opportunity to tell them for days, but there was no privacy on the boat. It didn't seem right to blurt out her omission in front of Olivia and Bridget. Quakers or not, they were still the servants, after all.

As was Gwen—except Gwen was bound by an indenture.

Would Faye be able to visit her sister? Or would Gwen's master demand that she not? After all, her sister was at the moment owned by another human being. She wasn't free. She hadn't been free for years.

Unlike Faye.

With a thump of certainty settling in her chest, Faye understood her reluctance to contact her sister. How could she look Gwen in the face and tell her that she'd been freed upon purchase? That she'd been made a member of the McClure family while Gwen had been made little more than a slave? How would Gwen react to that? Would she be hurt? Feel betrayed? Abandoned?

The same emotions Faye had bottled up when Gwen had been pulled away from her.

It wasn't that she was ashamed that her sister was a servant, it was that she was ashamed to have been spared that life while Gwen had not. Guilt—an emotion she'd never named before—settled over her like a mantle.

She brushed tears from her cheeks and stared out over the river, mind numb with her revelation.

Bran scrambled onto the wagon and stood beside Mark Allen. "That it?"

"Looks like it."

"Ain't much."

That might have been the understatement of the month. Mark Allen hadn't expected a town like Pittsburgh, but Roberts Landing wasn't even a village, much less a port. One dock thrust out into the river channel with two keelboats tied to it. The shoreline was dotted with smaller crafts beached or tied to trees. A cluster of houses huddled behind a line of storefronts. Several children ran barefoot along the riverbank, waving to those on the boat.

"This ain't goin' to make someone happy," Bran said.

Everyone on both boats knew Faye wasn't happy about moving west. Mark Allen had given the girl a wide berth since their last encounter that ended with their tentative friendship in shambles.

He'd seen her brushing away tears that morning. She hadn't moved from the trunk and hadn't spoken to anyone other than Paul. She'd looked like a lost waif, in some ways more pitiful than Bran when he'd discovered the boy. Bran had been self-assured and cocky. Faye seemed to have lost hope.

Gone was the feisty young woman who had tried to rationalize her refusal to answer her sister or even acknowledge her existence to the McClures. She'd been spitting mad at him then.

But he didn't like thinking about that conversation.

About Gwen's letters to Faye.

Gwen hadn't contacted him. Surely, she knew he'd come to her as soon as he was free.

He'd promised.

The sailors cut loose the keelboat and poled both vessels to the dock. After the flatboat bumped against the wooden pier and was tied snugly, the sailors ran a ramp out and started shoving trunks onto the dock.

Bran followed Mark Allen to the horses. Paul was already there, stroking Storm's neck. The black gelding tossed its head and snorted, restless from the long journey and made nervous by the sudden rush of activity.

Mark Allen untied Jughead and passed the rope to Bran. "Lead him down the ramp, and I'll follow with Storm. Unless you would rather lead him yourself, sir," he said to Paul.

"I had best tend to the women. I know the horses are in good hands with thee." Paul gave Storm one last pat before striding toward the cabin.

"I would take these horses over them women any day." Bran spat on the deck.

"Do not spit." The boy had picked up some less-than-savory habits from the sailors. "Go on with Jughead now."

Storm danced and tugged at the rope in Mark Allen's hands. The black horse crowded behind Jughead, but the steady gray didn't hurry or twitch an ear. His calm demeanor and Mark Allen's soothing voice got them off the vessel and down the dock without incident. They tied both horses and returned for the teams.

"That ramp is too narrow to take them down side by side. You take Ben and I shall lead Buster." The pair of heavy sorrels who pulled the wagon stepped off the boat without a fuss. Mark Allen and Bran returned for the carriage team, Dolly and Skip, the matched pair of black-legged bays. Dolly danced and tossed her head, but finally followed Skip down the dock to join the other horses. Bran made one more trip to fetch Ginger, the docile extra riding horse Mr. McClure had insisted on bringing west.

"How are we goin' to get the wagon and carriage off the boat?" Bran stood by Skip's flank, absently scratching the gelding above its tail.

"Good question." Mark Allen wished he had an answer. Roberts Landing's dock wasn't half the width of Pittsburgh's. There wasn't going to be room enough to roll them down the ramp and turn them onto the dock.

"Look." Bran pointed to sailors on shore pushing a flat barge into the river. Within minutes, they had it backed up to the flatboat, and the carriage was rolled onto it. The sailors poled it to the shore, offloaded the carriage, and returned for the wagon. "If that don't beat all."

Mark Allen nodded. "We best fetch the tack trunks from the dock so we can harness the teams."

The rattle of wheels and jingle of harness caught his attention as he walked toward the dock. A Negro man stopped an empty wagon beside them.

"I'm looking for Dr. Paul McClure."

"He is around here somewhere." Mark Allen looked toward the flatboat.

"He took the ladies over there." Bran jerked a thumb toward a tall building in need of whitewash with a wide boardwalk and a covered porch.

"I thank thee." The Negro touched his hat. "Are thee loading the doctor's belongings on that wagon?"

"We are," Mark Allen said.

"I shall park this one beside it. We can divide the load."

"Are you from the village of Mount Pleasant?"

"I am. Name's Zachary Brown."

"I'm Mark Allen Teed and this here is Bran."

"Bran Hogan." The boy stood straight and pulled his shoulders back.

"Pleased to meet thee." Zachary touched his hat again. "I best find the doctor. We shall need to hurry if we are to make it to Mount Pleasant before dark."

Zachary parked his wagon, hopped off, and made his way to the building Bran had pointed out.

"You ever heard tell of a darkie talkin' Quaker?" Bran leaned over and spat.

"Do not spit."

"Well? Did you?"

Mark Allen shook his head. "We are in free territory now. I expect there are plenty of things here we are not used to."

"Don't seem right, him talkin' all Quaker." Bran screwed up his face as if to spit, shot Mark Allen and look, then wiped the back of his hand across his mouth. "Well, it don't."

"I expect we shall get used to things being different. They are free here, after all. Free to live as they wish, same as us. He must have wished to be Quaker."

"I don't understand that, for sure."

Neither did Mark Allen. "We got wagons to load."

But if the Negro from Mount Pleasant was a Quaker, did that mean everyone there was Quaker?

Even Gwen?

Faye sipped the tepid excuse for tea the innkeeper had provided them and grimaced. Paul had secured the ladies a private room and left them to freshen up as best they could under the circumstances. Madam sat across the little round table from Faye while Olivia and Bridget took their turns at the washbasin.

"'Tis glad I am to be off that boat." Madam held her tea cup without drinking. She stared into its bitter depths. "Tonight, we shall see our new home."

And Gwen?

It was time to tell Madam about Gwen. The other women wouldn't overhear from across the room. Faye cleared her throat, but a knock on the door stopped her.

Madam glanced at the maid and cook. Bridget folded the towel she held and placed it on the washstand. Both women had finished refreshing themselves. Madam called out, "Enter."

Paul poked his head around the door. A huge grin slashed across his face. "We have a visitor."

"Do we?" Madam stood.

Paul opened the door wider, and a Negro followed him into the room. "This is Zachary Brown—from Mount Pleasant. He has come to escort us home."

"I'm so very pleased to meet thee," Madam said.

Zachary inclined his head. "As I am to meet thee."

Paul thumped him on the shoulder. "He has already met Mark Allen and Bran. This is Olivia, Mother's maid, and Bridget, the best cook Pittsburgh had to offer." Both women nodded. "And this," he extended a hand toward Faye, "is my ward, Faye Morgan."

Faye met the man's gaze. The intensity of those dark eyes bored into her, tripping her heart against her ribs. He looked startled. He must know Gwen, and her resemblance to her sister would give her away.

"Zachary is also a Friend." Paul thumped him on the shoulder again, oblivious to Zachary's reaction to Faye.

"Are all those in Mount Pleasant Quakers?" Madam asked.

"Almost. The town is growing faster than we ever imagined, though. I expect we shall have all sorts moving in soon."

Faye listened to their chatter without comprehending it. He knew who she was. She'd missed her opportunity to confess her omission to Madam. At any moment, he would blurt out a question regarding Gwen.

"Best we hasten to load the wagons and ready the carriage," the dark man said.

"Right." Paul nodded to the women. "Can thee be ready to travel in half an hour?"

"Of course," Madam said, "but thee will need dinner before we leave, or tea at least."

"Ask the innkeeper to wrap some cheese and bread for us. We shall eat on the move." Paul all but bounced on his toes in his eagerness to get going. "We must arrive tonight or else we shall miss Meeting tomorrow."

Before Zachary followed Paul out the door, he sent a puzzled glance back at Faye. Had he wondered that she didn't inquire after her sister? Of course he had. What sort of sister wouldn't? Guilt—it hurt more since she could name the emotion—pinched her.

"Bridget, please obtain the bread and cheese from the innkeeper. Olivia, we must visit the mercantile we saw two doors down. I would like to take a bolt of mattress ticking with us. After those horrid beds on the boat, I would feel better knowing we are equipped to produce our own when we arrive. Faye, dear, come with us." Madam took charge like a little general on the battlefield.

There would be no more chances for a private talk.

How could she have messed things up so badly?

What Faye wouldn't give to hobble to the boat and sail back to Pittsburgh.

Chapter 19

H ALF AN HOUR FLEW by. The women met the men at the wagons.

When Faye handed Zachary the bolt of mattress ticking, he leaned closer to her than necessary to take it.

"Does thee have a sister named Gwen?"

Her hand shook as she tucked a stray lock of hair back under her bonnet. She cast a glance at Madam and Paul near the carriage. "I do."

"I thought so." Zachary's grin spread. "Thee are almost her image. I cannot believe she said nothing about thee joining us."

"She does not know."

His grin sagged. "No?"

"Nay. And the McClures know nothing about Gwen either."

Zachary pushed his hat back and scratched the front of his head. "I do not understand."

"'Tis a long story. Please, say nothing about Gwen for now."

"Gwen searched for thee for so long. When she heard thee had sailed abroad, she was devastated. Did thee receive her letters?"

"I did."

Grin gone and brows drawn, Zachary settled his hat on his head.

Faye picked at the edge of her shawl, casting another glance at Paul, who was watching them. "'Tis a long story." She hurried away as fast as her limping gait would allow.

"What were thee discussing so earnestly with Zachary?" Paul looked from her to the man at the wagon and back again.

"Nothing important." Faye pushed as much cheer into her voice as she could muster. "Shall we begin this last leg of our journey?"

Faye took her seat in the carriage across from Olivia and Madam. The vehicle rocked as Mark Allen climbed onto the high seat to drive the team. It had been decided that Bridget would ride beside young Bran on the wagon, because, having been raised on a farm, she was skilled enough at driving to handle the team should the boy encounter a problem. Zachary drove his wagon at the head of the line. Outside the carriage window, Paul controlled a jigging and side-stepping Storm. No doubt the horse was picking up on its rider's eagerness to get moving.

"Let us move out!" Paul shouted.

The carriage lurched beneath her. Faye pressed her back into the brown fabric of the carriage. A sigh slipped between her lips, and she curled her fingers into the folds of her skirt. How was she going to explain Gwen now? She glanced at Olivia. Perhaps if Faye had been alone with Madam, she could have mustered the courage. Perhaps not. How did one confess to hiding a secret for five years from the very people who had pulled her from a life of drudgery and possible abuse?

It wasn't that she'd lied to them. She'd never done that. Madam had asked her if there were any family they could contact for her. Of course she'd told them no. She'd had no idea where Gwen was or how to find her. And she had believed in her heart that her sister was lost to her, as surely as her parents and little brothers. To hope otherwise had been unthinkable. Never once had she allowed herself to dream that Gwen would come back into her life.

As the land rolled by the window, emotions tumbled inside her, swinging from despair at being caught in the omission to a new, burgeoning anticipation of seeing her sister again.

Her sister the servant. Guilt squeezed Faye until it was difficult to draw a full breath.

"Is thy ankle painful?" Madam leaned forward. "I can shift over that thee might rest it on the cushion between Olivia and me."

"Thank you—thee." It felt better to put her foot up. She gave Madam a wan smile.

At least in a backwater village, if Madam and Paul were furious with her for not telling them about Gwen, the gossip sure to follow wouldn't ruin her chances of finding a good husband.

One couldn't ruin a chance that didn't exist.

Mark Allen took some pride in watching Bran handle the wagon. Ben and Buster were a well-broke team, and the boy had learned well during their practice sessions and was handling the lines like a seasoned teamster.

Teamster was a good occupation, something Mark Allen had thought he might like to do before he'd hired on with the McClures. But if he did, he'd always smell of horses.

Why had Faye's comment bothered him so? She was spoiled. Her opinion was the least of his concerns.

The chief concern was Gwen.

Would he find her that very evening? Or would he need to wait for daybreak? Because he couldn't wait any longer than that. He had to know that she was well, and cared for, and... and waiting for him.

Not that she'd promised to.

But in his heart, Mark Allen had always assumed she would. He'd worked out his indenture, he'd found Gwen's sister and brought her, just as he'd said he would. She'd be happy to see Faye, of that he had no doubt. But...

What if she wasn't *his* Gwen anymore?

Pain laced through him, but he clicked to Dolly and Skip, who were lagging behind the wagon, taking advantage of his distraction. "Hup, you two. Pick up your feet."

The horses leaned into their harnesses and caught up to Jughead and Ginger, who were tied to the back of the wagon.

"Everything all right up there?" he yelled to Bran.

The youngster turned back with his wide grin. "I told you I would be good at this."

Mark Allen snorted. He couldn't help admiring the boy's high spirits and confidence, things Mark Allen was in increasingly short supply of.

As they got farther from Roberts Landing, the road turned into little more than a track, sometimes weaving between trees or wild brush and sometimes crossing open land. The wider wagon wheels were handling the rough ground better than the lighter, narrower carriage wheels, which were made for fast travel on good roads. Mark Allen had his hands full guiding Dolly and Skip through the labyrinth of ruts.

It helped keep his mind on the task at hand.

Even so, his heart dropped along with the carriage when they hit a trench in the earth he hadn't seen in time. Both right-side wheels dropped into it, but it was the crack and splintering of wood that had Mark Allen hollering, "Whoa!"

There were cries from the ladies inside.

Paul raced toward him on Storm. No doubt he'd heard the wood give way. Ahead, the two wagons stopped, and Zachary jogged back his way.

"What happened?" Paul called even before he got his horse stopped.

"We hit that rut." Disgust filled Mark Allen's voice, and he shook his head. "'Twas my fault, I did not see it in time."

Paul vaulted off Storm while Mark Allen climbed down from the carriage.

Olivia opened the carriage door and poked her head out.

"Was anyone hurt inside?" Paul asked.

"Just a little shaken," the maid said.

Mark Allen glared at the wheel—the shattered rear wheel.

Zachary reached him and shook his head. "'Twill require a wheel-wright."

Four spokes were broken, the rim cracked. If fixable at all, it would take someone with more knowledge than Mark Allen had.

Paul joined them, positioning himself to block the women's view. "What should we do?" He looked at Zachary.

The dark man scanned the sky, then squinted to the northwest. "'Twill be dark before long. Thomas, the wheelwright in Mount Pleasant, could not repair it before tomorrow, and that being Sunday, not until the day after."

"Then we must move the women to the wagons and hurry on," Paul said.

"We can saddle Jughead and Ginger," Mark Allen said. "That would make room in the wagon and two of the ladies could ride."

Paul rubbed his jaw, glancing at the wagon and then back. "I shall work out the seating arrangements. Mark Allen, saddle the horses. Zachary, would thee tell young Bran to make room for the women in the back of the wagon? If there is room, he may need to shift a trunk or two to yours, if that suits thee."

"We will make room." Zachary strode off.

Mark Allen cleared his throat. "I am sorry about this. 'Tis truly my fault it happened."

Paul gripped his shoulder. "Worry not. Thee did not plant the ruts in the road. And thee are not schooled in wilderness driving. 'Twas an unfortunate accident. No one was injured. 'Tis but a wheel. Feel no remorse over this."

But Mark Allen did. And perhaps more keenly because he knew his thoughts and emotions had been taken up by something other than driving.

Gwen.

A broken wheel. They were stuck in the wilderness without a building in sight. Stranded, while the men shuffled trunks between the wagons.

Paul approached them. "We are set until I can return with the wheelwright."

"Can it be repaired?" Madam asked.

"Indeed. Zachary informs me they have a skilled wheelwright in Mount Pleasant."

"Will we wait for him to arrive?" Madam asked.

"We shall have to travel on. Thank the Lord that Zachary brought his wagon. If not, we would be stuck here, for we are only halfway." Paul pointed to the wagons. "The men are making room for thee to ride in Zachary's wagon. I know 'tis not as comfortable as the carriage, but we must make haste. This road is not fit to travel after dark."

'Twasn't fit to travel at all. Faye wasn't sure her teeth would survive the rattling they'd taken in the carriage. No wonder the wheel couldn't take it either.

"Would thee prefer to ride on the wagon seat or in the back, Mother?"

"I believe I would like to ride next to Zachary. 'Twould give me the opportunity to ask questions about our new home."

At least Faye would be spared sitting next to him. His disapproval all but solidified the air between them whenever he glanced her way.

"Then Bridget and Olivia can take the back," Paul said. "And Faye, if thee would ride next to Mark Allen on our wagon then—"

"Certainly not."

Paul blinked at her. "What?"

"I would prefer to ride in the back of the wagon." Nowhere near that stableman.

Paul frowned. "There is no more room in the back. Perhaps thee would rather ride on Mark Allen's horse. I understand the beast to be a perfectly safe mount."

Faye took a step back. Beast indeed. She wasn't getting on the back of any horse. Paul knew her feelings on horses in general and horses underneath her in particular. The challenging glint in his eye stiffened her backbone.

"I shall ride next to the stableman."

"His name is Mark Allen."

She limped past Paul and pretended she didn't see the humor in his smile as he escorted his mother and the other women to Zachary's wagon. Faye stepped up beside the McClures' wagon and waited for Mark Allen to assist her onto its high seat.

He should have enough manners to do that much, at least.

Mark Allen hefted Jughead's saddle onto the gray gelding's back. He tightened the cinch as Bran arrived by his side.

"Ain't you the lucky one."

Mark Allen raised a brow and grabbed the bridle out of the wagon.

Bran poked his thumb toward where Faye waited next to the front wheel, arms crossed and tapping her foot. Heaven's mercy. Was he going to have to ride the rest of the day next to that disapproving scowl?

"Ain't you lucky to ride next to Miss High and Mighty herself?" Bran tugged the bridle from Mark Allen's grasp and slipped it onto Jughead.

"You did a fine job handling the wagon. Why don't you—"

"The boss don't want me drivin' her. You know it." Bran swung aboard Jughead. An unholy grin exposed the gap between the boy's teeth before he wheeled the horse around and trotted away.

Mark Allen dusted off his hands on his pants. Might as well get on with it. He walked to the front of the wagon.

"Do you want me to help you up?"

"That is why I am waiting here."

He stifled a cringe. It was going to be a long afternoon. He grasped her forearm and steadied her as she climbed onto the seat. He waited while she arranged her ridiculously full skirts before he climbed up beside her, pulled on his gloves, and gathered the reins.

She scooted as far to the opposite side of the bench seat as she could get without falling off.

He probably could use a bath, but it wasn't like she was all roses and lilacs herself.

At Zachary's backward glance, Mark Allen touched the front of his hat, and the wagon in front rolled out. He clicked, and the well-trained team of sorrels leaned into their harnesses.

Faye uttered a small gasp as the wagon lurched into motion.

"If your ankle is paining you, you can rest it on the kickboard."

"As if I would expose my ankle for more of your scrutiny."

"Suit yourself. I was just thinking you would be more comfortable."

"My comfort is none of your affair."

Mark Allen planted his feet on the kickboard and braced his elbows on his knees. No reason he couldn't be comfortable. He shot a glance at his unwilling companion.

Even after a full week on the boats, she was a fetching sight. Dark curls, so like Gwen's, peeked from under her bonnet. Her cheeks, sun-kissed from the time she'd spent on deck, sported a rosy hue. Road dust dulled her already drab Quaker garb. Quaker. She used the Quaker *thee* around the McClures. Mark Allen rubbed the back of his neck.

"Are you Quaker?" he asked

She gave a little start at the sound of his voice. "Of course I am."

"Then why do you not say *thee* all the time like the rest of them?"

Faye shifted on the seat, her face forward. "'Tis rather new to me.

We were not Quakers before we went to Scotland. While over there, Paul felt the need to convert."

"And you did not?"

That time, she jerked so hard Mark Allen worried she might fall off the wagon.

"What makes you—thee—say that?"

He shrugged. "Mrs. McClure and the doctor have no trouble speaking Quaker."

She tightened her lips into a flat line. Silence rolled off her like a wave. Not like the little lapping waves on the river, but like a curling wave on the ocean that threatened to swallow anything in its path. For an hour they bounced and bumped along in that stifling silence.

"What is she like?"

This time it was Mark Allen's turn to startle at her softly spoken question.

"Gwen?"

Faye sighed dropping her chin against her chest.

"She is beautiful. You favor her that way."

Faye's eyebrows shot to her hairline. She looked at him for the first time since the wagon had started rolling.

Mark Allen wanted to swallow his tongue. What on earth had made him say a thing like that? Heat sizzled from under his collar. "Sh-she is caring and gentle. She works hard. Her smile is like a slice of sunshine on a cloudy day." He rubbed his hand over his burning face.

"You love her?"

"I told you, everyone loves Gwen." He tugged his hat lower over his eyes.

"I suppose you—thee—find me much lacking in comparison."

How was he supposed to answer that? He didn't know much about women, but he was pretty sure when one asked that type of question, a smart man kept his mouth shut.

"I wish I had answered her letters." Her voice had gone soft again, reminding him of Gwen.

"She will be surprised to see you." And happy. She would run into Faye's arms.

But would she do the same for him? Was the feeling that lingered in the back of his throat jealousy? Was he jealous of Faye and her reunion with Gwen while almost dreading his own?

"I love her, you—thee should know that."

"Of course you do, she is your sister."

"And as I told thee, she was more than that." Faye twisted to face him. "She was my best friend and my protector. Even from our father, at times. After he started drinking."

Anger stirred in his gut. Mark Allen knew all too much about a father who drank. He closed his eyes against the memory of his father lurching into the shack where they lived, bellowing and raging, crashing into the wall. Mark Allen would escape to the barn and hide in the hayloft until his father had slept off his drunkenness.

"I was relieved when we boarded the ship. Gwen said he wouldn't be able to buy whiskey there." She dropped her gaze to her hands, gripped in her lap. "But somehow he did."

Mark Allen slipped the reins into one hand and with the other he squeezed her clasped hands.

She snapped up her head to stare at him and he let go. With those brown eyes, she reminded him of a wounded dog he'd found once, a combination of determination and hopelessness behind the sheen of unshed tears.

He knew that feeling.

"With my father, 'twas the rum." He gritted his teeth. The feather-light touch of her fingers against his sleeve shocked him. When she removed her hand, he gathered the reins back and clicked to the team.

Faye lifted her injured foot onto the kickboard and settled her skirts around it as best she could.

Good.

She tucked her chin and shielded her face with the brim of her bonnet, but not before he saw the rosy hue on her cheeks deepen. He caught sight of Bran trotting up beside the wagon on Jughead. When the boy rolled his eyes, Mark Allen ignored him and slapped the reins against the broad rumps in front of him.

Silence settled between himself and Faye. A comfortable silence. He sensed a depth to Faye he hadn't glimpsed before. The depth born of an old hurt. A festering hurt in the soul.

Something he understood all too well.

It didn't excuse her rudeness toward him or her ignoring Gwen's letters, but it sparked a flame of compassion.

Chapter 20

F AYE SNUGGED HER SHAWL around her shoulders and shivered against the cool breeze. She wrinkled her nose at the dusty smell of the fabric. Once they unpacked, everything would need washing. Hopefully, they could hire a washerwoman right away.

She cast a glance at the man beside her. Taller than Paul, he was lean to the point of skinny. His coat stretched across his shoulders but hung like an old sack to his hips. He could use some feeding up. His brown hair needed cutting, the long ends straggling from the leather tie at his nape. He smelled of horse and dust and sweat.

She wrinkled her nose again.

He loved Gwen. He said everyone did, but his blush and stammer hadn't fooled her. Did Gwen love him too? She hadn't mentioned anyone in her letters, but they had been short, lacking any true details. And she did say she had a lot to tell Faye. Maybe Mark Allen was part of that.

Sunlight slanted across the land from the west. Faye tilted her bonnet to shade her eyes. The landscape rolled gently. The road, if one could give the rutted path such a grand name, wove between trees and along the edge of a large pond. They came around a curve and the horses pulling Zachary Brown's wagon picked up their pace.

Mark Allen spoke to his team, and the massive beasts tossed their heads and caught up with the lead wagon.

Bran cantered back on the gray horse until he was beside Mark Allen.

"We be almost there." The boy leaned over and, of all things, spat on the ground. "Zachary says we can see the settlement around the next bend."

Mark Allen shot her a glance before glowering at the boy. "Do not spit."

Faye didn't know whether to be annoyed at the boy's complete lack of manners, amused at Mark Allen's response, or frightened at the prospect of finally seeing where she would doubtless spend the rest of her life as an old maid.

"Sure hope whoever is expectin' us has somethin' cookin' on the stove. My belly is rubbin' against my backbone." The boy leaned sideways again, but at Mark Allen's pointed glare, he hitched himself straight in the saddle and shrugged.

"Zachary said he had been waiting in Roberts Landing for several days," Mark Allen said. "I doubt anyone is expecting us to arrive tonight."

Faye sagged against the back of the wagon seat, his words striking like a reprieve. She'd speak with Madam and Paul that evening. She'd tell them about Gwen and the letters. Her stomach tightened, but it had nothing to do with hunger.

The wagons rolled around another bend, and Zachary pointed to the settlement before them on a low hill.

Faye couldn't hear what Paul said to the Negro over the distance, the creaking of the wagon, and the jingle of harnesses. Paul clapped his heels to Storm's sides and galloped ahead. She could only imagine the joy on her guardian's face. As much as she dreaded their arrival, Paul relished it twofold.

She sighed rather noisily and not at all ladylike.

"You wished to remain in Pittsburgh." A wry smile tweaked Mark Allen's lips. "But surely now that we are here, you shall make the best of it."

Faye lifted her chin. "I'm very much afraid there will be no 'best of it' for me in this place."

"Why do you say that?"

"I'm sure you—thee—would not understand."

"They say this territory is like none other. They say a man can make what he wants of himself here. They say—"

"They can say whatever they want, but it changes nothing. We are in the wilderness. There is no opportunity for a woman here, except to work herself into an early grave. I know what that is like. I watched my mother do it, dying abed with her fifth child because her strength was gone, used up trying to scratch a living out of the dirt on the outskirts of civilization in Wales." Faye clenched her fists in the folds of her skirt.

"'Twill be hard work, but to be my own person, free to own land, have a family, and build a future. I have no words to explain what that means to me."

"For a man, maybe. Men marry and use a wife up, then bury her and take another." Faye turned away from the bright hope on Mark Allen's. "Or take to the bottle."

"There will be no bottle for me." Determination strengthened his tone.

She hoped not and then wondered why she cared. Who was this stableman to her? Paul's hired man. Someone who would doubtless leave them to follow his dreams. But someone who had sometimes shown her kindness.

Someone who loved her sister.

The teams leaned into their harnesses on the uphill climb. The houses perched along the side of the road ranged from squat log structures to board-sided homes of varying sizes and shapes. Paul had ridden on ahead, and his horse stood tied to a hitching post in front of a two-story house with two stone chimneys tapering toward the sky, one at each end. Beyond the house were a barn and field, and beyond them the land fell away into rolling hills blanketed with trees.

The house itself, while not grand, was a far cry from the shack Faye had envisioned. Whitewash coated its board siding and curtains peeked from real glass windows, their shutters open and inviting. It bore no resemblance to the wattle and daub house she'd lived in as a child. A small sigh of relief escaped her.

"'Tis a fine-looking house." Mark Allen set the brake and wrapped the lines around the handle before hopping down. He came around to her side of the wagon and assisted her to the ground.

Paul grinned at them from the open doorway, sheltered by a roofed porch that ran the width of the building.

Faye hung back as Madam joined him, Olivia and Bridget on her heels.

"Come, Faye." Paul held out a hand in her direction. The pride and purpose encompassed in his smile contrasted sharply with the cloud of fatalism washing over her.

Her shoes rang as hollow as her hopes on the porch boards as she crossed over the threshold.

"Did you see everyone gawpin' at us from them other houses?" Bran asked.

Mark Allen had noticed it but figured folks were giving them some space before they came to greet the new doctor. And it was the dinner hour, attested to by the delicious aromas coming from the same windows and doors as the lookers-on.

His middle rumbled.

"Sound like we made it here just in time." Paul joined them. "Have thee looked in the stable?"

"Not yet."

Paul motioned him and Bran to follow, then threw the door open wide.

It smelled of fresh wood and dust. There hadn't been a horse near the building yet, or Mark Allen would have smelled that too. Paul gestured to the door at the back, shooing them into the living quarters beyond. On the table, cheesecloth-wrapped bundles sat on a table so new the wood was almost yellow.

"Food!" Bran pushed past him and unwrapped half a wheel of cheese, a crusty loaf of bread, and a bowl of dried apple rings. "'Tis a feast!"

"Thee can fill thy bellies after the wagons are unloaded." Paul raised an eyebrow at Bran. "But tear off a crust of bread now to plug the hole in thy middle."

Bran put those words into action, cramming a handful of bread into his mouth.

Mark Allen would have to work on the boy's manners.

Paul spread his arms to indicate the space. "Are thee satisfied with this, Mark Allen?"

"'Tis more than adequate." A set of bunks were built against one wall, a small fireplace on the other. "Bran and I will be comfortable here."

"Good." Paul slapped him on the back. "Good. Now let us finish the unloading and thee can settle the horses."

Mark Allen took one more look around the space that was to be his home for the time being. He hoped not for long. He hoped that once he reunited with Gwen...

Dare he hope for anything at all?

The weak evening light filtering through the windows had faded before all the trunks and boxes were shuffled inside.

Faye walked through the house with Madam while Bridget and Olivia dug through their belongings to find lamps and oil and the men tromped in with yet another load of crated goods for the kitchen.

Madam stopped in the hallway upstairs. "'Tis a good thing we left most of our furniture behind. 'Twould not have fit in here." Madam clasped her hands in front of her and faced Faye. "Which room do thee favor? One in front? Or one with the view to the back?"

Faye lifted a shoulder to shrug but changed her mind. If she was bound to live there for the rest of her life, at least she could pick her prison. There were four bedrooms off the hallway. She stepped into the closest back bedroom and peered out the window into the darkness. A lantern spilled a path of light from the open stable door. Beyond that, she couldn't see much.

Mark Allen stepped into the stable doorway, a box on one shoulder. He paused and turned toward the house. The lantern behind him highlighted the determined angle of his jaw.

Faye stepped away from the window. "This one will do." She touched the smooth plastered wall. At least it wasn't rough boards. A roped bed frame rested in one corner, its mattress most likely stuffed with straw.

Closing her eyes, the vision of her canopied, four-poster bed with its mattress of down feathers pushed against the backs of her eyelids. To sink into its cloud-like softness—

"Glory be!" Bridget's shout swept up the stairs.

Madam hurried downstairs, leaving Faye with nothing to do but follow.

"Where are thee, Bridget?" Madam called as she reached the bottom step.

Bridget poked her head around the corner of the kitchen doorway. "We have a pantry off the kitchen, and 'tis full to bursting. Why, every woman in the settlement must have pitched in."

"What a blessing. Thee can find something to feed everyone tonight then?"

"Aye, and right away. Some kind soul left a ham, bread, and a wheel of cheese on the table."

Zachary eased a crate onto a growing stack along the wall. "The entire settlement has been anxious for thee to arrive and determined that thee feel welcomed here in thy new home."

The lines around Madam's mouth and the stoop of her shoulders bore evidence of her fatigue from their long journey. But her eyes shone in the flickering lamp light. "Indeed. We are home."

The loss of her dreams crashed around Faye at Madam's words. There would be no dances in this place. No charming young men looking for a refined wife to parade on their arms. She would have but two choices—to be an old maid or to work herself to death as her mother had, too worn out to birth her last babe.

Either way, the future stretching before her was bleak.

Faye followed Madam from the kitchen to a dining room of empty walls with a plainly built table in the middle and six plain chairs surrounding it.

"The townsfolk will be by tomorrow, I expect," Zachary said. "'Tis late to call, and they will know thee must be tired from thy journey."

"Of course." Madam motioned to the table. "But thee will join us for supper, surely."

"I thank thee, but I have things that need attending to at my place. I have been away for a few days."

"Then join us another time." Madam smiled and walked with him to the door.

Within minutes, Bridget readied sliced ham, bread, and cheese. The table was covered with a plain white cloth and set with plain pewter dishes and cups. The letter to Paul had said the house would be furnished. Faye should have realized that meant furnished in the Quaker way—without a speck of decoration or color or whimsy.

"Paul, come and eat with us," Madam called into the other front room, which would serve as their parlor.

"In a moment."

Faye fiddled with her fork. A very plain fork, of course.

When Paul joined them, they bowed their heads for the silent prayer. For once, it ended far too soon.

It was time. Faye needed to tell them about Gwen.

Madam eyed her across the table. "Does the house displease thee?"

Faye realized she'd been pushing her food around her plate. "I have something to tell thee." At least she'd gotten the thee out without a stammer.

Madam set down her fork and leaned forward. "Then please do."

Faye glanced at Paul, swallowed at the frown that marred his brow, then focused on Madam. Simple was usually best, they said. "I have a sister."

"What?" Paul's voice bounced off the empty walls.

Madam gave him a quick shake of her head. "Thee have a sister?"

"I do." She swallowed again. "And she lives here, in Mount Pleasant."

Paul tossed his white napkin to the table and leaned back in his chair. "Why is this the first we have heard about her?"

"Paul." Madam shot him a *let me handle this* look. "Do tell us, dear. The whole story, as thee are able."

"You—thee know most of it. My mother and brothers died in Wales, and my father on the ship crossing the ocean." Faye lifted her cup with an unsteady hand and took a sip. "My sister Gwen was also on the ship. We were both sold into indenture because the captain claimed our father had not paid for our passage—which was a lie." She raised her chin and her voice. "He did. I saw him hand over the money."

"I'm sure he did, my dear." Madam's eyes were misty. "I'm very sure he did."

Her reassurance brought a lump to Faye's throat. Having Madam believe the best of Father, a man she'd never met, touched her deeply.

"As am I." All sternness had disappeared from Paul's voice.

Faye cleared her throat. "We were kept in a different ship until the day of the auction." She shuddered. "Then we were shoved into a chute with many others, mostly Negroes but not all."

"Were thee separated from thy sister there?" Madam asked.

"Not at first. But when we reached the end of the chute, Gwen was pulled away from me and sold first." The lump in Faye's throat tightened at the memory of her sister, crying her name as she was dragged away. "I never thought I would see her again."

"But why did thee not tell us?" Paul's voice remained gentle, his eyes creased with concern. "Did thee fear our reaction?"

"Nay." Never had she worried over that. "But 'twas easier to not speak of her, to not think of her, than to face the reality of her loss."

"Because, unlike the others, she was still alive?" Madam asked.

Faye nodded. Even though she knew it to be irrational, deep down, she'd blamed Gwen for leaving her that day. And that shamed her more than not telling Madam and Paul about her.

Paul covered her hand with his. "Then how came thee to know she is here?"

"She sent me two letters while we were overseas. They were given to me upon our return."

Paul's hand stiffened over hers. "And still thee did not tell us?" Was that a note of hurt in his voice?

"I should have." Faye raised her eyes to meet his. "I was afraid."

Madam pressed her hand to her chest. "Of us?"

"Not of you. You—thee have been nothing but kindness to me."

"Then what caused thy fear?" Paul asked.

What indeed? She hadn't wanted to leave Pittsburgh, but that was only a part of it. She wanted to marry a man who would take care of her, but that was also only part of it. Mostly, she hadn't wanted to ever be hungry and afraid and vulnerable again. Ever. She'd wanted security. A security Gwen couldn't provide.

She still wanted it.

But how to voice that without sounding selfish and shallow?

A knock at the door interrupted, followed by a voice. "Help! We need the doctor!"

Chapter 21

A YOUNG MAN HAD tumbled off the back of a horse before it stopped. He rushed to the porch, pounded on the door, and hollered for the doctor.

Mark Allen set the crate of extra stable gear he'd just lifted from the wagon back onto the tailgate and hurried to the house.

The door opened, and Paul appeared. "What has happened?"

"'Tis Gwen." The youngster pointed into the darkness behind him. "Micah bid me to fetch thee, Doctor. All know thee have arrived."

Gwen?

Mark Allen's heart stopped for a moment, then galloped like a charger. The name was uncommon enough for him to hope it was her—his Gwen. But if this boy had come for the doctor, then she must be hurt or ill. Fear spiked through him as he ran the last steps to the edge of the porch.

"Mark Allen," the doctor called. "Saddle Storm, make haste."

"Aye, sir." Mark Allen swung around until the next words stopped him in his tracks.

"'Tis her time, Doctor. 'Tis the babe."

"Ah, good." Paul's voice shifted from worry to calm. "Wait for me here, I shall require an escort." Paul shut the door.

'Tis the babe.

It couldn't be his Gwen then. Nay. It couldn't be.

Mark Allen stumbled into the stable, past the harness horses to Storm's stall. He saddled the gelding as if in a fog, then led it to the house.

Paul stepped onto the porch, leather bag in one hand, speaking to someone behind him. "I will send word if I can."

Faye filled the doorway behind the doctor. "How many Gwens can there be here? Please, allow me to attend with thee."

He turned and faced her. "Even if it is thy sister, thee are not prepared to attend a birthing."

Birthing.

Faye clutched the front of her shawl, her face a study of conflicting emotions.

Mark Allen's face may have looked the same. He did his best to school his expression as he approached.

At least Faye felt something for the sister who had worried over her day and night for as long as Mark Allen had known her...

Oh. She must have finally told the McClures about Gwen.

"Send word if thee can." Faye stepped back into the house but kept the door open.

The doctor took the reins from Mark Allen and swung into the saddle. "Do not expect it. But I will tell thee all when I return, this I promise."

Mark Allen stumbled out of the way as the black horse whirled and sprinted after the young man on his mount. Sprinted into the darkness of the strange town. And sprinted to the aid of someone named Gwen.

A Gwen who was having a baby.

His eyes met Faye's, hers as bleak as he felt. She believed the Gwen involved to be her sister, he could see the truth and compassion on her face. She shut the door, keeping eye contact until the wood broke it.

As severed as his heart.

Pacing the floor of her new room did little to calm Faye. The third board from the door creaked when she stepped on it. She'd learned that early in the evening. Someone's dog down the street barked off and on. Not a yappy bark, but the deep-throated bay of a hound. Who knew what sort of varmints prowled along the edge of the wilderness after dark? A pair of cats had yowled at each other from somewhere behind the house but must have tired and moved on or gone to sleep hours past.

If only Paul would return.

Faye knew little about childbirth aside from the basics, and she had only a foggy understanding of those. She'd been too young when they'd left Wales to have learned much, and the society in which she'd been brought up frowned on young ladies knowing about such matters. CeCe, always one to test the boundaries of society, had imparted her wisdom on the topic freely on several occasions.

Of course, CeCe was awaiting the birth of her own child, so perhaps she had known more than Faye had given her credit for, at least about the conceiving part of the process.

And what about Mark Allen? The poor man's stricken look had more than confirmed her opinion. He loved Gwen. But Gwen must be married to another. After all, she was having a baby and one didn't...

Although CeCe had.

But Gwen was nothing like CeCe.

Faye flopped onto the bed and let herself fall across its surprisingly comfortable mattress. Predawn light traced the edge of the window as she closed her eyes.

The thump of the front door closing brought her upright with a gasp. Brilliant sunlight flooded the room. Faye rubbed her grainy eyes and glanced around the unfamiliar space.

The Quaker village. Ohio. Their new house.

Gwen!

She shot off the bed and rushed to the stairs, half-hobbling and half-running their length.

"Be easy, Faye." Paul appeared at the bottom and steadied her as she reached the last step.

"Is it my sister, Gwen Morgan?"

"Come and sit." Paul helped her into a straight-backed chair at the table, then took the one beside it. "'Tis indeed thy sister, but her name is Gwen Pike now." He raised a brow at her. "I did not inform her of thy presence here. I thought it best to come directly from thee."

Faye pressed the heel of one hand to her forehead. Of course. She must face Gwen—and soon—before she learned of her presence from anyone else. "She is married?"

"Indeed. Thee has a baby girl and a toddler named Owen to call thee aunt."

"Owen." Faye sat back until her shoulders whacked the chair's high back. "Our father's name."

"'Tis common among Friends to name the first son after the mother's father."

Friends. The second letter had included *thee* and *thy*, but still, the truth came solidly home at the news of a husband and a family. Her sister was a member of the community at Mount Pleasant.

And now—so was Faye.

Married.

Mark Allen leaned against the wall of the house next to the window where he'd been listening.

His Gwen. The woman he'd followed into the wilderness. The woman he'd tracked down an ungrateful and infuriating sister for.

The woman he thought would be waiting for him.

Emotions bombarded him. He couldn't hold on to one before another shoved it aside. Hurt. Anger. Sorrow. Despair. They spiraled like a funnel cloud, ripping apart Mark Allen's hopes and dreams.

Storm snorted, pausing the onslaught. The horse needed caring for. Needed to be unsaddled, watered, curried, and turned into a stall with an armful of hay. Chores Mark Allen could do by rote. Something to get him moving again.

He led the beast to the stable, one leaden step at a time, the familiar activities loosening his thoughts and making sense of what he'd learned. Confirmation of his deepest fear since the rider had hammered on the door.

What should he do?

Mark Allen was employed by the doctor. He wasn't an indentured servant anymore. He could leave the employment as he wished. He could saddle Jughead and be on the road in ten minutes. The doctor was a good man and would probably keep Bran on.

He ignored the pang at the thought of leaving the boy behind.

But where would Mark Allen go? What future would he ride toward? Or would he only be riding away from his past? Away from the might-have-been? Away from his shattered hopes and dreams? After all, how could he stay and see her with another man and their children? To pass her on the street or meet in the mercantile, the chandler, or the butcher shop? Could he handle that when...

When Gwen was lost to him?

"Are thee sure about going alone?" Madam lingered in the doorway to Faye's room.

"I am." Faye smoothed the only presentable dress she had over her hips and adjusted the white shawl across her shoulders. "'Tis best if I reconnect with her first, before introducing my... my new family."

"Of course, that does seem more appropriate." Uncertainty traced the wrinkles in the dear woman's face. "Thee does not believe she will resent Paul and me, does thee?"

"Nay." Faye swept across the room and hugged the older woman, holding tightly for a few heartbeats. "Gwen is not that way. She will love thee as I do. But she has just given birth, and Paul chastened me not to overtax her this afternoon."

"Of course, Paul would know best." Understanding and relief colored Madam's tone.

"Thank thee for allowing me the wagon." While she'd rather have ridden in the carriage, it had yet to be repaired and brought to the house. And Paul had cautioned her to present herself in a less grand manner. While he hadn't said as much, he'd implied that Gwen and her husband lived a humble existence.

Old memories of their cottage in Wales threatened to overwhelm Faye. Sadness, fear, and hunger were her strongest impressions. And Gwen. Gwen, who had never left her side until wrenched away by forces beyond her control.

For which Faye had turned her back on her. Grief and guilt poured over her—again.

"Mark Allen is bringing the wagon around now," Madam said.

The creak of the vehicle drifted through Faye's open window with the light spring breeze.

"I shall return before long." Faye plunged into the hallway and down the stairs, a firm grip on her reticule and a firmer grip on her resolve—lest she turn around, throw herself on her bed, and refuse to emerge ever again.

Or face the mess she'd made of everything.

Paul had given Mark Allen precise directions to the Pikes' place. It wouldn't be difficult to find. But why was he sitting in the wagon waiting for Gwen's sister? Why wasn't he miles away on Jughead, leaving the area as fast as the old horse could take him?

Because it was Gwen.

He needed to see her one last time—or so he told himself. Needed to be sure she really was his Gwen, that it wasn't some horrible misunderstanding. He had to be sure, and that meant seeing her with his own eyes.

No matter how much it hurt.

Faye marched with barely a limp through the front door, letting it slam behind her.

Mark Allen leaped from the wagon and assisted her onto the high seat without a word.

Equally wordless, Faye took her seat, adjusted her skirts, and sat stiff as a hoe handle.

Mark Allen climbed aboard, gathered the reins of Ben and Buster, then chirped to the heavy team of sorrels to start them clomping into the street.

It wasn't a street by city standards, but it wasn't a farm lane either. Houses lined it at regular intervals, most sided with milled boards like the doctor's, but a few made of rough logs and even one of brick. When he reached the end of the houses, he turned to the east as the doctor had instructed.

The landscape opened up into a series of rolling hills dotted with fields and woodlots. When they topped the first hill, a homestead came into view nestled below in the horseshoe loop of a creek. The house was made of logs, two stories high, and large enough for at least two rooms on each level. Smoke rose from the fieldstone chimney on one end. A log barn and three smaller buildings flanked it. In all, it looked like the perfect place to settle down with a wife and children.

He stopped the wagon. The twist in his chest called him a fool for being there. But he could hardly deposit Faye on the side of the road and move on.

A very quiet Faye, whose ashen face had not turned to look at anything they'd passed. Nor had her posture relaxed an inch. If anything, she appeared to have frozen in place.

He cleared his throat. "'Twill be nice to see your sister again." For her, anyway.

"Aye." The single word was short, sharp, and doubtless meant to discourage further attempts at conversation.

But Mark Allen didn't care. "Are you not excited to see her again after... how long has it been?"

"I do not see 'tis any of your business."

"Your—not thy?" Why was he baiting her? Because it was easier than thinking about what awaited at the bottom of the hill.

"What do you care? You are not a Quaker."

"And neither are you."

She finally moved, sending him a searing glare that should have stripped the skin from his face. "What do you know about it?"

"I know a fraud when I see one."

"I will not be spoken to by a... a hired lackey in such a manner. Paul will hear of this." She flounced on the seat. At least the color was back in her cheeks. It was better for Gwen to not see her sister looking so sickly.

But that wasn't all that prompted him to goad her further. He was angry. A deep anger that needed an outlet, and heaven knew, she'd unloaded her anger on him more than once. Even knowing he was behaving poorly, he said, "I'm a free man. I can make my own way in this world now. I have paid my debt. What have you accomplished, Faye Morgan?"

It may have been his imagination, or he may have heard her teeth grating together.

"I will have you know that I am considered a very accomplished woman."

"By Pittsburgh's standards?" He barked a rude laugh. "What good are your haughty manners in Mount Pleasant? Can you handle a horse? Can you plant a garden? Can you preserve food and launder clothing and—"

"When I require a lecture from the *stable boy*, I will let *thee* know." The words came out quiet, deadly, and intended to put him in his place.

And it worked.

Who was he to lecture anyone?

She may have neglected to answer her sister, even denied that sister's very existence, but it didn't give him the right to take out his anger and hurt on her.

With a sick feeling in his middle, he clicked to the horses, and they started down the hill.

Toward Gwen.

Chapter 22

F AYE SEETHED AS THE wagon pulled to a halt in front of the rough log cabin. She barely noticed the buildings or the fields and pastures beyond or the creek babbling nearby. As soon as the vehicle came to a full stop, she stood.

"Allow me to assist thee." A Quaker man appeared beside her. Dressed in the usual plain manner she was becoming accustomed to, he reached up to her.

She slid her hand into his, eager to avoid touching the infuriating stableman and unwilling to land in a heap in the dirt next to the wagon. Until they found a laundress, she had no other clean dress to wear.

The man steadied her as she climbed down, then let go of her hand and took a step back, looking her over from bonnet to shoes and back again, a slow smile adding sparkle to his startling blue eyes. "I know we have not met, but if thee tells me thy name is Faye Morgan, 'twill not surprise me in the least."

"How...?" All sense of time and place returned. She wasn't there to fight with Mark Allen or defend the choices she'd made in her life. She looked at the house, truly seeing it for the first time, then back at the man before her. "You are her husband?"

He nodded. "Thy brother-in-law, Micah Pike." He shook his head. "She said thee resembled her, but she never said how much. But for thy eye color, thee could be twins."

They'd heard the same growing up many times. The memory brought a smile just as the door to the log house opened and out stepped—

Gwen.

Mark Allen's heart worked its way into his throat at the sight of Gwen in the doorway, looking as lovely as he'd remembered but with a swaddled babe in her arms. Perhaps even lovelier. Motherhood obviously suited her, as he'd always known it would.

He'd just always assumed—hoped, at least—that she'd share it with him, not the man speaking with Faye.

A gasp, and then Gwen started forward, one hand clutching the babe, the other covering her mouth.

"Be easy, Gwen." The man—her husband—rushed to her side, a young boy with golden curls sprouting from beneath a straw hat followed her. "Have a care. The doctor bid thee rest." The man took the infant.

But Gwen ignored him and once the babe was secure in his arms, rushed to Faye, arms coming around her sister. "My darling Faye," Gwen chanted the words over and over again.

How many times had Mark Allen dreamed of this moment? Dreamed of reuniting Gwen with her long-lost sister? Dreamed of the very sisterly hug happening before him? Dreamed that it would be followed by her arms opening toward him next?

His hands must have tightened on the reins because Ben and Buster each took a step back, drawing attention to the wagon—and him.

Gwen opened her eyes, and over her sister's shoulder, she spied Mark Allen.

His emotions clogged his senses and slowed everything down as if he were running through deep water. Each breath extracted with effort. Each heartbeat too loud and too long.

Gwen's blue eyes pooled with tears, the hand rose again to her mouth. She released her sister and took a step toward the wagon.

"Mark Allen?"

Her husband, who had been walking toward the house, whipped around.

His name meant something to the man.

Gwen must have spoken of him.

Mark Allen wasn't sure if that pleased him or not.

She took another step, then stopped and waited.

He touched the brim of his hat. "Gwen."

"I cannot believe..."

An awkward moment stretched between them.

"Cannot believe that I would keep my word?" Hurt crowded into his voice, even though he tried to suppress it.

"Nay. Never that. Thee were always a man of thy word, even as a boy."

He wanted to say the same of her, but there she stood, married to another. She hadn't waited for him.

Not that she'd never said she would. It hurt to admit it, even to himself. His hopes and dreams had never been hers.

"You look well, Gwen."

A flush climbed her cheeks and, for a moment, it reminded him of Faye, only the flush wasn't caused by anger at him.

"Gwen." Faye pulled on her sister's arm and shot Mark Allen a glare. "Come away. We have much to catch up on."

"Indeed." Gwen gave her head a little shake. "Indeed, we do. But thank thee, Mark Allen, for bringing her. Thee has always known how dear she is to me."

The wealth of gratitude in her eyes almost—almost—eased the ache in his heart.

"He did not bring me." Faye tugged on her sister's arm again. "'Twas the doctor."

"Paul?" Gwen's attention swung back to Faye, her eyebrows raised. "He gave his last name, but I was rather distracted at the time. I never connected it to Martha McClure. Is it possible?"

For once, the Quaker habit of using only first names had worked in Faye's favor.

"More than possible."

"Then I needn't have searched for thee." Gwen laughed, the joyful sound Faye had long remembered. "I should have trusted God would bring thee to my door."

Faye's head spun with all the talk of God and use of *thee*. Her sister really was a Quaker.

"Come into the house. Thee must tell me everything." But even as Faye walked beside her, Gwen glanced over her shoulder at Mark Allen again.

Faye wasn't the only one who witnessed it. Micah had planted himself near the porch, babe still in his arms, eyes locked on the wagon and its driver, with the little boy beside him.

Good. Someone else could deal with the insufferable stableman. Faye would rather walk back to the house in the village rather than ride next to Mark Allen again... but she wasn't sure she could find her way. She'd not paid any attention to their route, so she had little choice but to return with him. Later. Much later if it were up to her, but Paul had warned her not to overtax Gwen.

Gwen retrieved her daughter, and they left Micah and the boy standing guard outside the door.

The house wasn't fancy, but then, it wouldn't be. The logs were chinked with what looked like dirt, the furniture handmade of local materials most likely. A huge log split right down the middle and laid side by side, sanded and polished to a shine, served as a table. The hearth at the end of the single room that served as both kitchen and parlor filled most of the wall. Two doors opened off the back, a bed visible in one, shelving in the other. A rope ladder swung from an opening in the rafters overhead. Two glass windows let in light, one on either side of the door, and a fire blazed in the hearth. But the interior was still dim.

Faye swallowed her dismay—or tried to. The stables in Pittsburgh had been grander, constructed of bricks and finished inside with milled boards and many windows to let in the light.

"Sit, please." Gwen pointed to the half of a split log that served as a bench beside the table. "'Twill be a moment to brew tea."

"Nay, sister. Paul said for thee to rest. Do not bother with tea."

"'Twas such a blessing to have the doctor arrive when he did." Gwen stroked the cheek of the babe in her arms. "Sally Faye arrived a little early and the midwife was concerned. As were Micah and I. The poor man was more frightened than I have ever seen him. He ran to our neighbor's house and begged them to send their son to fetch the doctor."

"Sally Faye?" The name almost stuck in her throat. Gwen had named her daughter... after her?

"Oh, aye." Gwen's smile more than made up for the lack of light. "How could I not name my daughter after my sister? And Sally after Micah's mother."

Faye couldn't have forced another word from her throat if she'd tried.

"Would thee like to hold her?"

Faye hadn't held an infant since her brothers. Fear paralyzed her. What if she got attached to the little girl, only to lose her too? But Gwen rose and laid the bundle in her arms. Arms that came around to cuddle the babe as if they knew what to do when Faye herself didn't.

The perfect curve of her cheeks, the button of a nose, the smattering of black wisps around the cloth cap on her head, and the scent of a newborn resurrected memories of another time, another place, another life.

"She is perfect."

"Indeed." Gwen's smile resembled their mothers' so much that it almost hurt to look at her.

"And she is your second? The boy outside?" The boy with golden curls and eyes a far lighter blue than Gwen's. He must favor his father, and yet, the man outside had been nearly as dark as Gwen.

"Owen, my son."

"Named after Father."

"Aye." Gwen looked out the window, then back at Faye. "His story I will save for another day. Today it is enough that my sister is here with me again at last."

Faye had done nothing to deserve such honor and devotion. She did her best not to squirm on the bench, but she made a vow that one day she'd live up to Gwen's esteem.

Somehow.

Gwen's husband approached the wagon where Mark Allen waited, the little boy tagging along. There was something about the boy—

"So thee are Mark Allen, from the Whitefords'?"

"I was. Now I'm Mark Allen Teed, freeman, employed by Dr. Mc-Clure."

"Micah Pike." He drew the boy to his side. "And this is my son, Owen."

In polite society, under normal circumstances, the proper response would have been to say it was a pleasure to meet them. Only it wasn't. It wasn't pleasant at all. Mark Allen should have saddled Jughead and ridden away. But it was too late for that.

"Married to Gwen, I assume," he said instead.

"Indeed." The man all but puffed out his chest. And why wouldn't he? Mark Allen would have done so had the roles been reversed. "'Twould appear we owe thee a debt of gratitude, Mark Allen, for the delivery of Gwen's sister."

Mark Allen shrugged. "She would have arrived even without me." He wouldn't be petty enough to withhold the truth. "'Twas already in the works when I discovered her in Pittsburgh."

"How did thee discover her?" Was that suspicion in the man's voice?

"By riding halfway across the country in the dead of winter and nearly freezing to death." All attempts to be polite had slipped from his grasp.

Micah waved a hand in the direction of the town. "If thee wishes, I will see Faye returned to the McClures. Did they state a time she was to return?"

Why would they? Oh, of course. He'd assume Faye was a servant—the same mistake Mark Allen had made. Well, that was for them to figure out. Mark Allen wasn't going to speak out of turn. "'Twould suit me fine. She can tell you when she needs to return."

With a chirp and a tug on the reins, Mark Allen had Ben and Buster turning the wagon around.

The little boy, Owen, waved as he passed by. Mark Allen touched his hat in return and searched the boy's face for any hint of Gwen, but the tow-headed child didn't favor her at all.

Not that it mattered.

In the back of his mind, he'd always pictured a boy with his light brown hair and a little girl with Gwen's dark curls. Another dream gone.

On the road again, he slapped the horses with the reins and moved them into a steady trot. What was he going to do? Stay and watch Gwen's children grow? Or strike out on his own?

To do... what?

Chapter 23

AFTER THE SHORT VISIT with her sister the day before, Faye awoke with a sour feeling in her stomach. The kind that came from doing something she wasn't proud of. Or from not doing something she should have. Or both.

Yet Gwen still loved her.

Faye had confessed to keeping Gwen's existence a secret from Madam and Paul. Her sister had blinked back the hurt, but not before Faye had seen it. She'd also confessed to not wanting to come to Mount Pleasant—even after she knew Gwen was here. She'd even confessed to having ambitions to marry well and live in comfort with a husband who could support her and their children in a gracious manner.

Gwen had taken it all in stride, assuring her that if their circumstances had been reversed, she might have done the same.

But they both knew it wasn't true.

Which was why—as Mark Allen had said—everyone loved Gwen.

The one thing Faye hadn't been able to bring herself to confess was her resentment, anger even, at Gwen's abandonment. How could she confess to that? It made no sense, even to her. The memory of

Gwen's grief-ravaged face as that horrible man had dragged her away. Gwen hadn't abandoned Faye, Gwen had been forced away into a life of servitude.

While Faye had been given a life of ease.

During which time, she'd done her best to forget she ever had a sister.

And hence, the sourness of guilt in her stomach that hadn't lessened upon learning Gwen had been freed from indenture. Which Faye should have known. Quakers wouldn't have kept a person in bondage of any kind.

She swung her legs over the side of the bed. A breeze flowed through the open window carrying the scent of freshly turned earth, reminding her of home and the kitchen garden outside her beautifully furnished bedroom. She rose and padded to the window.

Mark Allen and Bran—were they brothers?—worked with shovel and hoe on a level area between the house and barn. Their voices carried, but she couldn't make out the words. Mark Allen stuck his shovel into the ground, then leaned against it and stared into the distance.

Bran appeared to be arguing with him.

And then it hit her.

Mark Allen was in love with Gwen—and Gwen was married to Micah.

While he sometimes made her mad enough to spit, he'd also shown her true kindness. He'd understood about her father and his drinking, something she'd never shared with anyone else.

Had his needling of her on the ride to Gwen and Micah's been borne of a broken heart?

The same way her behavior on the boat had been borne of her disappointed hopes?

He said something to the boy, turned another shovelful of dirt, and glanced up at her window.

Caught looking and dressed only in her shift, Faye backed away, flustered.

What was wrong with her anyway?

And him? He was just the man hired to tend the horses and the garden. He had no business looking at her window.

She slapped her palm to her forehead. It was time to stop thinking like that. They were on the frontier where everyone—low-born or high—worked side by side to scratch out a living. Gone were the upper social levels she'd worked so hard to fit within. She wasn't some princess in a tower waiting for her prince to ride up on a charger.

She was Faye Morgan, the ward of the town's doctor and sister to Gwen—and nothing more. It was time to make the best of what she had.

As Gwen was doing.

But how?

"And you will stay until this here garden be planted?"

Mark Allen turned the last clump of ground over and patted it with the back of his shovel. "I told you I would." He glanced at the window again—although Faye wasn't there. When he'd seen her, for a moment, he'd thought she was Gwen. The pain that hadn't left since he'd learned Gwen was married tightened in his chest.

He needed to leave. Even seeing her sister was too much, but he'd agreed to work for Paul, given his word. It didn't sit right to abandon his job almost before he began. If he could get the garden started and Bran trained to tend it, then he could ride away without feeling as if he'd let anyone down.

"We been here only a day, but I think it be a good place." Bran wiped his sweaty face with his sleeve. "A man could start at the bottom here and move himself up like you was talkin' about."

"That was before." Mark Allen entered the stable and hung the shovel in its place. The town had outfitted the stable as well as the house. The Quakers had done everything they could to welcome the new doctor.

If only Gwen had been free to welcome him. He paused, hand still on the shovel handle. Had her husband purchased her indenture and then married her? It happened. But even if she'd met him that way, she seemed happy. And they had two children. Gwen was forever beyond his reach.

Bran hung his hoe and then crossed his arms. "'Tis about that other gal, ain't it? The one who had the baby."

"What if it is?"

"There be a passel of womenfolk in this town. I seen a bunch of 'em when I scouted round yesterday." He looked Mark Allen up and down. "You ain't half bad-lookin'. I reckon one of 'em would put up with you by and by."

Spoken like a youngster who'd never been in love.

"Come on." Mark Allen headed toward the house. "We should ask Bridget about the kinds of seeds she wants us to purchase."

He opened the kitchen door and entered to the tantalizing aroma of freshly baked bread.

Bran whistled through his teeth.

Mark Allen elbowed him. The boy had no manners whatsoever.

"There be the young man I need to test a slice of this bread." Bridget wiped her hands on a cloth and reached for one of the round loaves, cutting off a thick slice. "Garden work brings on a terrible hunger." She handed it to Bran with a fond smile.

"Yes, ma'am." He started to shove the piece into his mouth, then caught Mark Allen's glare. "Thank you."

She cut another slice and handed it to Mark Allen.

"Thank you." He took a bite and smiled his appreciation, even though he wasn't hungry. Might never be hungry again. A broken heart did that to a man, he supposed. He swallowed and cleared his throat. "Paul said to check with you about what seeds to purchase."

"I have the list right here." She grabbed a piece of paper off the table behind her. "If they have more than one variety of anything, just ask them which they think will do best. Until we learn the ways of the soil here, 'twill be trial and error to put forth a good garden."

"Yes, ma'am." He took the list, but even being able to read much of what was written didn't lift his spirits.

She clucked her tongue. "And none of that in a Quaker household. 'Tis Bridget and only Bridget thee needs to be callin' me." She winked at Bran and cut him another slice of bread, his having disappeared. "That goes for thee too."

"Yes, ma... Bridget." He grinned at her.

Mark Allen chewed on his bread during the walk to the mercantile, mostly to avoid having to engage in Bran's steady stream of chatter. He seemed to have something to say about everything since they'd arrived. Like a child in a candy store, he saw Mount Pleasant as the best place on earth.

And maybe it was for Bran, but it couldn't be for Mark Allen. Not with Gwen married.

They reached the mercantile and waited in line behind several women purchasing yard goods. Plain yard goods, of course. Gray, dark blue, black, and white seemed to be the only colors allowed by the Quakers, gray being prominent.

"How can I help thee?" a man around Mark Allen's age asked, the long apron covering his front marking him as a clerk.

He handed over Bridget's list. "We need garden seeds."

"I can help thee with that." He bustled around behind the counter and pulled jars off the shelves behind, measuring and weighing the different seeds onto paper that he creased and folded, marking the name on each piece.

Bran wandered off to look around.

"Thee must be with the new doctor's family," the clerk said.

"I'm his stableman and gardener."

"Welcome to Mount Pleasant. I'm Andrew Griffin." He wiped his hand down his apron and then offered it.

Mark Allen shook his hand. "Mark Allen Teed. Folks call me Mark Allen."

"'Tis a pleasure to meet thee." Andrew paused his weighing and packeting and cocked his head. "Gardener, thee said? Are thee interested in apple trees? Planting an orchard?"

He'd never thought about it, but having a source for their own cider would be welcome. "I am."

Andrew leaned over the counter as if delivering a secret. "There is a man just north of town, John Chapman, who is something of a character, but he is knowledgeable about orchards, apples being his specialty. Thee will wish to speak to him directly and without delay. He has a tendency to move on from place to place."

"I appreciate the information." Something of a character?

A clatter on the other side of the store took Andrew's attention, and the clerk frowned.

Mark Allen turned around, dreading what he'd see. Bran was sprawled on the floor surrounded by a pile of work boots and two overturned crates.

Just what he needed, one more *character* in his life.

Faye placed three wrapped loaves into a basket Bridget had provided for the bread. "Thank thee for baking them."

"'Tis the least we can do for a new mother." Bridget dipped her head toward the door. "Be off with thee now and enjoy the visit."

Basket in hand, Faye joined Madam, who waited for her in the front room. "All set."

"'Tis good of thee to invite me along."

Guilt picked at her. "I am so sorry I never told thee about Gwen. 'Twasn't that I wished to keep a secret, truly. 'Twas more like I could not speak of her."

Madam squeezed Faye's arm. "I think I understand."

"I'm sure thee will love Gwen. Everyone does." Faye suppressed a twinge of emotion she didn't want to ponder.

"Of that, I have no doubt."

The wagon rumbled to a stop in front of the house. Faye stepped outside and shaded her eyes. It was the boy handling the reins, not Mark Allen.

He'd gone with the men to repair and retrieve the carriage. Thankfully, they'd taken the local wheelwright's wagon.

Maybe it was best if Mark Allen didn't return to Gwen's house.

The boy jumped down and assisted Madam onto the high seat, then handed Faye into the back, the seat not being wide enough for three.

"Mark Allen gave me directions." He took up the reins. "Me and Ben and Buster will have you there in no time." He slapped the reins against the broad rumps in front of him, and the wagon lurched into motion.

"Do get us there in one piece, young Bran," Madam said, but there was a merry note to her voice even as she clutched the wooden seat.

Faye bit her tongue rather than give voice to her thoughts, though the young upstart could use a lesson in driving ladies.

Something moved behind the newly planted hedgerow separating their house from the one next door. A very dark boy in a floppy hat. A slave? It couldn't be. Quakers did not keep slaves, and they were in the free territory. Just a boy then, but why was he skulking around in the hedgerow?

The wagon rolled over a rut. Faye grasped the board sides to steady herself. "Can thee not keep the wagon on the road?"

"'Tis a very bumpy road," Madam answered quickly, perhaps to stave off whatever Bran might have said, the impudent boy.

They arrived no worse for wear, and Gwen greeted them at the door. Faye introduced Madam and then insisted Gwen sit and chat with her while she finished the tea.

"I cannot thank thee enough for what thee has done for my sister." Gwen's voice trembled with unshed tears.

"Oh, no, my dear. 'Tis we who have been blessed to have her in our family. Not that we are true family, of course." Madam hastened to add. "Not as thee are."

Faye set the tea on the table along with the basket of bread.

Gwen laid her hand over Madam's. "I must introduce thee to Thomas and Betsy Baldwin, the couple who took me in. I consider them family, as I am sure Faye considers thee. 'Tis no disrespect to our mother and father. They are gone, and they would not wish us to be alone in the world."

The lump in Faye's throat wouldn't allow her to speak, but that was for the best. She hadn't any words. It was no wonder everyone loved Gwen.

She did too.

So why, deep down, did Faye continue to harbor resentment and guilt?

Mark Allen gave a mighty shove alongside Paul as Thomas Baldwin, the wheelwright, removed the block from the carriage's axle. Then they eased the vehicle onto its repaired wheel.

"Well." Paul dusted off his gloved hands. "Looks as good as new."

"'Twas an easy enough repair." Thomas removed his hat and wiped his brow before resettling it. "But thee were wise to leave it here. Moving it would have compounded the damage." He patted the carriage. "'Tis a fine vehicle."

Paul studied it. "Probably too fine for Mount Pleasant."

"Nay, I did not mean it in that way," Thomas said, "only that 'twas solidly built by someone who knew their craft well."

"Will the good people of Mount Pleasant deem it unseemly for their doctor to own such a carriage?" Paul asked

What did it matter? Mark Allen glanced over the landscape but didn't really see it. There wasn't anything to see anyway. No buildings. No farms. Nothing but unsettled territory. They were all stuck in the middle of nowhere.

When he thought he'd be stuck there with Gwen, it'd sounded like paradise. Without her, it was more of a prison.

Only if he let it be.

He was a free man. He could saddle Jughead and be on the way back to... to where? Not to his father's house, supposing the man still drew breath. Certainly not back to Daniel Whiteford. Where would Mark Allen go? How would he earn a living?

Thomas tugged on the end of his beard. "There will always be some looking to find fault, even among the Friends, and while 'tis finely built, 'tis not too fancy for our town."

Mark Allen was struggling with what to do with the rest of his life, and these two men were discussing whether or not a carriage was a good fit for the town doctor. He wished his problems were that small.

"What thinks thee, Mark Allen?" Paul studied him with sharp eyes.

"Me?"

"Aye. Thee will be living here as well, and thee will be driving the carriage when my mother and Faye have need." Paul tipped his head a fraction to the side. "Do thee believe it too grand for Mount Pleasant?"

Mark Allen eyed the carriage for a moment and collected his thoughts. Paul had been good to him, and he deserved an honest answer. "I believe 'tis a sturdy, serviceable vehicle, and 'twould be a waste not to use it as it was designed."

Thomas chuckled. "The young man has good sense."

Paul gripped Mark Allen's shoulder. "Indeed, he does, and he is wonderful with the horses. Bridget says he is industrious with the garden as well. We are lucky to have him with us."

With us, not working *for* us. Mark Allen swallowed a lump that might have been gratitude. After all, Paul and his mother had treated him and Bran almost like family since they'd showed up on their doorstep.

Like family—for the first time in his life.

Could Mark Allen turn away from that?

Should he?

"I will see to the team." He busied himself with untying Dolly and Skip from the back of Thomas's wagon and hitching them to the repaired carriage.

Within minutes, Thomas had pulled away in his wagon, and Paul joined Mark Allen on the bench rather than ride inside the carriage by himself.

"I cannot help but notice thee have been quiet since we arrived." Paul glanced at him. "Is there something that troubles thee?"

Honesty was always the best policy, Mark Allen believed that. Not that he hadn't skirted the truth a time or two in the past, mostly when he'd been sure it was for the greater good. "I'm not sure how long I will stay in Mount Pleasant."

"Does it not suit thee?"

"'Tisn't the place." How much should he say?

"'Tis the people then?" Paul leaned forward, elbows on his knees, looking forward as if seeing into the future—or maybe the past. "I had trouble understanding the Quakers at first. Their speech, of course, and their manner of dressing plain, but even more, their belief that anyone could speak directly to the Lord God and hear back from Him. Even women. Even slaves." He shook his head. "'Twas far different from what I had learned as a boy."

"Nay, 'tis not the Quakers. You have been nothing but kind to Bran and me." Having had no formal church experience of his own, Mark Allen didn't understand their religious views or anyone else's. His father had never attended a church, and Mr. Whiteford had not required his servants to attend.

"Then is the difficulty of a personal nature?"

"Aye." He shifted on the hard seat. "But I will not leave until the garden is planted and the seedlings well on their way."

"I will be sorry to see thee leave."

It wasn't the words, but the sincerity behind them and his reaction to it that had Mark Allen fumbling for something else to talk about. "Have you considered an orchard?" he blurted out.

"An orchard?"

"Apples, for cider. The clerk yesterday told me of a man named John Chapman who resides north of Mount Pleasant and is well-versed in the ways of apple trees."

"Our own cider. Now that sounds like a wise investment." He turned to Mark Allen. "But would thee stay long enough to see the saplings in the ground and started?"

Would he? He clicked to the horses, urging them to a faster trot as the road leveled out. If he agreed, he'd be in Mount Pleasant for a year, at least. He didn't know a lot about trees, but he knew they needed time and care to get a proper start.

A year of being close to Gwen.

But also a year before he had to make decisions about his future.

"I would agree to that."

"Then meet with this Chapman fellow and see what he has to say."

And so, Mark Allen was committed to staying—for a year.

Chapter 24

A T THE TAP ON Gwen's door, Faye set down her cup. She was startled when the door opened before anyone had bid entrance.

"Where is that granddaughter of mine?" a bearded man asked as he stepped over the threshold.

Gwen chuckled, shifting the baby from her shoulder to face the older couple who entered. "Waiting for thee, of course." She returned her attention to Faye and Madam. "These are Thomas and Betsy Baldwin, the couple who took me in when I left Daniel Whiteford's service." Gwen finished the introductions.

Thomas whisked Sally Faye into his arms and beamed at her through the bristle of his gray beard.

Betsy came to Faye's side. "We searched for thee for so long, 'tis hard to believe thee have come to us with the doctor we prayed God would provide."

"Indeed." Gwen said. "When I think of all the worry and tears only to have God deliver thee to me in the end."

Faye didn't know what to say. Had God delivered her to her sister? If He had, it had been with her digging in her heels the entire way.

But Gwen obviously believed it. She'd become a true Quaker—not an impostor like Faye.

The sourness in her stomach returned.

What was it about these people? Thomas cooed over Sally Faye, Madam and Betsy talked as if they'd known each other all their lives and had never been separated by social standing, Gwen tended to Owen, who had burst through the door declaring his thirst.

Faye was left to her own thoughts. Ever the outsider looking in.

"Tell us, Faye." Betsy turned to her. "What does thee think of our small town so far?"

"I have seen very little of it." And even less that she could enthuse over.

"Is the house suitable?" Thomas looked from her to Madam. "Does thee have any need?"

Other than husband prospects who didn't smell of horse and dirt? Faye managed to keep her mouth shut and let Madam answer.

"The house is perfectly adequate, and the setting offers such a lovely view out the back. Bridget keeps exclaiming over the kitchen and all its modern conveniences." Madam chuckled. "She'll have us letting out our garments with that clever brick oven built into the hearth. So much handier than what we had in the house in Pittsburgh."

House? *Home.* What'd they'd had at home.

Gwen touched her shoulder, and she startled.

"Is something wrong?" her sister asked.

She should have known she wouldn't be able to hide her thoughts well enough to fool the sister who'd all but raised her. "Nothing."

Gwen glanced around the room. "Come. Let us take a walk outside. I could use the fresh air, and the children are in the best of hands."

Reluctantly, Faye rose and followed Gwen out the door. The air was damp, a promise of rain in the heavy clouds that gathered against the horizon. It suited her mood.

"Tell me, sister, what lies so heavily on thy heart?" Gwen kept her measured steps and led them around the cabin toward a line of trees that followed the creek.

"'Tis nothing, as I said."

"Most might believe thee." Gwen's voice held a note of sadness. "But we have been through too much together, thee and I. So much loss and pain."

"Which is why I wished for a husband to provide for me as Madam's husband—whom I never met—provided for her before his death."

Gwen paused, her fingers a gentle brush against Faye's arm. "Micah provides for me." She pointed toward the field on the other side of the cabin where her husband walked behind a team of horses, arms bared to the elbows as he steadied the plow.

Faye could almost smell the sweat and horse from where they stood. And yet, she could not dispute the adoration in Micah's expression when he spied Gwen. Nor could she dispute the returned regard from her sister. A part of Faye even envied them.

But love didn't put food on the table or a leak-proof roof overhead.

One accident, one illness, or one misfortune, and it was lost. Then how was a woman to pick up the pieces? Or a man, for that matter. Their father hadn't managed his losses. Love was all well and good, but if it came without security, Faye wasn't interested.

She'd have to wait and hope that Mount Pleasant grew quickly enough to attract some more well-to-do inhabitants.

Before she became known as the doctor's spinster ward.

The wind had picked up by the time Mark Allen pulled the team to a halt and set the brake in front of the doctor's house, where Bran was sweeping the front porch. Mark Allen had driven Paul to see three couples before returning to the house, people Paul had heard were ailing in some way. He was getting off on a good foot as a conscientious frontier-town doctor.

Paul climbed down. Holding onto his hat with one hand, he scanned the clouds. "Thee did not wait for the women to drive them home?" he asked Bran.

Bran propped the broom against the house. "Micah told me to skedaddle. Said he would fetch 'em home when they was ready."

"He would have to stop working to do that, and time is money to a farmer." Paul stepped away from the carriage and faced Mark Allen. "The horses have plenty of energy left, so thee can bring them home. And should it rain, they will appreciate this sturdy, serviceable vehicle being used as it was designed." He chuckled as he stomped his boots off on the porch and entered the house.

Bran approached the carriage. "I can fetch 'em for you if you like, so you don't need to see that other gal."

As if not seeing Gwen would remove her from his thoughts.

"Paul told me to do it, so I will." Mark Allen released the brake. "Besides"—he tipped his chin at mud Paul had knocked from his boots—"you have sweeping to do."

"Aw, I was just helpin' Bridget." The brash youngster actually blushed. "If I did the sweepin', she said she might have time to make doughnuts."

The surest way to the heart of a young man was through his stomach, and Bran was flourishing under Bridget's care and cooking. He'd filled out the clothes Mark Allen had bought him months ago and would need a new set soon. Aside from threatening to burst his seams, the sleeves and pant legs were getting too short.

But dawdling over thoughts of Bran wasn't getting his job done. Mark Allen clicked to Dolly and Skip and turned them in the direction of Micah's farm. He let them set their own pace, but it wasn't far, and they arrived all too soon. He'd barely had time to steel himself to face Gwen again.

Rain splattered in wind-driven drops as he drove the carriage into the yard.

Micah was unhitching his team of red roans from a plow in front of the barn. He approached the carriage. "I told Bran I would return the women."

"Paul sent me to fetch them." Mark Allen pulled his hat lower to shield his face from the rain. "The carriage was already hitched."

"'Twill be more comfortable for them." Micah shielded his face with his hand. "Does thee mind taking the Baldwins home? They walked over earlier."

"Not at all." He was already soaked through, so another stop would make little difference.

In moments, the wheelwright and the lady who must be his wife hustled from the cabin along with Martha and Faye while Gwen watched from the doorway.

Beautiful Gwen, with a babe in her arms.

Mark Allen's throat knotted.

Thomas helped the women into the carriage, then looked up at

Mark Allen. "'Tis glad I am that thee happened by. Foolish of me to insist on the walk." He grinned. "And now I have a chance to ride in a fine vehicle."

"Yes, sir."

"Thomas, not sir."

"Of course."

Thomas patted the side of the carriage. "Thee will get used to our ways, and perchance, with time, come to join us. Thee would be welcomed."

The carriage rocked as he entered and settled into a seat. With one last glance at Gwen, tucked under the eaves out of the rain and holding her babe, Mark Allen slapped the reins and got the team moving. They were more lively heading home toward the barn, neither liking the chilly rain any more than he did.

As the water sluiced down around him, he couldn't help but ponder Thomas's words about joining the Quakers. He'd never belonged to any group of people, not even a real family, and the idea—while foreign to him—held a certain appeal. Even Bran was fitting in with Bridget acting like his big sister. And it was obvious Gwen had found a home among them.

Could he live so close to her and ever be truly happy?

Finding John Chapman turned out to be harder than the store clerk had indicated. Mark Allen urged Jughead to the top of a small rise, resolved to return to town if he didn't find the man from there. He'd been gone since midmorning, and he didn't need the angle of the sun to know it was nearly supper time. His stomach growled like a bobcat. He should have snagged a couple of Bridget's doughnuts on his way out of town.

Jughead topped the rise, and a shallow valley spread before them, washed clean by the previous day's rain and so green it almost hurt Mark Allen's eyes. The kind of green that only springtime and fertile soil could achieve. The perfect place to grow things.

A man moved on foot near the middle. He had a haversack over one shoulder and walked stooped over as if examining the ground. Was this the man he'd been searching for? The threadbare shirt and tin-pot hat would certainly mark him as a character, as the clerk had described.

Mark Allen urged Jughead forward.

When the man spied them, he raised his hands, waving them wildly and shouting, "Come no closer. Stay where you are. I will walk to you."

You. Not a Quaker then. The man was beyond lean, downright skinny, and in need of a bath and a razor. But if he could instruct Mark Allen on starting an orchard, none of that mattered.

"Ho! What brings you to my valley?" the man called as he drew near, his bare feet not slowing him down.

"Are you John Chapman?"

"I am he." He hooked his thumb under the haversack's strap.

"Andrew Griffin from the mercantile said you were knowledgeable about orchards, apples in particular."

"And he would be correct. Get down and tether your beast so he does not trample my seedlings."

So that was why he'd stopped Mark Allen from riding in. On closer inspection, the tender spring leaves of skinny seedlings were visible above the native grasses.

"I would like to start an apple orchard," Mark Allen said once Jughead was munching grass a safe distance away.

"Then you have come to the right man." Chapman swept an arm to encompass the valley. "This is my latest orchard, started last year. Acres of future cider producers spread before you."

Mark Allen could picture it in a few years, round fruit hanging from each tree, shining red in the fall sun. Would he be here then?

He squinted at the seedlings. "They are planted so closely together, won't that be a problem?"

"I can see you have the makings of an orchardist." The oddly dressed, barefoot man seemed pleased. "Not every seedling will prosper, so I always plant more than I need." He patted his haversack. "I have plenty of seeds, you see."

"Could I purchase seeds from you?"

He held up one finger. "I can do better than that. I will give you a sackful of seedlings that need to be thinned out."

"And explain to me how to plant them so they will thrive?"

"Aye, lad. Be happy to." Chapman rubbed his hands together. "No time like the present. Let us start."

Mark Allen's stomach rumbled, but he followed the orchardist. They walked between the rows of seedlings, and he listened carefully as Chapman extolled the virtues of his variety of apples—which he called "spitters"—their value for producing the best cider, and how to manage the soil around them for a bountiful harvest.

So engrossed was he in the man's horticulture lecture, Mark Allen barely noticed the fading daylight.

Chapman dusted off his hands after poking fingers into the soil around the base of a seedling and explaining, once more for clarity, what he was looking for. Then he eyed Mark Allen up and down.

"Come back in the morning, and I will have the seedlings in a sack for you." He named what sounded like a fair price and marched off in the direction of a tent Mark Allen hadn't noticed before.

It was a lengthy hike back to Jughead, who dozed beneath the tree where Mark Allen had tethered him. Head swirling with all the talk of trees and soils and water and insects and blights, Mark Allen swung into the saddle and pointed the horse toward home, letting him pick his way through the gathering darkness.

Somewhere between the discussion of apple varieties and proper soil drainage, eagerness had taken hold of Mark Allen. Being able to start with yearling trees—did one call trees yearlings like a horse?—would hasten his efforts to start an orchard.

If he did well, perhaps he could start a second orchard, a larger one, if he could claim a tract of land for his own. That would mean putting down roots in the frontier.

He snorted quietly in the night at the double meaning.

But he also smiled for the first time in days.

Chapter 25

I T'D BEEN THREE DAYS since Faye had seen her sister, and she was at a loss as to what to do with herself. Three days spent mostly in her room staring out the window. But she couldn't run to her sister's every day and become a nuisance.

When it wasn't raining, which it seemed to do far too often, she watched Mark Allen and the boy work in the garden. Not that garden work interested her, but she had nothing else to fill her time, and there was nothing else to see from her bedroom.

She considered trying to contact CeCe. If she sent a letter to her friend's parents in Pittsburgh, they would forward it to CeCe's Boston address. With careful wording, Faye might receive an invitation to visit. And from there, maybe she'd find a husband of means.

Elbows propped on the windowsill, the damp breeze washing over her, she indulged in a daydream of a stately brick house, servants to keep it tidy, delicious smells simmering from the kitchen, and a broad porch surrounded by a lawn managed by a gardener and bordered with rose bushes. She could almost smell it. She breathed in deeply.

Ugh!

The acrid tang of horse manure ripped her daydream away.

Mark Allen entered her view, pushing a barrow laden with the smelly stuff, Bran following with a shovel over one shoulder and a coarse sack clutched to his scrawny chest. Nothing could be farther from the dapper gardener of her dreams.

What were they doing?

She leaned out the window to follow their path past the new garden and around the side of the barn to where the land sloped away from the house. The land behind the barn had been fenced for the horses, but Mark Allen and Bran didn't enter the paddock. They stopped, and Brad handed the shovel over to Mark Allen.

They were close enough that Faye could hear the *shurf* of the shovel biting into the damp soil. How much garden did they need to feed their small household? Did Paul know that his hired man was digging up the place?

If it wouldn't have been so unladylike, she'd have yelled out to the window at them. But she wasn't some fishmonger's wife to be screaming from a windowsill.

Instead, she wrapped a light shawl around her shoulders and headed for the stairs. She'd find out what those two were up to and put a stop to anything that didn't have Paul's approval. It was the least she could do to help out.

And it would get her out of the house.

Madam had gone to visit Betsy Baldwin and taken Olivia. Bridget was singing in the kitchen. Paul was who knew where introducing himself to the farmers in the outlying area. As if they hadn't all had a good long gawk at the new doctor at Sunday meeting the day before.

Faye stepped off the porch and headed for where the men were working. The low rumble of Mark Allen's voice was answered by the scratchy tenor of Bran, but she wasn't close enough to make out the words. Then the *shurf* of the shovel started again.

The breeze blew up the hill, carrying the odors of damp earth and horse manure. Faye wrinkled her nose but marched on.

"What are you doing?" She almost changed *you* to *thee*, but *you* sounded more like someone in charge.

Mark Allen emptied the shovel, rested its tip on the ground, and put his foot on the back of the spade. "Digging a hole."

Anger scaled her backbone like an ivy vine, sending out shoots all along the way. Why was the man so difficult? She crossed her arms, the ends of her shawl tucked under them. "You know what I mean."

"'Tis none of your business, as I see it," Mark Allen drawled, "but we are starting an apple orchard."

"Does Paul know of this?"

Bran snorted but looked away when Faye scowled at him.

"Indeed, he does." Mark Allen forced the shovel into the dirt and lifted another load of the dark soil, knuckles white on the handle, muscles straining against the linen of his shirt sleeves, cords tightening along his neck above his narrow neckcloth. His hazel eyes fairly sparking with irritation.

Why did he always treat her as if he were somehow above her? It should be the other way around. He was the hired man, she was...

She was the penniless ward.

The younger sister of the girl he'd been indentured with.

He wasn't fooled by her veneer. He knew where she'd come from. The anger drained from her in a rush of self-awareness that left her embarrassed.

Who was she to think of Boston and a fine husband? She was Faye Morgan—orphan. Nothing more.

She turned to leave but stopped at Mark Allen's touch, his fingers light on her still crossed arms.

"We have a habit of starting on the wrong foot," he said.

Bran snorted again but ducked his head when Mark Allen frowned at him.

Mark Allen's hand fell away. "I got the idea of starting an orchard while at the mercantile purchasing garden seeds, and Paul approved of it. To grow apples for making cider."

"What do you know about tending an orchard?" Faye cringed at the sharpness of her words. "I mean, have thee grown trees before?" That was better. And the gentle Quaker *thee* added another level of calmness.

Mark Allen shook his head. "But the clerk told me of a man who does, and he gave me these seedlings." He pointed to the sack Bran had carried. "He explained how to plant them in a mix of soil and manure, how to keep them properly watered, and what sort of bugs to watch out for and signs of blights that may harm them."

She looked from the twigs sticking out of the sack to the smelly dirt and manure. "And from that, thee can produce a drinkable cider?"

His low chuckle should have aggravated her, but it didn't. It wasn't mocking, it was... she wasn't sure what it was, but she didn't bristle at it. Maybe she even enjoyed the sound.

"Not for a few years."

A few years. The enormity of her position once again landed on her shoulders. Years spent wasting away on the frontier, waiting for civilization to catch up to them. What a horrible thought.

"Would you like to help plant them?" he asked.

"You want me to put my hands in the dirt?"

Mark Allen must have misunderstood what he'd thought was a softening of Faye's attitude. Her voice had risen, tone sharpened, and her use of *you* capped it off. Why must she get all prickly when they'd been on their way to a civil conversation?

"Do I look like a farmer to you?"

Bran snorted, coughed, and looked fit to swallow his tongue, but Mark Allen didn't correct him.

Faye turned on the boy like a cat with its tail jerked.

Mark Allen stepped between them. "I thought maybe you were looking for something to do." He shrugged. "After all, you walked down here from the house."

"I am not a farmer."

"Neither am I. But I like to see things grow." He pointed to the sack. "And I think I shall enjoy tending to trees. 'Tisn't like they need plowing or planting every year."

She hesitated, then took a step closer to the sack and examined the seedlings. "And tending them will not require a horse."

"What do you have against horses?" Bran asked, stepping beside Mark Allen.

"They smell."

Mark Allen grabbed a handful of Bran's shirt and pulled him back, the boy fairly bristling at the insult to horses.

"They do have their own scent." He jerked Bran's shirt when the boy opened his mouth. "But it can be comforting when you are familiar with it."

She pointed at the loaded barrow. "I fail to see how that mess can be comforting."

"Perhaps not. That part of the horses is for growing things, like these seedlings."

Faye glanced at the house, then back at the sack, and finally turned to the hole he'd finished digging.

"So what will thee do next?"

He found it intriguing that she slipped into the Quaker speech when she calmed down, or maybe when she was interested in something. With her curly hair escaping its pins and the wind playing havoc with it, he could almost mistake her for Gwen. And then she turned her eyes to him.

Brown—not Gwen's blue.

Disappointment struck him in the middle.

Faye should march back to the house and mind her own business, but the idea didn't appeal to her. Neither did dirtying her hands in whatever muck those little trees needed. But she couldn't deny that the prospect of doing something had caught her attention.

And held it.

Whether it had been the excitement in Mark Allen's voice or the sparkle in his eyes while speaking about the trees, or if it were simply her need to out of her room—her need to do something—Faye didn't know. But in her mind's eye, she could see the square of land beside the paddock with neatly spaced rows of trees bearing apples each fall.

Then, out of nowhere, came an idea so preposterous she almost burst out in laughter.

"What do you call someone who owns and operates an orchard?" she asked.

Mark Allen rubbed the back of his neck. "An orchardist, I think."

"Are there women orchardists?"

Bran snorted again, but it turned into a howl of laughter.

Faye paid him no mind, keeping her attention fully on Mark Allen. The tall, lean man didn't move a muscle. Not so much as the flicker of an eyelid or twitch of a lip. He appeared to be considering her question seriously.

Was she serious? Well... why not? She needed something to do. Bridget and Olivia kept the house clean and neat—not that Faye had offered to help them with any tasks. Growing trees that would produce apples sounded interesting. It didn't require the use of a horse or spending the day bent over in a garden. One looked up at trees, not down. And they provided shade during the summer. The more the idea swirled in her head, the more eagerly she awaited Mark Allen's answer.

"I do not know," he finally said.

"How difficult can it be if thee and Bran are learning it?" As soon as the question slipped past her lips, she wished it back.

Lids dropping to darken his eyes, Mark Allen turned back to the work she'd interrupted, forcing the shovel deep into the damp earth without a word.

"Best you leave this to us men," Bran said. "Ain't no work for a woman."

"How do you know?"

"Women should keep house for a husband and have babies." The boy crossed his arms. "Everyone knows that."

"Bran." Mark Allen pointed to the sack.

The boy dropped to his knees and separated one of the saplings, handling it as if it were made of blown glass.

In spite of herself, Faye took a step nearer. She should be furious with the boy for talking to her in such a way, but could she fault him for describing the life she'd dreamed of? Keeping a house for a husband and raising his children were exactly what she'd forfeited when she'd left Pittsburgh.

If she could grow trees that would produce apples, then she could provide for herself. She could earn enough money to feed and clothe herself at least, and maybe at some point provide a house of her own. Not that Paul would turn her out, she had no fears of that. But she could be independent.

Maybe she didn't need a husband.

The thought shocked her.

Then it took root.

But with her unbridled tongue, she'd just burned the bridge that would have helped her reach that goal.

"Mark Allen?" He didn't answer, but he shot a glance in her direction, so she continued. "I only meant that I can learn as well, not that thee were limited in the ability to learn. I chose my words poorly when I spoke."

Bran harrumphed, and she bit her tongue to keep from responding.

Mark Allen took the spindly tree sapling and—to her disbelief and dismay—grabbed a huge handful of the manure from the barrow with his bare hand and slapped it into the hole. Then he shaped some of the dirt he'd taken from the hole into a mound over the manure. Onto that, he spread the wispy roots of the sapling before covering them with dirt he loosened and crumbled between his fingers. Then he filled the rest of the hole and packed the dirt down with his hands, leaving a shallow indent around the little tree's trunk. Still kneeling by the newly planted tree, he looked up at her.

"Are you willing to do all that?"

Faye swallowed. Was she?

Chapter 26

E ATING DINNER WITH THE house servants had been their practice since the first full day after arriving in Mount Pleasant, but it was still uncomfortable for Faye. Bridget and Olivia added little to the conversation, so perhaps they weren't entirely comfortable with the arrangements either, but Madam and Paul carried on as if it were the most natural course of events. At least Mark Allen and Bran continued to take their meals separately, Mark Allen claiming that it took too much time out of their work day to clean up and change to be presentable at the table.

Faye was reluctant to bring forth her idea for discussion with such an audience. After all, it was sure to be received as a preposterous notion.

Since Mark Allen had asked her if she could plant the trees, a full week had passed in which Faye occupied herself with visiting her sister and accompanying Paul on his "getting to know people" rounds. Even with things to distract her, the idea of owning an orchard hadn't let go. If anything, it'd gotten harder to ignore.

The only time both Madam and Paul were together for any length was at their evening meal. So if she was going to broach the subject, it would have to be under the scrutiny of Bridget and Olivia. Why their opinions mattered, she wasn't quite sure, but Faye pulled in a steadying breath and set her fork beside her plate.

"I have been thinking."

Four pairs of eyes rested on her, forks suspended halfway to mouths, several eyebrows raised. For heaven's sake, did they not consider her capable of thought?

"I wish to do something more than just... just occupy this house."

Madam dabbed at her mouth with a napkin, then folded and laid it aside. "What do thee have in mind, my dear?"

"Thee has been a help to me," Paul said. "My patients seem as eager to see thee as they do me. I would be pleased if thee accompanied me more often. Perhaps thee could even master the basics of nursing in time."

Faye did her best to suppress a shudder. Nursing—blood and sickness and dying—held no appeal to her whatsoever.

"There is a group of ladies among the Friends here working on projects to benefit—"

"I wish to learn to run an orchard." Oh, she shouldn't have interrupted. But none of them laughed, which gave her the courage to plunge on. "I wish to learn how to tend the trees and make cider and perhaps one day own an orchard of my own." She sat back in her chair, shoulders smacking into the unyielding wood.

Open-mouthed astonishment graced the faces around the table. Bridget and Olivia turned to Madam, but it was Paul who answered.

"A woman orchardist?" He rubbed his chin and studied her. "The Friends are comfortable with women holding roles in society that others would disapprove of. I see no reason why thee should not explore the possibility." He shrugged. "However, I have no knowledge of such things. We would need to find someone willing to train thee."

Faye was shocked but pleased at his acceptance. Maybe she shouldn't have been. No one had embraced being Quaker more wholeheartedly than Paul.

"Mark Allen is learning with the trees he planted for you. I could learn alongside him."

"My dear." Madam cleared her throat, "I agree with Paul that the Friends are more willing to accept a woman doing the unconventional, but for thee, an unwed woman, to work side by side with an unmarried man..." She shook her head. "I cannot believe that would go unnoticed, even among the Friends."

"Mother has a point."

"We would not be alone," Faye hastened to assure them, warming to her cause despite their tempered response to her announcement. After all, they hadn't rejected her idea out of hand. "Bran is always there, and we would be in sight of the house, just out the kitchen window. Bridget has a fine view of the orchard."

Bridget shot a glance between Faye, Paul, and Madam. "'Tis true enough that I see the garden and orchard and have watched the men working."

Faye blinked at the calm confidence—perhaps even approval—in the cook's tone. Did she have an ally?

"The best way to settle the matter is for me to speak with the elders," Paul said. "I shall inquire as to a convenient time to address the matter with them." He pulled his pocket watch from his waistcoat and clicked it open. "I have to leave, but I will attend to this at the proper time." He rose and left the room.

"Whatever prompted thee to wish to work with an orchard?" The bafflement in Madam's voice matched the wrinkles in her brow. Perhaps she wasn't as accepting of all their life changes as Paul.

"I'm not entirely sure." Faye picked up her fork and pushed the remaining asparagus spears around her plate. "But once the idea took hold, I could not shake it."

"A woman orchardist." Bridget smiled at Faye. "Who better to grow and nurture a livin' thing than a woman? If thee be askin' me, I say it makes perfect sense."

"'Tis stepping outside the norm," Olivia said without disapproval.

"Indeed." Madam rose. "I suppose the elders will know what is best. If thee will excuse us, Olivia and I have a meeting with the women's council. Betsy invited us to join them this evening." She turned to Faye before leaving. "I shall mention thy desire to work in the orchard to the women. In some matters, their word carries more weight than even that of the elders."

"Thank thee, Madam."

"I cannot say I understand. In my day, a young woman would not have dreamed of... But then, I have learned to see things differently since we embraced the Society of Friends." She shook her head. "'Tis not as if thee were purposing becoming a muleskinner or an undertaker." She left the room with Olivia.

Bridget glared at the half-emptied plates on the table. "While I support thy proposal, I might wish thee would have waited until they finished the meal. Why is it that a new idea stops a person's appetite?" Then she grinned at Faye. "But I suppose those chickens Paul brought home yesterday will eat well of the scraps."

Faye scrambled to her feet. "Let me take out the scraps and feed them since 'tis my fault there is so much."

Bridget's eyebrows soared to her hairline. Of course, Faye had never offered to help with the housework before. Not once. Yet another thing that had to change. If she were to one day have her own house, she'd need to learn everything about taking care of it. And she'd need to learn to cook as well.

Oddly enough, those thoughts didn't depress her spirits one bit.

The swish of cloth against grass was the only warning Mark Allen had of someone approaching. Squinting into the brightness of the rising sun, an image formed, and his breath caught in his throat. Then he blinked and the woman coming toward him, sunlight framing her in a brilliant halo, took the shape of Faye Morgan—not Gwen.

"Good morning, Mark Allen." Her voice was crisp and clean in the early morning stillness. She glanced at Bran. "And thee as well, Bran."

"Good morning." Bran barely glanced up from a seedling.

"You are out and about early." Mark Allen rose from where he'd been pulling grass and weeds away from the little apple trees. John Chapman had said to keep the other growth away from them for the first year so they would have no competition for water.

Faye folded her arms across her middle. "Would it harm thee to simply return my greeting?"

She was lecturing *him* on how to speak to another person? But she was right, and that kept his tongue civil. "Good morning, Faye." He touched the brim of his hat. "What can I do for you?"

"Maybe 'tis what I can do for thee." She smiled, and the resemblance to Gwen faded a bit. It was a genuine smile, maybe the first he'd ever seen from her, but her mouth quirked in its own shape, not a mimic of her sister's smile.

"How is that?"

"Paul has given me his permission, pending the consent of the elders, to learn to be an orchardist alongside thee."

Mark Allen stared at her for a long pause, sure she would burst out laughing at such a joke. But she didn't. In fact, her smile slipped, and a frown that bordered on a glare replaced it.

"Well, what have thee to say?" The haughty demand he'd come to associate with her was back in her voice.

"You want to be an orchardist?"

"Is that not what I just said?"

"I have never heard of a woman orchardist."

"Just how many orchardists do thee know?"

She had him there. Counting John Chapman, the sum total was exactly one. And he was a character if ever there was one. Perhaps a woman orchardist would be no more an oddity.

"Have you nothing to say?" Her voice has risen and hardened, dropping the Quaker thee.

"Are you willing to put your hands in the dirt?"

That reminder of her comment brought a deep flush to her cheeks that—if he were being honest—added to her beauty. How could she not be beautiful when she resembled Gwen?

"Of course I am." She brushed her hands down her dress. "'Tis why I am wearing this old dress. And I brought an old pair of gloves." She pulled a dingy pair of white leather gloves from the pocket tied at her waist.

White. For working in the dirt.

As for that dress being old, it looked plenty fashionable to Mark Allen, not that he knew the first thing about women's fashions. Gwen had always worn a servant's dress at the Whitefords', but it hadn't changed her loveliness. Not one bit. His hesitation must have come across as disapproval because her frown firmed into an eye-snapping glare.

"I am perfectly serious." One booted foot stamped the ground.

"Oh, I can see that." How was he supposed to approach the situation? "But for how long?"

"What do you mean?"

He could have shaved with the sharpness of her voice. He was making a hash of things, but what was he supposed to do? It was not a good situation.

Especially when she was a constant reminder of Gwen.

"We both know what you really want is to marry a rich man. What rich man is going to seek you out in an orchard?"

Her skin blanched to an alarming shade before she whirled and fled to the house.

Mark Allen wanted to kick himself.

"Guess you done put her in her place."

Bran's gleeful chuckle made Mark Allen wince. Not only had he been rude to Faye, but he'd been a poor example to Bran of how a man should treat a woman.

"I will need to apologize to her."

"Why?" Bran's eyebrows hiked and his voice broke on the word. Yet another sign that the boy was growing up—and needed a better role model than Mark Allen had just been.

"Because I was rude."

"Likely you was right."

"Even so, I should have been kind."

Bran snorted.

"Heed me on this—'tis always better to treat others with kindness. Your mother's book says as much." There were a lot of words in it about how to behave and other advice on living well. Mark Allen had read enough of it to have understood that much, and he'd not even reached the middle of it yet.

Bran hung his head for a moment, then looked up at Mark Allen. "Aye. 'Tis true."

"Maybe we both need to do some more reading in that book."

Maybe it even held some advice on how to get past a broken heart.

Gwen opened the door, surprise written across her face as she peered beyond Faye. "I did not hear the carriage."

"Because I walked." Faye pushed through the door and sank onto the bench beside the kitchen table. "The whole way." And she'd pay for that later if her aching feet were any indication. But at least the long walk had worked out most of her anger.

"Whyever did thee not ask for the carriage? 'Tis almost two miles."

"Because Mark Allen would have driven it, and I needed to get away from him."

"Oh?" The babe fussed, and Gwen lifted her from the cradle and soothed her while watching Faye.

"He is such a... an infuriating man."

"I never knew him to be that way." Gwen's tone grew puzzled. "He was always helpful, always considerate and kind."

"Because he was in love with thee." The words rushed out before Faye thought them through. She cringed. "I should not have said that. Thee are a married woman now."

"Aye." Gwen sat in the rocking chair Micah had made for her. Micah had made most of the furniture—as he'd built the entire cabin—for Gwen. "Mark Allen was my only friend for those years at the White-fords'. He wanted to be more, but I was focused on gaining my freedom and finding thee. I had no desire for more than his friendship. And then Owen entered my life and everything changed."

What was her sister saying? That Owen had come before Micah?

"I can see that I have shocked thee. 'Tis time I told thee the whole story."

Faye listened without uttering a word while Gwen explained the oath she'd given to take an unwanted babe and make him her own and how that had led her to the Quakers—including Micah Pike.

"I understand now that what I did was wrong, even if I did it for all the right reasons. But I did not. 'Twas a selfish thing that I thought would reunite me to thee."

"Thee may have saved the child from a much worse fate."

"Perhaps. We will never know. He may have had a better life. He may have ended up with a wealthy couple who could have lavished him with everything money can buy."

Faye reached across the space between them and squeezed her sister's hand. "Have I not seen thee and the boy together? Never have I witnessed a more loving example of mother and son." She straightened and clasped her hands together in her lap. "Not even our own mother and brothers."

Gwen's eyes grew misty. "Some days, I can barely remember what they looked like, our brothers."

Blinking back an answering dampness, Faye nodded. "Or Mother. What she smelled like, or the softness of her hair."

"'Tis what made me so desperate to find thee, my only living family."

Faye cringed inwardly. Her sister had been desperate to find her, while she'd been living a life of leisure and doing her best to forget she even had a sister. No wonder Mark Allen admired—loved—her sister and seldom had a kind word for Faye.

But when he did, those kindnesses had been unreserved and genuine.

Maybe that was why this morning's verbal scuffle had hurt so much. Or perhaps he'd just come too close to the truth. She'd wanted the husband and the standing and the perfect family in Pittsburgh. But she'd never get that now, and she could either weep her life away, or she could learn to run an orchard and stand on her own two feet.

Whether Mark Allen would help her or not.

But a part of her very much wished he would.

Sally Faye had fallen asleep during the story, so Gwen rose and laid her in the cradle. Then she joined Faye on the bench, arm around her back, bringing their heads close as they'd so often done as children.

"Mark Allen is a good man, he always was, but he was not the man for me. Perhaps, Faye, thee should decide if he might be the one for thee."

Faye didn't wrinkle her nose, even though the scent of horse came to mind with Mark Allen's name. "He does not care for me, sister, that much I can assure thee."

"Oh?"

"'Tis rare when we speak without it coming to raised voices."

"Why is that, do thee suppose?"

"The man thinks he knows what is best for everyone."

Gwen smiled, a soft chuckle following. "Aye, 'twould be like him." She gave Faye a squeeze. "But it comes from a good heart, remember that."

"Or perhaps from a broken one." Again, the words were out before Faye had thought them through.

Her sister sighed. "I cannot tell thee how much I regret that. I should have been more honest with him back then. I should have been more honest with everyone back then." She leaned against Faye. "I'm so glad thee have come here, however thee managed it. If not Mark Allen, I hope thee will find a man to settle down with and stay forever."

"I am planning on staying."

Gwen sat upright, her smile wide and bright.

"But I have no illusions that I shall find a husband on this frontier. I plan to make my own way by running an orchard of apple trees and producing cider."

Disbelief, confusion, and then, at last, joy sparked from her sister's dark blue eyes. "Thee always were the independent one. I have no doubt thee will succeed."

The pride in Gwen's voice rekindled Faye's resolve.

Chapter 27

"**A** WOMAN ORCHARDIST?" JOHN Chapman stuck a finger in his ear and gave it a good wriggle as if cleaning it, then he pulled the finger out and cocked his head. "Is that what you said?"

Mark Allen was second-guessing his decision to mention the situation to Chapman. "Indeed, and she is serious about it."

The laughter that followed was something between a donkey's bray and a coonhound's bawl. It carried across the shallow valley and likely right up to the doorposts in Mount Pleasant. When Mark Allen was convinced the skinny man would never stop, he let out one last gasp, bent double, and slapped both knees before straightening and mopping his eyes with the back of a sleeve.

If Faye were there, she'd have taken mortal offense. Mark Allen could almost see the fire in her dark eyes and her hands planted on her hips.

Chapman let out one last chuckle. "If that don't beat all."

"Then you think a woman cannot handle the job?"

"Nay." Chapman waved a hand. "I never said so. But you must admit, nobody but those Quakers would allow it."

"They look at things differently, 'tis a fact."

"The work she can do, but the land… are they willing to sell property to a woman?"

That hadn't even occurred to Mark Allen.

As he understood the matter from overhearing talk, the Quakers had purchased a large tract of land surrounding Mount Pleasant from the man who'd started the town. Many of the Quakers had purchased additional plots for houses in the town itself, those who wouldn't be earning their living off the land, like the wheelwright, Thomas. Those who would be farming would purchase the surrounding land from the Quaker Meeting—what they called their church—over time, as Gwen's husband was doing.

Mark Allen ignored the disgruntled feeling thoughts of that man always produced.

Faye would have to purchase land, as would Mark Allen if he stayed and made his life in Mount Pleasant. A man purchasing land was one thing, but a woman, that was something altogether different.

A woman could inherit land if her husband died, of course, but it would be handed down to their children, preferably a son, in due time. If it were handed down to a daughter, it would become her husband's property upon their marriage. If there were no children, then a brother or nephew or some other close relative would inherit. If none of those, the land would become the county's upon her death.

How was Faye going to talk the Quakers into selling her the needed acreage to start an orchard?

"But you think, if they do sell her the land, that she could manage an orchard on her own?"

Chapman squinted into the distance, then scrubbed his jaw as he looked back at Mark Allen. "Aye, a woman could handle most of it, especially at first when the trees are young, if she be not with children to chase after. Should she come to need a mature tree felled or a stump dug out, she could hire a man to do that."

If her property were close to his, Mark Allen could be that man. He wouldn't mind helping Faye. As irritating as she could be, she was also different from Gwen in a way that wasn't displeasing. He rather liked her spirit and feisty temper—when they weren't aimed at him.

Every twist and turn of his thoughts tightened him like a screw to this Ohio landscape. But looking over the valley, he could see the potential. If he could secure his land, get his trees planted, and continue to work for Paul until the apples matured enough to produce cider, he'd be a man of property and some importance within a decade.

He, Mark Allen Teed, son of a drunkard and former indentured servant.

Spurred on by that thought, he paid close attention as Chapman described the proper pruning, demonstrating on willow twigs, that would mean the difference between a proper orchard and an unkempt patch of trees.

By the time Mark Allen dragged himself into bed that evening, he'd decided on two things. He was going to make his living as an orchardist. And he was going to do it in Mount Pleasant, Ohio Territory. Therefore, he must resign himself to Gwen being there—married to someone else.

Faye rocked back and forth with Sally Faye against her shoulder, the infant sound asleep. It'd been two days since she'd confessed her desire to be a businesswoman to Gwen. Two days in which to worry and wonder if it would actually happen. Two days of Paul's advice to be patient and pray for God's will in the situation. Two things Faye knew herself to be incompetent at—patience and prayer. But the gentle rocking motion and the unique smell of her newly born niece combined to give her a sense of at least momentary contentment.

"She rests easy with thee." Gwen stirred a pot of pea soup at the hearth, its savory aroma adding to the peace and tranquility of the humble cabin. "I pray that someday thee has one of thy own."

"That would require a husband, and as discussed on my last visit, the prospects for one of those here on the frontier are slim." At least, the type of husband she'd always dreamed of.

While Gwen and Micah's cabin had a certain charm, it was a long step down even from the new doctor's house in Mount Pleasant. The walls were solid logs from trees Micah had cut to open more land for farming. The logs had been hewn square on all four sides, but there were still spaces between them that had been chinked with—of all things—a mixture of river clay, dried grass, and horse manure.

There was no way Faye would ever live in a house even partially constructed of horse manure.

"And I shall have my orchard to run."

"What excites thee so about tending trees?" Gwen crossed the room and sat in a chair near the rocker.

"'Tisn't really the trees, although I am interested in them. 'Tis the chance to provide for myself. To have something that will produce both food and income. 'Twill ensure I shall never be hungry again, or dependent upon another person for my survival."

Understanding dawned in her sister's eyes. They shared a look that required no words, the long, hungry days and nights while their father drank away what money he had before they'd boarded the ship that would take their father's life. And the hungry days of waiting on another ship to be sold like animals on an auction block. The shared grief, helplessness, and hopelessness they'd endured.

Gwen had overcome it, with her husband and her humble cabin.

Faye would overcome in a different way. Her way.

If the Quaker elders would agree.

He couldn't say that he'd grown entirely comfortable with the plainly dressed men seated in the meeting house discussing his future, but Mark Allen had grown to respect them. Listening to the elders discuss the available properties left in their land purchase, and which tract would best lend itself to an orchard, deepened that respect.

Knowledgeable men, as one would expect of elders in any form of a church, they were also kind and caring. They listened to him when he explained the needs of the land as he'd learned from Chapman. Suggestions were offered and discussed, and questions were raised. It was an unhurried, thoughtful, and thorough process.

So unlike Mark Allen's privately held convictions about religious people.

He'd not been around anyone religious as a child, his father having no use for those kinds of folks. The Whitefords had attended church every Sunday, but they hadn't encouraged any of the staff to attend. Arthur, as their driver, had sat in the balcony with the rest of the servants. He'd sometimes shared a bit about what was said with Mark Allen, but it hadn't made much sense.

The people Mark Allen knew who went to church on Sunday looked down on folks like him.

But not the Quakers. And it meant something. He wasn't exactly sure what, but it was something good. Something different. Something... right. He'd even learned while listening that they didn't hold with indentured servitude and more than slavery.

These men were willing to sell him a tract of land—to be paid when his cider business was up and running—and they barely knew him. Of course, Paul's word on his behalf was a large part of their trust in him. But deep down, Mark Allen was sure that wasn't the whole reason. These men of age and wisdom didn't see Mark Allen Teed as the son of a drunkard or the former indentured servant. They saw someone they thought would succeed in operating his own business for many years to come. Someone who would be a contributing member of their community.

It was a humbling and gratifying experience.

"And now, if we are agreed on that parcel, we should address the other issue," one of the elders said. Mark Allen couldn't remember all their names, but he made a mental note to do better in the future.

"Indeed." Thomas Baldwin stood and leaned over the map on the table, held flat with smooth river rocks on each corner. "In the case of Faye Morgan's request for a tract of land, it occurs to me that the land between Mark Allen's new claim and Micah Pike's farm would do nicely." He straightened and glanced at the other elders. "Micah, her sister's husband, would prove a good overseer of her assets until the girl comes of age, along with her guardian." He nodded to Paul. "And Mark Allen would be nearby to assist and advise with the business of her orchard—supervised by both Paul and Micah, of course." He resumed his seat.

"But the girl cannot own the land," another elder said. "As I under-stand, she is both unmarried and has not reached the age of majority."

Paul rose from the bench beside Mark Allen and cleared his throat. "The town has been so gracious to me and my family—including my ward, Faye Morgan. We are most appreciative of the house and barn thee provided for us. I would like to purchase the land for Faye's orchard. I will pass it off to her at the appropriate time, either when she reaches the age of majority, or when she marries."

"Do thee truly think she can make a success of an orchard?" Thomas asked.

"Indeed," Paul said. "Our Faye is a very determined young lady. If she sets her mind to it—and I believe she has—then she will see it through."

Determined. That certainly described her. Feisty and spoiled were also apt descriptions, but Mark Allen agreed that she could handle the orchard. She could do almost everything Chapman had explained to him, and he'd assist her with the rest.

The discussion that followed was short. They deemed Paul's idea a workable one, and all were in agreement.

Mark Allen rose when the others did and followed Paul from the meeting house to the horses. He swung aboard Jughead and waited for Paul to mount Storm before turning the gray toward home.

"Thee were quiet back there," Paul said.

"I was listening."

"And something more, I think." The man was perceptive. Maybe that made him a better doctor.

And maybe it was time to tell the whole truth.

"I have reservations about working with Micah Pike."

"Has thee an issue with the man?"

An issue? One could put it that way. Mark Allen rubbed the back of his neck. "I was indentured with Gwen Morgan—now Pike—at the Whitefords'. I arrived at your home in Pittsburgh looking for her sister, for Faye, to reunite them."

"Oh." Paul pulled Storm to a halt and faced him.

Mark Allen stopped Jughead. It was time to tell him everything. "I had promised Gwen years ago to help locate her sister. She was sold off, but I never forgot my promise."

Paul squinted in the dim evening light. "Thy promise? Or Gwen?"

"Both."

"Ah. I think I see the issue."

"My decision to start an orchard and stay in Mount Pleasant was difficult, but I believe it the right course for me."

"Made more difficult by this situation, the shared overseeing of Faye and her orchard with Micah? Will it change thy mind?"

"Nay." Once Mark Allen set his mind on something, he followed through with it. "I have decided to stay."

Even if it meant working alongside Micah Pike.

"Do sit down, my dear, before thee wears a path in our new floor-boards." Madam glanced at Faye over the top of her needlework.

Faye dropped onto the chair opposite the fireplace from Madam. "What is taking them so long?"

"They are men, dear." Madam chuckled. "While they claim 'tis women who chatter like magpies, the truth is, they are prone to do the same when gathered together."

"I dislike waiting."

"Everyone does. But I believe it builds character, not having everything at thy fingertips the moment thee wishes it." Madam let her needlework rest in her lap. "All those years I spent doing frivolous things, things that mattered not in any true sense of importance, things that helped no one in need."

It hurt to watch Madam reflect on her former life in such a way. "Thee helped me."

"Oh, my dear. That was one of the few truly good deeds I ever did. How I wish now I would have known of thy sister at the time, but, of course, I could not have attended the sale myself." She fanned her face with one hand. "To even think of being there in the vile place—"

"Which is why I desire a business of my own so much. With a business to support myself, I shall never again face an uncertain future."

"If only that were true."

Faye stiffened in her chair. "What do thee mean?"

"My dear, businesses are not easy to manage." She shook her head. "Many fail, leaving their owners in a poor state, indeed."

"Mine will not." If determination alone could secure her future, Faye's orchard would be the richest of them all. "I am willing to do whatever it takes to make my trees the best producers."

Before Madam could reply, the clomp of hooves reached them.

Faye bolted from the chair and opened the door as Paul dismounted. "What did they say?"

"A moment, Faye." He handed Mark Allen his reins. "Have Bran tend to the horses so thee can join us."

Mark Allen took the beasts away.

"Paul—"

"When Mark Allen returns, I shall tell thee all, but it involves him, so we must wait." He gave her an encouraging smile. "Be patient. 'Tis good news."

More waiting. But at least she knew she was waiting for good news.

Paul took the chair Faye had left, so she sat on the chair beside Madam's.

And waited.

How long did it take to pass the reins to the boy?

At long last, boots thumped on the porch.

Faye hurried to the door and flung it open before Mark Allen could knock. "Come in, we are waiting." She didn't even try to keep the impatience from her voice.

His eyebrows raised, but he slipped off his hat and entered.

"Come in, please." Paul motioned to the chair beside his. "Have a seat."

Mark Allen looked as uncomfortable as Faye was impatient, but he sat and turned his hat in his hands.

Faye returned to her chair and fiddled with the worn edge of her sleeve.

"Now that thee are both here," Paul said, "let me explain to Faye what has been decided. The elders are in agreement with thy orchard, Faye."

Faye clasped her hands under her chin and waited for the "but" that lingered in his tone. He'd said good news—not *all* good news.

"But..."

And there it was.

"Thee are still my ward and have not reached majority age." When she hauled in a breath to respond, he silenced her with raised a finger. "Thee are nearly eighteen, but still a full three years short of the mark. Therefore, I have purchased the land for thee, and 'twill remain in my name until thee marries or until thee reaches thy majority. On this, there will be no argument."

"That is very good of thee," Madam said. "A perfectly acceptable way to provide for Faye."

But the whole point was—Faye wished to provide for herself.

"There is more." Paul gestured to Mark Allen. "Mark Allen's land will border thy land on the west while Micah Pike's land will border thee on the east. The Elders agree that thee shall be under my guardianship, supervised by myself and thy brother-in-law, and under the tutelage of Mark Allen. I believe this to be a very agreeable arrangement."

Faye wanted to sputter out a whole list of disagreements, but in truth, the settlement the elders had reached was more than fair. Far more than she'd have gotten in a non-Quaker community. Their generosity in allowing a woman—a young unmarried woman—such an opportunity wasn't lost on her.

Neither was the brooding look directed at her by Mark Allen.

Chapter 28

MARK ALLEN RODE JUGHEAD through the tract of land he'd been allowed by the elders. Hardwoods and conifers littered the landscape, along with willow, assorted low-growing brush, and brambles. Plenty of brambles. It was typical of the countryside, nothing special except for the creek that wound through it. The same creek that hooked around Gwen's farm.

Gwen and Micah's.

He stopped Jughead and surveyed the clearing that fell naturally in the middle of his land.

His land.

The old horse jerked up its head, ears swiveled to the front.

"What is it, boy?" Mark Allen patted the gray neck.

Jughead blew out a breath, and movement caught Mark Allen's eye. A youth, for he was too small to be else, darted from behind a tree and dashed away, hand holding a floppy hat in place and bare feet visible as he leaped a fallen tree. Dark hand. Dark feet.

An escaped slave?

The free territory would attract them, for sure.

It was none of Mark Allen's business.

The land was. He'd have to clear a few trees and plenty of brush, but it wasn't dense forest, and if he got started right away, he could have it cleared by fall.

Something waved in the breeze in the middle of the clearing.

With a gentle nudge of his heels, he sent Jughead forward to check it out. The old horse perked his ears when they got close, nostrils flared. He snorted and shook his head.

"What is it, boy?" Mark Allen dismounted at approached the burlap sack wedged into the crotch of a small tree. Its top, above a strip of leather used to tie it shut, fluttered in a gust of wind. A slip of paper was caught beneath the leather. Mark Allen worked it loose and unfolded it.

Mark Allen,

Time for me to move on. More apples to plant. Here is a bag of seeds for you and the gal. I will return next year to see how you are faring.

J. Chapman

Mark Allen rubbed the back of his neck. How had the man known this was his land? Had he sent the youth to deliver the sack? Mark Allen opened it to expose its treasure of shining brown seeds, each one capable of producing an apple tree.

Jughead snorted behind him.

"They may smell like apples, but these are not for you." He tied the bag and secured it behind his saddle.

"Thee knows what is said about a man who speaks to his horse, does thee not?" Zachary rode toward him on a long-legged mule. The animal was harnessed, not saddled. "Some say that his saddle has begun to slip."

Mark Allen grinned. "Hello, Zachary." He tied Jughead to a tree and then approached the man and mule. "What brings you out here?"

"'Tis well known thee are starting an orchard." He patted a pack strapped to the harness behind him. "I have come with tools to lend thee a hand." He drew his leg over the neck of the mule and slid down her side. He patted the beast. "Annabelle is very experienced at skidding trees."

Mark Allen hadn't even thought about how to move the trees and brush he planned to cut. How unexpected—and humbling—that someone he'd barely met was willing to come and work alongside him.

"Can thee use one more?"

Riding through the brush came another man, sitting on a heavy draft horse. Behind him, he led another horse carrying a pack, and both were harnessed for work.

Micah Pike.

Mark Allen's first reaction was the wrong one, and he knew it, so he squashed it as surely as if he'd ground it into the dirt with his boot heel. This was Gwen's husband, but also a neighbor, and Mark Allen had made his choice to stay. If they were going to be neighbors, they had better be neighborly.

The way Micah waited for an answer, not dismounting, said he recognized the same thing. Perhaps he wasn't happy to have Mark Allen nearby. That would take some time to ponder, but this was a time for action. Mark Allen cleared his throat. "I'm much obliged for the help."

Micah dismounted and led the horses forward. "And perhaps when we are done here, we can start on Faye's orchard. The three of us can clear a lot of land."

"Indeed." Zachary seemed to size up both Mark Allen and Micah. Then he tipped his chin toward the sack Mark Allen had found. "What is that?"

"A gift of apple seeds from John Chapman. More than enough for both Faye and me to start our orchards."

Zachary rubbed his hands together. "I can almost taste the cider now."

"'Twill be a boon to the community to have an orchard—two even—for those who cannot produce their own apples," Micah said. "Or those of us who have not the time for making cider."

"'Tis true." Zachary agreed. "Milking cows and tending fields more than fills my days."

"You have a dairy?" Mark Allen asked.

"Indeed, he does. He brought west some of the best shorthorn cows ever seen." Micah raised both hands. "Not that I want to milk cows. Happy I am to be able to purchase milk from thee. I will content myself to raising corn, oats, wheat, and next year I shall plant flax."

Zachary's brow wrinkled. "I thought thee seed to plant flax this spring."

"I did." Micah wagged his head. "But my wife's goat ate it. Every last seed."

Zachary's laugh filled the clearing. "'Tis why I milk cows—and not goats."

"Enough about that." Micah turned to Mark Allen. "Where would thee like us to start?"

And just like that, Mark Allen was thrust into the role of crew boss. He pointed to several areas where all they needed to cut and remove was brush, most not more than shoulder height, and they set to work with axes. The steady *thwack* of steel biting deep into green wood rang over the land.

Zachary used Annabelle to drag the growing piles of brush to one corner of the clearing while Mark Allen and Micah kept cutting. Sweat poured from Mark Allen, but each satisfying *thwack* felt good. He was working his own land beside men who knew what they were doing. Like a well-trained team of horses, they didn't need words, each moving in a pattern that made the work flow smoothly.

Micah arched his back and shielded his eyes from the sun. "My stomach says 'tis lunchtime, and the sun appears to agree."

Zachary removed his hat, wiped his brow, and resettled the hat. "Indeed. I could drink half that creek dry."

"I wish I had something to offer you—"

"Worry not." Micah raised a hand as he walked to his pack. "Gwen anticipated our needs."

Gwen. The name hit him, but it didn't hurt quite as much as it had before. That was progress.

"Zachary." He turned to the other man to take his mind off of Gwen. "There was a boy here, half-grown at best, when I arrived. Could be an escaped slave. He ran off in that direction." Mark Allen pointed.

Zachary glanced that way, back at Mark Allen. "Does thee wish to report it to the elders?"

"What?" Mark Allen retreated a step. "Nay. I have no desire to see any man—or woman either—kept in bondage."

"Then best to forget what thee saw." Yet Zachary's eyes were troubled.

Did that mean he knew something about the boy?

"Eat up." Micah returned and handed each man a cloth-wrapped bundle containing cheese, bread, and a thick slice of bacon.

Gwen had known there would be three of them?

So this hadn't been by happenstance. Mark Allen bowed his head for the long Quaker silent prayer. *"Thank You, God, for sending these men to assist me."*

It felt strange and yet right at the same time, both the help from two such different men and his first attempt at a prayer.

"I do not see why I was not allowed to join them." Faye jabbed her needle into the piece she was stitching, pricking her finger underneath. "Oh." She popped the offended digit into her mouth.

"Because thee has no business clearing land." Weariness filled Paul's voice, whether from the day he'd had or her refusal to let the matter go, it was hard to say.

"There must have been something I could have done."

"My dear, thee would have had to ride a horse to get there." Madam raised her brows in a silent plea for Faye to drop her argument.

And she was right. Faye rubbed her pricked finger against her apron, and when no blood appeared, she returned to stitching by candlelight. As any gently raised young woman, she was proficient at stitching. It was coming in handy here on the frontier, where every window was in want of a covering. And the house had a surprising number of windows.

In truth, the whole town was much more civilized than Faye had imagined. Even the houses made of logs had glass windows. Her house would too, once her orchard was running profitably and she could afford to build it. Of milled boards, not logs chinked with any nasty concoction.

She had little idea what went into the production of cider past pressing the apples, but she would learn. Barrels would be required, of course. Mount Pleasant had a cooper—a barrel maker—and Paul said the man had two apprentices in training, so proper barrels could be purchased from him. A press might be harder to come by, but there were two blacksmiths in town. Surely one of them would know how to create a press. Extracting juice from the hard apples would take a strong piece of equipment—and probably a strong man to run it, but she'd worry about that later. The general store would have cheesecloth for straining the cider and funnels for pouring and...

Excitement over her new occupation made it difficult to sit and hem a curtain in the glow of the candle beside her.

But she couldn't get her orchard up and running if she wasn't allowed on the property. Her property. Well, it would be her property when she turned twenty and one. Or married, but that wasn't going to happen. She could finally see a future for herself in Mount Pleasant, a future bright with promise, but a very different future than she'd imagined while walking the decks of the ship returning from Scotland.

Very different, indeed.

And when the men started clearing *her* land, she had every intention of being there.

Even if she had to walk the whole way.

"I don't know why you think you need to attend the meetin'." Bran sulked on his bunk in their room at the back of the stable.

Mark Allen straightened his clean neckcloth, using the jagged corner of a broken mirror that Bridget had given him. Then he brushed back his hair and secured it with its leather tie.

"I want to see what 'tis all about."

"I told you, I listened in once. They don't say much at all, and when one finally speaks, it don't make sense."

"You should not spy on people."

Bran snorted. "It ain't spyin' when they say 'tis a public meeting."

The boy was probably right.

"And they even let them women speak." Bran's face, just visible at the mirror's edge, scrunched into a frown. "Ain't supposed to let women talk in church."

Mark Allen spun around. "What?"

"Says so in the Bible." The boy patted his pocket where he carried the old book.

"I have not read that."

"You ain't read far enough yet." Bran stretched and put his feet on the floor. "Ma set great store by the words therein."

"Then why do you not attend church?"

Bran looked out the window, lips pressed together.

There was a lot Mark Allen didn't know about Bran. And things were probably best that way. Figuring the boy wouldn't answer, he reached for his coat.

"Wait. I will go with you."

"Make haste while I hitch the team and saddle Storm."

Bran hopped onto the high seat beside him as Mark Allen clicked to the team and drove the carriage to the front of the house. Paul assisted the ladies into the carriage before he untied Storm from behind and mounted.

Within minutes, they were on the road to the meeting house, the largest brick building on the far side of town. Men and women walked toward the building like a black and gray wave that sunny morning, the women's white shoulder scarves and bonnets fluttering like the white curls atop the wave. Others approached in wagons and on horseback.

The McClures' carriage looked out of place amid them. Paul had been right to question it, and there had been some tongues wagging, but by and large, the town seemed to have accepted their new doctor and his family.

They'd even accepted his hired help.

Mark Allen nodded to those he recognized, still a little surprised when others returned his silent greeting. Being an indentured servant meant being little better than a slave, it meant that people had seen right through him. These people didn't. And he knew that it wasn't his changed status from indentured to employed that mattered to them. They saw him as an equal in the eyes of their God.

The God he felt drawn to learn more about.

Faye squeezed onto the end of the bench next to Gwen and held her hands out for little Sally Faye. Owen, being older, sat next to Micah on the men's side. The babe was asleep but snuggled into her aunt's arms as if she belonged there. A stab of envy for what she wouldn't have pierced Faye for a fleeting moment, but knowing her niece would grow up next door to her was the next best thing to having a babe of her own.

How was CeCe faring? She must be heavy with child. Faye should write to her. She'd do it that very afternoon.

A familiar figure entered the room on the men's side. Mark Allen. What was he doing at the meeting? He wasn't a Quaker—a Friend. Faye needed to remember to use the term Friend, as those who were members of the Society of Friends did.

Bran entered behind Mark Allen.

Really, that was too much. She leaned over and whispered in Gwen's ear, "They are not Friends. Why are they here?"

Gwen whispered back, "Perhaps they will be soon."

Was everyone turning Quaker? And why did it irritate Faye? She swayed gently on the bench to soothe the sleeping babe while an elder called the meeting to begin and then took his seat. Silence fell over the room. As usual, it lingered for a while before someone stood to speak. The gentleman spoke at length on the topic of a servant's heart.

Wasn't that what Faye was aiming for? To serve her community by owning and operating an orchard to provide cider—a needed commodity?

Guilt picked at her.

She hadn't wished for the orchard to help others but to help herself. She shot a glance over her shoulder at Mark Allen, whose rapt expression said he was hanging on the man's every word. Young Bran, on the other hand, noticed her and smirked.

Faye jerked back around, startling her niece who protested by mewling.

Gwen took the babe and moved past Faye. There was a quiet room at the back where mothers could attend to their babes.

Her arms empty, Faye snuck another glance across the room, but Mark Allen was still engrossed with the speaker while Bran—the impudent boy—was grinning at her.

Was it because he saw through her and knew her to be a fraud?

Gwen was a true believer in the Quaker—Friends' way, as were Paul and Madam, Olivia and Bridget. Even the dark one who didn't like her, the man who'd met them at the river.

Why were they all so sure about God and she wasn't?

And why did it suddenly bother her?

Chapter 29

M ARK ALLEN WORKED IN the garden and tended to the orchard most mornings, so Faye was up early the Monday following his presence at the meeting and walking the short path to the garden by the time the sun was fully above the tree line.

Bran saw her first, his mouth dropping open.

"Close it or thee will swallow a gnat." She brushed past him and swatted at the annoying insects that hovered in front of her face. "Good morning, Mark Allen."

Mark Allen straightened and faced her. "What can I do for you?"

"'Tisn't what thee can do for me, 'tis what I can do for thee." She almost giggled at the silly rhyme the Quaker speech made of that sentence. She spread her hands. "I am here to help with the garden."

"You want to work? In the garden?" Disbelief colored his words. "In the dirt?"

She pulled gloves from her pocket and worked her hands into them. "Indeed, I came prepared."

"Know you the difference between a carrot and a weed?" Bran asked, then leaned over and spit.

"Do not spit." Mark Allen's words were for the boy, but he never took his eyes off of Faye. "Why?"

"I am ready to learn so I can be the best orchardist in this area."

Bran snorted.

"Bran, catch Storm and give him a good grooming. Paul may have need of him today."

The boy poked his thumbs through his suspenders. "Glad to." Then he sauntered away.

"Thee needn't have sent him away." But Faye wasn't sorry to see the impudent boy go.

"If you are here to *work*, two pairs of hands in the garden are enough."

She bristled at the stress he put on the word work, but then smoothed her apron with her gloved hands. "I am ready."

"Good."

Two hours later, with sweat dribbling down her temples, her knees aching, and smelly dirt covering her gloves, she wasn't sure she'd ever be able to straighten her back again.

To give the girl credit, Faye had done everything Mark Allen told her needed to be done. Even more surprising, she'd listened intently when he'd explained about the different types of seedlings poking through the soil. She'd jerked out one pea vine along with a weed, but he'd reseated the vine. They were resilient, so it should survive. Even if it didn't, they had plenty of peas planted. Losing one wouldn't hurt the harvest.

The kitchen door banged, and Bridget approached with a pitcher and basket. She often brought him and Bran a bucket of cold water and a dipper to refresh them as the day grew hot. Faye must rate a little more refreshment.

He glanced at the woman kneeling beside him. The pang that her resemblance to Gwen brought was still there, but faint.

Faye wiped the back of her gloved hand across her cheek to brush the wayward curls from its dampness, leaving behind a smudge of dirt. She was one of those women who even wore dirt well, looking industrious rather than frumpy. Hand pressed to the small of her back, she stood and knocked the dirt from her gloves before removing them.

"Bridget, thee are a saint."

"For sure and for certain, thee be needing a bit of refreshment by now." Bridget set the basket on the ground, then lifted out two mugs and poured amber liquid into both before handing them over. "There be bread and cheese under the linen if thee get hungry."

She'd never brought him and Bran bread and cheese. But then, Bran usually found a reason to visit the kitchen and bring it back himself.

Mark Allen accepted one of the mugs and drank down half its contents, the refreshing small beer that Bridget brewed two or three times a week. Its tang and slight fizz stripped the dust from his tongue and cleansed his dry throat.

"The garden has taken shape." Bridget walked down one side and back. "Thee has the knack for growing things, Mark Allen. 'Tis good to have such a man around the place, is it not, Faye?"

Heat crept up from his collar, intensifying when Faye turned a measuring stare at him, then looked at Bridget, and back to him, one eyebrow rising. Did she think he and Bridget...?

"Indeed." Faye sent a smile to Bridget. "For if we did not, we might all starve. Paul cannot pull his head out of his medical books long enough to poke a finger in the dirt."

"When he is home, poor man." Bridget pointed down the road. "Off to see more patients today, he is. How the citizens of Mount Pleasant survived without him is a mystery for the ages."

"I expect the novelty of the new doctor will wear off with time, and people will rediscover that they can make a poultice and bandage a cut without him." Faye finished the last of her drink. "Are we done for the day, Mark Allen?"

They hadn't even started weeding the corn patch yet, but Faye was pressing her hand to her back again, so she needed to stop. She wasn't used to hard work—not like her sister.

Not like her sister at all.

"Indeed." He handed the mug to Bridget. "I need to oil the carriage harness yet this morning, and then if you ladies have no need of me, I shall ride over to my property and spend the afternoon there."

"Very good." Faye lifted the basket and returned to the kitchen with Bridget. Stained skirts swishing in the grass, swaying with each step.

"Uh-huh."

Bran's voice pulled Mark Allen away from the mesmerizing motion. Where had the boy come from?

"Paul says I be free to go with you this afternoon if you want to work your land and ain't too busy watchin' those women."

Mark Allen cleared his throat. "You fetch the basket back from Bridget while I saddle Jughead." He strode to the corral and whistled to the horse. The harness would wait. There was work to be done. Work on *his* land. And he had Bran to help.

That added a little bounce to his steps—because it couldn't be for any other reason.

Faye moaned as she lowered herself into the warm water of the copper tub screened off in a corner of the kitchen. Everyone but Madam bathed there. Gone were the days when servants dragged a tub into her bedroom and carried water up and down the stairs. Olivia insisted that Madam still bathe in her room, appearing scandalized when Madam had suggested otherwise, but no one had offered to do the carrying for Faye. She'd resented it at first, naturally, but after working in the garden, she'd have willingly bathed in the creek beyond the corral.

Not the creek. She gave a soft snort.

"Is the water too hot?" Bridget asked from the other side of the blankets strung over a length of rope that formed the screen.

"'Tis perfect." And it was, seeping into her muscles and probably to her very bones. Although the day was warm enough, her aches enjoyed the water's additional heat.

Who knew garden work would be so much... work? Every stretch and pull and chopping at weeds with the instrument Mark Allen had given her—she didn't even know what it was called—had taken its toll. How did the man do it day after day? And the boy. Surely she should be able to keep up with the scrawny likes of him.

"Hmmm, I wonder who that be?" Bridget said.

"Who?" Faye squished a wash rag in the water and let it dribble over her shoulders.

"A boy in a hat too large for him."

Faye paused. "A dark-skinned boy?"

"Indeed."

"I saw him once before. Do thee think he could be an escaped slave?"

"Poor dear, if so, he be in a good place now here in Mount Pleasant."

"Where even a woman can own an orchard." Faye smiled at the thought.

"Ah, yes. I overheard Mark Allen telling Paul that they should be ready to start clearing thy land on Saturday next," Bridget said.

The soreness fell away as Faye bolted upright in the tub, sloshing water over its rim. Water she'd have to mop up herself, but she didn't care. Not with such exciting news. "This coming Saturday?"

"Aye. They be making good time what with the extra help from Zachary and Micah."

"Then I must be there." She started to rise, dropping the hard bar of soap on the floor.

"Finish thy bath." Bridget chuckled. "'Tis five days away."

Five days. In just five days, her future would begin. She had to be there. She wouldn't let the men keep her away. She'd spend the rest of the week working with Mark Allen and proving she was helpful. Proving that she could do the work.

She sank back into the tub and raised her hands. Redness marred the skin. If she hadn't worn gloves, she'd have blisters.

Faye Morgan—with blisters.

What would CeCe say?

What did it matter? She wasn't the Faye Morgan who'd left Pittsburgh anymore. She was the Faye Morgan of Mount Pleasant, the future orchardist.

A woman who would take care of herself.

One lone tall tree remained to come down. Mark Allen had half a mind to leave it because of its size, not so big around, but very tall. It would shade too much of the new orchard, stunting the little apple trees. As intimidating as it was, he needed to bring it down.

Zachary and Micah had shown him how to fell the big trees. They'd also cautioned him of the dangers. He wet his finger and stuck it above his head. The wind was out of the west and not too strong. A strong wind might catch a tree and twist it, taking it down in a direction other than the one planned. He and Bran had cleared everything around the towering giant, so there was nothing to damage even if it did fall wrong.

Except for themselves, of course.

"Move Jughead over there." He pointed to the edge of the clearing, well out of danger.

Bran untied the horse and walked him clear before tethering him and returning.

Mark Allen still hadn't moved. He had a bad feeling about that tree. What was it the second man to speak had said at the meeting? Listening to a "small voice" when one needed guidance from the Lord. Mark Allen didn't know what that meant, and his bad feeling wasn't a voice, so he needed to get on with felling the tree.

"We gonna cut that thing down or ain't we?"

The boy was right. Mark Allen was just spooked. What happened in a Quaker meeting had nothing to do with felling a tree. He hoped.

"Stand back." He hefted the ax and swung, the iron biting deep into the green wood. His muscles, strengthened by days of such labor, strained at his shirtsleeves. He worked until he had a perfect notch on the east side of the tree about one-third through the trunk.

Bran brought him a bucket and dipper, then looked up into the tree's branches. "I wonder how old this tree be?"

"Old." Mark Allen drained several dippers of water, then removed his hat and poured more water over his head, shaking like a dog.

"Hey!" Bran danced out of the way. "It ain't Saturday night yet, and I don't need no bath."

Mark Allen sniffed but didn't answer. The boy had a true aversion to soap, but maybe he could shove Bran in the creek when they were done and get the worst of the sweat off him. It'd smell better in their room, at least.

He replaced his hat and chugged one last dipper of water. Then he nodded toward Jughead. "Best you wait over there."

"I ain't no kid." Bran hefted the smaller ax Mark Allen had brought. "I can help with the felling cut."

As a team, two men made alternating cuts slightly higher than the first notch on the opposite side of the tree, chopping until it tumbled.

That bad feeling returned and sent a quiver across Mark Allen's skin. "I think it best you wait with Jughead."

Bran's mulish expression settled over his features. "You don't think I can pull my weight."

That wasn't it at all. Bran was a good worker, a fast learner, and surprisingly strong for such a small youth. Mark Allen rubbed the back of his neck. He didn't like it, but he understood the boy's need to prove himself.

"If I say run, you drop that ax and run to Jughead, you hear me?"

Bran tightened his grip on the ax. "You do the same."

Mark Allen stepped to one side of the tree and planted his feet.

Bran did the same on the other side, facing Mark Allen.

"Ready?" Mark Allen asked.

Bran nodded.

Thwack. Mark Allen's ax bit into the wood, and then he wrenched it free. *Thwack.* Bran's ax followed suit. *Thwack. Thwack.* It became like a dance, each partner swinging in rhythm with the other. Blood pumped through Mark Allen, his muscles working, breath coming deep and steady.

Then a crack—louder than a rifle shot—split the air.

The Widow Maker.

Mark Allen shouted, "Run!" He looked up as he dropped his ax and ran. The top of the tree had broken and was plunging straight down toward them.

"Bran!" The boy was running, legs pumping, arms swinging—ax still in hand. "Drop the ax!" Maybe he couldn't hear over the crashing of the tree top through the lower branches, or maybe he was too terror-stricken to hear, but he didn't let go of the ax.

The weight of it slowed him down.

Mark Allen veered toward Bran who was behind him already, but the treetop got to them first. Branches fell around Mark Allen, blocking his view, one colliding with his shoulder and sending him to the ground. Two other branches landed on top of him.

Then came an unearthly silence.

Chapter 30

"BRAN?" MARK ALLEN SHOVED at a branch that held him to the ground. "Bran!" He shoved again, ignoring the spike of pain in his shoulder. The branch moved, not much, but enough for him to wiggle out from under it. He staggered to his feet, jerking his shirtsleeve free and ignoring the rip. "Bran!"

The only answer was the snapping of twigs as Mark Allen extracted himself from the tangle of branches, some broken free of the tree, others still attached to the treetop. Once he could see above the wreckage, Mark Allen rubbed the grit from his eyes and searched the area. The treetop had landed on its side, branches piled up all around, leaves blocking his view.

"Bran!" He forced his way through branches as the pounding of horse hooves reached him.

Micah raced astride one of the huge beasts, the two animals harnessed together. He must have been working a field close enough to hear the tree break. He pulled the horses to a halt in front of Mark Allen and jumped to the ground. "Are thee injured?"

"Not I. Bran is in there somewhere. He will not answer me."

A stricken expression flashed across the other man's face before he turned to his team. "I will tether the horses until we find him, then we will see how to proceed."

"Can we not start moving the debris?"

Micah turned to face him and shook his head. "Were we to shift the wrong piece, we could make things worse... if he is still alive."

If.

Bran had to be alive.

"Bran!" Mark Allen shouted again, then waded back into the tangle.

"Easy!" Micah called after him. "Move as little as thee can."

Mark Allen slowed down. *Lord, help me find him.* The words came to his mind—not his mouth—but the Quakers prayed in silence, so it seemed fitting.

A moan came from the dense tangle to his right.

"I heard him! Bran!"

"Where?" Micah yelled.

"There." Mark Allen pointed.

Micah ran around the bulk of the debris and worked in at an angle to Mark Allen, both of them calling the boy's name at intervals.

There was no answer.

Then Mark Allen spied a bit of fabric—Bran's shirt. "There he is." He pointed to the spot almost midway between them.

"I see him." Micah waded into a thick patch of branches, knocking the leafy parts out of his way.

Mark Allen's way was blocked by the main trunk of the treetop. Frustrated, he backed up and worked his way around it.

"He is breathing!" Micah hollered.

Relief washed over Mark Allen. He pressed harder through the tangled limbs. "Can you reach him?"

"Not yet." There was a pause followed by a loud snap. "There are so many broken branches, 'tis difficult."

"But you can see him?"

"Indeed. He appears to be hemmed in, but not crushed. There is a lot of blood in his hair."

Mark Allen plowed through a thick layer of smaller branches, crashing through like a bull moose. He had to see Bran for himself. Head wounds bled something awful, so it might not be as bad as it looked. *Please, Lord.* The words came to his mind as if on their own.

Or was it the small voice?

With a final heave against a large branch, he saw Bran.

Covered in blood.

It amazed Faye how the memories—memories she'd worked for years to bury—resurfaced as she plunged her hands into the bread dough, its stretchy softness giving way beneath her fingers. She could almost feel her mother's presence behind her, as if, should she turn her head fast enough, she might catch a glimpse.

"If thee keeps progressing, I fear I shall be in need of new employment."

It was Bridget's voice, not Mother's, but the praise still brought a warm flush. Once, long ago, Faye had been happy to do such work. How had she forgotten that? How had she let herself be changed into the selfish, shallow creature she'd been in Pittsburgh?

She'd become like the other girls her age growing up in a well-to-do household. And if she'd had her way, she'd still be there, her only ambition to secure a man to care for her for the rest of her life. A man who smelled nice and did little other than go to his club, attend social activities, and occasionally bet on the horses.

Not a man like Mark Allen, with his muscled shoulders and work-roughened hands. Mark Allen would help Faye obtain her dreams by teaching her, not giving to her. He could be extremely irritating, but also kind and thoughtful. When Bridget had told her the account of how he'd met and cared for Bran—the account Bridget had gotten straight from Bran himself—it had further softened Faye's heart toward Mark Allen.

She let her flour-covered hands rest on the kneaded dough.

As much as she'd resented Paul for hauling her away from Pittsburgh and all she'd thought were necessary for security and happiness, gratitude filled her for her guardian's insistence. Had he known how much better things would be for her here? In a place and among a people who would accept her for who she was—and who she'd been—and not for the persona she'd developed that had enabled her to blend in?

A persona she'd taken great pride in.

Dear Gwen hadn't changed—not one bit. Her sister had remained true to herself while a servant as well as after she'd been set free.

It shamed Faye that she had fallen so far short.

"What be the cause of that long face, I wonder?" Bridget's voice cut through Faye's thoughts.

"Woolgathering." Faye brushed away the regrets, firm in the knowledge that her sister loved her, Paul and Madam loved her, Bridget was becoming the friend CeCe never could be, and Mark Allen was going to help her start her orchard.

Pounding on the door startled her and Bridget.

"Let me see to that." Bridget wiped her hands on a towel as she left the room.

"We need the doctor, now."

Micah's raised voice shot fear through Faye, and she rushed to the door. Was it Gwen? Sally Faye or Owen?

"...the treetop broke off above them and came down like a spear," Micah was explaining.

Not Gwen or the children then, but the fear didn't dissipate. "Mark Allen?"

"Scratched and bruised, but young Bran"—Micah looked past her and Bridget as if he'd find Paul behind them—"is in a bad way."

It wasn't Mark Allen. Faye pushed the wave of relief away as Bridget paled at the news of Bran.

"Paul rode out about fifteen minutes ago," Faye said, "heading for William and Elizabeth's place."

Micah whirled and shouted over his shoulder, "I will catch up to him there."

Bridget stalked to the kitchen and stripped off her apron. "I'm going to hitch the team and drive the wagon out there."

"Shall I go with thee?"

Bridget gripped her upper arms. "Stay here and start a restorative broth with the chicken hanging in the larder."

Faye must have grimaced.

"Thee can do this. Cut the bird up and put it in the pot with plenty of water, stoke the fire and swing the pot over it until it boils, then back it off but keep it boiling. I will help thee finish it when I return."

Not sure her tongue would form any words, Faye nodded. She was being left in charge of the kitchen, and she wouldn't let Bridget down.

The woman was attached to Bran as if he were her own family.

Bridget hurried out the back door while Faye blinked suspicious dampness away. Perhaps Bran had wiggled his way into more than just Bridget's affections. The scamp. If broth would help, then Faye needed to get moving.

But thank God, Mark Allen was all right.

Mark Allen crouched beside Bran. He and Micah had worked the lad free of the wreckage with the help of the heavy workhorses, but other than a single moan when Mark Allen had lifted him and carried him a safe distance from the unstable branches, Bran hadn't moved or made a sound. His chest rose and fell with comforting regularity, however, and the blood that matted his hair had clotted and stopped the bleeding.

But the eerie silence was difficult to bear.

One knee pressed into the fertile soil, the other supporting his elbow, Mark Allen bowed his head and prayed. He begged the Lord Bran's life. He didn't stop or move until the thunder of hooves and rattle of wagon wheels reached him.

Bridget held the reins of the horses as if she'd been born to it, the expression on her face a mixture of gritty determination and fear.

He rose and grabbed Buster's bridle as she pulled the team to a halt. Before he could offer assistance, she vaulted to the ground and rushed to Bran's side.

Mark Allen set the brake and secured the lines before joining her.

Tears streaked her face as she smoothed Bran's hair from his face. Her lips moved without words. Was she praying too? He hoped so. God was more likely to listen to her than he was to Mark Allen, her being a Quaker and all.

Micah and Paul rode up a few moments later. Paul swung off of Storm, tossed Micah the reins, and ran to their side.

"How is he?"

"He breathes," Mark Allen said, "but he has not opened his eyes or made a sound other than a groan."

The doctor worked his hands up and down Bran's body, pausing and probing in several places, undoing his shirt and examining his skin. "Has anyone water?"

"I do." Mark Allen sprinted to Jughead and removed the canteen behind his saddle, then raced back, fumbling to remove the cork. "Here." He pressed it into Paul's waiting hand.

"I have cloth in my—" Paul's words hung in the air as Bridget tore a strip from her petticoat and handed it over. "Thank thee." He didn't look up but kept his attention on Bran as he wetted the cloth and cleaned the blood from the boy's head.

So much blood.

Mark Allen wasn't squeamish, but this was Bran. He looked away and breathed in deeply through his nose.

Micah touched his arm through the almost ripped-off sleeve. "Let us give Paul more space." He ushered Mark Allen a few steps away. "Thee had blanched as white as dandelion fluff."

Mark Allen swallowed and glanced at Bran again. "'Tis just... so much blood. And Bran, he..." At a loss for words to explain, he finished with a shrug.

"Bran means much to thee. Anyone can see that."

"I should not have allowed him to help cut the tree."

"Blame not thyself." Micah moved to block his view of Bran so Mark Allen. "'Twas an accident, pure and simple."

"A Widow Maker."

"Indeed, that is what most call it. It happens sometimes. Even a healthy tree can have a weak spot. Thee were not to know this one would break off high up and come plunging down."

Mark Allen studied the toes of his boots. "I knew it was possible."

"Many things are possible. The boy could be injured every time he harnesses or saddles a horse, but thee cannot forbid him to do so."

"He is just a boy."

"Older than he looks, I think."

"Aye, he is. Small for his age, but with the heart of a man."

"A lucky man to have a friend so devoted." Micah cocked his head, a wry twist to his lips. "I can see why Gwen is so fond of thee."

That snapped up Mark Allen's head.

"Thy arrival unsettled me at first." The other man shrugged. "What husband would not worry when a man his wife has spoken highly of comes to town?"

Gwen had spoken highly of him? While the words were nice to hear, they didn't overcome Mark Allen's concern for Bran. He was resigned to the loss of Gwen, was learning to be content with his present situation, and was looking forward to his future in Mount Pleasant—a future that was supposed to include Bran.

"For years," Mark Allen said, "Gwen was my only friend. Once, I thought maybe more, but 'twas not to be. It pleases me to see her with a good man like you." His words came without thought, but Mark Allen meant them. "Faye tells me that she is happy, and what more could I wish for her?"

"I am glad we have cleared the air between us, Mark Allen, for I would like to call thee friend as well."

Mark Allen extended his hand and grimaced when Micah gripped it.

"Ah, thee are not unscathed, I see."

"My shoulder, but 'tis nothing, not compared to..." He glanced past Micah to where Paul and Bridget were still hunched over a motionless Bran.

"He is between God's will and Paul's skill now," Micah said. "I have been praying."

"As have I." His response drew a smile from his new friend.

"Mark Allen, bring the wagon close," Paul called to him. "We will get him home now."

"Has he come round?"

Paul shook his head, mouth in a grim line.

"Will he?"

"Only time will tell."

Within moments, Bran was transferred to the wagon, head pillowed on Bridget's lap, Paul on his other side. Mark Allen clicked to the horses, keeping them at a slow walk as Paul had instructed. He searched the road ahead for any hole or rock or crevice to avoid.

He couldn't imagine life in Mount Pleasant—or anywhere else—without Bran at his side. Even Faye was softening toward the lad. And the three of them had such plans for the orchards.

Bran had to survive.

Faye paced the kitchen, stopping every so often to stir the chicken she'd hacked into bits. She'd been too young to be trusted with a knife when they'd left Wales, so she had no memories to fall back on for that task. The mangled bits looked nothing like Bridget's neat pieces, but they were for broth so it shouldn't matter.

The front door opened and Faye hurried to see if Paul and Bridget needed help—but it was Madam and Olivia who entered.

"Oh," she said.

"Thee appear flushed, my dear," Madam said. "Has something happened?"

"Aye, 'tis Bran. The boy was injured cutting down a tree. Bridget left with the wagon and Micah to fetch Paul over an hour past."

"Oh, my." Olivia pressed her hand to her collar. "Bridget must be beside herself. She dotes on that boy."

"We should prepare a bed for him," Madam said, "in case Paul wishes to keep him close for the night."

"He can have mine." The words were out before Faye could give thought to them.

"Thee can share my room until he is well," Madam said. "And we should start a broth."

Olivia sniffed. "'Twould appear someone already has."

"I have." Faye might have been annoyed by the astonished looks they directed at her, but she didn't have time. "I will strip my bedding and put on fresh." She headed for the stairs.

"I will tend the broth," Olivia said.

"Then I shall assist Faye." Madam followed her up the stairs and into her room. "I must say, my dear, thee are becoming an industrious—and generous—young woman."

The praise in her tone warmed Faye to her toes.

"I think thee are right." Faye smiled at the woman who had shown her such kindness—even motherly love. "And I have thee and Paul to thank for it. If not for thee, I might have been—"

"Hush, my dear. Paul and I would have had it no other way. Thee are family to us."

Family. Madam and Paul along with Gwen—not in place of her. And Gwen had her extended family as well with Micah, the children, and the Baldwins. And then there were Olivia, Bridget, Mark Allen, and...

If she needn't worry about Bran, things would be perfect.

Chapter 31

"I WILL SEE THAT a bed is readied." Paul jumped from the back of the wagon as Mark Allen stopped the horses and set the brake.

Mark Allen climbed down and looked over the side of the wagon box. "I did the best I could."

"Thee are not to blame for the ruts in the road." Bridget's voice was strained, her eyes tight with worry.

Mark Allen let the tailgate down and reached for Bran. "Slide him toward me."

For a moment, he thought she might insist on carrying the boy herself, but with the gentlest of movements, she did as he said.

Mark Allen lifted Bran. He'd gained weight since the first time Mark Allen had pulled him up on Jughead. Grown too, like a leggy colt.

"All is ready." Paul called from the doorway. "Bring him in."

Inside, Faye waited at the top of the stairs, hands twisting the apron at her waist. "Bring him up here."

"To thy room?" Bridget asked, following Mark Allen up the steps.

"Indeed, we have readied it." Faye stepped aside and motioned Mark Allen through the doorway.

The room was filled with sunlight, the bed neatly made with the blanket turned back. Mark Allen lowered Bran onto it.

Behind him, Paul said, "Thee can wait downstairs while I give him a thorough examination."

"I will stay." Bridget planted herself at the foot of the bed, chin lifted as if daring Paul to throw her out.

"Of course." He bent over the bed but spoke to the rest of them. "But only Bridget."

"Come." Faye tugged on Mark Allen's sleeve. "Give Paul room to work." There was something like... tenderness in her voice.

He looked at Bridget, but her eyes never left Bran's face. If Paul would only allow one to remain, it should be her. She had grown so attached to Bran. Mark Allen had, too, but he would step aside for her. After all, Bran didn't have a mother, and when one was ill, a woman's touch could make a difference.

Or so he'd been told.

Faye tugged at his sleeve again, and he followed her from the room, waiting while she eased the door closed with a slight click.

"She practically ran out the door when Micah arrived," Faye said. "She hitched the horses by herself and had whipped them into a run by the time they reached the street."

"Bran is in good hands with Paul and Bridget." Mark Allen glanced back at the door. "She is quite a woman."

Silence followed his words.

Mark Allen's words of admiration came at Faye as if they'd been fired from a cannon, crashing through her outer layer of newly found confidence and purpose. Or maybe it was his tone, so full of admiration for Bridget. She was quite a woman, all right, and quickly becoming a good friend, but to hear her praises from Mark Allen... stung.

Why?

A moment of clarity silenced her.

Mark Allen had chastised Faye, lectured her, criticized her, and even belittled her on occasion, but he'd never once admired her.

It stung that he admired someone else.

No. She had to be fully honest with herself. It stung that he admired another *woman*.

"I have broth to see to in the kitchen." She whirled and scampered down the stairs, very aware of the thump of his boot heels behind her. She whisked through the doorway and straight to the hearth, grabbing the wooden spoon and giving the concoction a vicious stir. Some of the liquid splashed out and sizzled on the logs.

"Are you cooking?" Mark Allen's voice rose on the last word.

She dropped the spoon back into the pot, folded her arms, and faced him. "Thee think me too inept?"

He took a step backward, hands half raised. "I did not say so."

"Thee may as well have."

"'Tis just that I did not think you were—"

"Quite a woman?"

A flush rose from his collar and washed across his face. "I meant no disrespect."

"Did thee not?"

"Nay." He stood straighter. "I have never been disrespectful to you."

She glared at him. "Never?"

He rubbed the back of his neck, not quite meeting her eyes. "Never intentionally."

"Even when lecturing me about my sister?"

Olivia entered the kitchen, looked from Faye to Mark Allen, and then backed out of the room.

Tongues were going to wag under this roof tonight, but Faye didn't care. She stepped close enough to Mark Allen that she had to crane her neck to see his face, his waistcoat almost touching her apron's bib, her toes between his.

"I may have been selfish, I may have been useless, I may have had my hopes set in the wrong direction, but in case thee have not noticed, Mark Allen Teed, I am not that same woman anymore." She jabbed her finger at the floor. "I can make broth. I can bake bread. I can tend the chickens." She jabbed her finger into the fabric of his waistcoat and the hard muscles beneath it. "And thee well know I can work in the garden and tend to the saplings. In fact"—she gave his chest one more poke—"I am quite a woman too."

Words spent, she turned and gave the broth another stir.

Mark Allen retreated and the front door banged shut.

Then she wilted, one hand on the mantel to keep her balance.

"Well done." Olivia's voice was soft, but firm. "Thee are indeed a young woman to be reckoned with, Faye Morgan, and glad I am to have seen thy transformation."

Faye cringed while staring into the fire. "'Twas a long time coming."

"Nay, I think 'twas at exactly the right time." Olivia looked over Faye's shoulder. "Let me help thee with the broth."

"I wish thee would." She lifted her eyes to the older woman. "I have no idea how to finish it. Bridget only told me how to start."

"'Tisn't difficult." Olivia gathered what she needed, then faced Faye. "Seeing thee stand up for thyself was inspiring. Never let anyone speak down to thee. As the Friends have taught us, we are all equal in God's sight."

"Do thee believe that?"

"Indeed, I do. And thee should too." The older woman handed Faye an odd-looking bowl with wire mesh in the bottom. "Now let us finish this broth before that youngster awakens."

"Will he awaken?"

"Only God knows for sure, but Martha and I were just praying for him."

Madam and Olivia had been praying. Bridget was assisting Paul. And Faye had gotten into a shouting match with Mark Allen.

The last of her righteous indignation fled, along with what remained of her newly acquired self-confidence.

The chores done and daylight gone, Mark Allen sat at the table in the back room of the stable and stared at the wooden walls. Alone. After the dressing-down from Faye, he'd busied himself with every chore he could think of, alternating between worry for Bran and simmering anger.

Anger for the harsh words Faye had hurled at him, punctuated by her finger in his chest. Anger at himself for being guilty of everything she'd accused him of. And anger that he didn't know what to do to make things better.

Because although he hadn't realized it until then, he'd come to enjoy time spent with Faye.

When had she stopped reminding him of Gwen? Had it been when she'd plunged those ridiculous white gloves into the dirt for the first time? Or when she'd knelt beside him, pulling grass away from the saplings? Or maybe when she'd laughed at something Bran had said while they worked instead of scowling at him.

Whenever it had happened, it had.

Her lashing out at him had come from the pain he had caused her. Shame washed over him.

"Mark Allen?" Bridget's voice jerked him from his thoughts. "Are thee back there?"

He rose and opened the door to the stable. "Is it Bran?"

"Aye." Her smile was wide, her eyes shining. "He be talking to Paul and hungry as an ox."

"Then he was not hurt too badly?" Relief rolled over him.

"Nay, but a curious thing, he remembers nothing of the accident." Her brow wrinkled. "Paul says that may be temporary—or not. But either way, he will recover."

"Thank God."

"Aye, and I have." She gestured to the house. "Come and see for thyself."

"I do not think..."

"Come. The row between thee and Faye will blow over, as such things do."

"But I have said some things I should not have."

"And what person among us has not?" She gestured again. "Bran will rest easier after he sees thee. He awoke worried for thee, although he could not say why."

For Bran, Mark Allen would go to the house. He followed Bridget across the yard, into the house, and up the stairs.

Nestled in the bed, head swathed in bandages, Bran glanced up when he entered the room. The boy's cheeks were pale, but his eyes were bright, and his gap-toothed grin greeted Mark Allen. A sight for sore eyes, for sure.

"They told me you took no harm." Bran pointed to the spot on Mark Allen's shoulder where blood had soaked through his shirt.

"'Tis not but a scratch. You, on the other hand." Mark Allen cleared his throat of the emotions that threatened to choke him.

"I'm sorry." Bran's voice wobbled on the last word. "I forgot to drop the ax. Guess I ain't ready to be much help to you in the orchard."

Mark Allen strode close to the bed and dropped to his knees, clasping Bran's hand. "There is no one I would rather have beside me helping to build the orchard."

Bran's grin returned. "Not even Faye?"

Bran needn't worry about that. Whatever might have been building between Mark Allen and Faye, he'd squashed in the kitchen earlier.

Faye sat on the top step of the porch. Cricket song filled the air and frogs croaked at each other from the creek. Voices drifted from upstairs but were too low for her to understand. She could pick out the low rumble of Mark Allen's voice and the Irish lilt of Bridget's. Both were relieved that Bran had awakened—and so was Faye.

But the harsh words between her and Mark Allen hung heavily around her. Why did they so often blow up at each other? She no longer looked down on him and was ashamed she ever had. He was honest and straightforward, and he'd demonstrated his loyalty by his promise to Gwen. He kept himself clean and tidy, and even though he smelled of horses, she was getting used to it. His kindness came through in a way that sometimes left a lump in her throat.

And something else—a yearning in her heart.

But he loved Gwen.

The door opened behind her and shut with a click.

She didn't turn. The faint odor of horse announced who approached.

"Faye." His voice was soft and maybe a touch uncertain. Was he afraid she'd turn and snap at him again?

"'Tis a peaceful evening to sit outside." Her training in the art of small talk kicked in. When one didn't know what to say, it was always safe to discuss the weather.

"Indeed." The porch boards moved beneath her as he approached. "May I join you?"

She scooted to the side of the broad step. "Paul says Bran will recover fully in a few days."

"Aye, and I'm glad to hear it." He rubbed the back of his neck, facing away from her. "'Twas my fault he got hurt."

She touched his sleeve. "'Twas an accident. Micah and Paul both said so."

"I should have insisted he stay back with Jughead. He is just a boy."

"Were thee chopping trees at his age?"

He faced her. "Nay, I was indentured as a stable boy."

"And could one of the horses in thy care have injured thee?"

"Of course, but 'tis not the same."

"How is it different?"

"Because..." His word dragged out. "Because I was the one who could have prevented it."

An old feeling welled up that she had suppressed for years. A feeling she'd never even spoken of to Gwen. Guilt. Deep and strong and as wrong-headed as what the man beside her was feeling. She pressed a hand to her middle, the memories almost a physical pain.

"When my father died on the boat, I knew 'twas my fault."

Mark Allen leaned closer to her, his voice soft. "I thought he died of an illness?"

"The boat was cold at night, and I had begged him for another blanket to cover Gwen and me." She lifted her face to the sky, the stars bright overhead. Did Father look down at them? Was he listening? Did he forgive her? "He gave us his blanket to stop my whining. Six evenings later, they slid his body into the sea."

Mark Allen put an arm around her shaking shoulders and drew her to his side.

She leaned against him and let the tears flow silently, not bothering to wipe them away. At length, the shaking stopped and the tears dried.

Mark Allen's chin rested on the crown of her head, his breath moving her hair. "You were a child, Faye. Your father gave you the blanket because he loved you. He was an adult and knew the risks. He loved you enough to risk dying for you. There is no greater love than that."

No greater love. She'd heard that phrase before. "'Tis from the Bible, is it not?"

"I believe so. Someone quoted it at the meeting. I learned to read from Bran's Bible, but I do not remember reading that. I admit, most of the things I read made little sense, but now, hearing your story, I understand that one."

She moved away from the heat of his body. "And would thee have risked your life to save Bran's?"

His hazel eyes were clear in the moonlight. "Aye. I would."

"Then perhaps all is well between thee and him."

He hung his head for a moment. "And between you and me? Can all be well?"

Her heart fluttered against her ribs. "Indeed. I wish I had not spoken as I did in the—"

"Nay. 'Twas my fault. I spoke without thinking."

"Thee were upset over Bran."

"'Tis no excuse."

She held out her hand. "Friends again?"

His work-roughened and warm hand enveloped hers, holding and not shaking it. "I would like that."

A flurry of uncertain emotions swirled within her. She needed to get control of them. She was finally learning she didn't need a man. In fact, she was on the verge of earning her independence.

And besides, Mark Allen was in love with her sister.

Chapter 32

T HE DAYS SETTLED INTO a routine for Mark Allen. In the mornings, he worked at the McClures, caring for the horses and equipment, working in the garden and tending the young orchard trees, and driving the women whenever they needed him. Once his duties to Paul were fulfilled, he mounted Jughead and headed for his property. On Saturdays—which Paul had deemed his day off—Mark Allen was joined by Zachary and Micah. Even with their farms to work, they carved out that day each week to chop trees and skid them away from the future orchard site.

But this Saturday was different. They were to start clearing Faye's property.

Which probably explained her waiting outside the stable as he stepped through the door, saddle and saddle blanket hoisted on his shoulder, ignoring the flush of pleasure just seeing her brought to him.

"I wish to go with thee." Her chin was tilted up, her eyes catching the early morning light.

"Paul says Bran must stay in bed for a few more days." He walked past her toward the corral. "You can ride behind me if you like." He whistled to Jughead, and the old gray perked his ears before heading toward the gate. In the full heat of summer, the horses stayed out all night and grazed while it was cooler.

Her skirts swished in the grass behind him. "Mark Allen, I am perfectly serious."

"As am I." He shook the bridle off his arm, entered the corral, and slipped it over the gray's head. After all, he couldn't take the wagon without Paul's permission. Or maybe he enjoyed teasing her too much—because of course Paul would give his permission if Faye wished it.

"Thee knows full well that I cannot ride."

He tossed the saddle blanket and then the saddle across Jughead's back, reaching under to pull up the cinch. "All you need to do is sit." He grinned at her. "Jughead and I will do the rest."

"I cannot get on that"—she stabbed a finger toward his horse—"beast."

"Why are you so afraid of horses?" He led Jughead out of the corral and closed the gate. "Jughead here is as gentle as a lamb."

Her nose wrinkled, but her eyes tossed flames at him.

And he liked seeing it, that feisty side of her.

"'Tisn't that I am afraid. 'Tis only that I have an aversion to their smell."

He hiked an eyebrow, and her face flamed scarlet. The little liar. She was scared spitless but would rather stamp her foot and pretend anger.

He liked that too.

"Maybe you could borrow a bit of Bridget's cotton wool and plug your nostrils until we arrive." He did his best to keep a straight face as he lifted each of Jughead's feet for cleaning.

"Mark Allen Teed, thee are the most—"

"Faye?" Paul came around the corner of the stable. "What are thee doing out here at this hour?"

Mark Allen dropped the horse's last cleaned hoof and dusted off his hands, looking from Faye to Paul and back again. Things could get interesting.

She planted her hands on her shapely hips as she swung to face her guardian. "I wish to oversee my land being cleared. Would thee please allow us to borrow the wagon and horses for the day?"

Paul rubbed his chin, and Mark Allen had the sneaking feeling he was hiding a smile by the action. Perhaps he had heard their conversation before he made himself known.

"Well, I do not suppose thee should ask poor old Jughead to carry both of thee plus the ax and shovel and whatever other tools thee needs." He nodded. "If Micah will be there, then by all means, take Faye in the wagon."

It was no wonder Faye'd been so spoiled. Paul didn't seem able to refuse her anything—other than remaining in Pittsburgh, of course.

"Do you need Storm saddled?" Mark Allen asked.

Paul waved off the question. "'Tis thy day off, and I know thee are anxious to get started on Faye's land. I can saddle him myself."

He was anxious to get started, but as he stripped the gear from Jughead and brought out Ben and Buster, the bounce in his step might have had as much to do with the feisty woman waiting for him to get the team hitched as it did clearing the land.

He almost stumbled at the thought.

They had smoothed things over the night of Bran's accident and agreed to be friends, but when had he started looking forward to spending time with her?

With her skirts secured beneath her on the hard seat, Faye waited for Mark Allen to load the tools he needed. Tools to clear her land of trees. Tools to start on her future.

Bridget exited the kitchen door with a basket in her hands and approached the wagon. "Thee will have need of a proper meal."

Mark Allen took the basket, giving a soft grunt at its weight before he placed it in the back. "Thank you."

Bridget stepped closer to the wagon seat and whispered to Faye. "'Tis good thee are going to see thy land. Well done." Then she winked and whisked away, returning to the kitchen.

Faye warmed at the woman's approval. She'd been making an effort to be more helpful around the house as well as in the kitchen over the past weeks. She'd discovered she enjoyed cooking and baking—at least with Bridget supervising so she didn't mess up.

Or maybe she just enjoyed the time spent with Bridget, who had become more friend than servant. Or perhaps, more Friend.

She pressed her lips together as Mark Allen climbed onto the seat and untied the reins. But it was no use. She was going to ask the question that had been needling her since they'd talked on the steps and mentioned the Bible.

"Why did thee attend meeting last Sunday?"

He shot her a glance, then clicked to the horses and got them moving.

Faye waited, but all he did was fiddle with the reins between his fingers.

"Will thee answer me?"

"Why do you attend?

She stiffened at his question. "Because I am a member. I joined the Society of Friends with Paul and Madam while in Edinburgh."

He turned to her, hazel eyes probing and earnest. "But you do not believe as they do." It wasn't a question.

And she couldn't deny it.

It wasn't the conversation Mark Allen had planned to have with Faye on the drive. He'd thought they'd talk of their future orchards, and maybe he'd even get her eyes flashing again with a little teasing. She was fetching when her dander was up and the color bloomed on her cheeks.

Instead, she grew pale at his accusation that she was not a true believer.

"I meant no disrespect." He didn't want a repeat of the disaster the other night. "I am not a believer either, as you well know."

"Then why did thee attend?" Her voice was softer, almost pleading, as if his answer mattered to her.

He took his time and collected his thoughts. He didn't want to tell her less than the truth, but he wasn't sure he knew the whole truth.

"Thee does not need to answer if 'tis something private."

"Nay. 'Tisn't that. 'Tis just a difficult question to wrap my mind around."

"Why?"

Indeed. Why? "Because I felt... drawn." He shook his head. "I suppose that sounds odd enough."

"Nay. 'Tis how I felt in Scotland."

Mark Allen pulled the wagon to the side of the road. They'd moved past the town, and they wouldn't be blocking anyone's way.

"You did?"

Color rushed into Faye's cheeks, but she didn't lower her face. Her dark eyes remained on his, and in their depths might have been understanding.

"Then why do you not believe now?"

She looked across the rolling hills. "Paul's excitement was contagious, at first. Madam's, too, as she followed his lead. To listen to them speak, one thought becoming a Quaker would solve all of life's problems."

"But it didn't." Of course it didn't, or she'd be in Pittsburgh instead of Mount Pleasant.

Faye shook her head, several dark curls escaping from beneath her cap just like what used to happen to Gwen.

As Gwen's name came to mind, he braced for the familiar rush of pain. But it didn't come. And the memory of her gentle blue eyes turned into the snapping brown eyes of her sister

"I was disappointed," she said. "But I think I am changing my mind on that."

"Because?"

"I have decided that coming to Mount Pleasant was the best decision for me." She wrung her hands in her lap. "'Tis hard to explain, but everything I thought I wanted for my future now seems"—she shrugged—"not so very important after all. Paul was right to bring me here. The Quakers, they are right to believe that people are equal—as God intended—and not separated by class."

The dark boy in the floppy hat crossed the road in front of them, holding the hand of a young girl and towing her behind as they slipped into a grove of trees. Who was he?

"Or the color of our skin," she finished after the pair disappeared.

That was the last thing Mark Allen had expected to her say. Had he truly heard her correctly? "You think you will be happy here?"

The smile she gave him was sincere and open and entirely Faye without a trace of Gwen. "I do. And I have thee to thank for much of it, for thy help starting my orchard, even for the very idea of an orchard at all."

Mark Allen sat a little taller on the seat.

Zachary and Micah were waiting when they arrived. Faye'd been the reason Mark Allen was late. Next time, she'd make sure he knew the evening before that she'd be attending so he could have the wagon ready.

She hopped off without waiting for his assistance and steadied herself against the wheel in surprise. What would CeCe have to say about that? What would Madam? Then she laughed and headed for the two men leaning against their axes.

"Good morning. 'Tis exciting to see my land be cleared. I cannot thank thee enough for thy help."

"Pleased to be of service." Micah gave her a half bow and a smile. "Besides, my wife would pin my ears should I neglect the needs of her beloved sister."

Faye pushed down the guilt that still pricked her when she thought of how she'd treated Gwen.

"Excuse me, it looks as if Mark Allen could use a hand." Micah left Faye and Zachary.

It was time to clear the air between them, but Faye was at a loss on how to start. After all, he'd clearly disapproved of her when he'd first met her at Roberts Landing. Maybe small talk would bridge the gap.

"I have seen a young man with very dark skin and a large hat around the area. This morning, he had a little girl with him."

"Where did thee see him?" Zachary's voice was calm and measured.

"On the way here, not far outside of town. They went into a woodlot. Do thee believe he could be an escaped slave?"

The sides of his mouth pulled down, but his voice came with the same measured calmness as before. "There are many who will make their way to this free Northwest Territory. And many will die in the attempt. Others will be hauled back into bondage and wish they had died."

A shiver crept over Faye's skin. "They risk everything for freedom."

"They have nothing, if they have not freedom."

"Gwen took a great risk for her freedom." At his raised brow, she continued, "She told me her story, about Owen, about lying to the Friends, and about being forgiven."

"She was repentant, and we Friends forgive those who are." His lips pulled to one side in a half smile. "But I am biased where thy sister is concerned. She saved my life."

"Oh." Gwen hadn't mentioned that.

"Thee should ask her sometime. 'Tis more her story to tell than mine." He picked up his ax as if to leave.

Faye touched his sleeve. "We did not start off on the best footing, thee and I. For my part in that, I wish to apologize."

He cocked his head, dark eyes searching her face. Then he gave a single nod. "Thee have grown since arriving here, which has been noticed by many."

"Indeed, in many ways. I believe..." She took a deep breath and plowed ahead. "Perhaps the most important being a new understanding about what it means to be a Quaker. That is, what it means to truly believe."

His smile was wide and welcoming. "Then welcome, Faye Morgan, to Mount Pleasant and to the Society of Friends here."

"Are thee going to chatter all morning, or cut trees?" Micah called.

Zachary hollered back, "Shall we see who can fell the most this forenoon?"

Faye followed Zachary to where the other men had unhitched the team and unloaded tools. "What shall I do?" she asked.

"Do?" Mark Allen gave her a blank look.

"Indeed. I did not come to stand and watch."

It was Zachary who answered. "Thee will need to stand far back when the trees start to fall, but thee can show us where thee would like us to stack the logs for future use."

"Future use?"

"For building," Mark Allen said. "You will need a building for the cider press. Not for some time, of course, but we can stack the logs near where you wish the building to be."

Not for a house then. What a relief. She may have reconciled—embraced even—her new way of living and working with her hands, but she wasn't going to live in a building of logs chinked with some nasty

FREEDOM'S PRIDE 257

concoction. Plenty of Quakers owned nice houses.

"Do thee have any suggestions?" Because she really had no clue what an appropriate site would be.

"Someplace near the creek, I should think," Micah said.

"But not in the marsh," Zachary added.

"And not too far from where we are cutting." Mark Allen glanced around the area. "The farther we have to move them, the longer the process will take."

Faye ticked off their advice on her fingers. "Near the creek, not in the marsh, close by. I shall see what I can find."

"Once that is settled, thee can always walk over to visit Gwen and the children. They would be happy to see thee." Micah winked at her before shouldering his ax.

"Perhaps I shall."

She studied Mark Allen's face as he reached for his ax. If Gwen's name had caused him any pain, he didn't show it. Yet while Zachary and Micah walked away talking and pointing to trees, Mark Allen silently followed in their wake.

Would he ever recover from loving her sister?

Chapter 33

F AYE ROCKED SALLY FAYE as Gwen prepared their tea. After stomping around a large portion of her property to find the best spot for a building, and then the walk to Micah and Gwen's house, she was happy to be off her feet. Perhaps her boots, so stylish back in Pittsburgh, would need to be replaced with something sturdier.

She and her boots had something in common. Both had to be more practical to be successful in Mount Pleasant.

"What brings such a smile to thy face?" Gwen asked as she placed a teacup on the table beside the rocking chair.

"Woolgathering." She didn't need to rehash all her former short-comings with her sister.

"Ah, I had hoped it might be thoughts of a certain young man who is at this moment working to clear thy land."

"Zachary has been most helpful." Faye took a sip of tea, watching Gwen over the rim of her cup.

"Thee knows I speak of Mark Allen." Gwen sat and picked up her own cup. "And should two people I care deeply about come to find happiness with each other, 'twould please me greatly."

"Thee still care deeply for Mark Allen?" The idea unsettled Faye.

"Indeed. And if he were to become my brother-in-law, I would welcome him with open arms."

"What would Micah say about that?" The attitude she'd witnessed between the two men that morning had been one of manly cama-raderie, quite unlike their first meeting.

"I should think he would be pleased to have Mark Allen as a broth-er-in-law. 'Twould seem the two have made their peace."

"And thee?" Faye had to know. "Thee have let go any tender feelings for Mark Allen?"

Gwen set her cup down and stared out the window for a moment before turning back to Faye. "If I ever had such feelings, they were fleeting. He was my best friend, my confidant, and much more a brotherly figure than ever a romantic one. It saddens me that I failed to express that adequately to him when I had the chance. 'Twas unfair to him to leave him with such expectations."

"Thee could never be unfair to anyone. 'Tisn't in thee."

Gwen bowed her head, hands clasped in her lap. "I almost was once."

"Tell me about it." Anything to turn the conversation away from Mark Allen.

Gwen poured out a story of slave hunters who had planned to kidnap Zachary, and how she had kept secret what she'd overheard in an effort to protect herself. But in the end, she hadn't been able to sustain her deceit. It was like some fanciful fairytale, so unlike the sister Faye knew, she'd have had trouble believing it if Zachary hadn't hinted earlier that Gwen had saved his life.

"I am ashamed of what I almost let happen." Gwen ended her story.

"But thee did not go through with it. Thee did the right thing in the end." Sally Faye sighed in her sleep against Faye's shoulder. "Zachary told me thee saved his life."

"I could not have without the support of Thomas and Betsy, without the faith and support of the Friends."

"And now the Friends are supporting me in my endeavors, and I am finally beginning to understand their faith."

"But, did thee not join the Friends while in Scotland?"

"I did, but it did not take hold." Faye took a moment to sip her tea, trying to find the right words. "I floundered when things did not go my way. I fear my pride and willfulness were too much."

"As happened with me." Gwen nodded. "Do not let thy pride and willfulness get in the way with Mark Allen. He is a good man."

Oh, must they talk about him again? After Faye's obsession with finding a husband in Pittsburgh, she'd finally come to terms with taking care of herself—come to relish the prospect. And now her sister was intent on driving her into the arms of a handsome frontiersman...

Who loved Gwen.

Mark Allen dug his fingers into the rich soil. He pulled up a clump of sod, a fat earthworm dangling from its underside. "'Twill be good for an orchard."

"As good as thy plot of land?" Micah asked.

"Perhaps even better." Mark Allen replaced the sod and stood. "Between them, we should eventually produce enough cider to supply Mount Pleasant and sell the excess to the riverboats."

"Not a tree planted, and already thinking of expansion." Zachary thumped him on the back. "I like a man with the vision to better himself."

"A man with property needs a wife to help him keep it." Micah glanced toward his place, although the roll of the land and trees hid it from view. "And a wife with the same vision is always a blessing."

Was he thinking of Gwen... or Faye?

"I suppose," seemed the safest answer.

Zachary tapped his fingers against his chin. "Thee makes a good point, Micah. Two people learning to be orchardists together would be an advantage. Taming the land side by side."

They were speaking of Faye. The idea brought heat up from under Mark Allen's collar.

"Think on it," Micah said.

"But I am not a Quaker. Are not Quakers required to marry other Quakers?"

Zachary's laugh boomed in the stillness of the early evening. "That is easily remedied. Did thee not attend meeting last Sunday?"

"I did."

"Will thee attend again tomorrow?"

"I plan to."

"Then thee are seeking, which means thee are on the path." Zachary raised a finger. "'Seek, and ye shall find,' 'tis from the Bible."

Was it truly as easy as that?

Becoming a Quaker, maybe, but Faye? She didn't want to marry anyone like him. She wanted a rich husband who would take care of her.

However, she was earnest about her orchard. And she was touching dirt—while wearing gloves. He hadn't been able to convince her to ride on Jughead, but there was progress.

"Think on it." Micah picked up his ax and looked around at the progress they'd made that day. "Thee would make a good brother-in-law." He touched the brim of his hat and headed for his team.

"'Twould seem thee has his blessing." Zachary wiped his brow and replaced his hat. "He is no longer concerned over thy presence here."

"Nor should he be." Mark Allen wanted his new friend to be assured of that. "Gwen is happy with Micah, and so I am happy for her."

"Thee are a good man, Mark Allen Teed. I am happy to call thee my friend."

They stood shoulder to shoulder for a few minutes, fallen timber spread in front of them with many more weeks of work before the land would be ready for planting. Weeks he wouldn't need to labor alone.

The thought of being alone didn't appeal to Mark Allen. The thought of a wife did. A feisty wife with flashing dark eyes and a ready temper who wouldn't let the world keep her down. She'd changed so much since they'd left the boat.

But had she changed enough to accept a man who smelled of horses?

The sun beat down on Faye as she carefully plucked the weeds from between the stalks of corn. It was safe enough for her to do alone. Even she could identify between a corn stalk and weeds.

Mark Allen was removing the brush in her orchard—having promised not to fell any large trees while there alone—so she had offered to work in the garden in return. The plants were large enough to distinguish between weed and vegetable. Even so, Mark Allen had insisted Bran join her.

Just in case.

But the boy was nowhere to be found, and she had decided not to wait on him. She'd finished her fifth row when a noise caught her attention. On the far side of the horse paddock along the creek, Bran pushed through a hedge of native shrubs. Behind him, the boy in the floppy hat was just visible but stayed in the hedge. Was the young girl behind him?

They were talking, but they were too far away for Faye to hear.

Bran swung around and saw her. He straightened, and one hand went behind his back. She wasn't sure, but he might have been making shooing motions to the boy. What on earth? She stood and waited for him to reach her.

"I have seen that boy before." She shielded her eyes from the sun with her hand, but the boy was gone. "Who is he?"

Bran shuffled closer, eyes downcast. "'Tis probably best you don't ask."

His bold statement took her off guard. What was he saying? "Is he—or are thee—doing anything illegal?"

Bran's head jerked up, his jaw thrust out, shoulders back. "We are not."

She believed him, his reaction too marked to be false. But Paul should know about the stranger. Or maybe it would be best to approach Mark Allen.

"'Tis nothin', just a boy I met. Best to forget you saw him." Bran moved into the garden. "You are doin' good with the corn. I will start on the turnips."

She would approach Mark Allen. He and Bran were close. He'd get to the bottom of whatever was going on.

And it would give her a reason to speak to the man. She grabbed a weed and pulled it from the base of a corn stalk, its white roots exposed to the sun. She hadn't been able to pull Gwen's words out so easily. Her sister's gentle but less than subtle suggestion regarding Mark Allen had taken root. Or maybe it had watered roots that had started to grow on their own.

Faye—the Mount Pleasant Faye—needed to be more practical. She needed to change more than just her boots. While she could, maybe, become a successful orchardist in time, there was as much of a chance that she'd fail. Hadn't Madam herself said so? All of Faye's determination might not be enough. So it was good to think practically.

Better to think that way than about a pair of broad shoulders, or warm hazel eyes, or an endearing grin that she saw all too infrequently. Because while Mark Allen might see the practical side of a union between them, would he only ever see her as Pittsburgh Faye? Or worse—as Gwen's sister?

What was she thinking? It wasn't as if she could propose to the man, after all. A lady waited and hoped and then waited and hoped some more.

What had that accomplished for her in Pittsburgh?

She finished weeding around the corn and stood, hand pressed to her back.

"Bran!" Bridget called from the kitchen door. "I need thee to run an errand."

The boy took off without a backward glance. He'd walk over hot coals if Bridget asked him to, and smile the whole way across.

Out of the corner of her eye, she spied Mark Allen on his gray horse. The beast was heading to the creek. Mark Allen would likely water him there rather than draw buckets from the well.

Maybe... maybe it was time to put her thoughts into action. Waiting for someone else to provide for her hadn't worked. It was standing up for herself that had changed things for her. That and coming to Mount Pleasant, which she had done in obedience to Paul, who said he was being obedient to the Lord. Life was complicated, a series of knowing when to follow and when to move forward in faith. And right then she felt nudged to stand up for herself again.

She stripped off the dirty gloves and dropped them by the last row of corn.

Gwen had no claim to Mark Allen.

It was time to see if that claim could be hers.

Hot, sweaty, and covered in dirt, Mark Allen rode Jughead to the creek behind the barn where shrubs grew thick near the water and a curve of the creek had created a deep hole, making the perfect private bathing pool.

He let Jughead drink his fill, then tethered him to a sturdy branch at the water's edge before he shucked out of his clothing. Leaves, bark, and other debris flew from his shirt and britches when he shook them. He dropped them over his boots, rolled off his sweaty socks, stripped out of his small clothes, untied the leather string that held his hair back, and waded into the chilly water. The drop-off to the hole was close to shore, and he submerged himself, his feet touching the sandy bottom before he kicked his way to the surface. Gulping a breath of air, he shook his hair to clear it from his eyes and stepped out of the hole.

Faye stood on the bank of the creek, one hand over her mouth, and the other holding her skirts as if to flee. But she didn't move.

Neither did she look away. Her eyes were dark and wide and lovely.

The water lapped at Mark Allen's waist. Oh, no. He dropped to his knees, letting the water swallow him to his neck. A very hot neck despite the cool water.

"What are you doing here?" He hadn't meant the words to be so harsh, but he hadn't meant to be caught naked in the creek either.

"I came to see thee."

"Well, you have certainly done that."

"I did not mean that I meant to see…" She pointed a finger that wasn't quite steady in his direction.

"What did you think I was doing here?"

"Watering the horse." She poked a finger behind her and jabbed Jughead in the rear.

The startled horse stepped forward into the shrubs and then backed up, right into Faye's backside.

Mark Allen watched in disbelief as her arms windmilled in a futile attempt to catch her balance. A scream ripped from her throat before she splashed into the creek's bathing pool.

Chapter 34

F AYE TWISTED BEFORE HITTING the creek, her right shoulder smacking into the river's surface, her feet in the air, and then she was below the water looking up at diminishing light. Her skirts billowed and blocked her from the air above. No, not just her skirts. She was sinking.

Panic set it. She opened her mouth, and it filled with water. She thrashed her arms, one of them tangling in the yards of wet fabric that encircled her like a shroud. Like the shroud that had wrapped Father when they slid him into the ocean.

But she was alive!

Kicking to free herself from the clinging fabric, she struck something solid. Then an arm came around her front, and her back was pressed against someone. Still flailing her arms, she felt bare skin.

Mark Allen.

They broke the surface of the creek, and she spit the mouthful of water and hauled in a full breath. She continued to flair her arms. She didn't know how to swim, but instinct said to keep moving.

"Be still or you will drown us both." Mark Allen's breath fanned her ear.

"I cannot swim."

"I can swim for both of us if you will just stop kicking my shins and splashing water in my face."

Oh. She stopped thrashing.

"The hole is deep but not wide. 'Tis just a few strokes until you will be able to touch the bottom."

Then she was tipped onto her side, he kept her head above water, his arm reaching and pulling... and naked.

She was in the creek with a naked man.

A naked man who had saved her from drowning after that horrid beast had tried to kill her.

He stopped and moved his hands to her waist, lifting her until her toes touched a sandy ledge. "Walk forward, the water is no more than waist deep there."

Waist deep? Maybe his waist. It was closer to her armpits. But it didn't matter, she was upright and walking and breathing the most delicious air she'd ever tasted. She turned.

"Faye, nay." Mark Allen held out his hands. "I am not—"

Faye launched herself into his arms. "Thee saved me."

His arms came around her then, his hazel eyes filled with some emotion she'd not seen before. Something she knew she'd like to see again. They flicked from her eyes to her lips and back again, the reflection from the creek making them shimmer with that tantalizing emotion. Her skirts floated near the surface of the water encompassing them both. His breath came fast and ragged. After all, he'd just swum for the both of them. His brown hair hung loose, more hair furring his chest. A chest that rose and fell against the stiffness of her stays.

"Faye!" Paul's voice cut through her thoughts. "Faye! Where are thee?"

Mark Allen stepped back, sliding into the hole but keeping his head above water. "You should answer him. He must have heard your scream."

She'd screamed?

"Answer him."

She turned toward the bank where Paul came charging around hedge.

"Faye!"

"I am fine." She waded toward the bank. "No thanks to that"—she pointed at Jughead—"vicious beast."

Paul swung his head from her to the horse. When he turned back toward Faye, he spied Mark Allen. His mouth opened, but no words emerged.

Faye suppressed the urge to giggle. How shocking it must look. She should be shocked—and she would have been back in Pittsburgh—but all she could do was grin and shake her head.

"'Tisn't what it appears, I vow." She held her hand out for Paul's assistance in leaving the creek, her saturated skirts weighing enough to require his help lest she lose her balance again.

He hauled her out. "Go to the house."

"Paul, I can—"

"I will speak with Mark Allen, and thee will go to the house." Paul's brows were drawn into a line that said further discussion was unwanted and unwise.

She hesitated.

"Faye, leave us." His words were a definite command.

Faye cast a glance at Mark Allen, still up to his neck in the creek, and he gave her the slightest nod. She gathered her sodden skirts and stalked off. Paul wasn't unreasonable and Mark Allen would set him straight.

But, oh, the feel of his arms around her left her wanting more.

"What have thee to say for thyself?" Paul's words were clipped and precise, arms crossed over his chest, frown deep across his forehead.

"I came to the creek to bathe after working in the orchard—Faye's orchard." Mark Allen took two strokes through the water until his feet touched the sandy bottom. Then he stood and smoothed his hair back from his face, eyeing his clothing on the bank by Jughead and wishing he were dressed for this discussion.

"How did Faye come to be here with thee?"

"That I know not. I climbed from the bathing hole and there she was, on the bank near Jughead."

"She saw thee"—Paul pointed to where the water lapped gently at Mark Allen's waist, its clear surface only partly hiding what lay beneath—"like that."

Sweat broke out across Mark Allen's forehead despite the cool water. "She did."

Paul looked away then, hand moving to his chin where he tapped his lower lip.

Mark Allen took a step toward his clothing but stopped when Paul turned to him again.

"And how, pray tell, did my ward end up in the water with thee?"

Paul's face darkened, and Mark Allen raised both hands, palms out. "She said she thought I had come to water Jughead. She was shocked to find me..." He looked down at himself, still waist-deep in the creek. "She started Jughead, and he backed into her, knocking her into the creek."

Paul paced along the creek's bank. "Faye has been gently reared and protected. She has certainly never been alone with a man, much less a naked man." His voice rose with each word. "How could thee have been so careless?"

Careless? He'd been filthy, nothing more. But it didn't seem the time to point that out. Not to the man pacing and raking his fingers through his hair.

"If I could go back and undo—"

"Which thee cannot." Paul spun to face Mark Allen, then pointed at his pile of clothing on the ground. "Get thee dressed. I shall go and speak with Faye and see if we can recover from this or if thee will need to..." He shook his head and stomped off.

Need to... what?

Move on. That was the only logical end to the sentence Paul had not finished.

Mark Allen would be fired from his employment in disgrace.

He'd be run from town as if he were some... scoundrel.

He'd lose the only family he'd ever known. His land. His friends. The boy who felt more like a brother every day would choose Bridget and these kind people.

He'd lose Faye. Not that he'd ever had her.

Mark Allen waded to the shore and let the slight breeze dry most of the water from his skin before pulling on his clothing. He glared at Jughead, dozing in a spot of sunshine that beamed through the branches.

"Thanks to you, we might be on the road before nightfall."

No, Paul was a fair man. He'd let Mark Allen stay until the morning before he tossed him out on his ear. Unemployed. Riding off to who knew where. Alone.

Leaving Faye behind.

And that hurt the most.

"Young lady, thee are not taking this seriously." Paul's voice rose to the rafters. No doubt, Olivia and Bridget heard every word from the kitchen.

It didn't bother Faye in the least. She had done nothing wrong and had nothing to be ashamed of.

Dressed in dry clothing and seated by the window in the parlor, she pushed damp hair over her shoulder and folded her hands in her lap. "'Twas nothing but an accident. 'Tis true that the beast pushed me into the creek, but I may have startled him."

Madam fanned herself in the chair across from Faye. "Thee could have drowned."

"Not with Mark Allen there."

"I will ask thee again." The tension in Paul's voice was tight enough to pluck like a fiddle string. "Why did thee follow him to the creek?"

Should she—could she—tell the whole truth? Maybe not yet. "I wished to speak with him."

Paul let out a sound between a growl and a groan, but Madam leaned forward. "To what end, my dear? What did thee wish to speak to him about that caused thee to follow him and not wait for him to return here?"

Oh, she could not dance around such directness, especially given the distress on Madam's face. The poor woman had hovered over her since Faye had returned, drenched from the creek. And Madam had nearly fainted when Paul told her about Mark Allen being there... unclothed.

"I wished to speak to him... privately." Faye's courage sputtered out. How could she admit that she'd been determined to ask Mark Allen to marry her? If the orchard idea had shocked Madam to her core, this might lay her in her grave. A lady simply did not take the initiative. Ever. It wasn't done. Not by a properly brought-up young lady, for sure.

But an orphan from Wales? Well, that was something different.

Madam wouldn't see it that way.

Yet it was the truth.

With two pairs of eyes on her, Faye closed her own and remembered Gwen's story. Not telling the truth had gained her freedom, but nearly lost her everything else. If anything the Quakers had taught Faye had stuck, it was the importance of truth. The truth could set her free. It might be messy. It might even hurt the ones she loved. But in that moment, she knew that if she took the easy way, if she lied, she'd never recover from it.

She'd never fully embrace the beliefs of the Quakers—the belief in a God of all truth.

"I was going to ask him to marry me."

Madam gasped and slumped against the back of her chair.

Paul half-sat, half-fell onto the settee.

The stomp of boots on the porch was their only warning before the front door opened, and Mark Allen barged into the parlor.

Mark Allen slicked the hat from his damp hair, which he'd neglected to tie back after turning Jughead out to pasture and changing into his best clothes. He must look like exactly what he was, a hired man in the employer's parlor. But he didn't care. What he had to say was going to be said—whether it got him booted from the house that very night or not.

"Nothing that happened between Faye and me at the creek was planned. It was happenstance. And neither of us did anything to be ashamed of."

Paul's mother fanned herself.

Paul ran a hand down his face.

But Faye, beautiful, feisty Faye, beamed a smile at him that knocked the breath clean out of his lungs.

"As thee can imagine"—Faye's smile didn't waver—"we were discussing that very topic."

"Faye." Paul looked at the ceiling and then at his ward. "'Twould be a good idea for thee to wait upstairs."

Faye stood and crossed the room, but instead of leaving, she joined Mark Allen, standing at his side with her chin raised in a look that he'd been on the receiving end of too many times to count. "I think not."

"Faye, dear." Martha dropped her fan in her lap. "Thee should listen to Paul. I will go with thee—"

"Nay, Madam. I am not leaving." Faye's voice was soft, in respect for the older woman who'd taken her in, no doubt. "What will be said will pertain to me and my future."

How did she know what he'd planned? He'd only just decided himself after leaving the creek, and he hadn't been able to talk himself out of it while he tended to Jughead or changed his clothes.

Emboldened, Mark Allen stepped farther into the room, and Faye moved with him.

"I am not a Quaker," he said, "but Zachary assures me that I am a seeker. You"—he gestured to the two watching him, then toward the window, the entire town—"have something I have lacked my whole life. I have known other religious people, but you are not just religious. You truly believe and live as though you do. 'Tis what I want as well." Should he tell them all of it? Why not? A person couldn't be too honest.

"Bran and I stayed with a couple last winter, and they prayed for us. They said we had been sent by God to help them. They said God had used us. I thought they were... well, maybe not crazy, but I was not sure. Looking back... They were not Quakers, but they also believed and lived as though they did. So this God you worship, He is more than a Quaker God. He is the real God. And He cares about us."

Paul stood as though to approach, but Mark Allen raised his hand.

"There is more. I want to be part of this community, both as a Quaker and an orchardist and..." He fumbled for Faye's hand and placed it in the crook of his elbow, and meeting her dark eyes, spoke the rest of his thoughts to her. "And a husband."

Madam gasped, grabbed her fan and applied it vigorously, but a gentle smile accompanied the action.

"Aah. Well, then" Paul approached and rested a hand on each of their shoulders. "I cannot think which makes me happier. To welcome thee into the family of God or into our family."

But Faye said nothing. Her dark eyes swam with emotions, or was that his wishful thinking?

Why did she not say something?

Mark Allen found it difficult to draw a full breath. He daren't not look away from her, fearing her refusal.

The parlor grew quiet, only the ticking of the mantel clock could be heard.

"Tell him you will have him. Put the poor sot out o' his misery."

Over the top of Faye's head, Mark Allen saw Bridget clap a hand over Bran's mouth and haul him out of the doorway.

"Come, Mother," Paul said. "Let us give them the room." They left, the door shutting with a click.

Faye shifted to stand in front of Mark Allen and smoothed the front of his waistcoat, straightened his neckcloth, and tilted her head to the side, her lips parted ever so slightly.

Oh, how could he ever have mistaken her for Gwen? She was... She was all Faye, and in her eyes lurked amusement and... wonder.

He slid his arms around her and pulled her close.

"'Tis different when you have clothing on." Her voice was little more than a whisper.

That didn't sound like a no, so Mark Allen brought his lips down against hers. Once, long ago, he'd stolen a kiss from Gwen, but what he'd felt then had been nothing, *nothing* compared to the flame that surged through him at the softness of Faye's lips. And when she slid her hands behind his neck and drew him closer, he discovered the difference between infatuation and love.

There was no doubt that he loved the woman in his arms.

He drew back. "Will thee have me, Faye Morgan?"

"Thee?"

"Indeed. Will thee?"

"I will." She giggled, her mouth pulled into that smile that made his heart race. "Someday, I will tell thee why I followed thee to the creek. But not today."

"It matters not, as long as thee have agreed to be my wife."

"Wholly and truly, I have." Then she raised on her toes and drew his head down again for another kiss.

Which suited Mark Allen just fine.

Author's Historical Notes

Durgantown, North Carolina, was a stopping place along Swift Creek between Greensboro and New Bern. The small town is called Vanceboro today.

Travel on the Ohio River back in the day was largely seasonal. When the spring runoff raised the water levels, the keelboats could navigate the waterway. But it was still dangerous traveling, with Indians threatening passing boats in search of food, clothing, guns, and ammunition.

John Chapman is known today as Johnny Appleseed. While his folklore character has been embellished in many ways, he was a savvy businessman who knew orchards and planted apples across the states of Pennsylvania, Ohio, Indiana, and into Michigan. He was known for wearing a tin pot hat and ragged clothing—and going barefoot. He planted his orchards from seed, believing that grafting harmed the host plant. He was an early animal rights convert and a vegetarian. He remained unmarried, leaving no heirs to his 1,200 acres of orchards at his death.

Chapman's apples were used to make cider, an important drink from Colonial America up to prohibition. Water wasn't always potable, but hard cider was. During Prohibition, the FBI chopped down many of Chapman's apple trees to prevent locals from brewing their own hooch. Only in recent years has hard cider started to make a comeback in popularity, although many of the modern versions have higher alcohol content.

Along with cider, small beer was a common drink for every household. Unlike beers made in a brewery, it was stirred up quickly in the kitchen and fermented for only a day or two. It was a low-alcoholic drink that even children drank. Water during the Colonial and Federalist periods often contained harmful bacteria. Even a small amount of alcohol from the fermentation in small beer and cider sterilized the drinks.

PATH TO
FREEDOM

3

FREEDOM'S
PROMISE

PEGG THOMAS

Freedom's Promise - Prologue

F RAGILE BLACK CREPE CRUSHED beneath his fingers as Daniel Whiteford removed the wreath from his front door. What used to be his
front door. He handed the wreath to the butler, who accepted it with
a solemn nod. Cook sniffed and his wife's maid wiped a tear from the
groove in her cheek.

"I know you shall take good care of this place for the new owner."
Daniel cleared his throat and pivoted to face the trio. "You have always
done your best for me."

"Good luck, sir," the butler said.

"When you find them, tell Gwen hello from all of us." Cook's chin
wobbled on the last word. The maid wiped another tear without re-
laxing the stiff set of her shoulders.

"Indeed." Daniel stepped off the porch and strode to the carriage
without another backward glance.

Arthur held the door open. Daniel collapsed onto the plush seat
and buried his face in his hands. The soft click of the door closing

barely registered past the fog of grief clouding his mind. The carriage rocked as the bandy-legged old coachman climbed onto the high seat. It jerked into motion with the clatter of iron horseshoes striking cobblestones.

He pulled his hands from his face but refused to look back at the house. The house his children had grown up in. The house his wife had died in. An empty shell awaiting the new owner's arrival.

Why had everything gone so wrong? His wife's death, as much from a broken heart as from the influenza, had been the last straw. Their daughter's horrendous scandal, caught with that low-life captain in the very bedroom she shared with her husband. Daniel pressed his fingers to his throbbing temples. And Jonas, his only son, the one on whom he had leveled such hopes. The one he had planned to take over the shipping business he'd labored his whole life to build. Jonas would rather make his money running after slaves.

Slavery. He'd never agreed with the practice. They'd never had a slave in their home. Daniel hired his employees or bought their indentures. He couldn't abide the thought of one man owning another as if a horse or a cow. He shuddered and drew in a long breath.

Daniel Whiteford had one more chance to do things right. He knew where Thomas Baldwin had settled, in the Quaker community of Mount Pleasant in the Ohio territory. There he would find Gwen Morgan—and reclaim his grandson.

Reviews are Golden

R EVIEWS ARE THE LIFEBLOOD of authors. Leaving a review on **Amazon**, **Goodreads**, and/or **BookBub** means that more readers will find our books! Reviews can be long or short - your honest opinion of the book. Shout-outs on any social media platforms also help!

Pegg Thomas lives in Michigan's Upper Peninsula with Michael, her husband of *mumble* years. She creates American stories with real history and fictional characters inspired by her ancestors who immigrated here in the early 1600s.

Pegg won the 2019 FHL Readers' Choice Award for novellas, was a double-finalist for the 2019 ACFW Carol Award for novellas, and a finalist for the 2019 ACFW Editor of the Year. She was a finalist in the 2021 FHL Readers' Choice Award for novellas. Pegg won the 2022 Selah Award for historical romance and placed 2nd with her second entry. She was a finalist for the 2023 FHL Selah Award, placed 2nd in the 2024 Selah Award, and won the 2024 Will Rogers Silver AND Bronze Medallion Awards. Pegg spent 3 ½ years as the managing editor of Smitten Historical Romance.

When not writing or editing, Pegg can be found in her garden, her kitchen, or sitting at one of her spinning wheels creating yarn to turn into her signature wool shawls. https://PeggThomas.com

PeggThomas.com

Facebook

Goodreads

BookBub

Amazon

Newsletter signup

www.ingramcontent.com/pod-product-compliance
Lightning Source LLC
Chambersburg PA
CBHW052030240626

47153CB00006B/2026